KU-621-238

XX 0670 913359 8009
Leabharlanna Atha Cliath
LIBRARY
Invoice : 02/4230 Price EUR26.49
Title: Seven sisters
Class:

The Seven Sisters

By the Same Author

FICTION

A Summer Bird-Cage

The Garrick Year

The Millstone

Jerusalem the Golden

The Waterfall

The Needle's Eye

The Realms of Gold

The Ice Age

The Middle Ground

The Radiant Way

A Natural Curiosity

The Gates of Ivory

The Witch of Exmoor

The Peppered Moth

OTHER WORKS

Arnold Bennett: A Biography

A Writer's Britain

The Oxford Companion to English Literature (editor)

Angus Wilson: A Biography

The Seven Sisters

MARGARET DRABBLE

VIKING
an imprint of
PENGUIN BOOKS

VIKING

Published by the Penguin Group
Penguin Books Ltd, 80 Strand, London WC2R 0RL, England
Penguin Putnam Inc., 375 Hudson Street, New York, New York 10014, USA
Penguin Books Australia Ltd, 250 Camberwell Road, Camberwell, Victoria 3124, Australia
Penguin Books Canada Ltd, 10 Alcorn Avenue, Toronto, Ontario, Canada M4V 3B2
Penguin Books India (P) Ltd, 11 Community Centre, Panchsheel Park, New Delhi – 110 017, India
Penguin Books (NZ) Ltd, Cnr Rosedale and Airborne Roads, Albany, Auckland, New Zealand
Penguin Books (South Africa) (Pty) Ltd, 24 Sturdee Avenue, Rosebank 2196, South Africa

Penguin Books Ltd, Registered Offices: 80 Strand, London WC2R 0RL, England

www.penguin.com

First published 2002
2

Copyright © Margaret Drabble, 2002

Extract from 'Two Songs' by C. Day Lewis reproduced
by permission of Peters, Fraser & Dunlop Ltd
Extract from 'Thalassa' by Louis MacNeice, published by Faber & Faber.
Reproduced by permission of David Higham Associates Ltd

The moral right of the author has been asserted

All rights reserved
Without limiting the rights under copyright
reserved above, no part of this publication may be
reproduced, stored in or introduced into a retrieval system,
or transmitted, in any form or by any means (electronic, mechanical,
photocopying, recording or otherwise), without the prior
written permission of both the copyright owner and
the above publisher of this book

Set in 12/14.75 pt Monotype Dante
Typeset by Rowland Phototypesetting Ltd, Bury St Edmunds, Suffolk
Printed in Great Britain by Clays Ltd, St Ives plc

A CIP catalogue record for this book is available from the British Library

Hardback ISBN 0-670-91335-9
Paperback ISBN 0-670-91336-7

For Ann, Kay, Pat, Per, Viv and Al

Are not five sparrows sold for two farthings?
And not one of them is forgotten before God.

PART ONE
Her Diary

I have just got back from my Health Club. I have switched on this modern laptop machine. And I have told myself that I must resist the temptation to start playing solitaire upon it. Instead, I am going to write some kind of diary. I haven't kept a diary since I was at school. *En effet*, we all used to keep them then. Julia, Janet and I, and all the other girls. It was the fashion, at St Anne's, in the Fourth Form. Nothing much happened to us, but we all wrote about it nonetheless. We wrote about our young, trivial, daily hopes, our likes and our dislikes, our friends and our enemies, our hockey games and our blackheads and our crushes and our faith in God. We wrote about what we thought about Emily Brontë and the dissection of frogs. I don't think we were very honest in our diaries. Blackheads and acne were as far as we got in our truth-telling in those days.

She sits alone, high on a dark evening, in the third year of her sojourn

Nothing much happens to me now, nor ever will again. But that should not prevent me from trying to write about it. I cannot help but feel that there is something important about this nothingness. It should represent a lack of hope, and yet I think that, somewhere, hope may yet be with me. This nothingness is significant. If I immerse myself in it, perhaps it will turn itself into something else. Into something terrible, into something transformed. I cast myself upon its waste of waters. It is not for myself alone that I do this. I hope I may discover some more general purpose as I write. I will have faith that something or someone is waiting for me on the far shore.

Leabharlanna Átha Cliath

I sometimes have fears that my Health Club may not be very healthy after all. Since I started to swim there, one of my toenails has begun to look very odd. It has turned a bluish-yellow colour, and is developing a ridged effect that I think is new to me, though it is true that I see more of my toenails now that I swim more often. And I sometimes fancy I hear the words 'legionnaires' disease' hanging in the air, though I know they whisper only in my imagination. I mustn't get paranoid about it. It's very clean there, really. Spotlessly clean, expensively clean. A far cry from the chlorinated municipal pool we visited once a week from St Anne's. Schools, even quite good schools, didn't have their own pools in those days, as they do now.

I love my Health Club. It's saving my life. Isn't it? The water in the pool isn't chlorinated, it's ionized. I don't know what that means, but the result is that the water is pure and soft to the limbs, and odourless to the nostrils.

You do overhear some odd conversations there, though. I heard an alarming one this very evening.

I wasn't eavesdropping. There was no way I could avoid hearing it. We were all within a few feet of one another, in a small space, in varying stages of undress. I tried not to look at them, and I knew they weren't looking at me. Why should they? There is an etiquette. It's easy to avoid the eyes and bodies of others. But you can't help hearing what they say. Unless you've got your Sony Walkman plugged into your brain, or a mobile phone clamped to your ear. And I haven't got a mobile phone or a Sony Walkman yet. I don't think I want a mobile phone, but I'm thinking of getting a Sony Walkman. I never thought I'd even think of it. But then, so much of what I think of now would have been unthinkable to me ten years ago, five years ago. Some of it would have been unthinkable to anyone, I suppose. Some of the things most people seem to have now hadn't even been invented ten years ago.

Actually, I'm not sure I mean 'Sony Walkman' – 'Sony Walkman' is just a phrase to me. I may mean something else. I haven't dared yet to ask what it is that I do mean. Perhaps I mean a 'headset'. Nor do I know what kind of shop I'd get this thing in, even if I knew what it was that I was getting. Out of my depth, that's what I am. Though the pool isn't very deep. *No diving. No children. No running. No outdoor shoes.* We keep the rules.

The thing I mean is that earplug device attached to a headband that people stick on their heads and into their ears in order to listen to the television monitors or to Classic FM or Radio 2 while they pound along on the treadmill or pedal away on the bicycle. I quite want one, but I don't know where to buy one. And I'm in some way ashamed to ask. I grow ever more cowardly with age. Shame is a word that haunts me.

The chat of these two women began harmlessly. They were talking about exercise, workouts, stress, back pain. It's odd, the way young people seem to get so much back pain and shoulder pain these days. We never did, when we were their age. Health Clubs hadn't been invented, when I was young. There were tennis clubs, and those echoing public swimming pools where some people were said to catch polio, but there weren't any Health Clubs.

These were two young women, not close friends, possibly meeting for the first time – I didn't hear the beginning of their conversation. They were already talking to one another when I dripped my way along the white tiles from the pool to my locker. One of them, the younger, was a professional in Health Club matters; the other, like me, seemed to be an amateur and a beginner. The younger one was skinny and dark and fit, with an oval face and a long thin pointed nose and slanting doe-like eyes and a breastless body like a ballerina's. You could see her ribs. She wore her dark hair in curiously childish bunches which stuck straight out from her head. She was advising her plumper companion about which classes to join, and how long to use the treadmill. The plump woman, whose naked blue-white flesh was soft and dimpled and bulging, listened attentively as she towelled herself dry and pulled on her workaday cotton vest and pants. Then she must have asked the bunchy lady for more specific advice, for the conversation turned to a lump in her lower back. The thin dark bunchy lady ran her hands over the flanks and loins and back of the pale plump lady, and said that she could indeed feel the lump. It was a knot of muscle, she affirmed, and would soon submit to massage and exercise.

I remember thinking that this sounded like the vaguely optimistic advice that so-called professional healers usually offer, as a prelude to asking for money. I'm afraid I've always been sceptical about the virtues of massage and exercise, and anything that involves the laying on of hands has always seemed to me to be particularly suspect. Reiki, aromatherapy, yoga, shiatsu. I don't know even what they are, but I distrust them. However, as the two of them went into more detail, as the one with the bunches asked the one with the lump to stretch this way and that, I began to think that maybe the professional was taking this probably fictitious and attention-seeking complaint seriously, and with kindness, for she was listening patiently, and offering what sounded to me (though I wasn't really listening) like sensible advice. And then I noticed an almost imperceptible change in the tone of the younger person's voice. She continued to speak calmly and soothingly about stress and muscle tension and the dangers of sitting too long before a computer, but a kind of distant and muted caution had entered her tone. Had she, I wondered, suspected that an unwelcome or over-friendly overture was about to be made by the older woman?

I call the plumper woman 'older', but she was probably under thirty. They were both young. Most people at the Health Club are young. I'm no longer very good at judging the ages of the young. I'm not bad at teenagers, because of all those years as a headmaster's wife, but I'm not good at those prime decades between twenty and fifty. I wonder where they get the money from, these young people. The Health Club fees are expensive. I wouldn't be able to afford them without the special discount. If I don't get the discount next year I won't be able to keep it up. I have to count my pennies now, since my change of status. Are they all working? And if so, what at? Do their employers sometimes foot the bill, as I believe they do in Japan?

The change of tone in the younger thinner woman's voice wasn't due to a brush-off. It wasn't that at all. It was something quite different. It was fear and concern that I heard in her voice. The younger thinner woman was playing for time, as she said, yes, she could feel the lump, it was quite large, she agreed, and it did indeed move up and down under the skin, just as its owner had claimed it did. She was sure it would respond to the right kind of massage and exercise regime, she said, but meanwhile she really thought the other woman ought to take it to her doctor. Go and see your GP, the ballerina said.

Both fell quiet, as they considered this suggestion, and I pulled my navy-blue sweatshirt over my head and pretended I wasn't there. I don't think they had noticed me anyway. I'm not very noticeable.

When I emerged from the temporary muffled deafness of my garment, they had reverted to a more normal tone, and were already discussing something else. I can't remember what. Something neutral and harmless, like the new seafood restaurant down the road. The young do eat out a lot. Again, I wonder how they can afford it. Are they all earning a lot of money? This isn't a very affluent area. Well, it's what's called mixed. Some of it's awash with money, and some of it begs on the street corner. I'm still not always very good at telling which bits of it are which, though I'm getting better at it. My eye is adjusting, gradually. To the dark life of the city.

These two didn't sound very well off, from the way they spoke. But they must be. Or, as I said, they wouldn't be able to afford the fees. I don't understand these modern accents. Young people today don't speak very well, do they?

I could still hear the anxiety in both their voices. I wanted to say, It's probably only a lipoma, but that would probably have made matters worse, and, anyway, what on earth did I know about it? I hadn't laid my hands on that stranger's body, had I? I didn't know what lay beneath the skin.

She encourages herself to continue, despite misgivings

I've just read what I wrote yesterday, about the Health Club. I am quite interested in the bleating, whining, resentful, martyred tone I seem to have adopted. I don't remember choosing it, and I don't much like it. I wonder if it will stick. I will try to shake it off. I will try to disown it.

I didn't go to the Health Club this evening. I don't go every evening. Tonight was my Wormwood Scrubs evening. My man complained about the meatballs. My Wormwood Scrubs man is a murderer. He and a gang of his friends raped a woman and drowned her in the Grand Union Canal. He complains a lot about the food in Wormwood Scrubs. He says he's thinking of pretending to become a vegetarian. I suppose pretending to become a vegetarian and becoming a vegetarian come to the same thing, don't they? He is a lost soul. And so, perhaps, am I.

I never thought I would join a Health Club. I never thought I would find myself living alone in a flat in West London.

The Health Club wasn't a Health Club when I joined it. It was a College of Further Education during the daytime, and in the evenings it held adult evening classes in subjects like German Conversation and Caribbean Cookery and Information Technology and Poetry of the First World War and Modernism in the Visual Arts. But you could tell the demand for that kind of programme was falling. We were an ageing group of students. Even the computer students were old – I guess the course was for slow elderly beginners, inevitably a dying breed. I was one of the younger students in my class. Now that the building has been transformed into a Health Club, to care for the body rather than the mind, the age ratio has been reversed. I'm at the upper age limit now. When I go there, young shameless naked female bodies assault my eyes. I can't remember when I last saw young naked female bodies. I haven't seen the bodies of my daughters for years, not since they reached the modest age of puberty, and in later years I avoided the school boarders and their bedtime rituals. I wasn't paid to be a school matron, was I? And I wasn't very good at being motherly. I sometimes think of poor little Jinny Freeman, and her superfluous hair. Her legs were covered in fur. I ought to have made a helpful suggestion, but I couldn't bring myself to speak. I wasn't *in loco parentis*, was I? Her mother should have said something to her about it.

I want to make it clear that I haven't joined the Health Club in order to consort with the young. I don't expect their youth to rub off on me and to prolong my life. I don't plunge into that blue pool as into a fountain of eternal youth. The evening classes were more up my street, but they closed down on me. The building was sold from under our feet. Learning was taken over, bought out, and dispossessed.

I didn't choose to do German Conversation or Computer Skills. I'd already done some word processing at the IT College in Ipswich. I'd already learnt about laptops and playing solitaire. The class that I attended in that tall late Victorian building was on Virgil's *Aeneid*. You wouldn't think you could go to an evening class on Virgil's *Aeneid* in West London at the end of the twentieth century, would you? And in fact you can't any more, as it's closed. But you could, then, two years ago, when I joined it. It was a real lifeline to me in those first solitary months of my new London life. It was an excellent class. I enjoyed it, and I was a conscientious student. Why did I join it? Because its very existence seemed so anachronistic and so improbable. Because I thought it would keep my mind in good shape. Because I thought it might find me a friend. Because I thought it might find me the kind of friend that I would not have known in my former life.

Already I was wary about making friends with the kind of person who would want to be friends with a person like me. You even get some of them in my youth-oriented Health Club. On my second visit, in the changing room, a woman said to me, 'You've got your bathing costume on inside out.' I was mortified and embarrassed. I'd already made a fool of myself on my first visit by being unable to work out how to use the locker padlock, and then forgetting the number of my locker. I'd been given – well, I'd *chosen* – a combination number for the padlock – but I couldn't see how to make the padlock fit the lock. I asked a young woman, who then showed me, and she said she'd also been unable to work it out the first time, so that was all right. We laughed and parted, no offence or obligation. But then I forgot the locker number, and when I got back from the pool it took me ages to work out where it must have been. I found it in the end – I'd remembered it was at the end of a row, at the mirror and hairdryer end, not the corridor end, but there seemed to be lots of mirrors and hairdryers, an endlessly multiplying refraction of alleys of them, and I dreaded to be appearing to be interfering with other people's combination numbers.

I found my own locker and padlock in the end, without being spotted in my uncertainty, but it was a bewildering moment. I'd used the first three numbers of my birth year, 194. At least I wasn't likely to forget those. I've been more careful since then. Sometimes I leave a thread of the fringe of my red woolly scarf peeping through the door when I lock up. As a clue. Like Hansel and Gretel lost in the dark wood. But mine isn't a dark wood, it's a bright and glassy corridor.

That woman who told me on my second visit that I'd got my costume on inside out was lying. I hadn't. It was a ploy. She wanted to engage me in conversation. She wanted to latch on to me and use me and be my friend. I had stared down at myself, fearing to see exposed stitching, perhaps even that horrible white sanitary-towel effect strip of lining that covers my plain black swimsuit's crotch, but could see, after a moment's self-doubt, that there was nothing amiss. I said, coldly, something like, 'No, I haven't', and pulled one of my towels around myself before striding off towards the stairs to the pool. To be honest, I probably also said, 'Thank you.' I'm not very good at being very rude. But I am quite good, for better or for worse, at avoiding people, and I've made sure that I never change in the same section as her again.

She was an older woman, like myself. She had hoped she had spotted a weakling in need of protection. I avoided her. In fact, come to think of it, I haven't seen her for months. Maybe she's moved away, or died.

I'm wary about making new friends because I'm so bad at shaking off old ones. One of the reasons why I moved to London was to avoid the demands and the pity of those people I used to know in Suffolk when I was married to Andrew. I couldn't face them. I ran away. I still can't decide whether courage or cowardice prevailed in me when I made that choice.

The man in Wormwood Scrubs makes few demands on me. He is safely locked up, and he can't get out. That's the kind of friendship one can control, on one's own terms. A satisfactorily uneven relationship, in which I wield the power. I wield the power because at least I am free to come and to go.

She remembers the building years and the oxhide of Dido

My Health Club hasn't been open very long. It was a blow to me when the takeover bid was announced and the Virgil class closed, because I knew I would lose my new Thursday-evening friends. We were all promised concessionary membership rates if we chose to join the Club, but it wasn't going to be the same, was it? We Virgilians hadn't got to know one another well enough to stay in touch naturally. We hadn't had time to build up an easy extra-mural social life. And some of us just weren't Health Club types. We were made homeless, and turned out to wander our ways.

Nevertheless, there was a fascination in watching the transformation of the old building into the new. They kept the red-brick façade of the old college and gutted it inside. It was interesting to watch the scaffolding go up, and the internal structures crumble and vanish. The dark blue night sky was brilliantly illuminated by security lighting, and from my eyrie I could see the new building rise up, floor after floor, shining like a cruise ship afloat in the city. There were rumours that the top floor was being made into a swimming pool. I didn't believe them, but they turned out to be true, and that's where I now swim, six floors up, beneath the high clouds. But for many months the site was a little city of builders in hard yellow hats. Monstrous chutes and tubes depended from the roof, and temporary structures filled the forecourt. There were little buildings encamped within bigger buildings. False panelling with large graphics portraying athletic future clients fronted the street. I walked past the site daily, past the skips full of broken masonry that lined the pavements, and by night I watched from my window.

I thought of Dido and the building of the city of Carthage. Like seething bees in early summer the Phoenicians built their new hive on the African shore. (That's an Epic Simile.) They claimed the land from the indigenous shepherds, enclosing it in a boundary of strips of a stretched oxhide, and they dug and quarried and excavated, and on the citadel rose a vast temple to Juno, a temple of rich bronze. Even so rose up my Health Club, lofty and proud.

I would like to see the ruins of Carthage. But of course I haven't got the money for that kind of thing nowadays. Andrew has, but I haven't. I'm told there's not much left of Carthage, but I'd like to see it just the same. And I'd like to see the cave of the Sibyl at Cumae. That's probably not very nice either. But I'd like to see it, with my own eyes. They say that the wizened remains of the deathless Sibyl hung there for centuries in a basket, and the only thing that she would say, when questioned, was, 'I wish to die.' In a hollow voice like an echo she would utter these words. When the village children asked her what she wished, she said, 'I wish to die.' Or so they say. I'd like to hear her say that to me.

Andrew and I went to Delphi once. On a coach trip from Athens. That's a long time ago. We were on reasonably good terms in those days, or so I thought. The oracle there didn't warn me of Andrew's intentions. Or, if it did, I wasn't paying attention.

The Health Club opened before it was quite ready. The lifts hadn't been installed, and we had to use a bare concrete stairway. There was builders' rubble everywhere, the showers were temperamental, and the whirlpool kept going wrong. But the staff were very friendly. They welcomed me in. It was a new world in there, an amazing new world. I would never have dared to enter it had I not had a passport from the old world of Virgil. I would not have felt that I had the right. I am not very bold.

She tells the sad story of her marriage

I see I have mentioned Andrew three times already in this diary. I think that means that I should try to give some account of him and of my marriage to him. I am not sure that I will be able to tell the truth. I am not sure if I know the truth. I will try not to whine and bleat too much.

Let me try to describe him. He is a very good-looking Englishman. He is correct in every way. He is six feet tall, and he has neat, regular Anglo-Saxon features, and clear blue eyes – a little faded now, but still a vivid blue – and a fair if crinkled northern skin. His hair was once a strikingly rich yellow. It is now a bright silver white, but it is still thick and springing, and it still catches the eye. He shows no sign of growing bald. His hair does not recede. He is very clean, indeed almost ostentatiously clean. He is a very visible man, though he is not what one would call showy. He is in good taste. His face is lined now, but attractively, with little laugh-lines around the eyes. His skin is pleasantly weathered, for he likes his outdoor pursuits. He looks wholesome and healthy. He has a quizzical, friendly and entirely reliable expression. He is neither solemn nor dull, but he is known to be a good man. He sits on many committees and he does good works. He is good with both men and women. Most children like him, and the parents doted upon him and on public occasions vied for his attention. He exudes reliability, good nature, good humour, common sense, kindness. He is good, good, good. I have come to hate him. I think it is hate that I feel for him now. I hate him, of course, because he betrayed me. That is what other people think. They think it is as simple as that. I doubt it, but I suppose it may be so. I would not be a good judge of that, would I?

We were a happy couple when we were young. People probably thought I was lucky to catch him, though I too was pretty enough when I was a girl. *I* thought I was lucky, but that's because I was lacking in self-esteem. Also, in those days I loved him, and one tends to overestimate the value of a loved object.

I haven't aged well. People say women don't. That's not always true, but it has been true in my case. I too was fair, and blue-eyed, and I had a delicate English complexion and as good a figure as any girl in our year at St Anne's. I wouldn't say I was one of the belles of the school, because that would imply a certain art of presentation which I have always been anxious to avoid. I was brought up in a religious family, and we did not believe in improving on nature. But I was reasonably attractive, and I did not lack admirers. I suppose you might say I was an English rose. Now I look faded and washed out. My skin is weathered, and wrinkles and crowsfeet don't look as good on a woman as they do on a man. I'm not overweight, but I droop and I sag. I don't know what colours to wear. I used to look good in pastel shades, but they don't suit me any more. So I wear navy and grey and brown. They don't suit me well either, but at least I don't look as though I have been trying too hard. At least they look appropriate.

I see I am writing about myself, and not about Andrew. I don't think of myself as self-centred, but maybe I am.

I can't go back into all that old history. I'll begin with the story of our marriage in Suffolk. We'd already been married for nearly ten years when we moved to Suffolk. It wasn't a part of the country that either of us knew well, but we were willing to like it there. (I was born in the East Midlands, and Andrew in North Yorkshire.) It was a new start, for both of us. It meant promotion for Andrew, and security for me and the children, and it was something of an adventure. Andrew's post was tailor-made for him, and the small Georgian house that went with the job was beautiful. It wouldn't be ours, but it would be as good as ours, and I liked the idea of refurbishing it and making it look pretty. And the girls liked it. They liked the idea of living in the Big House. They were already fearsome little snobs, our three daughters.

Andrew was not only appointed headmaster of Holling House School, he was also now the Executive Director of the Trust. The Trust was a philanthropic institution with a not inconsiderable amount of money behind it, invested in the eighteenth century by a Nonconformist banker, principally for the care and education of the blind. (Its terms have been substantially bent during recent years, but there is still a residuary charitable link to visual impairment.) Under Andrew's management, the Trust prospered and the School flourished. Andrew's father was a lawyer and Andrew has a good legal mind: he saw ingenious ways of attracting new investment and new pupils without breaching old blind Hamilcar Henson's original intentions. Andrew was very good at marrying philanthropy and money. He and Hamilcar Henson would probably have got on well, had they inhabited the same time-frame. Andrew was very popular with the Henson descendants. And there wasn't anything remotely suspect about his management of the Trust, or of the School. So I don't know why I'm sounding so sour. So suspicious, and so sour. Andrew is an honest man.

I never really grasped the relationship between the School and the Trust and the Hamilcar Henson estate, in the grounds of which the School stood. Unlike Andrew, I haven't got a good legal brain.

Andrew and I met at school. He went to St Barnaby's, which was the brother school of St Anne's. He was everybody's heart-throb, in those days. He was a year older than us, as was correct, and we all swooned for him. We eyed him in church and at school dances. He was head boy, of course. We all wrote about him in our diaries. And I pulled the short straw and married him.

She counts her friends upon her fingers

I did like Suffolk, to begin with. It was so clean and airy, after our grubby years in Manchester. I liked the large skies, and the yellow fields, and the spacious school grounds. I liked playing Lady of the Manor, and arranging flowers, and ordering curtains. I had been so tired and so busy, in Manchester, with the two little girls in hot squabbling heaps in a small suburban house, and now they were growing up and the efficient machinery of the School contained and embraced them and took them from under my feet. I didn't have to worry about domestic matters much. The School provided its own ready-made system – cleaners, cooks, gardeners, a matron, a secretary. I felt less housebound because the house was not mine. I walked the dog along the riverbank. I have always liked walking by water. Occasionally I helped out in the School, in one way and another, but I did not involve myself deeply in School affairs. It was not an arduous life. I was able to be gracious at public events, when called upon to be so. I was quite good at that. I went to concerts and I presided over wine-and-cheese parties. It was all rather unreal but not unpleasant.

I allowed two women to befriend me. I had two friends in Suffolk. They were – indeed they still are – called Henrietta and Sally. I use this passive construction to describe our relationship because I cannot remember any moment at which I made any friendly step towards them. They co-opted me, and I failed to prevent them from doing so. That is how it happened. I have always been a passive person.

Yes, I had two friends in Suffolk. I suppose they still call themselves my friends, although I have left them and Suffolk and moved to this foreign land of urban barbarians. Henrietta is the wife of a solicitor in Bury St Edmunds. She works as a volunteer with the partially sighted. We still had a few of those at the School, though the supply of suitable blind paupers has begun to dry up of late. (That is one of the reasons why Andrew has been so busy rewriting the terms of the Trust.) Sally is a social worker employed by the County Council. Henrietta Parks is bossy, querulous, lank and long-faced. Sally Hepburn is fat and noisy. They are both do-gooders. I used to have a respect for do-gooders, but I do not like having good done unto me, and I became very suspicious of the motives of Sally and Henrietta.

Sally and Henrietta overwhelmed me with their sympathy when Andrew played me false and left me. Well, Andrew didn't actually leave me – he couldn't leave his post, could he? – but he certainly betrayed me. I was the one who had to leave. I was driven out of what had seemed to be my own home. I went further afield than I was expected to go. I was expected to stay around in Suffolk, in pitiable condition, being comforted by Job's comforters. By fat Sally and bony Henrietta.

There was always a large sky above me in Suffolk, and space around me. There were green and yellow fields, and bathing huts, and striped canvas chairs, and blue sky-reflecting estuaries flooding and spreading towards the silver main. I became an expert in cloud formations. I liked the large mauve and ochre and white cumulus clouds that sailed high over the ripe corn, and the long low yellowy-white clouds that lay parallel above the horizon like Magritte baguettes. It was a picturesque landscape, and it composed itself in oil-colour tints and formations. There were pink houses and thatched roofs and windmills and riverbanks and shingle beaches and spiked purple flowers growing in the sand dunes. There were sheep and horses and herons. An innocent, rural, backward, open land.

Now I live trapped beneath an enclosing grey gloomy London canopy. It is better so. In this trap is my freedom. Here I shall remake my body and my soul.

Everyone felt very sorry for me when Andrew's dalliance became common knowledge, when it became clear to the world that our marriage was over. I became an object of gossip and pity and contempt. Everyone loved and admired Andrew, or so the rubric went, and it was assumed that I above all others must love and admire Andrew. Nobody could guess at the relief I might be feeling. Nobody knew of the exhilaration I felt when I realized that I would not have to live with Andrew for the rest of my life. Nobody knew of my secret delight in his public guilt.

It is terrible, living with a man who is admired by all, when love has perished. Andrew had come to seem to me to be the vainest, the most self-satisfied, the most self-serving hypocrite in England. That kindly twinkle in his eyes had driven me to the shores of madness. The prospect of release, through the agency of Anthea Richards, was a delirious excitement to me. I embraced it and all its accompanying humiliations.

There, I have written down Anthea's name as well as Andrew's. I am making good progress with this account.

Henrietta and Sally, as I have said, are my Suffolk friends. I have two friends still from my schooldays at St Anne's. Janet and Julia are the names of my schoolfriends from St Anne's. They knew Andrew in his guise as head boy, all those years ago. He featured in their girlish dreams and in their girlish diaries. Though it has to be said that Julia always saw through Andrew. Julia was a wicked girl and now she is a wicked woman, and she is well placed to judge Andrew for what he is.

Two Suffolk friends. And myself makes three.

Two friends from St Anne's. And myself makes three.

Three daughters.

Three and three and three.

I am superstitious about numbers, although I know they are meaningless. It is almost an illness with me. I wonder if it is an illness with a name. Most things have names, if you inquire after them. I am lucky with numbers. One day I intend to win the Lottery, with lucky numbers. I haven't bought a ticket yet, but when I do, I shall win. Just you wait and see. It is written that I shall win. If ever I bother to play. (I bet that form of belief has a name, too. I might look it up one day. There must be a reference book called *Common Delusions*.)

The three girls sided with Andrew. Isobel, Ellen and Martha. Andrew alienated my three daughters. He seduced them and stole their hearts away.

I have written enough for today. Tomorrow I will write

about my friends from St Anne's. The prospect fills me with a slightly unhealthy excitement.

It is raining heavily, but I will brave the streets and go to my Club today. I haven't been for days. I must try to stick to some kind of routine, whatever the weather. If I break my routine I will die. I must measure out my days correctly, as I promised myself I would, or liberation will never be mine. Virgil has deserted me, but I shall remain faithful to his successor and his substitute and worship in his temple. Virgil's successor is the new god of Health.

Actually, I think Health must be a goddess rather than a god, but I don't know her name. Hygeia, perhaps? I must look her up when I go to the library.

I miss the reference books. I don't have much shelf space here. Life has become sparse. I like it, in a way, this thinness. But occasionally I miss something. Like a reference book.

She prefaces the stories of Janet and of Julia with more tales of the streets and of the Club

Well, here I am. I'm back. I didn't mean to go on writing tonight, but I don't see why I shouldn't. Nobody will know. I feel the need to continue. Though it wasn't a very eventful evening, nothing untoward. There was a moment as I walked under the motorway, when I felt nervous. A tall black man was walking towards me, straight at me, as though he meant to collide with me. I've been nervous ever since I had my bag snatched. Now I don't carry anything in my bag, except my bathing suit, and my trainers, and my Club Pass, and a fiver in case I think of something I need for supper on the way home. But he wouldn't know I hadn't got anything in it worth having, would he? Anyway, half the people around here look psychotic. You can't tell the muggers from the mad. I know I shouldn't say that, even to myself, but it's true.

When we were within a yard of one another, I veered to one side, trying to look as though I wasn't doing it deliberately. I didn't want him to think I was *avoiding* him. He might have found that provocative. But he didn't even seem to notice. He just ploughed on in his own lone furrow, without looking, staring straight ahead. He was probably out of his mind, or high, or drunk. No, not drunk. He was walking too straight to be drunk. Mad, probably.

No, I don't like walking under the railway, nor under the motorway. It's a double gauntlet. I don't like the pigeon mess, and the old mattresses, and the broken bottles, and the people who lurk near the bottle bank. My heart beats a little faster as I walk under those two bridges.

There was a black girl standing on the corner at the bus stop. She was wearing a black leather jacket and a short black skirt and high boots, and her hair was dyed that unnatural tawny colour that you see a lot around here. And her shoulder bag was like a grenade. I'm not joking. It was circular, and covered with long plastic or rubber spikes about three inches long. Like a mine or a grenade. Street warfare. Battle dress. And standing in the overgrown privet-hedge bottom was a pallid-faced, overweight child of about six years old, smoking the stub of a cigarette. He didn't seem to be with anyone. He certainly didn't belong to the black girl.

Indoors, in the Club, it's another world. It's all lightness and brightness and politeness. Hello, they say, using my name. Sometimes it's the only time I hear my name all day, the only time I speak to another person all day. I know they know my name only because it's written on my Club Pass, which they have to swipe every time I go in, but hearing it does remind me of who I am. It reminds me that I have a name. Sometimes they pronounce my name a little oddly, making me sound more like an illness than a woman, but I can't blame them for that. It's not a very common name. Or not in these parts. It may have been popular once.

They use – or try to use – my full name, not my nickname. They treat me as a grown woman. To them, I am an old woman. They do not know that I was once a child. The receptionists are very Smart Casual. They are well dressed and polite.

There are some beautiful women in the Club. Tonight there was one I don't think I've seen before. She looked like a painting by Gauguin, or a statue. A solid woman. A wide face, carved wide lips, like a wood sculpture, large breasts with large dark nipples and aureoles, and broad fertility hips. They're not all skinny, or even trying to be skinny.

I haven't seen that girl with the lipoma-lump for a week or two. Not since I first tried to describe her, in fact. I hope she's not in hospital.

I can't get used to all these nationalities. In Suffolk, we were all very white. We had some coloured people at the School, because all schools with very high fees take coloured people now, particularly schools like Andrew's that can dress exploitation up as multicultural philanthropy. But you don't see many coloured people in the streets of Woodbridge and Martlesham and Aldeburgh. There are Chinese and Indian restaurants, of course, and plenty of them, but there isn't what I'd call a community. Or if there is, I haven't seen it. It may be different in Ipswich. We didn't go to Ipswich all that often. Sally Hepburn knows Ipswich much better than I do.

Now I am going to write about my old friends Janet and Julia. I will begin with Janet because she is less interesting and easier to name.

Janet Milgram was a nice girl.

Yes, Janet was a nice girl. When she was twelve she had thick brown plaits and a centre parting and freckles. She was good at netball, and became team captain. I can't think of much more to say about Janet. She became a prefect. So did I. Julia did not become a prefect.

But a strange fate overtook Janet Milgram. She married a farmer who took to the bottle and died of drink. She became, for a while, a battered wife. She still lives in Lincolnshire, with her daughter and her son-in-law, on the very same farm where her husband worked, failed, beat her up and died. This is not what any of us would have expected. She had seemed set for a completely steady, unsurprising happy married life of sober industry. Her husband, Dick Parry, on the few occasions when I met him, seemed a regular, hardworking, sober kind of man. It just shows you can't tell what the cards hold.

(I haven't played solitaire for two days now. I congratulate myself. Writing is a good substitute.)

Janet has been cloyingly sympathetic about my divorce, which all too clearly delighted her, and asks me from time to time to go to stay with her. I do not go. But she does occasionally visit my mother in her care home near Lincoln. This I suppose is good of her, as my mother has become very difficult and talks a great deal about Jesus. But you can't expect me to be grateful to Janet, as I am sure she has her own selfish reasons for going to see my mother. Janet is now a big, plain, jolly woman, square and stocky, with a double chin and a round face and a head of bouncing grey curls and a belly which sticks out like a kitchen shelf. She still calls me by my school nickname, which annoys me. I am grown up now.

It's hard to believe that Janet, Julia and I were ever a threesome. But we were.

Julia once suggested that it was Janet, rather than agricultural subsidies and bad harvests and foot-and-mouth and the motorway bypass that drove Dick to the bottle. I wouldn't know about that. Maybe Julia goes around telling people that it was me that drove Andrew into the waiting arms of Anthea Richards. And who knows, maybe I did.

Julia Jordan is another matter altogether. Julia is rich, and Julia is famous, and Julia is a wicked woman. Julia lives in Paris, and she threatens to visit me soon. Julia is free. She is free to come and free to go. She is as free as a bird. She too was delighted by my divorce, though she was able to be much more open about her delight than Janet, being several times divorced herself. She approves of divorce. She never liked Andrew. She always saw through Andrew. She danced with him once when she was fifteen, and although she was flattered to be singled out by him, she didn't succumb to his slick vain well-mannered celebrated charm. She was cool about Andrew. We thought then that she was pretending to be cool, but now I think that she knew what she knew.

Julia was always a shocker, even at school, though I don't think any of us expected that she'd ever go quite so far as she eventually went. We were easily shocked, in those days. 'Juicy Julia' we called her, with admiration. How ugly and inappropriate schoolgirl slang is. I'm sure girls don't call one another 'juicy' now. I don't think it is a word my daughters have ever used. But, then, sex has become so commonplace these days. They call everything 'sexy' now, even quite inappropriate things like investment portfolios and computer software and electrical egg whisks. (At first I thought the thing about the egg whisk I heard on the radio on a food programme was some louche double entendre, but no. It was just Stupid Speak.) Sex was rare, when we were young. Julia was our pioneer. She went out, into all those dangerous places, and came back and told us about them. All the 'juicy' bits. She would entertain us with them, at night, after Lights

Out. Julia seemed to lack some kind of moral sense. She simply didn't think that what she was doing was wrong. Kissing, petting, heavy petting, letting the hands rove over her body, letting the fingers enter her body. We were all so timid and priggish and frightened. We listened spellbound to her stories.

There wasn't much scope for sex at school, as we were closely supervised during term time. Our parents paid good money for that supervision. Those formal school dances came but twice a year, one just before the Christmas break – 'The Winter Assembly', it was called, for some forgotten reason connected with the old days of the old town's social history – and one at the end of the summer term, which was known as 'The Leavers' Ball'. Serious impropriety at these time-honoured, public and carefully orchestrated events was almost unthinkable. We were all very well brought up. All our sex was in the head and in the pages of our diaries, and even there it was heavily monitored and edited.

Julia made up for the stringencies and deprivations of the school year with her activities during the holidays. When we were sixteen, and in the first year of the Sixth Form, she came back at the beginning of the summer term with the news that she had been what we called 'the whole way'. We were fascinated by this. Our knowledge of the sexual act was restricted to descriptions in the pages of the novels of Mazo de la Roche, Nicholas Monsarrat and D. H. Lawrence, and to hypothetical extrapolations from the discreet on-screen activities of actors like Gregory Peck, Victor Mature and Alan Ladd. (The clean-cut, well-shaven Gregory Peck was a great favourite.) We were very old-fashioned, and knew little of Elvis Presley and Rock and Roll. These things were kept from us, at St Anne's. So Julia's revelation that she was no longer a virgin amazed, intrigued and appalled us. We were full of admiration. We looked at her as though she had left the realms of the real and entered a fictional space. What did it feel like, we wanted to know, and how had it happened, and who was the boy, and had she enjoyed it, and when was she going to do it again, and how did she know she hadn't got herself pregnant? People just didn't *do* that kind of thing in those days.

Julia was proud and unperturbed. She dispensed rationed portions of her story night after night, in the dormitory. Julia and I were at that time sleeping with four others in the same room (it was called the Lilac Room) but those in adjacent chambers crept in to listen. From Magnolia and Rose and Myrtle and Hyacinth they came, bringing their eager ears and their pompon slippers and their candlewick dressing gowns. (Some even brought their teddy bears to listen. There were some pretty retarded people at St Anne's.) And night after night, Julia narrated. Even Janet Milgram listened, although she was by now a prospective head girl and ought to have tried to stop us. We were sick and green with curiosity. If Julia had asked us to pay to listen to her, we would have paid. We curried favour, and hung around, waiting for more crumbs. We had never known anyone our own age who wasn't a virgin.

I used to sit in Julia's narrow bed with her during these sinful episodes, with my arm around her and my feet tucked up under her thin tartan rug. We were close. I held on to the very flesh of her sinfulness. I was one of Julia's best friends, though I was never quite sure why. I don't know if we really liked one another. We used to walk to church together on Sunday mornings. We had paired off, as girls were obliged to do. In earlier years I had been Janet's pair, but by the Sixth Form Janet had splintered off and taken up with a hockey player called Smuts (I've forgotten her real name), partly because I was getting so thick with Julia. Janet, Julia and I were still considered a threesome for activities that didn't require pairs. I can't account for that. Perhaps it had something to do with the fact that we were the only three doing Latin S level. We were three, in our fashion.

As we walked to church, two by two, innocent and proper in our school uniforms and school hats, Julia would tell me about the boys she knew at home, and about the forbidden books she had been reading. She had read bits of *Ulysses* (she said her father had a secret copy he'd brought home from the war) and a lot of Colette. I'm trying to think of the other 'naughty' books she spoke of, but I can't remember any. This was before the days of the *Lady Chatterley* trial and even of the exotic revelations of Lawrence Durrell. We all read *The Rainbow* and *Sons and Lovers*, of course. But they were so high-minded that they didn't count as naughty. We were allowed to read them because they were English Literature. Our school, though prim, was not wholly unenlightened.

Julia said she was going to be a writer. Most of us weren't very ambitious, but Julia was.

I don't know where she got her confidence or her ideas. The environment was hardly very supportive of her kind of interest or experimentation. And it wasn't as though she was a striking beauty. In fact, she was rather odd-looking. She was of average height, about five foot four, and of average build, if anything slightly on the skinny side. Her breasts were small and high and far from voluptuous, and her belly was very flat, almost concave. (This we did envy: 'fat tummies', as we called them, filled us with an adolescent anorexic disgust. And this was before anorexia was widely diagnosed.) Her hair was a pale light mousy brown and slightly wavy: in later years she has taken to dyeing it in many different shades. Last time I saw her it was a rich dark chestnut, just a little too red to be real. She had a pale dun smooth skin, a sinisterly smooth skin, and a large black mole on her left shoulder. She was made up of tones of yellow and brown and pale pink. Her lips were pale pink, like the underside of a mushroom. Her most striking feature then was her very large, slightly protuberant eyes. They were uncanny. They were a light grey-blue and they had a strange, piercing, salacious expression, as though she could always read the worst of what you were thinking. Her eyes weren't very attractive, but they were compelling. Hypnotic, almost. She painted her eyelashes dark brown and she used blue eyeshadow. We weren't allowed to use cosmetics at St Anne's, but she did.

There was something voracious about Julia. She ate a lot, but she never put on weight, despite the heaviness of the school diet. She burned up the porridge and the shepherd's pie and the mashed potatoes and the syrup puddings and the piles of bread and margarine and jam. She was restless, and always on the move. She wasn't very good at sitting still. In church, she was perpetually fidgeting and leafing through her hymn book looking for traces of sublimated spiritual eroticism (she found plenty) and pulling at her gloves. (Yes, we wore gloves to church, in that lost era of good behaviour.) She had too much energy. But she hated sports. Alone of our year, she let it be known that she despised sports. This wasn't a fashionable attitude, but she got away with it.

She was also clever. She sailed through exams without too much effort, and took quiet satisfaction in her triumphs. Ours was a serious, old-fashioned, disciplined, ladylike school, and it should have been proud of Julia's successes – her A and S grades, her State Scholarship, and her place at Bristol, where she was to read English Literature. But Julia made our headmistress and even our broadminded English teacher uneasy. There was something not quite right about her, and they knew it. They were too nice to be openly snobbish about Julia, but they could sniff something in her and her background that they didn't like. I don't think they knew about her sexual escapades – she would have been expelled as a corrupting influence had the truth been known – but they suspected them. She made them feel uncomfortable.

I knew all and possibly more than all about Julia's escapades, and I also met her background. She invited me to stay with her for a long weekend at a half-term break – I think it must have been Whitsuntide – in the family home at Sevenoaks. I was pleased to be asked, and pleased to accept. I couldn't go home that weekend, as my father was ill, and my mother reluctant to have me in the house, and I was loath to linger at school, exposed as homeless, with all the other miserable unwanted girls who had nowhere to go. I grasped eagerly at Julia's face-saving invitation, and we set off together to Kent as on a spree.

It was very odd. Well, *en effet*, it wasn't *very* odd. It was just slightly off-key, in a way that I couldn't have defined then and don't think I can define now. Julia's home base was very suburban – her parents lived in an undistinguished 1930s bow-windowed semi-detached house in a crescent, with a lot of pleated curtaining and pelmets and wall-to-wall carpeting. It was deep-piled and a little lavish, in a way that seemed unfamiliar. I think a lot of us at St Anne's, including myself, came from middle-class families living in comfortable but modest circumstances – if we'd been better off, we'd probably have been sent to more celebrated schools. St Anne's was respectable, but it wasn't smart. Julia's family had the wrong kind of smartness. It sounds terribly snobbish to say that, but that's what I thought at the time, and I must try to be honest. Her father was a bank manager, and her mother talked a lot about the theatre. I think she may once have worked in the theatre in some backstage capacity. They both played golf and drank a lot of gin and tonic. We girls ate mostly in the kitchen, perched at a kind of American-style breakfast bar, though one evening during the weekend we had a more ceremonial meal *en famille* in the dining room with all the silverware and the napkins and the glasses. I helped to lay the table and Mrs Jordan teased me about the way I distributed the cutlery. I didn't like that. I did something wrong with the soup spoons, but I can't remember what.

Julia's parents made no attempt to control Julia. She did exactly what she wanted. Like myself, Julia was an only child (that was another bond between us) and (unlike me) she had clearly got the upper hand at home. She went to the cinema in the afternoon with local boys. She went to the pub, and stayed out late. Nice girls just didn't do that kind of thing in those days. She took me on these social excursions with her, and introduced me to her friends. One of them was the boy with whom she claimed to have had sexual intercourse. I couldn't help staring at him. He looked quite ordinary and, if I have to be honest, not all that attractive – he was not nearly as handsome as Andrew – but he clearly had hidden qualities.

I was out of my depth in Sevenoaks. It was a foreign country to me. I could see that Julia came from somewhere else. And she was already set on travelling elsewhere.

Julia published her first novel when she was only twenty, when she was still a student. I believe the authorities at Bristol threatened to expel her, or suspend her, or rusticate her, though in the event they failed to do so. Hers was not the kind of literary debut of which a university could then feel proud, though of course nobody would raise an eyebrow now. Things have changed. Her novel was a *succès de scandale*. I read it with some alarm, as I guess we all did. Janet Milgram pretended that she never even looked at it, but I didn't believe her. I think we all read it, avidly, surreptitiously, as we used to read the over-heated romances of Mazo de la Roche and Georgette Heyer and Dorothy Sayers by torchlight under the bedclothes.

We were all afraid that Julia would tell our secrets. I had told her some of mine. 'Don't tell anyone,' I had said to her, but I knew that she would tell. Writers have to tell. It's what they do. It's what they are for.

One day in gym, Mittie Bowling wet her bottle-green school knickers as she was doing some stupid split-leg exercise over the horizontal bar. 'Don't tell,' she whispered to Julia, who was standing next in line and who had seen the cloudy pale yellow urine drip. But of course Julia told. As I am telling now, forty-odd years later.

We of St Anne's needn't have worried too much, as it happened, about the contents of Julia's first novel. Our little secrets were spared. She had moved on from the confines of boarding school to a wider stage. She wrote about student sex, and her tone was worldly and authoritative. She had an uncanny mimicry of adult poise. She seemed so knowing. Perhaps she was knowing, though I was surprised she had had time to find out how to know so much in so short a space. My own discoveries were made so much more slowly. (I was a virgin when I married.)

Julia's narrator in this novel was a young woman called Celia, who recounted her sexual exploits with remarkable candour and panache. Her tone resembled Julia's own, but it was more mannered and more confident. Julia had hit on a fluent and distinctive narrative style that suited her, and she was to exploit it over her next few novels to great effect. This first novel must, I assume, have been heavily autobiographical, but to my relief I could not place most of the incidents or any of the characters. As I said, she had moved on from the dormitory. She had transformed St Anne's into St Bride's, but her references to it were fleeting. Bristol became Westhaven, and it was in Bristol that most of the action was set. Bristol, at that period, was not yet widely known for its bohemian tendencies, though they must have been already latent. Its reputation for bad behaviour took off in the next few years. Julia's novel was often, in the 1960s and '70s, cited as the beginning of something new and, to many, undesirable, both in terms of fiction and of city living. One can't turn the clock back now.

I don't think Julia's novel is cited very often these days as an example of anything. It has lost its power to shock. But it shocked then. It shocked me then.

In the novel, Julia/Celia described lying to her doctor at Westhaven in order to obtain contraceptive advice: clearly it hadn't proved effective, for the set piece of the work was a description of a back-street abortion. Not so back-street, *en effet*, although strictly illegal. Julia/Celia had herself fixed in a mews just off Portland Place, in London, not too far from Harley Street itself. (Harley Street was just a name to me then. I knew what it represented, but I didn't know where it was.) Julia/Celia gave many convincing and circumstantial details, about the price (exorbitant), the abortionist's manner (prurient), the reaction of her boyfriend (fainéant) and the view upwards through the sloping skylight (grey). She described the cramps, and the pain, and the blood. What she omitted to describe was any sense of fear or shame or guilt. The impassive neutrality of her narration was impressive. Reviewers commented with admiration on her calculated sang-froid. But I felt there was more – or less – to it than that. Her sang-froid wasn't calculated. It was real. She really hadn't thought an illegal abortion was a big deal.

The story ended with her ditching the student father of the aborted foetus and hitching up with a married university lecturer and his wife. That doesn't sound very bad these days, but it was pretty risqué then. There was a powerful scene in which the Celia character, at the end of a babysitting session for this married couple, found herself being propositioned, separately, in the space of quarter of an hour, by both husband and wife. She resolved the situation by suggesting that they all three repair to the bedroom together. Which they did. It was an erotic scene. Erotic, but not sensual.

Come to think of it, maybe that scene is still risqué, though in a different way. Lesbianism and troilism are just fine, but students and lecturers aren't supposed to have any kind of physical contact at all these days, are they? *Autres temps, autres moeurs.*

I don't think Julia was or is very sensual, although she's so interested in sex. People used to use the phrase 'cold sensuality' of men, which I've always taken to describe a sort of detached, uninvolved, impersonal interest in sensation and conquest rather than in emotion. Don Juan, Casanova. But you could use that phrase of Julia. *En effet*, our schoolgirl sobriquet, 'Juicy Julia', apart from being childish and ugly, was not even very appropriate. Julia was a dry person. She did once tell me that she loved the smell of the spermicidal jelly we used to apply to our Dutch caps, and I remember thinking – rather an odd thought for me – that she probably needed lubrication. She never sweated much, at school. Most adolescent girls sweat profusely, but Julia was cool and dry. I used to sweat a lot. I too am dry now. I have dried out. It is a great relief to me. Age has its delicacy.

Julia never had any children. Maybe that abortion damaged her. She has always said that she did not want children. Did

I want children? I don't know. I loved them, when they were little, in a programmed biological maternal manner, and I am hurt now they have rejected me in favour of their father. It is not their fault that he forced them to take sides, but I do feel, in an old-fashioned way, that they should have been more loyal to their mother.

In the Health Club, I look at the unstretched bodies of those young well-paid shallow Cockney-accented middle-class working girls, and I think, *Well, at least my body has been used for its proper purpose. It gave birth, three times over. No wonder it isn't as tight and firm as it used to be. It has seen some action.*

And then I think to myself, what an absurd, teleological way of thinking about the body. Julia used hers for sex, and bodies are made for sex too, aren't they?

She digresses to the forbidden subject of solitaire

I've just lapsed, and played solitaire solidly for half an hour. I got it to come out in the end. It's always so unsatisfying, that satisfaction. I quite like the orgasmic multi-coloured shuffle of the deck on the screen, but it doesn't really *satisfy*, does it? It can't, can it?

If you play solitaire with real cards, as we used to do at school, you can check on what your choices might have been had you made them, and where they might have led you. If you play on the laptop, you can't. I'm not talking about cheating on the laptop. I'm talking about checking. The laptop won't let you cheat, and that's fair enough, but it won't let you check either. It won't let you lift a card to see *what might have been*. It won't let you follow an alternative, unchosen route, even out of curiosity.

If you lay out a deck of real cards, of real, well-fingered, laminated, canvas, oblong cards, you know that the whole of the deck of the red and of the black is there on the table before you. You can't see them for what they are – that is the point of the game – but they are there, every one of the fifty-two, upon the table. Every single ace, every club and heart, spade and diamond of every denomination is there, in a particular pattern and permutation. I don't know how many starting variations there are, with fifty-two cards and a game of solitaire, but I'm sure somebody must. People who like numbers work it out, surely.

Whereas, when you play electronically, *there is nothing on the table at all except what you see.* When you first deal the deck for solitaire, there are the faces of seven cards showing, and the backs of twenty-one other cards, in gradated piles. My laptop version of solitaire actually shows the concealed cards overlapping as separate items, so you can count them, but I know that some versions of the game, less satisfyingly, simply display a face-down, dark, unreadable, undifferentiated mass. But the point is this. In the electronic version, those concealed cards do not exist *as cards* or even as numbers. They are merely notional. It is my belief that they have not yet decided what they are to be. I'm not sure at what point that decision is made, or by what.

There is more future freedom in the electronic version, although you are not free to cheat. But there is less reversibility. You can never rethink a past decision. The machine does not permit. It does not even permit a mistake.

She thinks of the seedless grapes, and of the sour

Enough of card games. They are a temptation to sin. That's what some people used to believe, and maybe they were right. My maternal grandparents were brought up in that faith, and I have inherited their sense of guilt.

Playing for high stakes is more dangerous and more sinful than playing alone, but playing alone is not good for the soul.

I wonder how the childless Julia feels about sex nowadays. I wonder whether she wishes that she had had children to shore up her old age. I think she has been married three times now. I've lost count. I met the second husband, but not the first. The one I met was something to do with television. I don't know if she is married at the moment, or whether she has a man in tow, but I think I shall soon discover, for she threatens to visit me. I wonder why she has kept in touch with me, over the years. I cannot think that my dull life can be of much interest to her, yet she is very faithful to me. She never forgets my birthday. These days, she is about the only person who remembers it. I am not sure that I like to be reminded of my birthdays, yet I have to admit that there is something reassuring in her fidelity. She always sends me a card, and on my fiftieth birthday she sent flowers. That was kind of her. I don't know why she bothers with me. I have nothing to offer. I was still in Suffolk, with Andrew, when I turned fifty. My daughter Ellen forgot my fiftieth birthday. Isobel and Martha remembered, but Ellen forgot. I do not blame her for that. She was living abroad. She has lived abroad for quite a long time now.

I don't send Julia cards for her birthday. I am very unreciprocal. I don't even know when her birthday is. I must have known, once, at school, because we all knew about such things. We knew each other's birthdays, star signs, horoscopes, favourite colours, favourite flowers, favourite names, favourite poems, favourite hymns. But I have long forgotten all these preferences. They don't print the date of her birthday in the press, or not that I've noticed. She's famous, but not famous in that way. Really, she's more notorious than famous. And maybe her notoriety is waning, now she is getting old. I wouldn't be a very good judge of that.

Yellow was her favourite colour when she was a girl, or so she said. Nobody else liked yellow. I think she liked yellow through perversity.

Come to think of it, she hasn't published a book for some years. No television series or films have appeared either, or not that I've noticed. Perhaps she's not well. Perhaps something has gone wrong. If it had, nobody would tell me.

Julia knows my new address, because I sent it to her, but I haven't seen her since I moved to London. I had a card from her last month, just before I began writing this journal, saying she was coming over and would like to see me. She said she'd ring as soon as she knew her dates. I expect to hear from her, because she really is, in her own way, oddly reliable. Dependable, even. She's a wicked woman, but she would stand by me, if I needed somebody to stand by me. And she would never be shocked. There's a lot to be said for people who can't be shocked. She wrote me a very funny letter when she found out about Andrew and Anthea.

There's the phone. Maybe that's Julia.

A false alarum

No, it wasn't Julia, it was Sally Hepburn from Suffolk. My fat Suffolk friend. She was ringing to check up on me. She wants to see me when she is in town next week. I seem to have agreed to see her. I find it very hard to say no to Sally Hepburn. Sally Hepburn is a pain in the neck. That's a coarse expression, but Sally is not a delicate woman. When she was my neighbour, I didn't let myself admit even to myself that I found her irritating. After all, she was supposed to be my friend, and she was supposed to be a suitable friend for a person like me. Andrew pretended to like her, too, in his superior, charming kind of way, his ostentatious 'see-how-nice-I-can-be-to-fat-middle-aged-single-women' way. And Sally is fat. She is gross. She must weigh twelve stone and more, and she is not tall. I wouldn't be surprised if she weighed fourteen stone. She is solid, and she has a vast spreading bosom. Is she really a suitable shape for a social worker? Many of her clients are overweight, and perhaps her heaviness and shapelessness make them feel at home with her. Is to be fat to be trustworthy? Somebody in classical antiquity thought so – was it Julius Caesar? I think it was, but I can't be bothered to check. Though I did bring my old school Shakespeare with me, to London. Anyway, I don't agree with Julius Caesar. I think fat people tend to be very manipulative. Moreover, I very much dislike the way Sally implies that I too have a weight problem. I am not as slim or as fit as I was, but I am not large. And I have lost weight since I started going to my Club. I take a size 12, occasionally even a size 10. Her clothes must be numbered up in the 20s.

I have my problems, but my weight is not one of them.

Sally has a maddening habit of assuming that I share all her problems and all her weaknesses. She is two years younger than me, yet she seems to go ahead, like a spectre with a corpse lantern, lighting the way to the tomb. Things can only get worse, says Sally. The hair on the face, the stress incontinence, the pelvic slack, the arthritic joints, the sagging boobs. (I hate that word, 'boobs', and could hardly bring myself to write it down, but it is a word she uses quite often, though I can't at the moment think why she needs to introduce it into our conversations.) I used to find myself inventing maladies of my own to keep her company, in the bad old days when we used to lunch together in Woodbridge. Just as I used to invent sexual misdemeanours in an effort to have something interesting to offer to Julia in exchange for her more sensational confidences. I really don't have to bother with Sally now, I tell myself. But, like Julia, she has a peculiarly pressing manner and does not easily take no for an answer. I know she wants to get her foot inside the door of this flat. She is so nosy. She wants to know how I live, what I've come down to over the past two years since I left Farlingham. The Lady of the Manor, in her pretty if borrowed grace-and-favour Georgian house, reduced to a two-room flat off Ladbroke Grove. She wants to inspect my misfortune. I've seen her in London a few times, since I left, but I've made sure that we met on neutral territory – lunch in the National Gallery, or at the British Library, or at the clerical Wren café attached to St James's, just off Piccadilly. Modest ladies' luncheon places. But keeping her out has only whetted her curiosity and her desire to get in, I can tell.

I am not ashamed of this flat. It satisfies me. And I am proud of my endurance in it, I am proud of the way I have parcelled out my life and controlled the empty spaces and filled up the time. It has not been easy, but I have worked at it, and I have made a shape to my life. I don't want that obese chatterbox barging in here with her huge chest thrust out in front of her, and her sensible shoes and her layers of woolly jersey and her too-tight mannish jackets and her *yack yack yack nose nose nose sniff sniff sniff*. Her great unused and useless dugs bear all before them. Talk about teleology. What was Sally Hepburn made for? It is not at all obvious.

She never stops talking. How she ever manages to elicit any information from her clients – her victims, *I* call them – God alone knows. Yet she does. And she elicits information from me too. Because every now and then I have to break in, to stop the remorseless flow of gossip and ignorant opinion and innuendo. That's how she tricks me into confessions. Maybe she has the same effect on those single mothers and battering stepfathers. The reverse of the psychoanalytic approach – not silence, but a battery of words. People tell her their secrets in order to shut her up.

I am so mean about Sally. But she has subjected and subdued me and I must fight back somehow. I fight back on this silent scroll of outrage, because I am bound to Sally for ever. I will never shake myself free.

Women's lives. How they entwine about one another and strangle one another.

Sally, like Julia, likes talking about sex, although, by her own account, she had no experience of it. She thinks nothing of discussing pornography, and words like 'orgasm' and 'clitoris' are frequently upon her lips. Unlike Julia, she is a virgin. There is not much to be said in favour of Janet Milgram Parry and Henrietta Parks but at least they do not talk about sex. They are ladies. What a relief it is to be able to write that sentence, that sentence that no one but myself will ever see. 'Janet and Henrietta are ladies.' I wonder how many people still know what that means? I wonder if I know what it means. I'll think about it.

She looks back on her arrival in this strange place

I was frightened when I first moved into this flat, alone. It is my own. I bought it, with the handout that Andrew gave me as the price of our divorce. Why did I choose this dark, dirty, menacing area, this street so unlike any street I have ever inhabited before, even in my imagination? Was it perversity? Was I setting myself a survival test? Was I punishing myself?

I knew I couldn't stay in Suffolk, although most people expected that I would. They didn't think I'd have the initiative to clear off so completely. (I don't think 'clear off' is a very ladylike phrase either – maybe I am losing caste by living here?) But I couldn't face the prospect of hanging around in a county where I might still bump into Andrew and my replacement. His new partner, Anthea Richards, now his bride. However careful I was not to bump into them, I'd still have to hear gossip about them, because Suffolk is a small (or perhaps I mean a thinly populated) county, and people in what was our world did talk about one another all the time. Andrew's second marriage has been newsworthy. I'm sure I would have talked about it myself, had I not been one of the parties. (That's an odd phrase too – 'parties'. Odd how writing things down makes all the phrases I take for granted look slightly off-key.)

Nobody expected Andrew to embark on an affair with the mother of one of his pupils. It wasn't as though she herself was *in statu pupillari*, but the connection nevertheless seemed more than vaguely unprofessional and improper – as though one or the other of them had taken advantage of the very thing that should have kept them apart.

People's sympathies were divided. I was an honourably loyal and washed-up wife, stranded, useless, ageing, as on a high and dusty kitchen shelf, so people felt sorry for me. But Anthea had twice been tragically bereaved. She had lost her husband, and then her daughter. Tragedy and compassion had brought Andrew and Anthea together. He had been too caring, too kind, and his own goodness had forged the bond between them. So it was seen. I know that's what people saw, and thought, and possibly said – though maybe they weren't quite crude enough, quite ungentlemanly and unladylike enough to *say* it. The circumstances of their affair were thought to be romantic rather than squalid or opportunist.

(Now isn't it interesting that my spellchecker on this wonderful laptop machine accepts the word 'unladylike' without protest, but doesn't like the word 'ungentlemanly'? Shall I try 'ungentlemanlike'? No, it doesn't like that either. A small triumph, or a small defeat, for the ladies. But which? I love my spellchecker. It is my friend and my companion. It speaks to me, and I answer.)

So I didn't want to hang around in Suffolk overhearing scraps of conversation about Andrew and Anthea, worrying about whether I would bump into them at parties or in the high-street shops, listening to speculation about how they were getting on. I didn't want to put my friends and neighbours to the trouble of trying to make sure they didn't ask us to the same events. I decided to remove myself and start a new life.

I did think, at one point, in those early days of shock, of moving back to the Midlands, but I didn't think about it for very long. There was nothing to attract me back. And after Father's death, I did not want to be too near my mother, for fear she would suck me in. A failing mother and a daughter shamed. This was not a scenario I fancied. Once the notion of moving to London occurred to me, I became increasingly fascinated by it. It started to glow at me in the darkness, with the dangerous nocturnal brightness of a new love. There was something erotic in my imaginings of London. I had never lived in the heart of a big city, and London is one of the biggest cities in the world.

I was warned about the expense, but I was not deterred. I pursued my fancy with more energy than I had felt in years. I signed on with estate agents, I read the property columns. My means would be restricted but I was not destitute. Andrew, as the guilty party, was moved to be generous, a movement made easier for him by the fact that Anthea was a fairly wealthy woman and brought new money with her rather than new financial demands. Two of the girls – our girls – were no longer dependent; only Martha was still living at home. The Trust was very forgiving and forbearing with Andrew, as it knew it couldn't do without him and couldn't afford the consequences of a posture of outrage. I, of course, was considered blameless, by all but my three alienated and disaffected daughters, so there was nobody to quarrel with what seemed, on Andrew's part, like generosity. But everybody thought I was mad to want to move to London. And the more they told me I was mad, the more stubborn I became in my resolve. I knew something exciting would happen to me in London. I still know it. It will. It will come. It will come soon.

She wonders if true change can still happen at her age

I couldn't afford anything grand, or anything in a nice district, so I explored grey areas, in Stamford Hill and Seven Sisters and Finsbury Park and Clissold Park and Camberwell and Brondesbury and Brockwell Park and Neasden. I looked at dozens of studios, bedsitters and maisonettes and flats in areas of London that I had never visited. I had never even known of their existence. Most of these places seemed profoundly alien and depressing to me, and I couldn't begin to think of myself living in them. I found this apartment by accident, through a conversation with the owner of one of the nicer flats I looked at. Her flat was in Crouch End, which is now very fashionable. I knew I couldn't afford it, and I told her so. This was a relief, after my life as Andrew's wife, in which I masqueraded as a lady who had no money worries. (We always had to try to appear to be better off than we were – I was never sure why.) This person was a very nice woman, and I could tell from the reading matter on her shelves that she was probably a social worker. I don't dislike all social workers. (I don't really dislike Sally. Sally is my friend. Well, sort of my friend, a sort of friend. Can I do better, for friends, at my age?)

This vendor-woman made me a cup of coffee, and asked me what brought me to London, and I said, 'Adventurous despair!', and she laughed. She said if I was really adventurous, I might try Ladbroke Grove.

(Now that's weird. My new friend spellchecker won't accept the words Ladbroke Grove, but it suggests as an alternative 'Ladbrokes'. I think that's a betting shop. Well, come off it, I *know* it's a betting shop, I wasn't born yesterday.)

This woman said she had a colleague whose daughter was moving in with her partner and was trying to sell something that might just suit me. Tell me about the neighbourhood, I said, and she did – very central, she said, compared with Stamford Hill and Brockwell Park. Central, and lively, and colourful. Of course, you may not want to be central, and lively, and colourful, she said. But I cried out that yes, I did. Suddenly the idea of being central and colourful rather than marginal and marginalized seemed to me to be infinitely luminous and numinous.

Also, said my new worldly wise adviser and go-between, if you buy direct from my friend's daughter Karen, you won't have to pay estate agent's fees. You'll both of you save thousands of pounds.

And so it proved to be, and here I am.

It's a strange little flat. It's high up on the third floor in a tall, not very well-maintained, late nineteenth-century end-of-terrace building, which adjoins and overlooks a dense low-built development of slightly kitsch red-brick Notting Hill Housing Trust in-fill. I look down on a network of new little flatlets and maisonettes and dolls' houses and terraces, separated by patches of communal garden. My solicitor made a great fuss about the neighbours and other tenants in this building, and who was responsible for what, but I didn't even listen. I don't care about that kind of thing. I told him I wanted it. I told him to get on with it. When he said that all those flights of stairs might prove tiring in years to come, I said that, on the contrary, they would keep me fit. As I trust they will. They and my Health Club. My Health Club and my stairs. (I don't use the step machines at the Health Club. I prefer the bicycle. I can go up and down stairs more purposefully on my way up to and down from what is now my home.)

I have two rooms and a bathroom here. It's enough. And I have a spectacular cityscape view of motorway and railway and distant council high-rise and night sky and morning sky. The sky is very different from the innocent Suffolk sky, but it is not always a deadly grey. At times it is awash with a lurid glow, with doomed and polluted sunrises and sunsets of orange and yellow and purple and bloody red. Although the stars are often obscured, I can watch the months and the seasons, and sometimes I can see the constellations. The Great Bear, Cassiopeia, the Seven Sisters, the Swan. All these I have seen, or fancied I have seen. The new moon even now hangs near me in the darkest of blues. And I can look down at the street life, of which there is much.

My daughter Ellen was the first of my daughters to visit, and she was, to begin with, disapproving. She pointed out all my apartment's conspicuous ill features – the damp in the bathroom, the cracks in the badly fitted double-glazing, the smell in the corridor, the irregular thumping reggae noise of the people in the top flat above. And, of course, the stairs. But Ellen is, in fact, the most reasonable of the girls, and when she saw that I was determined to stick here, she agreed that it had its points. Ellen, I feel, doesn't dislike me. Nor is she in love with her father. She sees through both of us. She has wisely decided to remove herself. She lives in a small town in Finland. So she's not likely to be popping in very often. I believe she has a lover. Or a partner, which, I gather, is the modern word for lover. I don't know what sex or what nationality this person may claim, and I don't ask.

Ellen is the most eccentric, as well as the most reasonable

of my daughters. She plays the violin. I picture her living alone in a wooden house on the edge of a lake on the edge of a forest, and dipping into a sauna from time to time, but it probably isn't like that at all. I've never been to Finland to see her, and I haven't been invited. I don't really know her very well, these days. She doesn't intend to let me get to know her very well. She doesn't speak about her father and Anthea at all, and I honour her restraint. She is wise to keep her distance.

Isobel and Martha are more censorious towards me and more obsequious towards their father. My oldest daughter Isobel, and I am sorry to have to say this, is a very self-centred and avaricious young woman. She expressed the view that I was wasting family money by insisting on living alone in London, when I could have lived much more cheaply in some hovel in East Anglia. She implied that I had got what was coming to me, and did not deserve what she actually had the audacity to describe as a golden handshake. She implied that I had been an inadequate wife. I had been frigid, remote, and unsupportive, both to her father and to the School. I think I once heard myself say that I hadn't married the School, and that she hadn't been very supportive of it herself. Isobel is one of those women who expect to be supported. She thinks she is the centre of every circle. It was her father that gave her this high opinion of herself. She was his first-born, and he spoiled her. She was very pretty, and is now very vain, although she is no longer as pretty as she was. Like her father, she glances at herself in every mirror. Nothing has ever been quite good enough for her. She is perpetually disappointed. She now has a tight, disapproving, contemptuous expression on her even-featured face for most of the time, though, like Andrew, she can turn on the charm when she wants to.

My daughter **Isobel**, my haughty first-born, thinks that I drove Andrew into adultery and into the arms of the wounded Anthea. In her eyes, her father can do no wrong, and I can do no right.

Ellen, the second-born and the least favoured, has removed herself from the blood-soaked family arena. She has denied her kith and kin and her inheritance. She is cool and dry and far away.

Martha, the youngest, the afterthought, the little baby of the family, is as thick as thieves with her stepmother, Anthea, and she endeavours day and night to steal the favours that were once awarded to her hard and grasping sister Isobel.

I wonder if they would recognize themselves from this harsh description. They were little children once, and all these plots and conflicts and vices were hidden in futurity. They need never have come to be. Yet now they are manifest, and now they cannot be undone. There is no way back to the shapeless tumble of the small nest of hopeful and unfinished people that they once were. Their soft limbs, their soft faces, their tender skin, their wounded tears. The reel cannot be wound back. The cards cannot be put back in the pack. The hidden is revealed. And yet it need not have been, surely? Sometimes I think that it could all have been quite different. I find it hard to believe that this is the bleak set pattern that I must live and die within.

It is not surprising that Martha is as thick as thieves with her stepmother, Anthea, for Martha was a friend of Anthea's dead daughter, and indeed it was Martha who found her floating in the Lady Pond. I felt sorry for Martha at the time, for this was a horrible experience for a girl of her age – well, for anyone of any age – but my sympathy was rapidly eroded by her hysterical enjoyment of the whole melodrama. Martha is an hysteric. She exaggerates everything. She is as demonstrative and as emotional and as verbose as Ellen is cold and hesitant and Finnish, but she is also, *au fond*, unconvincing. She took so much relish in that drowning, and in her own role as confidante and witness. I found her histrionics unpleasant, and I suppose I was not able to conceal my revulsion. So it is not surprising that Martha and Anthea fell into one another's arms over that dead body. And that Andrew also was willingly entrapped in the amorous blackmail of grief.

At least, that is how I interpreted the fateful course of events, though I may have been deceived. I may have misunderstood the time sequence. Possibly Andrew and Anthea had been carrying on with one another for some time before the 'accidental death', and simply used it as a pretext for making their entanglement public, hoping that a wash of sympathy would carry them along on top of the tide of public opinion. As it would indeed have done, had they so calculated. As, *en effet*, it did. For Andrew and Anthea did not drown, and neither did Martha. They flourished and their loves grew fat on that poor girl's death. Ellen has vanished to the Arctic Circle, and Isobel has turned into a self-regarding county queen, married now to the dull owner of many flat acres. Martha still lives with Andrew and Anthea, in a warm flushed emotional fusion of mutual condonement. It is all Darling This and Darling That and Dear Heart The Other. I don't like it. Andrew and I were never effusive with one another. We did not indulge in displays of endearments. I find such manners false. I am surprised by Andrew. But maybe this was what Andrew always wanted. Maybe he always wanted what I never gave, and could never have given. Maybe it is from my shortcomings that all these rank weeds grew.

I did not think to blame Andrew for my shortcomings. I

do not blame him now. But it is hard to live in the cold light.

There is no profit in such self-doubt. It is too late for regret and remorse.

She remembers the crossing of the threshold

When I moved to London, I was frightened by the choice I had made. I can admit that. I remember my first night here very clearly. In my adult years I had not had much experience of sleeping alone. I had moved from a dormitory in a girls' boarding school to a small bedsitter off a busy corridor in a women's college and then, after a short interlude teaching French in another girls' boarding school, I had moved into the marriage bed. When I travelled, I travelled with Andrew and I shared his bed. Andrew's work was home-based and he was rarely away. In the interregnum between myself and Anthea I had moved out of the Big House and lived in a spinsterly teacher's flat in the main school building, where I was surrounded by people who knew me and were intent upon being nice to me and sorry for me. I was eager to leave, but there were decencies to be observed, practical negotiations to be made, and Andrew's pride to be considered. As Andrew was, technically, the guilty party, I felt I had to be calm and gracious. It took some time to extricate myself from Suffolk.

So I was both nervous and exhilarated to find myself finally climbing this dingy ill-carpeted communal staircase with my suitcase, and crossing the threshold into my own life.

The furniture had already been installed. I'd sent on some of my own things, including a little desk dating back to my student days, but the place was so small that I didn't need much. I'd bought a new single bed. A brand-new single bed. Nobody had ever slept on my new bed. Nobody but me would ever sleep in it. I liked that idea very much. The removal men had picked up my sparse belongings from

Farlingham a few days earlier, and driven off with them and a set of keys. They were respectable, Suffolk removal men, from a reputable local firm. I trusted them with the keys. They'd offered to drive me to London with them but I couldn't face that. I didn't want to sit in their cab with them. It was not seemly. I felt too raw for company. I couldn't have taken either the banter or the deferential silence to which they would have treated me. Either would have been intolerable to me. So I'd gone alone, on the train, and met them at the other end of the journey, and watched them unload, and told them where to put the things. It was horrible. There are few things more distressing than the unpacking of old furniture into a new space. Then I went back to Suffolk for a night or two, to tie up the last loose ends. Then I came to London, again on the train, with my little suitcase and my sponge bag and my pills. Alone. I took the Tube from Liverpool Street to Ladbroke Grove. It's a direct line, though not a very good one. Hammersmith and City. It's a purple-pink colour on the map. I know it well now.

My friend Sally Hepburn had offered to come with me. My friend Henrietta Parks had offered to come with me. I had declined them both. My daughters had not offered. My daughters were treating me, at this stage, as a guilty fugitive. They were ashamed of me.

It was important to me to walk into that building and up those stairs and through my own front door by myself. This was to be the rest of my life, and I didn't want anyone watching me as I braced myself to greet it.

The door opens into an awkwardly shaped little landing space, on to which two more doors open, one into the kitchen-living room, the other into the bedroom which has a tiny bathroom *en suite*. It's a cheap but not ill-designed modern conversion. There are fitted cupboards throughout, fronted with a cold ivory-grey grained substance which might or might not be wood.

I went into the bedroom first, and put down my suitcase, and took a deep breath. (Well, I think I may have taken a deep breath, but as I write that phrase down on this remorseless laptop, I realize that I move from cliché to cliché. The machine hasn't got a cliché-spotter, but its cool objective format throws them into high relief.)

There was my single bed, and the cardboard boxes full of sheets and duvets and pillows and towels. There were my cases full of clothes and shoes. And that was about it. This was my little empire.

I took my sponge bag into the bathroom and tested the water. It was hot. So everything was connected. That was good. I opened a box or two, and hung up some garments. Then I went back into the other room, my living space. This looked less satisfactory than the bedroom – bleak, temporary, at once cluttered and empty. My student desk, an armchair, a bookcase. A small dining table, with four wooden chairs. I wondered if I would ever know four people, in London.

She remembers the unpacking of her household gods

It's interesting, what I'd chosen to salvage from the wreckage. I'd brought some books, of course, and my old wooden-cased bedside Roberts radio, and my digital clock. I sleep so badly now that I watch that clock for half the night. *Exsomnis noctesque diesque,* as Virgil put it. I'd brought a few old wedding presents that I'm sure Andrew won't miss, partly to compliment them for having survived better than our marriage – a Georgian silver soup ladle, a milk jug, an antique wooden coffee grinder which I have never used, an enamelled tray, a blue glass vase, a metal bird. The only framed photograph I've brought with me is a postcard-sized portrait of my long-dead father. I don't display it. I keep it in a drawer.

As I unpacked these objects, I found myself, for some reason, thinking about my childhood schoolgirl mascot. We all had mascots. We pretended to be very superstitious. For years I cherished a not very attractive glossy green plastic horse, about five inches long, which I called Emerald. She would stand on my desk, or by my bed. I couldn't go into a test or an examination without Emerald. It's interesting that I chose such a hard-edged and uncuddly object. I think I rather despised girls who favoured soft or fluffy toys, or ragged old comforters. Emerald, I thought, was more stylish and inspiring. She lasted until I was well into my teens, albeit with a broken leg. I glued the leg on again with a matchstick splint. I don't remember the moment at which I became bored with her, or lost her, or simply forgot about her. Where is she now? Has she degraded, or does some of her survive?

Julia had a more sophisticated mascot. It was a Turkish bracelet, designed to ward off the Evil Eye. I wonder if she has it still. We used to admire it greatly. We weren't allowed to wear jewellery at school, so she kept it in her sock drawer in a little white cloth bag. The bag had a drawstring, and was embroidered in white cotton with a white butterfly. White on white. She would get the bracelet out to show it to us and sometimes she would let us try it on. It consisted of twelve flat round clear turquoise glass beads, each thinly hooped with a slim band of silver, and linked together with a slender silver chain; in the middle of each bead was a little white glass circle with a black dot in it, like the pupil of an eye. I don't suppose it was of any value, but it had a magic to it, and was very different from any of the English trinkets which we had but weren't supposed to wear. She said she'd been given it by an uncle in the Navy who bought it for her in the Bazaar in Istanbul. It was delicate and fragile, and as I write of it I can see it on her wrist, and the way she turned her wrist to the light, to show off the beads. In later years, she was to acquire quite a collection of more serious jewellery, donated, as I supposed, by boyfriends, lovers, fiancés, husbands. All I've ever had is the Victorian sapphire and diamond engagement ring with which I was betrothed to Andrew, and which we bought in an antiques shop in Harrogate. Julia had knuckles full of diamonds. I wonder why I still wear Andrew's engagement ring. To ward off the Evil Eye, perhaps, though nobody would pursue me now. People would be more likely to snatch my ring than my person. There is no need for me to declare my marital status now.

Perhaps I'll sell it. It doesn't seem quite right, to sell it, but I don't really want it now. Do I?

I don't have jewellery. And when I arrived here, I didn't have much of anything. I hadn't brought much kitchen equipment. A couple of pans, a few place settings of stainless-steel cutlery, a mug, some plates, a kettle, some kitchen scissors, a pepper mill. I intended to buy myself some new crockery, when I settled down and found out what I needed. If ever I were to need anything more. I felt a relief in being so reduced. We accumulate too many objects, as we grow older. I had some hope that by stripping most of mine away, I might enter a new dimension. As a nun enters a convent in search of her god, so I entered my solitude. I felt fear, and I felt hope.

She takes her first walk around her new estate

I entered my domain in the early afternoon, and by five I had unpacked and made myself at home. It was February, well known as the dullest and dirtiest month of the year, but the weather was kind to me on that first day, and it was a clear, dry evening. I thought I would go out to buy some provisions. I had seen a grocery store of sorts near the Tube station, under the motorway. I would buy myself a little supper, and then I would watch my television. Yes, I have a television set. I am not a masochist, though it may appear otherwise. I would buy myself a bottle of wine, and some eggs, and some pasta, and some coffee, and some milk. Basic provisions for myself I would buy. A celebratory, solitary supper. I would never have to consult the taste of others again.

Walking along the pavement around here is a hazard and an adventure. You don't know what you'll see or what will happen. Then, on that first evening, I was an innocent. I am wiser now. But, even then, I knew to clutch my bag tightly and knot its strap around my arm.

I don't think I can recapture that first sense of disbelieving amazement I used to feel in these streets. I was an Alice in Wonderland.

The surface of the pavements is shocking. I recognize it now for what it is and will continue to be, but I still can't get used to it. It's filthy. It's particularly disgusting under the motorway, where the pigeons roost, and where strange large items of rubbish collect – they are too large to blow there on the high winds, so they must be deliberately dumped. Mattresses, abandoned pushchairs, old rugs, bicycle parts, motorcar parts. Car exhausts, broken wing mirrors, bumpers, sawn-off planks of wood. A sad and browning Christmas tree, which has been there since I first arrived. I saw it on that first evening, and it is there still. It has weathered two winters. Will it outlast my own sojourn? There are a lot of garages and mechanics and carpenters in the sheds under the arches of the motorway, and the emblems of their trade seem to spew out into the public pathways all around us. You have to pick your way carefully. There are always pools of standing water, even when it has not rained for days. Then there is the sputum, and the gum. The pavement, irregular enough in itself – it is always being dug up by an endless and unbroken cycle of water men and telephone men and television men and gas men – is marked with thick incrustations of expectorations and sediments of unidentifiable substances. Pigeon dirt, dog dirt, cat dirt, human dirt. City dirt.

I have made friends with a pet rat which lives up on Ladbroke Grove tube station. I must remember to record the story of my rat.

Some of the garden walls of the more regular houses that front the pavement are broken down. Slabs lie around. Then there are prefab huts cordoned off by barbed wire. God knows what is in them, or who would want to break in to steal any of it.

That first evening, I walked past the tall six-storey red-brick penitentiary of the college which is now my Health Club, and noted that it was offering Adult Evening Classes. I was surprised to find this archaic educational survival and thought I might perhaps join one of its offerings – and indeed, as I have already noted, a week or two later, I did. The advertisements for the college were easier to decipher than the casual and plentiful flyposters that were stuck all the way along walls and garage doors – I couldn't tell if these were announcing restaurants, or pop groups, or clubs, or services. I couldn't decode any of the messages. What were they, these things called SEA FOOD: SURVIVING THE QUEUE and EAT STATIC and DAY ONE? One trade sign seemed at first glance to read SHOCKS and EXHAUSTION, as though these were marketable commodities, but the objects on sale were, *en effet*, exhausts and shock absorbers.

FITTED WHILE U WAIT. I didn't wait. I couldn't quite absorb the shock. I repeat. I haven't absorbed it yet.

TRAINING FOR KILLS, that was another advertisement. I

worked that one out quite quickly. But many of the graffiti were impenetrable. Who was speaking to whom, on these city streets? Nobody was speaking to the person that is me. Nothing was aimed at me. The only message I thought I could understand was the one that said COMMUNISM IS ALIVE AND WELL AND FIGHTING IN PERU. This was applied to the wall in stencil, and it was accompanied by a hammer and sickle. It is so unlikely and so old-fashioned a message that it may well be an anagram for something else – some sexual perversion, probably. Like the dead Christmas tree, it's still there. It may be there for ever. It may be there when I am dead and gone.

She first hears them speaking in unknown tongues

The shop is called PriceCutter. It is a fair-sized grocery store, part of a cheap chain, and it sells food, newspapers, liquor. The people who work there are not white, nor are they black, and they speak a language that I do not know. The body of the shop occupies a long, deep oblong space, with shelves on both sides, and a central head-high block bearing racks of merchandise. The aisles are not quite wide enough and people are always banging irritably and sometimes angrily into one another. Londoners are not patient people. They anger quickly. That first evening, I was bemused by the shop's layout, as large cardboard boxes impeded access to many of the shelves, but I was to discover that this was a temporary (though recurrent) problem – I had come on some kind of delivery day, and groceries were piled around at random. Towers of lavatory paper, crates of tinned beans, pallets of packets of rice blocked the way at every turn. It was not like this in Woodbridge or Farlingham.

At first sight, the produce looked varied and quite tempting, but on closer inspection the charm palled. There were hard shiny bright green apples, and large round brown onions, and a choice of greenish or speckled bananas, and pallid browning lettuces balled up in Cellophane, and unnatural tomatoes. There was a wall of refrigerated shelves lined with small plastic pots of salad stuffs which looked enticing from afar but which, when challenged, turned out to contain pasta twirls coated in synthetic-looking mayonnaise in lurid shades of bright salmon or mustard yellow. There were also on offer some tubs of rust-tinted couscous spotted with dubious red and green specks of vegetable matter, and containers of lurid bathroom-paint-pink taramasalata. I am used to this kind of fare and ware now, and know how to avoid it or pick my way through it, but on that evening I felt mesmerized by the display. A sense of cheap poison prevailed. Everything was false and showy. It reminded me of my mother's warnings against the confectionery in Woolworths. Nevertheless, I risked an experimental little pot of stuffed vine leaves swimming in dark oil. We didn't get those in Suffolk.

I played safe after that, with a small block of processed Cheddar cheese, some milk, some Quaker macaroni, some bacon, a packet of cornflour and a bottle of Spanish wine. There was a whole wall of alcohol, with many bottles of unknown and brightly coloured drinks with names like Bacardi Breezer and Hooch and Dandelion. Pale chalk green and mauve pink and yellow gold and turquoise are these drinks, in their smart frosted bottles. To my surprise I couldn't see any of those delicious little Microwave Meals for One which I know make up most of Sally's not-very-slimming diet. It has taken me some time to realize that those meals are expensive. Those are a luxury. They don't stock them in PriceCutter, though they do stock turquoise beverages.

I have a microwave. Microwaves are sinful. Andrew didn't

approve of them and wouldn't allow the School to install them. That's why I got one. Andrew thought they might be bad for the children's health. He didn't approve of laziness and short cuts and aerosols. He may have been right. I'm not saying he was wrong about everything. But I don't mind if I poison myself, do I? What does it matter, at my age?

Near the checkout desk, where the attendants were speaking to one another in tongues, there was a heap of cut-price items in a dump bin – packets of food past their sell-by date, tins with dents or torn labels, that kind of thing. I picked out a heavily reduced wall calendar in a Cellophane wrap, portraying scenes of 'London's Tourist Sites', and added it to my purchases. Then I set off to my new home. I let myself in with some pride and some satisfaction. So far, so good.

(My use of that phrase 'dump bin' there is anachronistic. I didn't know those words when I moved here. I learnt them, at my Virgil class, from Anaïs Al-Sayyab. But I don't suppose that matters. Nobody will know. I don't have to be too careful about chronology, do I? This document isn't going to be used in evidence in a court of law, is it?)

A lot of the shops around here are covered in metal grilles. PriceCutter isn't, so I must suppose it has a complicated but concealed alarm and surveillance system instead. The video shop and the off-licence and the post office are all boxed in with this sinister grillwork. Like prisons. Like Wormwood Scrubs.

I boldly thought of buying myself some flowers, from the flower shop on the corner, which, as I now know, always has a fine array of blooms. (I didn't know that then.) But I hadn't got a spare hand to carry them with, so I didn't. I was glad, later, that I hadn't attempted to cheer myself with a bouquet on that first evening, because I found that I couldn't understand a word that the old flower man said to me. He was incomprehensible. Forget Eliza Doolittle. That old man doesn't speak in tongues, he speaks in English, but it's an extreme Cockney English, far more obscure than the English of any Shavian heroine I have heard, and anyway I don't know what the *words* mean. London flowers seem to have different names from Suffolk flowers. What is 'jip', I ask you? (I know the answer now.)

He calls his 'Alstro Marias' 'Ulster Marys'. I've learnt that one too. I like it.

When I got home, on that first evening, I opened the wine and poured myself a glass and stood and stared out of the high window. I switched on the radio, and found some music. Classic FM. The reception was excellent. I quite like that man who speaks to me in a friendly Irish accent between recordings.

This was the first evening of the rest of my new life. I was hungry. I hadn't had lunch. I started to prepare my supper, although it was so early. I hadn't brought a grater. I had to chop the cheese up into little chunks. I thought I'd get it all ready, then reheat it in the microwave later.

When I'd finished my second glass of wine, I hung up the calendar on the wall by the cooker, and crossed off all the used-up days in red pen. I crossed them out heavily till the paper was dented by the ballpoint. I obliterated them. All of January, and half of February. I told myself that I would cross off each day as it came. I would measure out my days.

As I sat there, on that first evening, I was suffused by a sense of what I can only call keen anticipation. I felt an intensity of anticipation for I knew not what. My destiny had no shape and no direction. It shone before me like the diffused radiance of dawn breaking over an unknown landscape.

My macaroni cheese was excellent. I ate it with relish. (I tried the vine leaves, but they were horrible.) Then I sat and stared out of the window from my one armchair. Mine is the most urban of views. Instead of the well-tended sloping lawn and the herbaceous borders and the distant glint of estuary that I could see from Holling House, I can see a two-tiered stretch of motorway, and blocks of high-rise council flats with their bright and intermittent lights, and the rooftops and skylights and aerials and satellite dishes and balconies and window boxes and windows of the nameless residents of these streets. Some of my third-floor neighbours hang their washing out on cleverly contrived lines and pulleys, and in the summer they put their shoes out to air at night. I can see geraniums, and a small palm tree in the middle distance, and pots of what Anaïs tells me is cannabis. I wouldn't know about that, but that's what she says.

The house I live in has a long untidy garden, to which I have no access. Occasionally I see a young yellow fox with a white apron walk delicately along the wall. At the bottom of the garden grows a tall London plane tree. Its branches spread on a level with my windows. The tree has never been pollarded, but its crown has been heavily and brutally pruned, and the branches end abruptly, like amputated limbs. On that first evening, I watched the silvery-grey tree in the blue night, and it seemed to me that as I watched the strangest bird in the world alighted upon it. It was as large as an egret, and its neck was as long as an egret's. I could not distinguish its true colour in the twilight, but it was a pale bird. I wondered if it had come to visit me from the Suffolk salt marshes. I wondered if it was an omen. It bobbed and stretched and preened itself upon the bough, and its neck seemed to stretch like a snake's. I peered at it, and its shape seemed to shift and change and alter before my eyes. After a while, curiosity overcame exhaustion and inertia, and heaved me out of my chair, and I got up and crossed to the window

– and behold, it was nothing more nor less than a common wood pigeon. I had been observing it through a flaw in the glass of the windowpane, and the glass itself had magnified and melted the form of the bird. I found I could make the bird's shape change at will. It was not a town pigeon, it was not one of those birds of grey and white with pink misshapen stumps for feet, it was an iridescent dove-grey pigeon of the dark and bloody London woods, and it was roosting in my tree.

I had power over the bird. It shifted shape at my command.

The flaw in the glass is always there. Sometimes I sit and stare through it for what seems like hours, making the outer world shift, marginally, at my will.

There aren't so many birds in London. The sparrows are dying or disappearing, nobody knows why. The omnivorous pigeons and the predatory magpies survive. I would like to visit the birdless lake of Avernus. Where no birds sing.

Why am I so certain that something exciting will happen to me in London? How can it, at my age? And what will it be?

I should feel powerless, but I do not. I feel more powerful than I did when I was married to that good man Andrew, the pillar of his community, the admired of all observers. I feel more powerful than I did then when I was a new and beloved bride, than when I became three times a mother and could rule over small lives. I cannot explain this sense of power.

One day soon I intend to put this sense of power to the test and buy myself a Lottery ticket. This will be a first for me, like so many things in my new existence. I'm not sure where they are on sale. Do people buy them at the post office, are they to be found at the newsagent's? I think it will be a question of First-Time Lucky. I haven't decided yet what to do with all the money. Anaïs may have some ideas. She has known riches in her time and she is still by temperament a big spender. She will be pleased when I win the jackpot.

Sally Hepburn will not be pleased. Sally wants me to be miserable. Sally wants to come and pry into my misery, and to report on it to those false friends in Farlingham. I should never have said she could come to this flat. What shall I give her for lunch? She's a fussy eater, although she eats so much. She has fads and phases. One year she is a vegetarian, then she suddenly decides she can't eat milk products but can accept white meat. One year fish is forbidden, the next it is the cure to all health problems. She even went through a phase when she decided she couldn't stomach wheat. It is all nonsense. These whims are designed only to swell her sense of her own importance. They are designed to make trouble for other people. Macaroni cheese is safe, isn't it? I can't remember what her position is on milk products at the moment, but I think she ordered a pizza last time we met in the Gallery, and it was covered with cheese. I pointed this out, and she didn't seem to know what I was talking about. She said she'd always liked cheese. So she must have decided dairy products are all right. And they are what she is going to get.

She introduces her friends in their persons to this story

Suddenly my thin life is thick. It has filled up. Sally has been to lunch, and I have survived her visit. And Julia Jordan is coming to see me next week when she is in London. My social life is almost too busy. Activity attracts activity.

A pleasant middle-aged woman in the sauna at the Health Club spoke to me this evening. She asked me where she could find some scales to weigh herself. I couldn't help her (oddly, I don't think there are any scales in the Ladies'

Changing Room), but it was good to be asked. We spoke a little about the merits of the Steam Room. She said she had high blood pressure and was not supposed to spend too long in the heat.

Then, on the way back, the elegant young man with dreadlocks who lives under the bridge spoke to me. My face must have been open, not shut. And so he spoke. He said, 'Good evening, Ma'am, and how are you today?' He was drinking cold Heinz chicken soup straight from the tin. I said I was fine, and that I hoped he was comfortable on his foam bedding. I gave him one of those new two-pound coins. He seemed quite pleased with it and turned it over several times as though it were a lucky charm. I used to be afraid to pass this man, and I would walk by on the other side, but I do not think he is at all dangerous. I am glad he spoke to me.

I gave Sally soup, but it wasn't cold, nor was it out of a tin. It was out of one of those fancy cardboard cartons, and I pretended I'd made it myself, or rather I didn't say I hadn't. This wasn't wholly cheating, as I did improve it – I added some mushrooms and parsley and cream. I don't know if she was fooled or not. I wasn't going to let on. Then we had our macaroni cheese. She ate that up all right, too, and I had made that from scratch. I hesitated over wine, but decided I'd better offer her some. I didn't want her thinking I couldn't afford it. But I didn't want her thinking I spent all my life drinking either. So I made a bit of a fuss about opening the bottle and not being able to find a corkscrew and told her I never usually drink at lunchtime. And that's true. I don't drink at lunchtime. I don't know if my performance was convincing or not. It wasn't a performance, as I was telling the truth, but she made me feel as though it was a performance.

Sally drank three-quarters of the bottle.

Sally had come by Tube, from Liverpool Street, and she'd

had a good introduction to my neighbourhood. It reminded me of my own first impressions and made me feel, in comparison, a seasoned Londoner. First of all, she had witnessed an unpleasant incident on Ladbroke Grove. There are many unpleasant incidents on Ladbroke Grove, though they take place more often in the dark than in the light of morning or the noonday sun. This one involved an elderly white man vomiting into the gutter by the bus stop. She didn't describe it very well, as vivid narration is not her forte, but I got the picture. Then she had had the added benediction of witnessing the man with the crucifix. I know that man well, by sight, and I watch him often. He is black, of short to medium height and of indeterminate age, with wisps of grey-black hair wandering over his balding scalp, and he walks the streets carrying a vast plain white wooden crucifix. It is hinged, so presumably he folds it away at night. His cross is taller than himself, and he carries it on his shoulder, as though he were climbing Calvary. He looks neither to right nor to left and he speaks to nobody. He does not rant, nor pray, nor proselytize. He simply walks the streets in silent dignity. He is a figure of penance. I think maybe he is saying penance for us all, for I cannot believe that he himself can have done anything bad enough to warrant so long an expiation. Anyway, Sally saw him, and reported her sighting, and I was able to lay claim to my long knowledge of him.

I think she was suitably impressed by my colourful neighbourhood.

She was certainly impressed by the unexpected apparition of Anaïs Al-Sayyab. I hadn't arranged for Anaïs to drop by in order to impress her, but that's how it turned out. I'd just wrested the cork out of the bottle when Anaïs rang to ask if she could pop round to borrow my radiator bleed key as she couldn't find hers and her central heating was full of airlocks.

(She lives very near.) Of course I said of course. I think we'd had some kind of discussion about plumbing and radiators a week or two ago, which had included a reference to airlocks. We don't always talk about such dull things but on this occasion it was lucky that we had. Anaïs didn't know I had company for lunch, and I didn't warn her over the phone. I wasn't quite sure how to put it. I could hardly say, 'For some reason I've got this embarrassingly enormous woman from Suffolk here in my flat', could I?

I hadn't seen Anaïs for a week or two. I know her from my Virgil class, and I sometimes bump into her at the Health Club. Not very often, for we keep different hours and she goes to classes, whereas I prefer to go alone. I do not like to impose on Anaïs Al-Sayyab, for she is a busy woman with a large circle of acquaintances, but I am always pleased to see her, and I am pleased that she bothers to keep up with me. I seem to play some role in her life. I am not sure what it is, but I am happy to play it.

We are not very close friends, but Sally Hepburn must have thought, from this somewhat unrepresentative meeting, that we pop in on one another all the time. I did nothing to correct this impression. I am not the kind of person to have close friends who pop in, but I think I wish I were that kind of person, and the illusion of being it is better than nothing.

I could see that Sally was much struck by Anaïs. Anaïs is striking. She is more than striking. She is spectacular. She ran up the stairs noisily, faster than Sally or I could have managed, and burst in dramatically, exaggerating her breathlessness. 'Wow, what stairs!' she cried, as she burst in, puffing and panting and blowing from her carmine lips. I could see Sally looking at her in wonder. For Anaïs is lustrous, and as exotic as her name. She is dark-haired and brown-complexioned, and she dresses in the gaudiest of garments. Even her bathing suit is striped and starred in splashes of mango and canary. Yesterday she was wearing a woollen coat of many colours, banded with green and red and blue and yellow, and cut in a surprising way that managed simultaneously to suggest a nomadic blanket and an expensive item of Japanese haute couture. She was also wearing a scarlet hat with a silver tassel, perched on top of her thick black curls. And her make-up was thick and lush and shameless.

Yet Anaïs is a lady. You can see at a glance that she is a lady. She's a different sort of lady from the refined and thoroughbred sort they tried to breed at St Anne's, but she is a lady.

I offered her a glass of wine, but she declined. No, she said, too busy, another day, she had to dash. So this was Sally from Suffolk? Heard a lot about *you*, cooed Anaïs in her slightly menacing way, which could have meant anything or nothing. Bless you, my darling, she said to me, as she put the bleed key into her bag. I'll give you a ring, she threatened, and she kissed me loudly and extravagantly, and then away she flew, clopping vigorously down the stairs and out of our hearing.

Anaïs wears short skirts and astonishing shoes. They are heavy, thick-soled and clumpy, and they add inches to her already considerable height. They are very smart and come from some designer shop in Knightsbridge of which I can never remember the name.

I don't mind it when Anaïs calls me darling. She calls everybody darling, and that's just fine by me. I don't think Anthea Richards ever dared to call me darling – it would hardly be proper, as a form of address to her lover's first wife – and I certainly wouldn't have liked it if she had.

Anaïs, early in our Virgilian acquaintance, decided to decide I was amusing company. And therefore, with her, I can be amusing. She summons up another self for me. She has that power.

This intervention from 'my friend Anaïs' (how proudly I write that phrase) gave a kick-start to my little luncheon party, and I found myself almost boastful about the contentment of my London life. Maybe it was my unsuitable air of self-satisfaction that made Sally drink so much and become so overbearing and, eventually, indiscreet. First of all, she displayed a brutally direct curiosity about Anaïs – who was she, what did she do, where had I met her, what nationality was she, did she always wear such outrageous clothes? Did I know many people like her? And why, when she wore such short skirts, didn't she bother to shave her legs? I never ask people direct questions because it's rude. And that last question of Sally's, about Anaïs's legs, was rude by any standards. I muffled my replies, but I did unwisely reveal that Anaïs worked in television. I suppose I was pleased to be able to claim to know somebody who works in television, but I should have kept quiet. It was none of Sally's business. (In fact, I don't think Anaïs does work in television any more, and I've never been quite clear what it was that she did when she did it, but she certainly used to have some professional connection with whatever it is that goes on or used to go on down the road at White City and Wood Lane.) And it was unwise to mention television anyway, on other grounds, because it gave Sally an opening for a speech about a TV programme she'd seen recently about prostitution in Pompeii.

She wasn't complaining that this Pompeii programme was pornographic. On the contrary. I might well have thought it was, had I seen it, which I hadn't, but Sally had thoroughly enjoyed it. Far from being shocked by it, she was praising it for its frankness and for the explicit nature of the erotic paintings of *hetairai*, priapic figures and bizarre sexual couplings which it had displayed. Sally claims never to have seen a naked man, in the flesh, though she seems to have seen many more on film than I ever have. I do not like talking about this kind of thing. I am squeamish and anyway I think these matters are private. But Sally has no shame. She became so excited about some of the depictions she had seen that she proposed that she and I should go on a coach tour to Naples and Pompeii. There are, she says, some excellent Art Tours with distinguished lecturers serving as guides, and handsome couriers who handle all the baggage and who probably, according to Sally, double up as gigolos. The word 'gigolo' amused her. She said it several times over, to make sure I got the point.

I could tell that Sally thought this was a very kind proposal, and one that would suit me well in my divorced and outcast state. I am supposed to be humbled, and grateful now for any overture. She said we could share a room and then we wouldn't have to pay the Single-Room Supplement and that it would be much cheaper that way.

I couldn't tell how serious she was. It's not the first time she's tried suggesting that we go on holiday together, and when I lived in Suffolk I did once let her drag me away for a short weekend to a rather low-key literary festival in Cromer. We stayed a night but we did not share a room. It rained all the time and we attended a very poor lecture by a man who writes about birds. Some of his slides were upside down.

I don't want to go to Naples with Sally. I would like to see Naples before I die, but I don't want to see it with her. I know more about Naples than Sally does. I would like to see the birdless realms of Avernus and the dark pit of Acheron. I would like to visit the Sibyl at Cumae and hear my endless fate. But not with Sally Hepburn.

I eventually diverted Sally from the subject of phallic

symbols by leading her on to Suffolk gossip. She was by now well through the wine, and although it was only a light white cheap Italian table wine (not from PriceCutter, but cheap enough nonetheless) it was turning her large face red and making her shout and spit. First she told me about Henrietta Parks and her new-born granddaughter, who, to Sally's ill-concealed satisfaction, seems to have a serious problem connected with her digestive system and is noticeably failing to thrive. A surgical operation may be necessary. I said that I was sorry to hear this. And so I was and so I am, I hope. I wish no harm to the innocents.

I sometimes think that *Schadenfreude* becomes a serious affliction for many of us as we grow older. We long for the illnesses and deaths of others. This is not pleasant, but I fear it may be so.

I have no grandchildren. Isobel, my married daughter, has not yet reproduced. I suppose I ought to wonder why not, but I never think about it, except when Sally obliquely raises the subject. It's no affair of mine. Is it?

Then Sally couldn't resist bringing me up to date with the latest news of Andrew and Anthea, and I couldn't resist listening. She had met them both at Ixham House at a lecture on penal reform and youth custody by the governor of Coveney Hall. (I managed not to tell her about my man in Wormwood Scrubs. I was tempted to tell her, but I kept him a secret.) Lady Westbury had laid on a reception with very nice nibbles. Everyone has to provide nibbles these days, said Sally, digging heartily into her macaroni.

I don't much like the word 'nibbles'. It reduces us to mice or hamsters. Sally seems very fond of it. Once Sally gets hold of a word, she does it to death. That day it was all gigolos and nibbles.

That woman doesn't nibble. She eats like a pig. She shovels

it in. And she messes it around on her plate, too. We were always told not to play with our food at St Anne's. She mushes and mashes hers with her fork, and makes little piles of it, and then eats it very noisily. I think she has dentures. Maybe that's why she mashes it all up so much. But it's no excuse.

Sally told me that at first she'd thought the Westbury nibbles were Marks and Spencer canapés, but they weren't, they were hand-crafted nibbles. Not hand-crafted by Lady Westbury herself, of course, but by some more personalized slavey than those employed by Marks and Spencer. (At this point I nearly told Sally about the carton soup, but again, I restrained myself. Why do I feel so powerful a need to betray myself to her? What hold does Sally Hepburn have on me? What are these games we play? And why, come to that, should a lecture on youth custody be so inappropriately accompanied by wine and canapés?)

Andrew and Anthea had been tucking into the nibbles too, according to Sally. They had even asked My Lady Westbury for the name of the caterer. They seemed to be thinking of having a party, says Sally, to celebrate their first wedding anniversary. They have been married nearly a year. It has all been very rapid.

How has Andrew got away with it? How has he managed to attract such sympathy and tolerance, in that gossipy, petty, backbiting little world? He and Anthea are invited everywhere. Nobody cuts them or gives them the cold shoulder. They were adulterers, and in the eyes of some churches they still are, but they go to parties and they give parties. Am I forgotten? Is my name forbidden? Is it a relief to all that I have left the county? Was I always a pariah, without my knowing it? Was this lofty solitude foreordained to be my destiny? A destiny stacked, laid, unalterably dealt?

Anthea, said Sally, was wearing a long woollen dress of a deep cherry red. Anthea is buxom and vivacious and elegant. I admit it. People smile when she enters a room. Whereas my Suffolk self was faded and wan, and the passivity of my self-pity made an ugly martyr of me. People turned away at my approach.

I must have been very bad, for them to have been forgiven so quickly for their transgression.

The binman at Farlingham once called me a tight-arsed bitch, because I asked him not to throw the bin lids on the flowerbed. Perhaps I am a tight-arsed bitch.

Sally says Anthea can't cook. Can't cook, or won't cook. Rumour has it, says Sally, that Andrew, Anthea and Martha eat out most of the time, or live on what's left over from the school kitchen. He'll be missing your good plain cooking, said Sally, scooping another great forkful into her wide mouth, and munching away.

She devours and insults my food simultaneously. She has always done so. I assume she must sometimes cook for herself, but she has never cooked for me. I wonder how she got to be quite so large. Those microwave meals aren't very substantial, are they? She probably eats double quantities of them.

I mean, literally, that she devours and insults simultaneously. She talks while eating. With her mouth full.

She couldn't think of anything else to say about Anthea. I thought, at one point, that she was about to raise the forbidden name of Anthea's dead daughter, Jane, but she didn't. She skirted the topic, with some reference to an article she'd read on the rising suicide rate for young males, and a client of hers whose son had taken an overdose, but then she ostentatiously drew back from it. I should try to be charitable and to remember that Sally probably behaves quite professionally with her clients. She does good, but I do nothing, and that is worse. Do Good, do Bad, do Nothing. I do nothing. Fainéant.

I made her some coffee – real coffee, not instant, though I didn't use my antique wooden grinder. I have never used my antique wooden grinder. It is useless. Then I sent her on her way. I was glad to see the back of her.

It was getting dark before Sally left. It's that time of year. The evenings are getting a little lighter now, but not very rapidly.

I think I got the better of the encounter. Sally was obliged to thank me for lunch, and when I told her to admire the view, she was obliged to admire the view. And she'd kept off the subject of sex, for most of the day, except for that Pompeian excursion, and that had been classical rather than personal. Overall, I'd given nothing away. When she had asked after my mother's health, I had stonewalled her completely. No change there, I said. I know Andrew hopes my mother will die shortly and leave me some kind of inheritance, and Sally probably senses this. He may even have mentioned it to her. I don't know what Andrew might tell Sally. I have no such expectations of my mother. I know more about my mother's finances than Andrew does. Like her, they are not healthy. Nursing homes are very expensive. They devour our estates.

Sally will be able to report back to Suffolk that I live in a shabby area full of drunks and psychopaths, but if she's any honesty in her she'll also have to say that I seem fine, gave her a nice lunch, and have made some interesting new friends. Thank you, Anaïs.

She remembers her hysteria and fretfulness and she regrets them

Re-reading my account of Sally's visit, I see that much of it is dictated by bravado. In truth, looking back over my behaviour in Suffolk, I have much to be ashamed about. I did not conduct myself like a lady in those last few years in Suffolk. I had small tantrums over small things and slept much in the afternoons. I behaved in a mildly deranged and menopausal manner. I refused to help in the School and I shouted at the groundsman when he mowed down the fritillaries. I withdrew my wifely support from my husband and gazed at my handsome daughter Isobel with envy and distrust. I should not have shouted at the refuse collector, even though I think he should not have thrown the dustbin lids on the flowerbeds. I moved out of my husband's bed and said that I preferred to sleep alone. I made the excuse that this was because I slept so badly. *Exsomnis noctesque diesque*. It is true that I slept badly. I still sleep badly. Things got worse when I stopped taking Hormone Replacement Therapy. I still have night sweats, though they should have stopped long ago. I no longer sweat during the day, but I do feel hot at night. Nobody warned me of this. Actually, it's not really a night sweat, it's more a night fever. I burn with heat, yet my skin is dry. I don't know what this means.

What would have happened to me and my marriage, if Jane Richards had not drowned herself in the Lady Pond? From that death, Andrew and Anthea took life, and now they are man and wife and one flesh. I think much about drowning. My man in Wormwood Scrubs drowned his victim. He says he didn't mean to, but I suspect he did. I know the very place. Anthea's daughter drowned herself. I know the very place. I wade in, but only up to my knees.

The coroner had said Jane's balance of mind was disturbed, which I guess it may well have been. I hadn't known Jane well, although – or perhaps I mean because – she was a friend of my daughter Martha. But I had liked her, or liked what I had seen of her, poor thing. Her name was Jane, plain Jane. She wasn't plain, she was not unattractive, but she did have an unfortunate problem. She was partially sighted, and she had a very severe squint. One of her eyes seemed to roll sideways, and it stared, as it were, right out of the side of her head. It was very disconcerting. I think an operation had gone badly wrong when she was a little girl. The School, of course, got some of its funding from the Hamilcar Henson Trust for the Blind, which made special provision for the partially sighted. That was why Jane had been sent to Holling House School in the first place. Some suggestion was made that it was Jane's poor vision that had led her to stumble into the water. But poor vision doesn't fill the pockets of your school blazer with stones, does it? Poor Jane. She was quite a bright little thing. She was in my class in 3C when Andrew bullied me into teaching French Conversation, that year when Mlle Fournier went back to France in something of a hurry. I remember hearing Jane recite a fable by La Fontaine. It was the one about the timid hare, *'Le Lièvre et les Grenouilles'*.

Un Lièvre en son gîte songeait
(Car que faire en un gîte, à moins que l'on ne songe?);
Dans un profond ennui ce Lièvre se plongeait:
Cet animal est triste, et la crainte le ronge . . .

That's a long time ago now. Poor hare.

Jane's death was hushed up, as much as was possible, and nobody blamed the School administration, or Andrew, or Anthea, or Jane's dead father, or the School groundsman, or the pond for not having any railings around it. As far as I can remember nobody blamed anybody or anything. I think

Andrew got off lightly, though of course I myself was not at all anxious for him to attract any bad publicity to himself or the School. There was a great deal of speculation about why she'd done it, but I tried not to pay too much attention to it. I didn't listen to gossip. I think I assumed that she'd simply suffered from an aggravated bout of teenage depression. There had been talk of a love affair that went wrong, but there is always talk of a love affair that has gone wrong. Once Sally tried to hint that Jane might have thought she was pregnant, but I didn't let her enlarge on this.

Jane drowned herself on my birthday. This was a meaningless coincidence, but the consequence of it is that I can never forget the date of her death. The fourth – or is it the fifth? – anniversary of it approaches. I remember Martha running up the lawn screaming, as Andrew and I were having breakfast. I was opening my birthday cards. I don't get many. There was one from my daughter Ellen in Finland, which had arrived a few days earlier: I'd saved it to open on the day. And there was a card from Julia Jordan, which had arrived that very morning. I was reading her message when I heard the screams.

Julia, as I have already noted, always remembers my birthday. I've never made much of a fuss about my birthday, although I'm so superstitious about numbers and always feel something significant might one year happen upon it. The only person who remembers it regularly, apart from family, is Julia, and that's because of some kind of flashback school memory. We used to mark birthdays at St Anne's. Cards, little presents, and an iced sponge cake with candles.

For my fourteenth birthday Julia gave me a tiny little bottle of perfume. It was of royal-blue glass, with a silver stopper. Oddly enough, I seem to have forgotten its name. It was called something like Eau de Paris, and it had a little picture of the Eiffel Tower on its label. I loved it. We weren't allowed perfume at school but I used to keep it under my pillow at night and sniff at it secretly.

I did behave badly and sadly in Suffolk. But I don't think Jane Richards drowned herself on my birthday to punish me. I don't think she was thinking about me at all, or about the strange consequences her death would have for me.

Julia is coming to see me next week. She rang to fix the date. Julia is a wicked woman. I am a wicked woman. Her sins are of commission, mine of omission. Both are grave.

I wonder what numbers I shall choose when I buy my Lottery ticket, the ticket that is going to bring me untold wealth. I believe a lot of people go by their own birthdays, or by the birthdays of their children. I'll have to think about that. Or maybe it's better to do it on impulse. I don't know how it works, at all. I don't even know how many numbers there are on a ticket, or what a ticket costs. Will I dare to ask? My heart beats faster at the prospect, even as I sit here alone in my tower, and I cannot tell whether it beats faster with pleasure or with fear.

She thinks of the new things in her life

I've done so many things for the first time in the last year or two. Like eating a vegetable samosa in the street on the way back from the tube station. We were taught that eating in the street was a crime. We weren't warned specifically against eating vegetable samosas, because they hadn't been introduced into England at that date, but we were warned against street eating. And I broke the rules.

I have also been into a pub on my own. I suppose I have been into country pubs on my own, in the past, but always to meet somebody, or to use the Ladies' Room, or to buy a sandwich. London pubs are very different from those Suffolk village pubs with pink walls and thatched roofs and hanging baskets of flowers and Meals of the Day and Pensioners' Lunches. Ladbroke Grove pubs are not at all the same. I don't know why I went in – to test myself, perhaps? Ostensibly, I went in for shelter, after getting off the bus. This was a year or so ago, now. It was pouring with rain, and I hadn't got an umbrella. It seemed stupid to walk home getting soaked to the skin. So I went into this pub, on the corner. It's called the Frog and Firkin, God knows why. It was horrible. The smell, the murk, and the people. A desolate conglomeration of desperate folk. I was one of them. This pub was more like a place of refuge than a place of refreshment. Aimless young men with small thin beards, a person of indeterminate sex wearing a baseball cap, a couple of old drunks, a crazed fat girl with a loud laugh. Jelly beans in a plastic container. A message saying *Have a Firkin Good Day*. Cigarette smoke. A man standing by himself at one end of the bar, talking to himself, and occasionally jerking his arm upwards in a meaningless gesture.

I smelt of wet wool. I ordered myself a tomato juice and boldly asked for some Worcester Sauce. I was offered ice. I declined it.

If I'd risked another hundred yards or two in the downpour I could have reached my Health Club and civilization. They do a good coffee in the Health Club. They know who I am in my Health Club, or at least they pretend to know who I am. They read my name off my swipe card and then wish me a good evening. It's a world away from the Frog and Firkin. I wonder if there are any Health Club members who also frequent the Frog and Firkin?

I realize now that all my life I've been an unthinking racist, and that I am one still. I simply cannot get used to all these foreigners in London pubs and on London streets. I don't expect to see black people buying mineral water in supermarkets, or pints of beer in a public house. (Actually, there was only one black man in the Frog and Firkin – I think the black men drink in the pub on the opposite corner – but you know what I mean.) Where do they get the money from? They don't look as though they've got jobs. But then I haven't got a job myself, have I? I've never had any money of my own, or I didn't have until Andrew bought me off. Come to think of it (and I don't know why I've never thought of this before) I never got paid when I stood in or sat in to take classes for members of staff who were off sick. It was just assumed that I would help out. I wasn't really qualified to do anything but teach fairly basic French, but I used to fill in for Religious Knowledge sometimes, and I often used to invigilate for examinations or superintend evening prep. I even took a PE class once, and I umpired a hockey match or two. But I was never paid. I was like an old-fashioned doctor's wife, or a vicar's wife. I was there when needed. And now I am not needed and I am not there.

She thinks of the many peoples of the earth

I wouldn't teach Latin. I remember that Andrew was quite cross with me one term when Miss Phillips was off for weeks with pleurisy, and I said no, I wouldn't take her class. I said my Latin wasn't good enough. And it wasn't. Latin is a serious subject. You can't play around with Latin. I have a respect for Latin.

The lumpen boys in big boots walk the streets. The ugly, heavy-footed spotted youths, in their gashed jeans. Two of them followed me last night as I walked back from the Club. They were singing some kind of stupid jingle, and I think they were singing it at me. It went something like this:

Jim Jim, Jim Jiminy
Jim Jim, Jeroo
I've washed all the dishes
And I've fuckall to do.

Then they overtook me, leering back at me, to see if they'd scored a goal. Or so I fancied. Maybe I imagined the whole thing. Maybe they didn't even notice me. I'm not very noticeable.

I sometimes think that my kind of washed-out genteel look – a look which I could not shed even if I tried – attracts a particular kind of aggression these days. The white lumpen boy ones are worse than the indifferent black boys, who do not notice me at all.

'Lumpen' means ragged. I read that in a book last week. I thought it meant something different. I think most of us think it means something different.

I am beginning to realize that black people come from many different kinds of social background, as well as from many different countries. I must always have known that, but in Suffolk I didn't see enough of them to be able to begin to make distinctions. There are very smart young black people on reception at the Health Club – a young woman called Tamsin who wears smartly tailored suits in strong plain dark colours, a good-looking young man called Chelsea who wears a white jacket and a red tie. They have a very pleasant manner, which I think of as faintly American, though they are not American. They come from another world from the man with dreadlocks who lives under the bridge by the howling monsters rattling their chains. They would not recognize the holy black man with the crucifix. I wonder what they would make of the elderly black woman I saw on the Tube this morning. She was sitting opposite me, tidily but cheaply dressed, reading a paperback book with a heavily laminated cover. Her boldly framed spectacles were held around her neck by a golden chain. She was elderly but not old, and she was dry and withered. It was her legs that attracted my attention. They were slim, and hideously scarred. I wondered if she had had varicose vein operations that had gone wrong. But far from hiding these once handsome legs, she was flaunting them. She was wearing a pair of semi-transparent toffee-tinted plastic shoes with high heels, of a curious elegance. The set of her ankles was superb. Now who was she, and whence had she come, and whither was she so proudly going?

I miss my Virgil evening class at what used to be the College of Further Education, and is now the Health Club. It was an interesting group. We were reading the *Aeneid*, in English, but with access to a Latin text. We compared our various English translations and suggested phrases of our own as improvements. We were an archaic, arcane little group. That's where I first met Anaïs. I'd like to ring Anaïs this evening, but I don't want to bother her. I don't want to become a bore to Anaïs. I'll wait for her to ring me. Anaïs was the most exotic and unlikely class member, but most of us were quite bright. We met on Thursday evenings. Our teacher was a fine woman called Mrs Jerrold. She was the widow of a legendary BBC Third Programme drama producer called Eugene Jerrold who had worked with Louis MacNeice and Dylan Thomas and George Orwell and all the great names of the 1940s and 1950s. Even I had heard of these writers. I had heard some of those programmes. *En effet*, I remembered them quite well.

As I've just said, I miss my Virgil class. It gave a better shape to the week than the Health Club, though of course I can go to the Health Club whenever I like, and Virgil was only on Thursdays.

Mrs Jerrold didn't boast about these famous people, or drop their names into our classes, but she had known them well. She was what I think might be called a game old bird, and she looked something like a bird, with a sharp, small, bridged beak of a nose, and dark darting eyes, and dyed boot-black tufty feathery hair sticking out at all angles from the confines of a brightly coloured bandeau. She had a good selection of bandeaux. She wore red lipstick, and green eyeshadow, and magenta earrings shaped like descending drooping flowers, like small hanging baskets. Fuchsia, belladonna, and dangling pagodas of pheasant berry. She was a parrot, a macaw. She was a sprightly old thing, and she knew her Virgil. I wonder how she is now. I wonder if she needed the money. Those classes pay terribly, I know, but they do pay something. (Unlike the supply classes I taught at Farlingham.)

I ought to look her up. But I'm not a social worker. I'm more of a social case than a social worker.

We were a nice class. We were nice even to our own mad member, an old man called Mr Wormald, who had a fixation on poor Mrs Jerrold. He tormented her. We were all very tolerant with him. I wonder what happened to him. I've never seen him since the class disbanded, though I suppose he lives locally. I don't think he'd have been interested in the Health Club offer, or a very welcome member had he tried to take it up. He was short and ill-shaven and yellow-complexioned and he looked as though he hadn't bathed in years. He was a pedant and an autodidact, and he delighted in correcting Mrs Jerrold whenever he saw an opportunity. He was sometimes right. He had ill-fitting dentures and a wife called Doris who worked for the Inland Revenue. He was retired, from what I know not. He had taken early retirement. He was a terrible man. He was the only man in the class. But we were kind to him, we made a space for him amongst us. I can't imagine why he was interested in Virgil. I don't think he was, really. He was interested in Mrs Jerrold and had latched on to her like a small persistent worrying dog. He asked her questions about Eugene Jerrold which we would have been too polite to formulate. She was very good at evading them.

I think Eugene had been killed in a car crash. I keep meaning to check on this. I could go to Colindale and look in the newspaper library there for the obituaries. But it seems a bit underhand and impertinent. More the kind of thing Sally Hepburn might do. Sally Hepburn has an unnatural and unseemly curiosity about other people.

At school, Julia, Janet and I all studied Latin up to A and then S level standard, only the three of us in the class. We had an excellent teacher. Maybe all Classics teachers are excellent. They sing in the dark and shore up the ruins. They play with tragic brilliance the endgame.

Our teacher at St Anne's was called Mrs Pearson. She was a sombre, sallow, heavy-browed woman, handsome and charismatic. Come to think of it, she too was a widow, like Mrs Jerrold. We thought Mrs Pearson a romantic figure, for she always dressed in black, quite stylishly, and she spoke frankly about erotic poetry. Maybe that's why Julia was so attentive in class. Dido and Lesbia. Mrs Pearson wasn't at all like Sally Hepburn, oh no, I don't mean that at all. Mrs Pearson was never rude or vulgar. But we knew that she had known and seen and suffered such things.

I don't want to go to Naples with Sally Hepburn, but I do want to go to Naples. I'd like to visit the Phlegrean Fields before I die. *I Campi Flegrei*, the Burning Fields. *Lugentes Campi*, the Mourning Plains. I love the Sixth Book of the *Aeneid*. I suppose I could afford to go on a modest coach tour by myself. I probably couldn't afford one of those very expensive ones with very expensive lecturers, but there must be cheaper ones for schoolmistresses and librarians and people like me. I'd have to have the Single-Room Supplement, because I don't think that at my age I could bear to share a room with a stranger, but maybe I could afford it. I'll look into it. I wouldn't have to tell Sally, would I? Even though it was her idea.

I live very cheaply most of the time, after all. I don't do much.

I don't think Sally knows anything about Virgil and the Underworld and the Golden Bough.

I wonder where I should arrange to meet Julia. There are some smart restaurants not far from here. Or I could cook her a little something or other. Some good plain home cooking.

I think that I first began to dislike Andrew when he made that remark about the Hungarian goulash I cooked for dinner for the Millers. Goulash was quite the in-thing in those days, and mine was usually quite nice. It was an economical way of making a stew look and taste a bit more interesting. So I'd done a goulash, with rice and peas and paprika. It was true that the beef wasn't quite up to Mr Bates's usual braising quality – it was a bit tough and, although I'd trimmed it carefully, there were residual attachments of a sort of yellowish gelatinous gristle or sinew – but it was perfectly edible, or so I thought. But Andrew played with his, ostentatiously cutting bits off and piling them on the side of his plate, and then he looked at me across the table and gave me that captivating smile and said, 'Well, sweetie, not quite one of your best, is it?' Then he took in Mr and Mrs Miller, into the smile, as he looked around and said, 'Just a wee bit on the disgusting side, I'm afraid', and pushed all the meat to one side.

Mr and Mrs Miller didn't say anything – how could they? They smiled back, in an embarrassed way, and went on eating. They made themselves eat all the nasty bits. I think they felt sorry for me. We didn't know one another very well, and they probably felt, as I did, that Andrew shouldn't have said what he said. I remember that I blushed. I used to blush, occasionally. Not very often – a blush always took me by surprise, as this one did. I said nothing. I smiled, in a propitiatory way, and bent my head over the orange-red mess, and went on chewing.

At such moments, one dies a little. I died a little, but I was also angry. I felt I had not deserved such treachery.

I won't cook a goulash for Julia. I'll ask her round here for a drink, and get some of those olives from the weird North African shop Anaïs has discovered, and then I'll take her out for a meal round the corner at Mr Gordano Black's. It's very smart there. She'll be impressed by Mr Gordano Black. I can afford it, for a special occasion. She'll probably try to pay, to show off about how rich she is, but I'll try not to let her. I'd better book a table right now. They get very busy.

I'm glad I don't have a spare room. I haven't even had to think about asking her to stay the night.

Julia will be here in an hour. I hope I look presentable. I wonder what she looks like, these days? I can't remember when I last saw her. But I think I've remembered the name of that French perfume she gave me all those years ago. It was called Evening in Paris, by Bourjois. I used to think the word was Bourgeois, and I thought that was a funny name for a Parisian product. But it wasn't. It was Bourjois. I wonder if it still exists. If it does, it must be very out of fashion. I wonder if she remembers that gift as well as I do. We didn't have so many things in those days. There weren't so many things to have. There was more to look forward to, but less to possess. It's the other way round now.

A dark, purple-blue glass bottle. A treasure. The fizzy water at Mr Gordano Black's comes in dark blue bottles. It's a good strong clear colour. We didn't have bottled water, in the old days. We drank water from the tap.

I'm wearing my old Liberty-print wool dress. Martha says it makes me look mumsy. I can't help that. What am I supposed to look like, at my age?

She tells the story of her reunion with novelist Julia Jordan

So Julia came, and Julia went. What a very strange woman she is. And what strange things she spoke of. I wonder what to make of it. There is some meaning in it, but I do not yet know what it might be.

Let me begin at the beginning. Julia arrived on the dot of our appointed hour. For a wicked woman, she is always surprisingly punctual. And she didn't seem at all winded by the stairs. The stairs are a kind of test, for people of our years. But she took them in her stride. No puffing or panting or exclaiming, even for show, from Julia Jordan.

But oh dear me she has aged. It's hard to say how, as it's not very obvious. She hasn't put on weight, and her hair is dyed, and her face is well concealed with careful cosmetics. But something has aged, something has withered. Julia has become bitter. She is sour and dry and she sets the teeth on edge.

She hasn't given up drinking. She made that clear at once, as she knocked back a gin and tonic and asked for more. I made the second one stronger.

I bought the gin for her specially, for the occasion. I don't drink gin very often. But I remembered that she does.

Her hair is now lion-coloured. It's wonderful. She has a

great tawny many-layered mane, waving and glinting with highlights and bushing around her small head. Can it be all her own? Mine has grown thin now, like my heart.

But she is not happy, despite her honey-coloured locks.

She was wearing what we used to call a little black dress. Not a conspicuous or a pretentious little black dress, but a plain jersey knee-length wool number, the kind, as the lower-middle-class magazines used to tell you, that you could 'dress up' or 'dress down' for the occasion. She hadn't dressed hers up much, out of respect, no doubt, for my lowly neighbourhood and poor estate, but she was wearing a lot of rings on her fingers. Julia was always fond of jewels, as I think I've already noted. I gazed, impressed, at her dangerous knuckles. She seemed to have graduated in late middle age to some even more serious sparklers than those she used to flash when we were still young. I couldn't help gazing at them, which pleased her, for she was able to tell me what they were and what they were worth. Diamonds, rubies, and some chunky modern gold craftwork. I've forgotten the details, even though I was told them only two days ago. But I did absorb the information that she had bought most of them herself, and was proud of having done so. She is an odd woman. Most women want to be given things, not to buy things. I've still got my old Victorian diamond and sapphire engagement ring. I keep meaning to get rid of it, but I've still got it. I'm not sure I want it, but I've still got it. I was given it, after all. It is mine.

Julia had brought me a present. It's an antique cameo brooch. She said she knew it was weeks early for my birthday, but she'd thought it was just Me and so she'd bought it and brought it. She said there was a story attached to it, but I now realize she forgot to tell me what it was. It's very pretty, in what Martha would no doubt call an old-fashioned mumsy sort of way. A cream-coloured neck-and-shoulder profile of a maiden with her hair in a fillet. Little twinings and twistings of creamy hair, against a pink-brown marble.

Shell pink, now that used to be a colour, when we were girls in the '50s. Shell-pink twin sets were considered very desirable. When we were in the Fifth Form I was very envious of Priscilla Beddoes's shell-pink Pringle twin set. I saw on television the other evening that twin sets are back in fashion, but I can't say I've spotted any yet around here in Ladbroke Grove.

Julia's career isn't going as well as it was. It hasn't ground to a halt, but it's begun to stall. She used to be able to call the tune, she says, but now she says she can't. She wonders if it's living in Paris that's causing the problems. She thinks she might move back to England. In order to be able to network, whatever that means.

She isn't married, at the moment. She's been having an affair with a big black American bit-part actor called Achilles. But it's coming to an end.

She congratulated me again, halfway through the second gin, on getting rid of Andrew. A self-righteous prat, that's how she described him. She asked about my finances, and I told her they were not too bad, considering. She pressed, and I gave her more details. The lump-sum pay-off from Andrew, the small monthly alimony cheque from Andrew, the pension my father set up for me which will mature when I'm sixty, the state pension I'll get when I'm sixty, the Freedom of London Bus and Underground Pass which will be mine at the same date. These are my assets. She seemed satisfied that I wasn't starving, but depressed by how much I'd had to pay for my flat. She says property is cheaper in Paris. She asked after my mother, and I told her she was still alive, though not well, and was still living in the care home.

I'd forgotten Julia had met my mother. My parents had invited her out for a meal with us at the Abbey Hotel at one of those half-term ceremonies, one of the few they had bothered to attend, and she had tried to flirt with my father, not very successfully. My father was not a flirtatious man. Julia asked me if the nursing home was expensive, and who was paying. She didn't ask, directly, about whether or not I stood to inherit anything from my mother when she died, but I think she had the impression that I might. I didn't disillusion her. My family probably had seemed quite well-to-do, to outsiders. Whereas, really, we were a case of genteel poverty.

Julia's mother is still alive and well, and living with her widowed sister in Hove. Her father, like mine, died some years ago. Women have a long afterlife, though not always a happy one.

Julia asked if I'd thought of getting a job, and I said yes, I'd thought about it a lot, but not to any great effect. What, I asked her, was I qualified to do?

When I was a girl, I wanted to get a job, to earn some pocket money, to learn about the world. Some of my school-friends did. They worked in bookshops and in cafés. Some of them even had holiday jobs at Butlins. But my mother wouldn't let me. She thought shop work wasn't ladylike. She had never worked. She didn't expect to work. I was an obedient child, and I did not resist her prohibition.

Julia liked Mr Gordano Black's restaurant. She ordered a salad of asparagus and artichoke, and then some kind of fish. It arrived upside-down, skin upwards, resting lightly on a little pillow of orange purée. I had a rocket and parmesan salad, and then a small light green risotto. We had a bottle of pale yellow wine and a bottle of dark blue water. It was a pleasantly coloured meal.

(I favour risotto and macaroni because of my teeth. I must do something about that upper left section. I still haven't found a London dentist. I've been secretly visiting Mr Chinnery in Ipswich, but I've begun to lose faith in him.)

I think we'd reached the second course when Julia suddenly got on to the subject of Naples and Pompeii. I was a little taken aback by the geographical coincidence, so soon after my conversation with Sally. I wouldn't have expected Julia to be interested in Naples and Pompeii. But she was, she was very interested, and she wanted to know if I'd ever been there, and if not, would I like to go. Now this did seem somewhat strange.

Julia's interest, unlike Sally Hepburn's, had not been attracted by the recent television programme about Pompeian pornography. It was, it seems, of somewhat longer standing. Julia has a project to write a novel set partly in Naples, and she says she needs to do a reconnaissance trip. She has been there before, but not, as she put it, for yonks. (For a writer, she does use some very vulgar expressions.) The novel hasn't been commissioned, but she's already had interest for a TV tie-in. (I think that was the phrase she used.) It involves an affair between an Italian newspaper tycoon and the expensive wife of an English libel lawyer. Or something along those lines. All Julia's novels are about adultery, sexual triangles, sexual foursomes, and other erotic and carnal permutations. I thought the milieu sounded a little high-pitched for Julia, who usually specializes in more suburban antics, but maybe she knows more about that kind of high-powered moneyed world than she used to.

Tuscany, apparently, is out of fashion these days. Tuscany has been done to death. Tuscany is old hat and overrun by yesterday's people. In other words, says Julia, the media are tired of Tuscany. They gave birth to it and now like Saturn they wish to devour it. Julia thinks Naples must be the coming place. It has a handsome new mayor called Antonio Bassolino whom all adore, says Julia. He has transformed the city. He has banished its beggars and adorned it with art. He is the herald of a new Renaissance. She says he has cleared all the traffic from the Piazza del Plebiscito and returned the square to its ancient architectural glory and dignity. He commissioned a pyramid of salt from an artist called Mimmo Paladino to fill the piazza as a celebration of its renewal. This sculpture is called *La Montagna del Sale*, and great black metal horses rear and ride up its crystalline slopes. Julia longs to see the pyramid, though she fears it may have melted by now. Salt wards off the Evil Eye, according to the Neapolitans. Julia believes that her television people will think Naples original and smart as a setting. She thinks they will buy Naples. She needs to visit Naples.

Naples, Amalfi, Sorrento. In and out of fashion they drift, over the centuries, over the millennia. Baia, Posillippo, Cumae, Avernus. The wheel of fortune has turned once more and the time of Naples has returned again, says Julia. She has read a book about Caravaggio and the Counter-Reformation that has given her some good ideas for locations. The ancient and the modern. The grandeur, the misery, the glistening pyramid of salt.

I might have assumed, from this scenario, that Julia's career was prospering, but I could tell, from the manner of her narration, that it wasn't. This project represents not an advance but a retreat. She is not happy about it, just as she is not happy about the big black Achilles. A last shot in the dark. The Evil Eye threatens her. The salt is melting.

She mentioned, very much in passing, the news that a young writer less than half her age – which is also my age, though Julia is four months older than I – has just been offered £500,000 for three chapters of an unfinished novel. I can see that she might find that worrying.

Over coffee, she got on to the subject of the loneliness of fame. I've had a very lonely life, said Julia. Oh, nonsense, I said, and pointed out to her that she had been married several times and never seemed short of a gentleman admirer. This gave her an opportunity to tell me that there is nothing lonelier than an unhappy marriage, as I ought to know, and that in her case *all* her marriages had been unhappy. The problem is, said Julia, I've had the *wrong kind* of fame. I've never been taken seriously. I never get invited to literary events or festivals or anything artistic. Nobody thinks of me as a literary writer. People just *use* me. They don't respect me. I changed publishers, because I didn't feel I was getting a good deal, and I don't like the people I'm with now. They are trash. I'm getting a new agent. I'm sick of being treated without respect. People don't respect women like me, who stand up for themselves. They treat me like shit.

She seemed in deadly earnest about all of this, and said she needed a brandy. Over the brandy, she became more and more confessional in mode. She told me about the neglectful and hurtful way in which various men had maltreated her over the years – how they had spent her money, and abused her body and her patience and her property. She had been obliged to resort to lawyers and injunctions. I sighed and sympathized, but in truth I was shocked, as I have been shocked over the years, by the lack of anything like normal human affection in her relations with men. They used her, but surely she also used them? I find Julia confusing. And of course I am myself confused, because I am no longer fond of Andrew, nor do I feel as much affection as I should for my three daughters, so I am as bad as she is. If bad it be. I *do* think I think it *is* bad, but she doesn't seem to have a sense of good and bad. And maybe there is no good or bad. It was all indoctrination.

We came back to my place for a last cup of coffee – I didn't see how I could avoid this, and had decided to go with it, as I couldn't reasonably resist it. We were followed, for a few yards, by an elderly drunken man weaving about on the pavement, but Julia didn't seem to mind that. She told him to piss off, and he fell back, muttering.

Julia paid the restaurant bill. She insisted. I was relieved, as I can't really afford to eat at Mr Gordano Black's. I've only been there twice, and on both occasions Anaïs paid. I don't understand a world in which black men buy fizzy water in Sainsbury's without hesitating about the cost, while I think I can't afford it. I suppose I could afford it, but I think I can't. Tap water is good enough for me. Nobody has died of it yet, as far as I know. Are they all B-movie actors, like Achilles, these mineral-water-drinking black men?

When we got back here, Julia returned to the theme of a trip to Naples and Amalfi. Surely I was free to go with her? She would pay. She was sick, she said, of battling around the world on her own. We could have fun together, she insisted. She had in her time endured some truly terrible holidays, she said. Once, when she was younger, exhausted by a long hard stretch on a TV series, and rolling, positively *rolling* in ready money, she had booked herself an exotic holiday in Jamaica – and those, she reminded me, were the days before every Tom, Dick and Harry flew off to Jamaica every year for a second holiday. And she'd hated it. She'd simply hated it. She'd been in this Luxury Complex by the sea, with palm trees, and there was no Room Service, and at night the dogs barked, and crabs scuttled under her door, and frogs invaded her de luxe bathroom, and insects devoured her, and all she did was sit and cry. Amidst the crabs and mosquitoes. It was hell, said Julia Jordan.

So she wants me to go along with her, as a sort of companion. To share her dining table and defend her from the eyes of strangers. I think she means it. It's very odd. I wonder if she really has no other women friends? I suppose it's possible. *En effet*, she's always been a man's woman. I am her only female friend.

I humoured her, I played along with her. I said I'd think about it. There was something desperate about her, and I felt forced to respond to it. I gave away more than I needed. I asked her if she remembered doing Book Six of the *Aeneid*, all those years ago, with Mrs Pearson, for our A levels. She looked blank at first, and I don't blame her for that – I'd have forgotten it all myself if I hadn't brushed it up recently with Mrs Jerrold. She remembered Mrs Pearson well enough, but she'd forgotten the text. I reminded her that Aeneas asks the Cumean Sibyl about his destiny, and asks her to allow him to visit the Underworld, and she tells him to pluck the Golden Bough and descend with it. And the Underworld, I said, that's just near Naples. Lake Avernus, the Burning Fields, the Sibyl's Cave. Good Lord, said Julia, are those real places? They certainly are, said I. Well, let's go and see them for ourselves, said Julia. I might be able to work them into the plot. OK, said I.

And then I rang for a minicab to take her back to her hotel.

I don't suppose she means it. I can't make her out, although I've known her on and off for most of my life. This poor-little-rich-woman pose of hers is a new one to me, but I have to admit it has a certain pathos. Poor Julia, she has outlived her looks, her popularity, and her fame. And it seems she never had the sort of fame and recognition that she coveted. And it's too late now. How can one sing the siren's song at sixty?

She says she will ring me about this Neapolitan project.

I can see that I could be a comforting companion. Shadowy, faded, yet entirely respectable. I can see us both, sitting on our little terrace overlooking the sea. I'd give her a touch of class, which is what she knows she needs. She'd probably be more fun as a companion than Sally Hepburn. Perhaps we could make up a threesome? Perhaps we should all three book ourselves on an art tour? God preserve me.

She wonders whether she should pluck the Golden Bough

I've been re-reading Book Six. It's an invitation.

> There stands a Tree; the Queen of Stygian Jove
> Claims it her own; thick Woods, and gloomy
> Night,
> Conceal the happy Plant from Humane sight.
> One bough it bears; but, wond'rous to behold;
> The ductile Rind, and Leaves, of Radiant Gold . . .
> Through the green Leafs the glitt'ring Shadows glow;
> As on the sacred Oak, the wintry Mistleto

I've been thinking a lot about Mrs Jerrold. And about whether she needed the money from teaching that evening class. And about why I haven't tried harder to get a job. Julia is right to be proud of her earnings. I ought to have tried harder to support myself. Part of me thinks that I ought not to be taking any money from Andrew at all, let alone thousands of pounds a year. I know the law doesn't see it that way, nor do my so-called friends, but I feel diminished by living on his money. I wonder if that's a feminist feeling. I never thought much about feminism, while I was married to Andrew. He, of course, was a fellow traveller on the subject of feminism. As soon as it became fashionable, so he adopted it. At least, he adopted it in all his public statements. But I don't think he ever thought about it very much.

I'm not really qualified to do anything except teach basic

French, and I'm so out of practice with my French that I don't think I could do even that competently. The methods are so different now. I feel a bit like poor Miss Matty in *Cranford*, when she lost most of her money in the joint stock bank. Like her, I have only a lady's accomplishments, and not many of those. Not much progress in more than a century. What was it that Miss Matty Jenkyns could do? She was good at making spills from coloured paper, and at knitting garters, and at covering babies' balls with rainbow stripes of worsted – not much money in any of that. But didn't she then go into business and start to sell little packets of tea? If she did, she was braver than I am. I couldn't. I couldn't work in a shop. It's not that I'd be ashamed to do so. It's just that I wouldn't know how to begin to set about it.

There's an unfortunate character in *Persuasion* – a lady, a fallen faded sick lady – who makes her living from some kind of handiwork. I don't even seem to be able to do that. I suppose I could babysit. I wonder if there's any call for that, in this neighbourhood? There are advertisements from babysitters on the Members' Board in the Club. *Non-smoker, clean driving licence, fond of children*, that kind of offer. I wonder what the rates are.

Sometimes I think I could do an unladylike job, a truly debasing and menial job. As I was sitting on the top of the number-seven bus the other day in one of those interminable traffic jams on Oxford Street, I saw an old man with a primitive wooden rake, scratching persistently away at the pavement. At first I couldn't think what he was doing, but eventually I worked out that he was engaged in trying to remove the blobs of chewing gum that bespatter the streets of our city. The stones of London are impregnated with dark blotches of gum. They lie thick like tears. And he was trying to remove them. He scrapes up the gum, and he deposits it in his plastic sack. The stains remain. I suppose somebody must pay him to do this.

I think his is an honourable calling. For some reason he made me think of Simone Weil. She was wedded to filth and lowliness. I don't know much about Simone Weil, but I do know something. I had to swat up on her once, when I was standing in for Betty Foy in the Religious Knowledge class. I did Simone Weil with the Sixth Form one week, and definitions of teleology and ontology with the Lower Sixth. I remember those lessons I gave rather clearly. I learnt something, even if the girls didn't. Betty Foy had made up a very odd syllabus. She went off to become a nun. She may have been given the sack, but her ostensible reason for leaving was that she was going off to be a nun. Andrew said she wasn't a good influence on growing minds. I don't know about that. I don't think a bit of Simone Weil can have hurt them.

Yes, I think I can remember the teleological and the ontological arguments in favour of the existence of God. 'It is because thou art, We are driven to the quest . . .', as the hymn has it. (We used to sing that hymn at St Anne's, and I always liked it.) That's the ontological argument. We wouldn't seek God if he didn't exist. I find it more attractive than the teleological, which argues that we must be going somewhere because everything has a design and a purpose. I don't see why we must be going anywhere and I don't think we are. But we *are* driven to the quest. I don't think that proves that God exists, either, but it does prove that there is something deeply unsatisfactory about the human condition. I was about to say that human beings are badly designed, but that of course would be to fall into the teleological trap. We weren't designed *for* anything. We happened to become. And this pointless but necessary yearning was part of the becoming.

I've just looked Mrs Jerrold up in the phone book, and I've found an entry that must be for her. It's not a common name, and the address sounds right. She appears to live in a mews nearer the Holland Park end of Ladbroke Grove. It's a better neighbourhood than mine. I wonder if I should give her a ring? Maybe it would be more polite to drop her a note. Shall I ask Anaïs? We could ask her round here for a drink.

I'm going to the cinema with Anaïs tomorrow. I'll ask her about Mrs Jerrold. And I'll ask her what she thinks of Julia. I'd be interested in her placing of Julia. Maybe she's never heard of her. I don't think Anaïs was in the drama bit of the BBC. I'm not sure what she was in. I think she had something to do with Design and Décor, but I'm not sure what. I think she advised on oriental matters. Though you aren't allowed to use the word 'oriental' now, for some reason, or so Anaïs tells me. It's gone out of fashion, like Tuscany.

And so has Julia. Twenty years ago, everybody had heard of Julia Jordan. Julia was a big name. But time is passing her by.

I don't like to think of poor Julia, alone in her Luxury Chalet with the crabs and mosquitoes, and no Room Service. It seems a sadly emblematic fate.

I will drop a line to Mrs Jerrold, saying that I miss the class. She won't think that intrusive, surely.

Goethe and Chateaubriand both went to the Phlegrean Fields. I wonder if Anaïs would like to come too?

I've just got my laptop solitaire game to come out twice running. That's very unusual. It can happen, but it's unusual. I suppose the more often I play the more often it will happen? Or not, as the case may be? I don't understand probability theory. Anyway, I choose to take it as a good omen. I'm warming up to the big event when I shall buy my first Lottery ticket. I've already got my eye on the shop where I'm going to do it. It's a horrible shop, one I would never normally enter. A dingy little newsagent-off-licence that sells crisps and snacks and very basic foodstuffs. I bought some milk there once. I bought it on the day before its sell-by date, and it went off before I'd finished it. I don't drink much milk.

It's the sort of shop that sells deadly wares. Nothing there could do you any good. Would I have to go back there to collect my winnings? Surely not. I must find out how the system works before it's too late.

She takes heart and revisits her mentor

Anaïs says she's already been to the Phlegrean Fields. I think she may have told us this in class, but I'd forgotten. She says, moreover, that Pozzuoli is a dump, and that the coastline where Aeneas landed is now an industrial wasteland. The Vale of Acheron. It's still hell, but it's a different kind of hell. I wonder if she's right. Sophia Loren was born in Pozzuoli, she says. And Chateaubriand went there in 1803. I've looked it up. 'All around, burnt lands, naked vineyards, with only a few pines, like sunshades, some aloes among hedges, and no birds sing.' Goethe thought it sublime. Onwards, stranger, onwards and upwards. *Nach Cuma, nach Cuma.* (Mind you, Goethe hadn't been to Italy when he wrote that poem about the Wanderer. He just imagined how it would be.) Anaïs and I talked about all of this over our Chinese meal at the Queensway Complex. I am quite good now with the chopsticks. There were many Chinese restaurants in Suffolk, but none of them were anywhere near as good as Queensway Chinese. But I'd never have dared to go without Anaïs.

It's very good of Anaïs to accompany me to the cinema. But I don't suppose I'm much trouble, as a companion. I don't make demands. And I'm very appreciative.

Anaïs hasn't heard of Julia Jordan. In vain did I recite the list of Julia's titles, her TV series, her films. They are all as dead as dust. No wonder Julia is down in the mouth. Anaïs is a modern woman, even though she is no longer young, whereas Julia already belongs to the past. I could see that Anaïs thought I was suffering from an apprehension distortion about Julia. She suspected that I exaggerated her fame because I had been at school with her, because she had been a big fish in a small pond. I didn't want to protest too much, because protestation never gets one anywhere, but I did want to make it clear that Julia was in a different league from Sally Hepburn – 'your fat friend Sally', as Anaïs has dubbed her. I told Anaïs that Julia's books must be in print and that she could check up on her in any bookshop. But I now begin to have my doubts. It may not be true. I used to buy her novels, as they came out, in hardback, but I left them all in Suffolk. As I've said, there isn't much room for books here.

Mrs Jerrold hasn't got much room for books either, but that hasn't prevented her from piling them in. I went to see her yesterday. She rang, as soon as she got my note, and said she'd be very happy to see me, and no time like the present, so round I went. And I had guessed right, which proves I am getting my bearings and learning to decipher postcodes correctly. She lives in a very desirable little cul-de-sac, all high painted wooden carriage doors and hanging baskets and window boxes and potted plants, a far cry from my grim eyrie. It is all bijou and rustic. She says she's been there a long time. I like these little corners of London, lingering on, expensively abandoned amidst the cataclysmic changes. Though Mrs Jerrold says she's not sure she likes living on the ground floor any more. She says she worries that people will climb up to her bedroom window at night and steal her jewels. I can't tell whether she means this seriously or not.

Not that Mrs Jerrold has any jewels, she assured me.

She has books, and knick-knacks, and cats. She lives in an overcrowded bohemian little nest. It's a bit dusty, and might give one asthma or hay fever, if one were given to sneezing. But I'm not so fussy about dust and dirt as I used to be. And I liked her accumulation of treasures. It was good to be in a room with a history. Maybe I've overdone the stripping down. Maybe I've thrown too much away.

She seemed as bright as ever, as she poured me a glass of red wine. She was drinking gin and water. She said she hadn't any tonic, and apologized for its absence, but I said I didn't much like gin. She said she didn't like tonic. Gin and water was her tipple, she said. Mother's ruin, she said, and laughed.

I don't know if she has children. We didn't get on to that. I thought we were going to, at one point, but we didn't.

She asked me how I was, and how I'd been filling my time since the college closed, so I told her about my routine – the Health Club, the cinema visits with Anaïs, the visits to see the murderous rapist in Wormwood Scrubs, the free lectures at the Tate and the National Gallery. (I didn't tell her about the endless games of solitaire I feel compelled to play. I'm sure she wouldn't approve of them. I don't approve of them myself.) She nodded, sagely, and said, 'Good, good, that's good.' She was curious about the Health Club. Who went there, how much did it cost, what did I do there? So I told her about the big reduction in fees that Anaïs and I had enjoyed because of the compulsory closing of the Virgil class, and I described to her the heavy dark women like fruits, the pale white women with cold mauve flesh, the skinny braided girls who wear no underwear, the bouncy girlish girls with bunches and hairclips, the social squawkers on their mobile phones, the bitter blondes and the sad starers. I described to her the brave ones on the brink, the flat ones in the sauna. I told her of the children in the crèche, with names like Xian and Lo and Amber and Mojo. I told her of the lily girls floating in the steam of the bubbling whirlpool, and the lean plodders on the treadmill, and those who stand around on one leg like storks or herons. I told her of the faraway look of those listening to distant music through plugged ears. They are all shapes and sizes, these women, I found myself telling Mrs Jerrold, as though this were a wonder. They are all ages, all shapes, and all sizes. That's good, that's good, nodded Mrs Jerrold, and urged me to eat another crisp.

I didn't tell Mrs Jerrold about the time I thought I had died in the sauna. I thought of telling her, but I didn't.

Mrs Jerrold's house is full of treasures, a record of her rich and embroidered past. The walls are covered with paintings – all tiny, all framed in gilt and silver and rosewood and ebony, a tapestry of bright images. Miniature landscapes, small still lives, cats and birds and fishes and children. (My walls are bare.) Photographs are propped up against her bookshelves and antique wineglasses with spirals in their stems march along her window ledges. (I have no photographs. My poor father lies face down in a drawer.) Cushions heap themselves upon the deep armchairs and the hard-backed couch. The cats have worn deep hairy hollows into the seats of the plump chairs they favour.

I told Mrs Jerrold that although I like my Health Club, I miss her class. I told her that I was still reading Virgil, and that I still saw Anaïs. I owe Anaïs to Mrs Jerrold's class, and I thanked her for that. She smiled and demurred. Mrs Jerrold says she's not teaching at the moment, apart from some private tuition to a friend's granddaughter who is working for university entrance. I think she may need the money. You can't live on trinkets, and I feel she belongs to a pre-pension age.

She tells me that she misses the class, too.

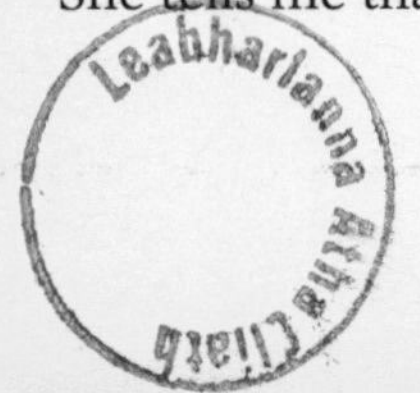
Leabharlanna Átha Cliath

Her husband, Eugene Jerrold, died over twenty years ago. She has been a widow for more than twenty years. (It is true that he died in a car crash in France. I checked. I'm a bit ashamed of this. I looked him up, a few days ago, and read the *Times* obituary in the Westminster Reference Library. I couldn't face going all the way to Colindale.) She spoke of him, a little. They first met, she said, when she was asked to read some of her poems for the BBC Third Programme. Mrs Jerrold, it seems, was once a poet. I hadn't known this. She said she published two slim volumes, just after the war, when she was very young. She had then been a rising star. She had met Eugene on the publication of her first volume. Those, she said, had been happy days. Comradely, poverty-stricken, post-war beer-drinking days. Though she had never liked beer, said Mrs Jerrold. She always preferred the gin. Gin and water. She got into the habit of drinking gin with water because the tonic was so expensive. 'We couldn't afford what you call mixers, in those days,' said Mrs Jerrold. 'And then I got a taste for gin with water. I don't like tonic. I don't see the point of tonic.'

I rashly asked if I could see her poems. This was forward of me, and if I hadn't had a glass of wine I wouldn't have dared. I couldn't tell if she wanted to show them to me or not, but she did. She clambered on to a little wooden stool, and reached up to a high shelf – it wasn't very high, her ceilings were low, but she really is very short – and pulled out a little volume still in its original dust jacket. She handed it down to me. It was a slim volume, very slim, and it was dusty. The jacket was dark blue, covered with an austere and distinguished pattern of small scattered white stars. Zodiac Press. I held the little book in my hand, as she clambered down again and settled herself once more. It was called *Moon*. That's all. *Moon*. I opened it, rather nervously. Opening it seemed a very personal, invasive act. It was her second volume, dedicated to Eugene. 'To Eugene' was all the dedication said. I shouldn't have been surprised by the titles of the poems, I suppose. But I was. 'Dido to Sychaeus', 'Dido to Aeneas', 'Remember Me', 'Dido in the Underworld', 'The Birds that Perched upon the Golden Bough', 'She Stands on the Sea Shore and Foretells Her Own Death'. These were her titles. I read them to myself, and then I glanced up at her.

She was sitting there, bright and neat, with a distant look on her sharp face. The look of a gypsy or of a sibyl, gazing far away. But she caught my glance, and leaped back into the present. 'Very derivative stuff,' she said, and laughed. 'I was full of fashionable melancholy, in those days. When I didn't know what sadness was, I could afford to be sad.'

I fingered the dry pages. I couldn't bring myself to try to read a poem. It didn't seem right, sitting there, in her presence.

Suddenly she said to me, in a completely different and much more sprightly tone, 'You don't see much of your daughters, do you?'

I think I put the volume down, at this point, on the flimsy rickety little round walnut occasional table at my elbow.

'No,' I said. 'I don't. I don't much want to.'

'Why not?'

'I just don't want to. I've left them behind. I'm living in another world now.'

'You *may* want to see them again, one day. You shouldn't exclude that possibility.'

She was looking very gypsy-like, as she said that: so much so that I retaliated with something like, 'Do you see a reunion in your crystal ball?'

She laughed. 'Who knows?' she said. 'I just said, don't exclude it. You can't tell what the future will bring.'

I was beginning to feel that it was time to take my leave. I didn't want to listen to any prophecies. I started making preparatory gestures, reaching for my cardigan and that kind of thing – I'd cast it off as it was very warm in her little front room, much warmer than in my flat. It was a heavy, thundery evening. Headache weather. I wondered if I ought to ask to borrow her poems, though I didn't much want to, but she seemed to have forgotten all about them. She was back with the Virgil class.

'I'm so glad you enjoyed it,' she said. 'Do you remember that I tried to find you all that Third Programme recording of Cecil Day Lewis's 1951 Festival of Britain translation of the *Aeneid*? I never managed to get hold of it. I think one of you had his text – was it you, or was it Mrs Barclay? No, you had the Penguin Jackson Knight, it must have been Mrs Barclay. I used to have the tapes, but somebody must have borrowed them and never brought them back. I rang up the National Sound Archives, but they didn't seem to know what they'd got. I even went into the British Library to look but I couldn't make head or tail of the electronic catalogue. It wasn't very well organized and the person who was helping me didn't seem to understand it very well either. He could only find a reference to the Funeral Games in Book Five. That wasn't really what I wanted. I'd have liked to hear Book Six again . . .'

Her sentence seemed incomplete, and I thought she was going to add 'before I die', but she didn't. To fill the pause, I said that I could well remember some of Eugene Jerrold's celebrated broadcasts – his Shakespeare productions, with Gielgud and Peggy Ashcroft and Jill Balcon, and those rare pieces by Beaumont and Fletcher, and early Ibsen, and Christopher Fry, and T. S. Eliot, and Giraudoux, and Anouilh. We'd been allowed to listen at school, on Sunday evenings. Poetic drama was considered semi-religious. (I hadn't known about Eugene Jerrold then, of course, but I'd checked on him later, after joining Mrs Jerrold's class. I don't think this was sycophantic teacher's-pet behaviour: I was just interested.) I said that I'd like to hear some of them again, and she seemed pleased by this, though she said she suspected most of them hadn't survived.

'Perhaps,' she said, 'we could have privatized our Virgil class. You and Anaïs and Mrs Barclay and one or two of the others could have come round here for Thursday evenings, instead of going to the College. We could have finished off Books Ten to Twelve. We could have squeezed in.'

She looked around, doubtfully. It would have been a squash. But I had had the same idea myself, though I hadn't liked to suggest it. We could have paid our term's fees direct to her. They weren't very high, but she would have got something.

I had timed my departure badly. As I started to take my leave, there was a crash of thunder followed by a sudden outburst of very heavy rain. I had a coat, but I didn't have an umbrella. I hesitated, in the narrow hallway, and peered into the cobbled mews through the thick glass pane in the door. Rain was descending in torrents. Mrs Jerrold said I couldn't go out in that, why didn't I sit down for five minutes and wait for it to pass over? I was embarrassed, and we got into a bit of an unseemly muddle as I tried to go and she told me I ought to stay. She knew perfectly well that I couldn't be in a hurry to go anywhere. So we went back into her little living room and I agreed to sit down again for a moment. The rain was drumming down and I could hear it sluicing down the gutter. It's a very ancient sound, rain. When I insisted I really would have to leave, she said she'd lend me an umbrella. I didn't want to accept this offer, but then she suddenly said such a charming thing. She said, 'If I lend you an umbrella, you'll have to come back. You won't be able to run away for another year. And I'd *like* to see you again.' Or words to that effect.

She said this in such a robust, no-nonsense way that I really couldn't refuse. There was a small drama over the umbrellas, but we were both relaxed again by now, and we were able to find it amusing. She offered me a choice between two umbrellas, both of which she displayed with panache. One was one of those stumpy, battered little objects, the sort you can shove in your handbag, and this one had clearly been stuffed into hers on many occasions, for its ribs stuck out awkwardly, and it would never fold up neatly again. It was a bright red, ill-kempt, scruffy, honourable little brolly, a brolly that had done good service. The other was a much more elegant piece of work, a finely scrolled and gold-tipped beige umbrella, with an ivory-coloured handle, a lady's umbrella, a fashion accessory, designed for display and for pointing at interesting objects as well as for sheltering from the rain. This, she said, was an end-of-term leaving present from her City Institute Tacitus class, and look, it had her initials engraved upon its stem. Of course I chose the scruffy one, but I was able to admire the treasured gift. I asked her if she'd ever used it, and she said only twice. She was afraid of losing it, she said.

After she'd restored the precious gift umbrella to its hallway hook, she suddenly darted back into the living room and came back bearing a small plastic bag. She'd suddenly remembered, she said. She'd got this tape that she knew I would enjoy. She wasn't going to tell me what it was, it could be a surprise. A secret, a surprise. I could play it to myself one evening. She just knew I would like it. And then I could bring it back when I returned the old umbrella.

You must come to me next time, I said, politely. We'll see,

we'll see, she said, finally sounding just slightly impatient, though it wasn't my fault I was still there, was it? And out I went, into the downpour.

I haven't played the tape yet. I wonder what it is. It isn't labelled – well, it just says I. J. on it. Her first name is Ida. She published under the name of Ida Kemp. But we all called her Mrs Jerrold.

The sand sticks in the hourglass and she thinks herself dead

I wonder what Mrs Jerrold would have made of my near-death sauna experience. I wanted to tell her about it, but I didn't. This is how it was.

There is a very pleasant sauna in the Health Club – the usual kind of thing, I imagine, though I don't have a very wide experience of saunas. It is a rectangular wooden room, with three tiers of slatted benching at right angles along two of its walls, and little movable wooden headrests, and lamps shaped like Olympic torches with shades of frosted glass. A wooden bucket of water, a wooden ladle, and two large quarter-hour glasses of sand and wood, which remarkably resemble the old-fashioned five-minute wooden egg-timer which my mother used throughout my childhood, until she replaced it with a series of much less delightful electric clocks and timers and pingers. People in the sauna time themselves on the quarter-hour glasses. I never stay in there for as long as a quarter of an hour – in fact the most I can take is four minutes. Some people lie naked on their towels, others keep their bathing suits on. I usually pull the top of my costume down, but I don't take it right off. I don't mind displaying my breasts, but I don't like people to see my pubic hair.

I like the quarter-hour glass because it is old-fashioned and silent and natural. I like the colours in that hot little room, the soft sweet shades of pinkish yellow and of brown. I like the resinous smell of the wood. I like the hiss of the steam in the pipes. Lying in there is peaceful. It's rather like lying in a large overheated airing cupboard. I did like the airing cupboards at Holling House, I'm afraid. I liked the orderly piles of towels and sheets and pillowcases. In my flat, I spin things in the machine or hang them to drip over the bath. It's not so satisfactory. I haven't got room here for a tumble-dryer.

I usually turn the glass in the sauna over, if I am alone, or follow its progress if someone else has turned it. I like the idea of dividing up time by numbers and the sand is soothingly numerate. Its dry grains sift and fall, as we lie there and peacefully exude drops of sweat. And on this occasion – last week, this was, just after Julia's visit – I was lying there calmly, as usual, on my back. I told myself I would wait until the glass emptied, for it had only three minutes to run. I shut my eyes, and perspired, and waited. I was alone in there. When I opened my eyes, I was surprised to see that only two minutes had passed, for I had guessed it had been longer. I shut my eyes again, and counted numbers to myself, for a timing of two more minutes, but when I opened them the sand had not moved. The sand stood still. And I thought, for a moment, that I had died. I thought I had passed from life to death and into eternal time. I thought this for only a second or two, but I *thought* it. Death was peaceful, and easy, and painless. I had died, and all was over. It was a relief to me, to know it was like that. And then my brain began to tick again, tick *tock*, tick *tock*, thump *thump* of the heart, drum *drum* of the pulse, one *two three* four *five*, and I realized what must have happened. The sand had not stopped, it had stuck, in the narrow glass artery. The hourglass had suffered a stroke, not me.

When I got up, I tapped it, and the sand began to drain away again. If only it were that easy.

So that was my Near-Death Experience. Not very dramatic, but revealing. And not, in itself, unpleasant.

Mrs Jerrold is in her mid-eighties, but she is sharp as a needle. She looks as though she is looking into the hereafter. This isn't fanciful. She really does look at times as though she can see across to the further shore. Perhaps, if one spends much time with the long-dead, one can see them clearly.

I wonder what happened to that girl with the lipoma. I haven't seen her for weeks. I can't ask after her, because I don't know her name. Moreover, it would be interfering and intrusive to inquire. And anyway, I don't care. I'm curious, but curiosity has nothing to do with caring.

I've just been down with the rubbish because the binmen are coming in the morning. One of the inconveniences of living on the third floor is the disposing of the rubbish. When I first moved in here it worried me a lot. At the Big House, it was all so well taken care of – the van would arrive on Thursdays, and Mrs Kay would have made sure that everything was ready and waiting for it. I didn't go near this operation, after that abusive interchange with the binman, but Mrs Kay was very efficient. The recycling would be placed in one sort of bag, the household waste in another, all neat and tidy and colour-coded. We used to produce a lot of waste. But here in London I don't produce much. One person doesn't. There's something pitiable about my leavings. I feel sorry for them. I can't even generate much rubbish these days. Small one-person-size low-fat yoghurt cartons, the peelings from two potatoes and a carrot, some onion skin, coffee grounds, tea bags, baked-bean tins, cheese rind, bacon rind, margarine pots, dead flowers, banana peel. Husks and crumbs and scraps. (I take bottles and jars down to the bottle bank under the bridge, where the man with dreadlocks has set up his camp.)

While I was down there, looking for the dustbin lid (either people don't put them back on properly, or children play with them, or neighbours steal them, or the wind dislodges them) while I was down there, I saw the man with the crucifix. He looks dreadful tonight, even more dreadful than usual. His hair is now that curious greyish-black colour that the hair of old black men becomes, and it is even sparser than it was when I first saw him. It is reduced now to one thick wadded clump which grows from low down on one side of his head only. The top of his head is bald, but this lump of hair wanders and spreads upwards over it, like a matted growth. It is like the wool of a sheep with scrapie. His lower lip and his jaw jut forward yet more terribly and tragically than they used to do. What would happen if I were to speak to him? I could ask his blessing. I have thought at times that I might be reduced to that. But I don't want to embarrass him.

Self-pity is a seductive emotion. One day soon I'm going to read through this diary and weed out all the passages contaminated by self-pity. If I recognize it for what it is. Which, of course, I may not. It deludes as well as seduces.

When I go down with my black bag of rubbish, I'm always afraid I'm going to lock myself out. I check for the key ten times before I go and as I go. I don't know the other people in this building. I wouldn't know what to do if I locked myself out. There is a police station, on Ladbroke Grove, but when my bag was stolen the police weren't very helpful. They seemed to suggest that I ought not to have had a bag at all, and that I certainly should not have been carrying it while travelling on the Underground. I don't think the other people in this building would be much help in a crisis. I sometimes say good morning or good evening to a solid elderly woman who lives on the first floor at the back, but a lot of the other inhabitants are foreigners. We don't even look at one another as we pass on the stairs or in the communal hallway. We avoid eye contact, as though we were all criminals.

There is something liberating about this total indifference. I think it must be intended to set me free. But free for what?

I think I might give my spare front door key and my spare flat key to Anaïs, in case I do lock myself out. She'll trust me not to be bothering her every five minutes. I think she's still got my radiator bleed key. I must remember to ask for it back one day.

While I'm into the subject of food and self-pity, I might as well admit to a very shaming episode. I think I've made it clear that the shops in my immediate neighbourhood are fairly unattractive. I often go to Sainsbury's just for the walk, and because I like the canal. And it's nice to see so many people who don't know me. There is one very friendly little Asian Minimarket round the corner, where a dark-skinned and gentle man with a smile of great sweetness always calls me 'dear', but the choice isn't great. (I'm not sure if that word 'dear' depresses me, or comforts me. It is intended to comfort, I know.) Most of the other shops are dreadful. But if you walk south from here, up Ladbroke Grove to Holland Park, the situation changes. On Holland Park, about half an hour's walk from here, there is the most expensive butcher's in London. It is a famous shop. 'Free-Range and Organic Meat and Poultry', it boasts, and I have no doubt its products are all they claim to be.

I don't eat much meat, but I must confess that the aura of this smart shop fascinates me, and one bright September morning a few months ago, I decided to go and treat myself to some small delicacy. A pot of rillettes, a lamb noisette, maybe even a quail.

It was a crisp day, with the low golden blue of autumn

and a faint smell of leaf and fire in the clear air, and I admired other people's gardens as I walked along. Some of them are very beautiful, and they are beautifully maintained. They give pleasure to the public. Some have little spiralling trees of evergreen topiary, and well-trained espalier trees with bright berries. I saw a pure-white rose, and a red dahlia looked at me in an inquiring manner through ornamental railings.

There was quite a queue at the butcher's, as there often is, but I joined it, still wondering what I would choose for myself. I didn't mind waiting. Why would I? The staff wear old-fashioned straw boaters and uniforms. The shelves on the right are full of bright rich jams and chutneys and preserves and oils. There are ducks' eggs and quails' eggs and cheeses of every description. And the meat is prepared in a variety of tempting cuts and marinades. It is an almost irresistible display. It is a far cry from PriceCutter.

The clientele is very different, too. There are expensive young people in designer jeans showing stretches of slim midriff, and there are distinguished-looking older gentlemen with grey hair who could be concert pianists. It is a cosmopolitan clientele, with accents from New England and France and Sweden and the Home Counties. These are not the tongues of the Goldborne Road. These high-grade carnivores make even the affluent young clientele of the Health Club look plebeian.

People were buying for large dinner parties. Free-range chickens, sirloins, legs of lamb, barbecue ribs, great pies of *boeuf en croûte*, wild boar and venison sausages. I was ashamed, to be shopping for myself alone. Once I too shopped for a family. If I had been a man, if I had been a concert pianist, I could have asked for a quail or a cooked chicken leg or a small pie. But I am a woman, and I was ashamed. And when my turn came, I found myself asking for a crown of lamb. A dish for a proud dinner table, adorned with its festive little paper frills and caps. I have never cooked a crown of lamb. I have always wanted to cook a crown of lamb. So I pretended I was giving a dinner party. I made the small talk of a woman who is about to give a dinner party. The man in the straw boater took me seriously, in this role, and served me with respect.

I walked home with my heavy crown, with its little paper thorns. I cooked it, and I ate some of it, but I was ashamed.

Now I'm going to play Mrs Jerrold's tape. I wonder what she's given me?

She does not understand the messages

Mrs Jerrold's tape is playing. But it doesn't make any sense. All I can hear is a sort of watery wailing, an underwater echoing sound. A wailing sound, against a watery bubbling and gushing. Am I playing it at the wrong speed or frequency? Has the tape perished? Is it a joke? Is it some very modern kind of music? Or is it a recording of whales or dolphins? Or of someone drowning in a well or a canal? Is it a recording of the death of Jane Richards in the Lady Pond?

Now it is beginning to squeak at a higher pitch, more like a bat in the upper air, or more what I imagine a bat might sound like.

Perhaps she has lent me a recording of the squeaking souls of the dead in the Underworld. It isn't a very interesting sound, but it's curiously distinctive.

We had a very good class discussion about the voices of the dead in Hades.

I'm going to switch this thing off. I think the tape is corrupted. And there's the phone. Perhaps it's Anaïs.

The comrades begin to gather for their journey

That wasn't Anaïs, it was Mrs Barclay on the phone. Quite a coincidence, when I'd just been talking about her so recently to Mrs Jerrold. Mrs Barclay said she'd been meaning to ring me for a long time but had lost my number, then found it again – guess where – in her Day Lewis Virgil translation. She'd written it in, with all our addresses and numbers, on the end papers. 'Well, it is *my own book*,' she commented, defending this small act of vandalism, but I hadn't said anything in reproach. I often write in books myself. She said she'd been thinking of me because she'd thought she'd seen Anaïs going into the Coronet Cinema at Notting Hill and had shouted after her but had been too late to stop her. 'And I didn't want to pursue her into the cinema without a ticket, did I?' said Mrs Barclay. 'Specially not a seedy old cinema like that!'

A pang of unreasonable jealousy shot through me at the thought of Anaïs going to the Coronet without telling me. Had she been accompanied by another friend? I could hardly ask, it would have sounded mad. I know Anaïs has lots of other friends, and that I am nothing special to her. I am lucky that she bothers with me at all. Anaïs and I don't often go to the Coronet. In fact, we've only been there once, to see that box-office-blockbuster romantic weepie, *The Springs of Dove*.

The cinema is, as Mrs Barclay said, seedy. It is vast and usually nearly empty, and is built like an old-fashioned music hall. It probably once was a music hall. The red velvet seats have broken springs, the clientele smokes heavily, and the staff are confusingly multi-ethnic and have a curiously intimate, offhand, joshing attitude towards their hard-boiled customers. The Coronet customers, including myself and Anaïs, laughed heartily at all the saddest moments of *The Springs of Dove*. (Incidentally, it was while we were queuing for our tickets in the shabby foyer that Anaïs burst out with one of her extraordinary anecdotes. She really has a vast repertoire of these, culled from Lord knows where – maybe her days in television. Darling, she said exuberantly, did I realize that this was the very spot where, in Edwardian days, no less than Bernard Shaw's sister Lucy learnt that her husband had been having a lengthy affair with the wife of the Coronet's manager, Eade Montefiore? The rest of the queue was much impressed by this, though perhaps not all of them knew who Bernard Shaw was.)

I wonder why Mrs Jerrold and Anaïs and I all call Mrs Barclay 'Mrs Barclay', and not Cynthia, which is her given name. She is no older than me, and considerably younger than Mrs Jerrold. Is it because of the air of eccentric and emphatic propriety which she carries with her, so at odds with the occasional impropriety of her utterances? Is it because the name of Cynthia does not suit her? Mrs Barclay has a theatrical manner, and has chosen Mrs Barclay as a kind of nickname.

Mrs Barclay then said, on the phone, that although she hadn't taken up the cut-price offer at the Health Club, as Anaïs and I had, she had maintained contact with the immediate area through AIDS and the London Lighthouse. What's the London Lighthouse, I asked, naively, as one might as a child naively ask, 'What is death?' I am much wiser now than I was when I picked up the phone half an hour ago. I cannot believe I walked past that other building so often, so unknowingly, on the way to my swimming pool in the sky.

Mrs Barclay – or Cynthia, as I shall now try to call her – lives way up in the smart part, beyond Mrs Jerrold. Near Holland Park. I have never been to her house, though I shall go there soon, now that I have been invited.

We often wondered if there was a Mr Barclay. Now I

know. Mr Barclay does indeed exist, he is not just an alibi. I wonder if I shall meet Mr Barclay too. I rather doubt it.

Cynthia was interested to hear that I had been to see Mrs Jerrold earlier this week. She too had been thinking about her, and about our Virgil class, after that glimpse of the person who might or might not have been Anaïs.

'Do you remember', said Cynthia, 'that plan that we had to get Mrs Jerrold to sail with us from Carthage to Naples and guide us round the ancient sites? I think we were half-serious until old Mr Wormald started to get excited about it. Imagine, a cruise with Mr Wormald!'

And then we chatted on for a while about the unhygienic Mr Wormald, and the romance of the idea of sailing from Carthage to Italy, in the wake of Aeneas. Cynthia Barclay seemed to have nothing better to do than to chat to me. And she has invited me to visit her on Thursday at six.

Her horizons begin to expand

Mrs Barclay's house is very grand and very exciting. I know a lot more now about Mrs Barclay and why she calls herself Mrs Barclay. I shall describe her first, and then I shall describe the man whom I met on the way home in the shop that isn't PriceCutter. I don't think he would have spoken to me as he did if I hadn't been energized by Mrs Barclay. He must have seen something new in my face. A ghost of my other self. I won't say my former self, because that's not what I mean. My other self. That's what I mean.

Cynthia Barclay used to be Mr Barclay's housekeeper. After a manner of speaking. And then he married her.

It's not quite a Jane Eyre and Mr Rochester story, I gather. But it's interesting.

She told me this story over a Bloody Mary in her vast tall first-floor drawing room which overlooks one of those private London squares. A *piano nobile*. This seems to me to be the height of dignified town living. Those houses must be worth a fortune. Perhaps not even Mr Barclay could afford to buy it now. I wonder if he owns it, or whether he has a lease? The outside of the house is painted a strong ochre, and the drawing room is decorated in lavish style. I've decided to call it Victorian Ottoman. It consists of lots of tapestry and cushions and patterns and huge chairs and deep low settees that seem to fit into the space quite easily. I think there was a chandelier but I was so dazzled by everything that I didn't take it in. Could it have been Venetian glass? I must remember to look up more boldly next time.

I'd never have asked for a Bloody Mary, because as a rule I'm not very keen on vodka, but she seemed very keen on mixing me one, so I let her. And I must say it was delicious. She gave me the works, as she put it. Lemon, ice, celery, Lea and Perrins, Tabasco, black pepper. It had quite a kick to it. Mrs Barclay says that one of the many things she did in her former life was to work as a barmaid. She says she loves mixing drinks.

I've never really had a job in my real adult life, but Mrs Barclay seems to have had dozens. She's been a waitress, a barmaid, a cook, a minicab driver, and a housekeeper. She's worked in a theatre and an auction house and a fashion house, and she's been paid to collect money for charity on railway stations. (I thought those people with collecting boxes were always volunteers, but she says not.) She's worked on a switchboard for a firm that sells fake handmade reclaimed bricks. She knows a lot about bricks: she says that was one of her more stimulating placements. She has a restless energy that might explain some of this strange pattern of employment. Also, as she points out, she has no skills, and isn't good with money. She plays life as it comes, and learns as she goes.

She's tall and bold and firm and mannered. She says she was kicked out of school at sixteen because of some escapade – we didn't go into that – and has never regretted it because she's enjoyed living by her wits. 'I'm a very resourceful woman,' boasted Cynthia Barclay, as she crunched loudly on her gory stick of celery.

But, says Cynthia, she's sometimes regretted her lack of formal education. 'I do like to use my brains,' said Cynthia. Hence, she says, the Virgil class. She took that up after she sailed into the calm rich harbour of Mr Barclay's protection.

'I was getting tired,' she said. 'And Mr Barclay doted on me. I came here as a temporary, through an agency, but I stayed on. He didn't want to lose me. He said that if I married him I could have anything I wanted. I could go out to as many evening classes and nightclubs as I liked, provided I always left him a nice meal ready for the microwave. He's not very demanding. He positively encourages me to spend my money and he approves of the time I spend at the Lighthouse. He's got lots of friends in the AIDS sector. But he did want to make sure of me. He didn't want me giving in my notice.'

Mr Barclay, she says, is seventy next year. He's a semi-retired art dealer and writes about art history. Hence, I suppose, the casual elegant opulence.

Cynthia says she is a spendthrift. That, she says, has always been her problem. Whatever she earns, she spends. She's been married once before, and had two children by her first marriage, but it had ended years ago. One of the children is in America, the other in Edinburgh. She didn't say anything much about her first husband, but I gathered he hadn't been very good with the money either. Mr Barclay, it seems, has enough money to cushion Cynthia from the ill effects of her own bad habits.

'Guess what I've taken up instead of Virgil?' said Cynthia, when she had sketched out this rapid map of her past history. 'I've taken up mathematics. I go to a class in Westminster. It's delightful. I went back to where I left off, when I was fifteen, and I'm catching up with things. They teach it much better now than they did when I was a girl. It's *much* more exciting. Mr Barclay is very impressed by my mathematics.'

I too was impressed. I do not think my brain could cope with mathematics now. *En effet*, to speak truth, I found the Virgil very difficult, even with Mrs Jerrold as our interpreter and guide. It stretched my brain to cracking point. I think Mrs Barclay's brains are in better trim than mine. She has given them more exercise.

Mrs Barclay didn't do all the talking. She asked me what I was doing, and I told her more about my visit to Mrs Jerrold, and the little books of poetry she had published when she was someone else called Ida Kemp. I told her that Anaïs and I sometimes went to the cinema together, and she asked if she might be allowed to come too one day. I don't know if I'd ever told her about my leaving Andrew and we didn't get on to the subject now, though I did admit to three daughters that I don't often see. Then I told her about the Health Club, and I said that I was surprised she hadn't joined. But she said she didn't need any more bodily exercise, she was always rushing around, it was mental exercise that she needed. Mathematics, algebra. She was thinking of taking up Japanese, as Mr Barclay was planning a trip to Japan to sell some paintings, and had suggested that she should go with him.

We had a long, nostalgic talk about our forcibly truncated Virgil class. Cynthia said the best evening ever was the evening when we did lines 490–94 of the Sixth Book. She remembered it so clearly. I had to look it all up again when I got home, though when I found it, it did all come back to me too. It's the bit where Aeneas in the Underworld meets the Greek generals and the followers of Agamemnon, and they flee from him in terror even though they are dead. They see his armour glittering in the gloom and they flee again to their ships to escape him. It's not a particularly interesting passage but I remember that we all became engrossed by the way the Greeks try to cry out but can produce no sound. *Pars tollere vocem exiguam: inceptus clamor frustratur hiantis.* That's the Latin.

> They rais'd a feeble Cry, with trembling Notes:
> But the weak Voice deceiv'd their gasping throats.

That's Dryden.

Day Lewis has 'their wide mouths only whimpered', and Jackson Knight has 'others raised a whispering voice; but their attempt at a battle-cry left their mouths idly gaping'. David West's new prose version says that they 'lifted up their voice and raised a tiny cry, which started as a shout from mouth wide open, but no shout came'.

I remember that we all found that phrase 'a tiny cry' very telling. We talked about it for some time. We spoke of nightmares, and trying to cry out in our sleep. We talked about sleep-talking and sleepwalking, and what the ancients believed about dreams and prophecies and the gates of ivory and the gates of horn.

'I talk in my sleep a lot,' said Mrs Barclay. 'Apparently I cry out the strangest things. Mr Barclay says I sometimes shout out things like "Earth, roll on!" or "Mother, sleep on!" Once I yelled out "Death in the tower! Death in the tower!" I think that's why I was so interested in those poor Greeks and their gaping jaws. Though mine isn't a tiny cry, he says. He says it's sometimes quite loud. It wakes him up. And the funny thing is that I can never remember what it is that I've been dreaming about.'

We were both laughing a lot by this point, and in my excitement I rashly bit on a pistachio nut. I felt yet another sliver of that risky tooth splinter and let out not a tiny cry but quite a loud one.

Cynthia has recommended a dentist. She says he is divine. He's expensive, she says, but divine. She's given me his number. I wonder if I can afford him?

I was feeling quite high as I walked home, despite my broken tooth. I've promised to suggest to Anaïs that we include Cynthia in our next Queensway outing. Perhaps Cynthia will be my third London friend. That would make my life more complete and more symmetrical.

She meets a divine stranger in the terrible shop and ponders on his question

The man in the Eurogroceries Minimarket will not become my friend, but he did speak to me. In London people do not speak to one another much. He spoke to me as I waited at the checkout with my meagre old-lady purchases of two bananas and a grapefruit and some kitchen roll. He spoke to me in French. This is very unusual. How did he know that I would understand French?

'*Madame*,' he said to me, very formally, as I rummaged in the bottom of my bag, with clumsy fingers, like an old lady, for an elusive fivepenny piece. '*Madame, pensez-vous souvent au passé?*'

I turned to look at him. He was tall, dark and dark-skinned, with a weather-beaten, pocked and furrowed face. He had once been handsome. He looked like an ageing *nouvelle vague* star of the '60s – the unkempt Belmondo roué look. We do not see many people of this style in our neighbourhood. He was unkempt but not ill-dressed. He was not a street person.

Though I would have replied to him anyway, even if he had been a street person.

'Oui, de temps en temps,' I said.

Then he said something that I did not catch – I think he may have said that he thought of the past more and more frequently, but I am not sure, and I would not like to misrepresent his important message by putting the wrong words in his mouth. I replied, saying something vague and indistinct, as I abandoned my search for the silver fivepence and handed over a five-pound note. Then, looking at me with a Gallic curiosity which in my youth I would have taken for gallantry, he said, *'Madame, j'ai cinquante-neuf ans.'*

I smiled, faintly, and told him my own age. It seemed a fair exchange. He nodded, as though that were the end of the conversation. And I pocketed my change, and my receipt, and nodded in return, and went on my way.

Since I got home, I have been thinking deeply about this strange incident. Who was he, and why did he speak to me? In my youth, I would have thought that he was making a sexual overture, and I feel it is possible that there was something in my appearance that called forth his address. I was better dressed than usual: I had dressed up for Cynthia and Holland Park. And an afterglow of our conversation and our cocktail may have hung around me.

I think he told me his age because he wanted to say that if he had been younger and I had been younger, he would have made a pass at me. He was remembering his own past, when he did such things. He was wondering if I remembered such a past too. He was regretting, for both of us, that we were no longer young.

I read in the newspaper last week an article about threatened species of flora. There was an account of the ghost orchid, which, the newspaper claimed, is so rare that it is seen only once in every fifteen years. (I suspect this is an exaggeration, but that is what the article claimed. Newspapers are not very reliable sources of information.) It is shy, and flowers only after a wet spring, and it grows deep in the beech woods. You must search for it in the undergrowth by torchlight. It is a pale yellow-mauve and it is solitary and nobody knows where it will be seen next, so you may search for it for years, indeed for a lifetime, without success. It disappears and reappears without warning or reason. Its ghostly pallor glimmers in the depths. I will not see it flower amidst the urban garbage by the towpath of the Grand Union Canal.

Perhaps the French gentleman saw a blossoming of my ghostly self. And I, in my turn, saw his ghostly spirit in flower.

I have been looking at my Virgil, and re-reading the passage where Aeneas thinks he sees Dido in the Underworld, but is not sure, in the moonlight, if it is she. She flees him, as once he fled her. The Dryden translation is the best. It is sublime. *Stay, stay your Steps, and listen to my Vows: 'Tis the last Interview that Fate allows!* But she will not stay. She shuns him, and hides in the forest and the shades of night.

And I have been remembering those evenings at St Anne's when we did what we called our 'prep'. I used to enjoy doing French translation. There was a pleasure in unravelling the grammar, in finding the right word. There was a deep pleasure in the correspondences. Cynthia Barclay is right. There is a lasting pleasure in the exercise of the mind. How strange that she should have discovered that, through all her vicissitudes. She does not look at all like an intellectual.

One cannot blame Jane Richards for being terminally bored by La Fontaine. I would have preferred to have been allowed to teach Verlaine or Baudelaire.

I look out of the window. It is a clear night. There is a

three-quarter moon lying drunkenly on its side. The glowing and luminous city calls from its dark heart. Tomorrow afternoon I will take my walk by the canal. I will not see the rare ghost orchid, but at this time of year the undergrowth has already begun to sprout over the polystyrene, and I if I walk far enough westwards I may see coltsfoot or even celandine. Perhaps there will be groundsel. Across the canal, in the trees that grow in the great grounds of the Victorian cemetery, I have fancied that I have seen great clumps of mistletoe hanging. Suspended, like the Sibyl in her wicker basket.

The mistletoe, like the ghost orchid, is magical, although it is not rare. It does not grow from the ground. It takes its green blood from a strange host. It is a humble plant with a mystic glamour. It protects against witchcraft and the Evil Eye. It is green in the cold midwinter. Its berries are yellow-white and succulent and fleshly, and its pallor is of the other world. When its sap dries, its dry leaves turn bright gold in death. The doves of Venus perched upon the mistletoe. It is the Golden Bough that leads us safely to the Underworld. These strange plants are plants, and no plants, and they live between the species. They are life, and they are death. I neither live nor die.

She seeks salvation in a plastic bag

So I went for a walk by the Grand Union Canal this afternoon, as I said I would. I set off from Sainsbury's, and walked westwards, past the gas-works and the cemetery and the slumbering trains of Eurostar. It seems to be too early in the year for groundsel, but the coltsfoot is in flower. The herons watch the water. I heard on the radio that many of them are suffering from some new kind of bone disease. It is not known what causes this disease.

I was a little cast down on my walk, although I like to be

by the water's edge. I was feeling well yesterday, cheered by my rediscovery of Mrs Jerrold and Mrs Barclay, and now I am feeling not so well. The sight of the shopping trolleys piled in the water of the canal beneath the bridge depressed me. And all the rubbish floating in the water reminded me of that afternoon I have tried to forget. I was really depressed then. I admit I was depressed. I will write it down, as it was.

It was a few months after I first arrived in London, when I was at my lowest ebb. The excitement of arrival had worn off, my brave and falsely high spirits had sustained several assaults, and I had not yet learnt how to cope with the length of the day. And the weather was appalling. It was June, but every day it rained. You may remember that year of rain. The afternoons were dark like winter. Water lay in puddles on the pavements, and in the gutters flowed. The sky was grey. From my high room I watched the grey clouds trudge and dredge across the high grey sky. I felt like a prisoner, up there in my tower. So I forced myself to go out. It was not easy. It took some courage to go out at all. It is easier to give up. Though that is not easy, either.

I must congratulate myself upon my courage, for no one else will.

It was raining steadily, on that afternoon nearly two years ago, but I thought it might clear up. I took the Tube, to Great Portland Street – it is a direct line, the purple-pink line again – and then I crossed the Euston Road and walked northwards towards the Rose Garden in Regents Park. I was wearing trousers, and the hems of them got wet. They soaked up the water, up to the knees, as I splashed my way through the standing puddles. The silky artificial fabric of my trousers seemed to have some kind of unfortunate capillary action. I must have looked ridiculous. The trousers were of a pale blue shade and the dark wet blue crept upwards, to the knees.

My shame was visible. Only the mad walk in such weather, beneath such skies. The rest of my body was dry, as I was wearing an old green long lightweight country jacket. I must have looked a fright, but there was nobody there to see me. The English do walk in the rain, but not in London. It continued to rain, unremittingly. It lightened, then it strengthened, then it lightened again, but it did not go away.

I was feeling desperate. What was it to me that the roses bloomed and the herbaceous borders blossomed? I plodded on, as the wet crept upwards. From time to time I looked at my watch, but the hands did not move. They had stuck. Time had come to an end. I walked through the dark underwater depths. Eventually I reached the large formal round pond at the end of the avenue leading from the Rose Garden. There was nobody on any of the benches. Rain fell on the wet statuary. A white plastic bag was floating in the shallow water of the fountain.

The plastic bag offended me. It seemed to sum up my despair. It floated, half submerged, yet not sinking, in miserable suspension.

I decided to try to remove it. My natural recoil from dirty street objects was mediated by the sense that this watery bag must have been washed clean by its immersion. Whatever filth it might have contained must have been washed away into or at least been diluted by the fountain waters. So I resolved to fish it out. I perched on the low parapet of the fountain's rim, and tried to stretch for it, but it was just beyond my reach. I looked for a stick, but I could not see anything suitable in that trim, well-tended public garden. I reached again, but in vain. Great drops fell on me, on the bag, on the pool's surface. I did not want to abandon my small project. I looked around me, but could see nobody. I was wet anyway, so what did it matter? I took off my sandals, and rolled up my wet trousers, and waded in. The water was shallow, and within two steps I had the bag in my grasp. I returned with it to the stone lip of the fountain, and clambered out. As I clambered out, I looked around again, guiltily, and saw that by now somebody was watching me. An elderly black man, muffled up in raincoat and hood, had arrived upon the scene, and was standing, hunched, as a witness. The expression upon his face was of unutterable dejection. It was not for this that he had come to the Mother Country. He had not been born here. I don't know how I knew that, but I knew it. I felt that we were kindred spirits, but I could neither speak nor smile. Solemnly, clutching the bag, I thrust my feet back into my wet slippery sandals, and then made my way across the gravel path to an elaborate black and gold ornamental dustbin, where I deposited the bag.

I felt better for this pointless act. I can recall it, now, without desperation.

But, looking back, this was a low point.

Things are better now. Aren't they?

She sees the girl with the lipoma crying and offers her succour

Things may be better for me, but not for that poor girl with what I hoped was only a lipoma. When I went to the Club this evening, I saw her again for the first time since I overheard that sad interchange about the lump in her back. She looked less plump than she had, but she didn't look as though she had lost weight through exercise. She looked poorly.

'Poorly.' That was a word my mother used to use. I don't know if it's a regional word, or a word still in common usage. Spellchecker doesn't mind it, so I guess it still exists.

The young woman was struggling to take off her tracksuit bottoms and sighing heavily as she did so, as though everything she did was too much of an effort for her. Getting dressed or undressed shouldn't be an effort, at her age, though I confess at my age I sometimes find it so. I looked the other way, because it is rude to stare, and continued with my own toilette, which consisted at this stage of stripping down to my bathing suit in order to set off for a swim. She was sitting down by her locker when I left her, groping in her tote bag.

I didn't swim for long because the pool was uncomfortably full. I did just six lengths, trying not to bump into people, then a couple of minutes in the whirlpool. I didn't stay long in the whirlpool either, because I was joined in it by an amazingly fat man who seemed to displace a lot of water. I have nothing against sitting in a whirlpool with a strange man but I think anyone would have agreed he was rather an extreme case. He looked like a Native American chief, but I don't suppose he can have been. We don't have many Native Americans around us, in our neighbourhood. He was wrapped up in a sort of sarong. I don't suppose that's any more unhygienic than bathing trunks. I hope he wasn't offended when I got out almost as soon as he got in. I wouldn't like to cause offence.

The urge to drop my sapphire and diamond engagement ring down the grating that runs around the edge of the pool is getting stronger. The blue water laps there so quietly and so enticingly. Maybe one day I will succumb to it.

When I got back to my locker after my shower and my three minutes in the sauna, the not-so-plump girl was still sitting there on the wooden bench. She had her head in her hands, and had replaced her tracksuit bottoms by a long purple skirt, but apart from that she hadn't moved. She didn't look up as I proceeded to towel myself and to begin to get dressed. There was a mobile phone lying on the bench beside her.

I felt I ought to say something. What if she was feeling ill? I blew my hair dry on full power and top heat with the blaring hot nozzle, and made a lot of disturbing noise as I pulled on my little black boots and packed up my training shoes. (Training for what, I sometimes wonder. It's a bit late for me to train for anything. I laughed when my 'personal trainer' asked me what my 'fitness aims' were. At my age, you don't have aims. You run in order to stand still.)

I made so much noise that she must have known I was there, and that I was observing her, and that the noise was directed at her. So she can't have been very surprised when I daringly said, 'Are you all right?' And she wasn't. She gave a kind of whimper, and muttered, 'No, not really.' I think that was brave of her. It was brave of me to speak, and brave of her to answer.

So I sat down by her and asked her if there was anything I could do to help. She said, again, 'No, not really', but she didn't say it with hostility, so I just continued to sit there in what I hoped was a companionable way. After a while she reached into her bag for a tissue, and blew her nose, and looked over at me.

'I'm sorry,' she said. 'I'm just feeling really rotten. That's all. I'll pick up soon.'

'Come and have a coffee with me downstairs,' I suggested. I thought she ought to move. It wasn't good for her to go on sitting there. I know what it feels like, to feel that you've just got to go on sitting there. Wherever 'there' may happen to be. It's not a good feeling.

She seemed to agree with me because, somewhat to my surprise, she said yes, she would. I must have looked very harmless.

So we went downstairs together, down the exposed and glittering glass catwalk of the turquoise and aquamarine spiral staircase, and in the healthy café I bought two cups of coffee.

'It'll do you good,' I said, vacuously.

She didn't say anything, so I filled in the gaps. I said I'd joined the Club when it first opened, indeed before it opened, because I used to go to the evening classes. I told her how I'd watched it being built. I told her about the gutting of the temple that had housed the Virgil class, the preserving of the Victorian red-brick façade, the bulldozers, the blasting, the hard-hatted workmen, the security lights. They'd done a good job, and in record time, I said. There must be a lot of money in Health Clubs, I said. The chain must be making a fortune. There was nothing like this around when I was young, I said. I nearly said that all this health faddism had gone too far, but luckily I stopped myself in time.

She was sipping her coffee while I chatted on like a social worker or a health visitor or a prison visitor or a Samaritan. She was a pale-faced, dark-haired, rather plain young woman. Her hair was cut straight and short and held back by little plastic clips. It was a fashionable style but it didn't look quite right on her. Her face was too round.

When she spoke, she said, 'You must live quite near, then', and I agreed that I did. A few minutes' walk away, I said.

She was like a poor fledgling, too young to be exposed. A child, really.

'Do you live near too?' I asked, risking a question that she might not answer.

'Not very far,' she said. Then she sighed, heavily, and said, 'Well, I'd better be getting back.'

'Will there be someone there?' I asked.

'I share a flat with some friends,' she said. 'It's all right, I'm not alone.'

'That's good,' I said.

'I suppose so,' she said. Then she made an effort, and smiled at me, quite convincingly, and said, 'You've been very kind. I'd better be going now. Thanks for the coffee.'

'It was nothing,' I said.

'No,' she said, 'it was kind.'

And she got up, and made a little sad waving gesture with her hand, low down and unconfident, from somewhere near her waist, and shouldered her tote bag, and set off into the evening.

Poor girl. I'm glad I spoke to her. I hope she isn't really ill. Maybe it's all in my imagination, and she's just had a row with her boyfriend. Rows can hurt, but they don't kill you.

We are surrounded by these miseries. London is suffused with grief.

There can be a luxury in grief. Sometimes I remember those great tides of self-pity that used to wash over me when I was a girl. I don't think there was anything very unusual about them. I used to hide in the attic at home, in that big dumped armchair that came from Grandma Green's old house, and I would cover my head with a towel, and cry. I thought everybody hated me. I used to see myself as an outcast, which I suppose, in a way, I was. But there was a kind of satisfaction in it. I relished the feeling of being rejected. The tears would pour down my cheeks, as hot as tea, and although I was utterly miserable, I was proud of being *so very* miserable. I used to go and look at myself in the mirror, all red-eyed and ugly and blotchy, and feel strangely satisfied.

And now I seem to be tempted to revert to a similar kind of adolescent behaviour pattern. I'm surprised by myself. I thought I'd grown out of feeling sorry for myself. I thought I'd become more of a stoic. What have I got to be miserable about, compared with so many?

I look at the London Lighthouse with a new eye, now that

Cynthia has told me its history. How astonishing that in all these months I never knew that it was there. Well, I knew it was there, but I didn't know what it was, did I?

Cynthia has been a volunteer there for years, she says. She fundraises, and chauffeurs, and fills in occasionally on reception. She used to visit there when it was residential. She has seen death in that building. She says I ought to go and see the garden. She says it is delightful. She says it is a nice place to sit. You can have lunch there in the summer, she says. I will, one day soon. If I dare to ring the bell.

Cynthia has so much energy. She looks after Mr Barclay, and the AIDS people, and she is learning mathematics. My life is so useless. I am redundant. Life has made me redundant. I am retired from it, though I have never had a job from which to retire.

I wonder if Cynthia and Mr Barclay share a bed. I could not tell from her account whether sex was or had been part of the bargain. I felt at one point that she was suggesting that Mr Barclay's sympathy with the AIDS cause was related to his own sexual orientation. I know that AIDS is not gender-specific, and I know that not all art dealers with a taste for Ottoman Victorian are homosexuals, but it would not surprise me to learn that Mr Barclay was gay. Mrs Barclay's manner is what I think is called 'camp', but I do not think she is gay. She said that he could hear her talking in her sleep, which might imply a shared bed. On the other hand, she did make it clear that she talked very loudly, not to say *shouted*, in her sleep. So he could easily hear her from an adjoining room. Perhaps she sleeps in a connecting room, with the door open between them in case he panics or is taken ill in the night. Why I should think this is likely I do not know. But I have a picture of this scene in my head.

The London Lighthouse is built of red brick but they seem

to be adding on some yellowish extensions. I think that's a pity. Cynthia is right, brick is interesting. Since she told me about her brick job, I have been studying the brickwork of London more closely. It repays study. Roman bricks, yellow stock bricks, red string courses, creamy-blueish bricks, moss-covered bricks, kiln-dried bricks, painted bricks, bricks set in herring-bone patterns. Coping stones, corner stones, arches, crenellations.

People used to die in that building. It had a morgue and a chapel. Now the patients are out-housed. It is nearly all Outreach now, says Cynthia. People survive on massive amounts of medication. Some of them have to take forty pills a day, says Cynthia.

I can't remember now whether Cynthia and I reverted during our Bloody Mary tête-à-tête to the subject of Mrs Jerrold's guided cruise from Carthage. I know we mentioned it on the phone, when she rang out of the blue to report on her sighting of Anaïs at the Coronet. We had so much else to talk about. I know I didn't mention Julia Jordan to her. I've slightly lost faith in Julia, ever since Anaïs said she's never heard of her. I've been to check on her in the bookshop, and she is still in print, though only marginally. There are a couple of paperbacks with lurid TV tie-in covers, but those once-so-famous early titles seem to have disappeared.

Julia hasn't rung about our trip to Naples. I don't know whether I'm sorry or not. In a minor way I had begun to fantasize quite pleasantly about a week or two in Italy with Julia, acting as her unpaid companion. We would divide our time between the classical antiquities and modern Naples with its pyramids of salt, between the beauties and horrors of the past and the world of newspaper tycoons, handsome mayors, Mafiosi and tax exiles. She would indulge me, I would indulge her, and she would pick up the bills. It's rather a shameful fantasy. Going on a cheap coach tour to Pompeii with Sally Hepburn is more within my range. And I won't even be able to afford that if I get my teeth fixed.

It would be good to travel in the footsteps of Aeneas. He stepped whole and unharmed out of the flames of Troy and abandoned the dead and the enslaved and went on his ruthless glittering way. (*Creusa, O Creusa.*) Some of us disapproved of Aeneas, but there's a ruthlessness about him that appeals. Virgil calls him Pius/Pious, but you can't really translate the word. He was pious, perhaps, but he was also a shit. (That was Mrs Barclay's word for him: it's not a word I've ever used, in conversation.) He was a shit and he followed his destiny.

We liked that bit when he arrives at Cumae and the priestess tells him to stop gaping at monuments like a tourist, and to get on with his mission.

Anaïs and Cynthia would be more fun as travelling companions than Sally Hepburn, wouldn't they?

She chances her luck for the first time and fails

When I win the Lottery, I can go to Italy on my own terms, and choose my own company. I found one of those things called Scratch Cards on my seat on the Tube on my way back from a National Gallery lecture last week and I have to admit that I took it home and scratched it. It said *Scratch and Win*, so I scratched. All it said to me then was *Better Luck Next Time*. I didn't think much of that as a message. It was clearer than Mrs Jerrold's tape, but even less encouraging. So perhaps I won't win the Lottery after all. Perhaps I'll never get to the Mourning Plains and the Sibyl's Cave.

I have, however, managed to get to the dentist. And Mr Wentworth is, as Cynthia promised, divine. He dwells in a deep basement very near Cavendish Square, in one of those rather pompous high-bourgeois Queen Anne-style red-brick side streets leading off Wimpole Street. I rang his bell nervously, and entered fearfully, and sat down anxiously in the communal country-house-style waiting room on the ground floor, amongst the copies of *Country Life* and *Vogue*, until he came up himself from his lair to usher me downwards. Oh, he is so charming. He is young and fair and beautiful and his eyes are of the most astonishing light greenish-blue. He wears a white coat and he looks as though he lives in the future. He comes from some brighter planet. It is surprising that he works away so far below the surface, but he has made his surgery cellar into a cavern of light. The walls are adorned with Hockney swimming pool prints – at least I imagine that is what they are, though they may be derivative imitations – and his musical tapes play the electronic music of the spheres. He was so sweet to me, so very sweet. No man has spoken to me with such kindness in months. I had filled in a form for him, while waiting upstairs, and he looked at it, and looked up from it, and looked into my eyes, and spoke to me with courtesy by my own name.

My clouded eyes were once clear and blue, but they were never as magical and as piercing as his are. He has a delicate, finely drawn face, girlish but not effeminate. He should be called Hyacinth or Narcissus, but his name appears to be Charles. Walter Pater or Burne-Jones would have loved him. I love him, and Cynthia loves him. His skin is very pale, as though he lives too much away from the natural light. He is bathed in a bright white neon glow. His hair curls, gently, and his lips curve, gently. He is, as Cynthia says, divine.

We spoke of Cynthia. Mrs Barclay, he said, was one of his most loyal clients. Mrs Barclay, he said, was very brave, and never flinched. *I* could flinch, he assured me, as much as I liked. Not everybody was made of the same strong stuff as Mrs Barclay.

I opened my mouth to him most trustingly and let him peer down my deep throat. He tapped and probed and gestured to his female accomplice to enter information about my teeth into a computer. He cupped my jaw in his hand so warmly and so softly. His was the soft touch of a lover, not the harsh grip of a technician. I lay back and thought of my sexual life with Andrew, of my fantasy sexual life with that raffish English teacher from Bury St Edmunds. Mr Wentworth tinkered and searched and explored my mouth. I lay back and willingly submitted. It is many years since any man has touched my face.

When he gently levered me back up to a sitting posture, he gave me a hand mirror and told me to look at myself. At first I did not wish to do so, for I was ashamed in his bright presence, but he cajoled me, and I opened my eyes and stared at my ageing face. He said it was no great matter to restore my broken tooth, and he pointed to what he would do, and where. He would extract the root, on my next visit, and create a bridge. He made this sound like a treat and an adventure.

He flattered my own poor teeth. He said they had served me well, and that I had cared for them well. He complimented me on those poor things that I have. And he said he would make me a new tooth, there, on those very premises. Of gold, and of the finest porcelain. He would make for me, he promised, a jewel of a tooth.

I did not like to murmur about expense. I would have paid anything to this magician, for I was under his spell. I would have paid the price of my voyage from Carthage to Sicily and the Aeolian Isles, from Sicily to Naples and Cumae and Caleta and beyond.

'I will send you an estimate,' he said.

I shall wait with interest but without anxiety for this billet-doux.

Why does he choose to work there so humbly in the artificial glow, when he could be glittering like a star on high? It is a mystery.

As I left, I saw along the corridor in other rooms men in blue overalls at work with kilns and furnaces. I saw white skulls and yellow jawbones. He has taken a cast of my jaw and it will join its fellow grinners in his underground gallery.

I wonder how many women fling themselves madly into the arms of Charles Wentworth? Cynthia and I cannot be the only ones among his clients to find him divine. I wonder if he is a married man. He seems too ethereal for such a bond as marriage.

It's a long time since I thought so fully or so intensely of that English teacher from Bury, whose mild gallantries of speech and subversive glances had once been my amorous refuge. I know that he had liked me, and had found me good company. Some did, some still do. He was disaffected with his wife, and I with my husband, so we had looked at one another at public events and private functions, and had woven dreams about one another. Further we had never ventured. Do I regret that now?

Madame, pensez-vous souvent au passé?
Oui, de temps en temps.

According to Sally Hepburn, rural Suffolk is rife with aberrations and perversions. Adultery, pederasty, group sex, bondage, and every kind of sado-masochistic practice. I never noticed such things. Like Rousseau, I never said what it was that I wanted. And now it is too late, and Andrew has left me for Anthea Richards. I don't know about Cynthia and Mr Barclay, but I do know about Anthea and Andrew. I know where they sleep. They sleep entwined in the bed where I used to sleep myself. In that same bed, in that same house. I think that is gross.

Sally Hepburn, of course, is a virgin and a voyeur. Whereas I am neither. I am a mother of three and a divorcée, the kind of person who imagines that she is in love with her dentist, because she has nothing better to occupy her mind.

I wonder when Julia will ring.

She chances her luck a second time and scales down her desires

Well, that was another disappointment. Yesterday I picked up my first Lottery ticket slip from my local newsagent round the back on Cranmer Road, not from that dreadful little sour-milk sour-grapes shop on Ladbroke Grove, and I at once saw how unlikely it was that I would win. I've filled it in, experimentally and randomly, without thinking. I won't pay one pound for this board. (That word 'board' is new to me. I don't think I'll be using it very often.) I'll try it out, and see what happens. But I do now see that it's impossible to guess right. I begin to understand the odds against me. These are the numbers I picked, entirely at random.

3 9 15 21 31 45

I hadn't realized there were so many numbers and permutations of numbers in the world. Of course I can't win. Nor does it seem likely that I shall ever get to Naples, even as Julia's lady companion, or on a coach trip with Fat Sally. I'd better scale down my expectations to something a bit more realistic.

I went to see my man in the Scrubs in the evening, and I told him about my failure of nerve with the Lottery. He laughed at me. He told me I ought to keep on persevering, not just give up at the first go. Feeble, he said I was. Then he tried to press on me a bag full of thousands of Coca Cola vouchers, saying I could win some prize for them on the Internet Auction. I refused them. He knows I don't do the Internet. He knows how to, but he's not allowed to. Anyway, I don't think I'd be allowed to take them out of the prison. Nothing in, nothing out, that's the rule.

Except stories, of course.

I also told him some of the things Mrs Barclay told me about the London Lighthouse. He couldn't believe I hadn't known about it before. It's been there ten years, he says. 'Oh Miss, you are a nice one,' he said. 'Born yesterday, that's you.' He didn't say this scornfully, but with a kind of mild wonder.

It's a nice evening tonight. I'll go for a short walk by the canal, and join the other no-hopers, killing time before time kills them. Killing time on their bicycles, with their fishing umbrellas, with their sad dogs, with their trailing grandchildren. Jogging, loitering, plodding. That's my proper place. That's my destiny.

She receives good news and finds her luck has changed

It is a long time since I had a chance to look at this diary. I have been too busy. Everything has changed. I have too much to tell, but I must try to put it all down in some kind of order before I go away. I must set the record straight.

The letter arrived on a Tuesday morning, like a bolt from the blue. Jove's thunderbolt. The gods play games with us, but at least this game is an amusing one. At least it begins well. Maybe I am after all a favoured daughter.

The letter told me that I had come into some money. Not through a Scratch Card or the Lottery, but in a manner that seems to me at least as unlikely and as arbitrary.

I suppose I have my father to thank for this change of fortune. My father, and Northam Provident. I've never thought very much about that little pension fund I started with his blessing and his little nest egg all those years ago. I got my yearly statements, and dutifully copied them for Andrew's income-tax return, and filed the originals in a folder, and thought no more about them. I could never understand them. I never knew what would be coming to me, or when. I suppose I expected that when I was sixty, the pension might supplement my state pension by a few pounds a week. But as inflation had been so extravagant over the past decades, and as I'd never increased the premium, I assumed any sensible person would have taken the money out and done something more modern with it.

Any sensible person, as it turns out, would have been wrong.

A year or so ago, Northam Provident sent me papers about voting on abandoning its co-operative status and becoming a PLC, whatever that is, but I didn't bother to vote. I didn't even think about it. I don't know anything about money matters. I felt my views were insignificant. Then I read in the paper that members who didn't feel so insignificant had voted overwhelmingly in favour of a take-over bid by a High Street bank. I had no idea what that might mean. *En effet*, I think I even thought it might compromise what little pension I might have expected. Eventually I got a letter stating that as a long-term pension-fund holder I would be entitled to a bonus, the amount of which had not yet been calculated. This promised bonus didn't seem to be replacing any pension and annuity I might one day receive. It seemed to be an extra. Did I want to re-invest, it asked, or did I want a cheque? I thought, that's nice, and wrote back saying I'd like a cheque. I remember wondering if it would cover my next year's

Health Club membership, or my new dentistry with Mr Wentworth. Then I forgot about it again.

Then, about two days after the last entry, above, in which I had resigned myself to the life of the canal bank (something must have depressed me, but I'm not now sure what it was), I got a letter from Northam Provident, with a cheque for £120,000.

I was completely astonished. At first I thought it was a mistake, and like a fool I rang up to query it. No, they told me, there was no mistake. The money was mine. Apparently, on my father's advice, I had taken out, all those years ago, a special With Profits Extra Bonus Scheme, and this large sum of money was legitimately mine. It had accumulated for me, silently and secretly, and the take-over bid had shaken it into my lap. A very nice homely woman with a Yorkshire accent explained to me that not only had I done very well from the take-over bid, I had also still got tucked away a fairly substantial annual pension, due to me shortly, when it and I matured. So it turned out that I was rich. Well, rich by my standards. Wealthy beyond the wildest dreams, in the world picture of the dreadlocked man under the bridge. Even Anaïs, I knew, would not sniff at a free gift of £120,000.

My first thought, after this initial shock, was that Andrew would be very cross. I thought that I would try not to let Andrew know of my luck.

My second thought was that I would go to Italy.

My third thought was that if Andrew got to know of my good fortune, he might try to cancel or reduce my alimony.

My fourth thought was: would it be legal for him to cancel or reduce my alimony?

My fifth thought was: *I will go to Italy.*

And so the fun began.

At first I kept the good news to myself. Furtively I collected brochures and bought maps and guidebooks, in a daze of excitement. It was clear that fate had long intended that I should go to Naples, Cumae and the Phlegrean Fields. The markers were all pointing in that direction. My journey, like that of Aeneas before me, was foreordained. My only hesitation was this: should I extend my travels further? Should I follow the wanderings of Aeneas from ruined Troy through the Aegean to Crete, to Sicily, and across the sea to Carthage, before embarking on the final voyage for Cumae and Pompeii and the descent into Avernus? How far could I afford to go? I pored over my Virgil, over Goethe's *Italian Journey* (I have the Auden translation), over a little school textbook called *The Voyages of Aeneas*. Outdoors, the rain dripped down the brickwork with its crusted city tears of salt and nitrate and lime and droppings: inside, I warmed myself in the glow of the bright horizons of the future.

Unexpected money is intoxicating. As I leafed through my brochures, or swam up and down the blue pool, or padded on my treadmill at the Health Club, I felt powerful. (I think the new word is 'empowered'. I have heard this word several times on the radio, and this must be what it means.) All sorts of wild notions crowded into my imagination. It was almost immediately obvious to me that I should invite some of my old classmates to accompany me on my journey. Cynthia and Anaïs, certainly. Not, perhaps, Mr Wormald. But maybe Mrs Jerrold would agree to be our guide? Yes, I could see the four of us, setting off bravely together, as good companions. I am not a very confident person, but I knew that they would like the idea, and would like to be invited to join me on my expedition. Well, who would not?

I did not at first think of my old friend Julia Jordan, for my encounter with her had been overlaid by more recent impressions of my renewed acquaintance with Mrs Barclay. But after a giddy day or two the image of Julia began to present itself more and more forcefully. It did not seem right not to include Julia in my projected party, for it was she who had put the idea in my head. She had even offered to pay my expenses. But would she fit in? Would she spoil the party spirit?

I thought a great deal about this matter.

Julia and I, as I have said, had studied Latin together at school. Julia had dimly remembered Mrs Pearson and Book Six of her Virgil, although she had seemed surprised to learn that one can still visit the cave of the Sibyl. I thought that Julia might find such an outing 'interesting'. She had boldly confessed herself to be lonely. She might welcome an overture. Who knows, she might even find it good copy for another book? Julia, I felt, would get on well with the robust Mrs Barclay. Anaïs is temperamental, but she in turn might find Julia 'interesting'. But then, perhaps Julia would resent my altered fortunes?

These were the thoughts that went through my head as I lay in the sauna, timing my remaining minutes, my remaining hours.

The first person I told of my good fortune was Anaïs Al-Sayyab. I rang her, and sprang it on her. Her reaction was more than satisfactory. She was delighted, extravagantly delighted. 'What a lark, darling,' she yelled, excited, down the line. And yes, of course she would come to Carthage and Naples with me. Why ever not? How soon could we set off? Should we charter a yacht and a captain and a crew? She would go and buy her cruise gear at once, and I should do the same. Some brighter colours, this time, darling, she instructed. Go for it. Go for it, darling. Celebrate.

Anaïs seemed very keen on the idea of contacting Cynthia Barclay and Mrs Jerrold. Why not? What fun! What an adventure!

(I did not at this stage mention Julia Jordan.)

Well, why not? Sudden money makes one reckless. I had nothing to lose. I rang Cynthia and Mrs Jerrold, and I propositioned them.

Did I think at this stage that we would ever set off anywhere? I really don't know. But all projects begin somewhere, and mine had begun, and it was gathering its own momentum.

The friends meet to plan their voyage

I knew that Cynthia would prove to be a good organizer. She at once suggested that we all meet, at her place, to talk the idea through. I rang Mrs Jerrold, and she seemed cautiously pleased to be included, though understandably, at this stage and at her age, non-committal. I told her that we all three longed for her to be our tour guide, and didn't she remember that we'd talked about it in class? Yes, she said, but we were joking, weren't we? It seems not, I said, in the new and challenging voice I'd acquired since my letter from Northam Provident. And she laughed, and agreed to come to Cynthia's for a planning session. I think the others still thought it was maybe just an excuse for a little reunion, for a drink and a gossip, but perhaps my own intentions were already more serious.

So we convened, in the large room overlooking the large and budding London square. Mr Barclay, Cynthia said, was very jealous, and said he wanted to come to Carthage too, but she had told him he couldn't. She said this as she mixed the drinks. The atmosphere was playful and festive, and everybody seemed overjoyed by my unexpected good fortune. I felt I was very lucky to have such friends. We were all delighted to see one another again, and we agreed that Mrs Barclay's salon was a much more congenial meeting place than the dingy little institutional room in the Further Education College where we used to gather on hard wooden chairs for our Thursday evenings. Mrs Barclay was in her element as hostess, we could see. Anaïs seemed particularly charmed by some of the items of the décor, fingering an embroidered silken table runner, and appraising the rugs with what seemed to be an expert eye. Mrs Barclay disclaimed all knowledge of the provenance of the rugs. She knew nothing about them, she said. Bricks and wallpapers she knew, yes, but fabrics, no. The fabrics were the province of Mr Barclay. He was the expert.

I had been so taken with Mrs Barclay's first Bloody Mary that I requested another, but Anaïs, from the wide selection of cocktails and mixed drinks that was on offer, selected a manhattan, straight up. It glowed with amber and ruby in its slim glass. Cynthia even managed to provide a pink translucent cherry to decorate it. Mrs Jerrold stuck to her usual gin and water, though she consented to an additional dash of Angostura Bitters. A pink gin and water, for Mrs Jerrold, over clashing rocks of ice. This was the life, I told myself. This was the way to do it.

I told my friends that I had set my heart on sailing across the Mediterranean, from Tunis to Italy. I needed to cross the waters on a ship. My heart and my soul demanded a sea voyage. We could fly to Tunis, I was happy to do that, but I wanted to sail homewards across the sea. I'd done some research into ferries, and we could sail from Tunis to Sicily, as Aeneas had done, or we could sail direct from Tunis to Naples.

Or, said Anaïs, we could hire a yacht.

Cynthia said that yachts were expensive. You needed more passengers, she said, to make it worth hiring a yacht. Cynthia said that people who hired yachts were in another league. Mr Barclay had known some of them, and they were different.

Mrs Jerrold said that the seas were uncertain.

Anaïs said that we ought to contact the whole of Mrs Jerrold's Virgil class and charter an aeroplane as well as a yacht, and while we were at it, why didn't we do a bit of recruiting at the Health Club? Or at the London Lighthouse, added Cynthia. We could go into business as Classical Tourists, and make a profit and pay Mrs Jerrold handsomely.

That's the way the conversation went.

Cynthia had provided some delicious snacks to accompany her fierce potions. She offered us little rolls of brown bread with asparagus and salmon and soft cheese in them, and tiny pastries filled with garlic cream cheese and chives. Cynthia's curved hair was gleaming with a new amber rinse, and Mrs Jerrold's spiky hair was encased in a special magenta bandeau embroidered with golden stars. I hadn't yet bought my new wardrobe, so I was still looking mousy and mumsy in Liberty print. Anaïs, as usual, was in many colours, and her stockings were green.

> The Isles of Greece, the Isles of Greece,
> Where burning Sappho loved and sung

intoned Mrs Jerrold, as she dusted crumbs of pastry from her bosom.

One can make anything happen, if one has the nerve. It has occurred to me, over the past weeks, that if I'd been a different kind of person, a person with initiative instead of the kind of person who always waits for things to happen, then I could have organized this trip without coming into £120,000 of unexpected and unmerited lucky money. I could have asked Cynthia and Anaïs and Mrs Jerrold round to my place, and we could have planned a trip over a bottle of Californian Chardonnay from PriceCutter, and done it all on the cheap. But the truth is that this project, without the unexpected wealth bonus, would never have occurred to me.

I suppose some people might soon have got used to the idea of this moderate sum of money and might have begun to find it inadequate for their needs or imaginings. After all, compared with some Lottery winnings, £120,000 isn't much. But I haven't reached that stage of dissatisfaction yet. It still seems a lot of money to me, although I've spent some of it already.

By the time we parted on that first evening, we had got as far as selecting some possible dates. This seemed like a semi-real commitment. We all of us seemed to be remarkably free and had various dates to choose from. I suppose that's not very surprising, at our age. We are of the third age. Our dependants have died or matured. For good and ill, we are free.

More surprisingly, I had also brought up the subject of Julia Jordan. I didn't mean to, but she just popped out of my mouth. I wonder if I am becoming as brazen as she is. She came up, if I remember rightly, while we were talking about Naples. Mrs Jerrold said that she had contacts from the old days on Capri and in Naples. One of Eugene's friends had been the British Consul there, and he was still alive, and retired, and living above Amalfi. He would give good advice about where to stay, she said. And I remembered what Julia had said about the handsome new mayor of Naples and the pyramid of salt, so I told them about it, and found myself in consequence describing Julia Jordan, her life and works. As I've recorded, I'd already tried her name and fame out on Anaïs, but with little success. Mrs Jerrold politely said she seemed to have heard of her, but with Cynthia Barclay she scored a big hit. Ten out of ten for Julia, from Mrs Barclay. She had read all her books, watched all her TV series, adored her work, and had even worked briefly for the film company that had made Julia's first big commercial success, *Charity Child*. She was too, too thrilled, she said, to hear that I knew her well. Why, she demanded, had I kept her so dark?

So, high on the shining recognition-factor of my old school-friend, I think I blurted out that I would like to ask Julia if she would like to come too. I was waiting for a call from her anyway, I said. Why not, why not, they all most readily agreed. That was the mood of the evening. It didn't commit us to anything, but we all said, why not? Julia, I rashly and disingenuously claimed, remembered Book Six of the *Aeneid* well from her schooldays and was as keen as I was to see the Sibyl's Cave and hear her destiny pronounced.

Mrs Barclay rightly expressed astonishment at this revelation of Julia's classical leanings, but she was too excited by the idea of meeting her heroine to cross-question me further about this matter. And Anaïs and Mrs Jerrold seemed happy to go along with us. The more the merrier, said Anaïs, lying back and smoking a thin brown cigarette amongst the opulent cushions, with her feet propped up on what my mother used to call a pouffe. The smoke of the cigarette was aromatic and illicit, but I think it was just a North African cigarette from the Goldborne Road. I imagined that we would smell more of that North African aroma in Carthage.

We were like schoolgirls, all of us, looking forward to a treat. And the treat was of my creation. I had thought of it. I had taken a lead. I was no longer a passive victim of my fate.

I felt I had done the right thing by bringing up the subject of Julia. After all, if she hadn't put the idea of Naples and Pompeii into my head, I'd never have become obsessed by it, would I? And I was amused by the thought of what they would all make of one another, if ever they were all to meet. I was childishly excited at the power I could exercise in bringing this disparate crew together. I would be the magician.

Julia is quite a character, I said to myself, as I set off on my walk home. They'll find Julia interesting, I reassured myself. Julia is quite wealthy, I said to myself, and won't mind buying a few rounds of propitiatory drinks.

It was only when I reached the bridge under the railway that I remembered that it hadn't been Julia who first put the idea of Naples into my head. It had been Fat Sally from Suffolk.

I stopped, literally, in my tracks. I stood there, under the bridge, under the railway tracks, arrested, like Saul on the road to Damascus. It's very odd that I hadn't thought of Sally before this moment, but I swear that I hadn't.

I couldn't invite Sally, could I? Sally just wasn't possible. Julia was, but Sally wasn't.

Yet I knew, even as I stood there beneath the rumbling arch, that I would have to give it a try.

I thought of Sally and that Literary Festival in Cromer, as I continued my walk home. She hadn't behaved too badly there, had she? She had an irritating way of button-holing strangers and asking them odd and unanswerable questions, usually about newspaper items about unusual illnesses, allergies, phobias and the like. This was the period at which she was particularly exercised by peanuts, and she had done a lot of survey work on this topic amongst the literary audiences. But she hadn't done or said anything really intolerable. And if she were to come along with me and Anaïs and Cynthia Barclay and Mrs Jerrold and Julia Jordan, she would be well diluted. We wouldn't have to pay her too much attention.

I'm not sure why I knew it was so important to me to try

to include Sally Hepburn in our plans, why the necessity of including her struck me with the force of revelation. Was it something to do with the balance of power, or with some concept of revenge? It can't have been simply because I wanted to give her a good time, can it? There is a curious symbiotic relationship between Sally Hepburn and me. Or do I mean a parasitic relationship? A parasite, the dictionary tells me, is one who eats at another's table. (We did parasites and saprophytes for O level Biology, Julia Jordan and Janet Milgram and me.) I think saprophytes feed upon the dead. And neither Sally Hepburn nor I are dead yet.

Maybe I wanted to patronize her. She has always thought she was patronizing me. I wanted to turn the tables. To make her eat at my table.

Or did I want to be kind? That seems unlikely. The human heart is black, so kindness cannot have been the explanation for my deeds.

I have no idea how it will all work out, but for better or worse, I knew at that point that I would have to contact not only Julia, but also Sally Hepburn. If both accepted, I knew that we would make a motley crew.

I rang Julia, that very evening. I don't often ring anyone abroad, though I do, very occasionally, speak to Ellen in Finland, despite Ellen's understandable fear and dislike of the telephone. But I braced myself, and rang Julia, and she was in, and she answered my call. She had the good grace to sound delighted by my good fortune. Her response was not as noisily spontaneous as the response of Anaïs had been, but it seemed sincere. I floated the idea of the expedition, which could so conveniently be combined with her desire to see Naples and meet its charismatic mayor, and I told her how pleased and honoured Cynthia and Anaïs and Mrs Jerrold would be if she were to join our group. She would add lustre to our gathering, I assured her. I told her, truthfully, that Cynthia was a great admirer of her work, and I described Anaïs in glowing terms, while trying not to make her sound too important. I reminded her that at school, on Sunday evenings, we had been allowed to listen to the radio dramas produced on the Third Programme by Eugene Jerrold. She said that she had some faint memory of these quiet sessions around the Bakelite Box in the Sixth Form Common Room. It came back to me, as we spoke, that Julia used to knit as we listened. Surprising, really. I bet she doesn't knit now. Not many people do.

So Julia agreed, provisionally, to come on board, and to come to London for a planning meeting. I realized that I ought not to broach the subject with Sally without consulting the others, so I waited until this second gathering to introduce her name.

We met, again, and again we met at Mrs Barclay's. I was a little nervous presenting Julia to my newer friends, but Cynthia did not let me down. Nothing could have been more respectfully rapturous than her welcoming of Julia, nothing more flattering than the ardour with which she offered her a bowl of cashew nuts and squeezed the lemon into her gin and tonic. Julia loves flattery. All writers love flattery, I believe, and Julia loves it more than most, because she doesn't get enough of it.

I could see Julia's eyes darting with approval around Mr Barclay's vast ornate spaces, and flickering appreciatively from the exotic and oriental Anaïs Al-Sayyab to the bird-like bardic Mrs Jerrold. I had told Julia that Mrs Jerrold was the Cumean Sibyl in disguise, and Mrs Jerrold, at this first encounter with Julia, was living up to her trailed foreshadowing by being even more gnomic than usual. I could see Julia thinking, Here is copy. Here are riches, and here is copy. Julia's diamonds sparkled, through the thin blue smoke of Anaïs's cheroot.

Julia has a professional novelist-and-screenwriter's agenda. Anaïs also has some concealed and possibly quasi-professional agenda of her own. I do not yet know what it is, though I trust it will reveal itself en route. I think it may be something to do with the purchasing of embroidered fabrics, but I may have got that wrong. Anaïs has a friend who is a traveller and dealer in fabrics. He has a small shop on Kensington Church Street and he sells at trade fairs and on the Internet. Anaïs was inspecting Mr Barclay's decor very closely, I noted.

Mr Barclay himself put his head round the door, during this last pre-departure gathering, and surveyed us all with a quizzical air. Mr Barclay is tall, thin, bald, formally dressed, and at once both clerical and dissipated of manner. 'Hello, girls,' said Mr Barclay, gazing at the gaggle of old ladies who had set up camp on his *piano nobile*. 'Can I join the ladies for a moment?'

'No,' said Cynthia, firmly, but she was of course overruled, and Mr Barclay settled down with a glass of Perrier water to cross-question us about our plans. He gazed with knowing admiration, I noted, at the jewels of Julia Jordan, and leered jovially at Anaïs. He and Mrs Jerrold treated one another warily. I am not sure what he made of me.

We described our proposed itinerary at his request. We had by this stage decided to fly to Tunis and stay there for a day or two, doing the sights, and then take the ferry, steering a straight course for Naples. We would not loiter in Sicily, as Aeneas and his crew had been forced to do. Mr Barclay listened, and nodded, and told us that he had been to Tangiers and Morocco and Tunisia in the 1950s, in the days before tourism was invented, when Tangiers was still the playground of the wandering rich. Tunis was disappointing, and Carthage was no more, said Mr Barclay. Carthage had been destroyed. *Carthaginem esse delendam.* The Tyrian queen would not be there to greet us, to proclaim a feast for us, to spread the silken towels for us, to entertain us with the purple robes and the golden goblet and the golden lyre. When he was in Tunis, he had bought several Tyrian carpets, he said – and there was one of them, even now, laid on the floor at our feet. Trample upon it, please do, do please feel free, said Mr Barclay, with a flourish. He was very gallant.

Carthage was destroyed, but Naples, after many centuries, had been restored, and thither, he understood, we would, after Tunisia, repair. Would we take in a few of the antiquities of the Ancient Africk Coast before setting sail for Italy with our minibus and our chauffeur on the Transmed ferry? El Djem, the third largest Roman amphitheatre in the world, was, he said, well worth the visit, and Kairouan also, if we had the stomach for that kind of thing. Was Anaïs, he inquired, of the Muslim faith, and if so, had she done her pilgrimages? Kairouan was a Holy City, was it not?

I thought that this line of suggestive interrogation was a little risqué, but Anaïs did not seem to mind it, though she replied to it quite briskly. Anaïs said that she was not a Muslim, she was a respectable postmodern atheist of Maronite Christian descent, but that she wouldn't mind seeing the Holy City of Kairouan and its blind camel if there was time. Ah, said Mr Barclay, if you do go to Kairouan, you must visit the man who sells embroidered shawls in the Street of the Weavers. I will write his name down for you and give it to Mrs Barclay before you go.

I think a knowing look may have passed between Mr Barclay and Anaïs at this point – a look, perhaps, of belated recognition.

I think I'm right in remembering that Mr Barclay referred to Cynthia as Mrs Barclay. What a strange couple they are.

Mr Barclay spoke to Anaïs with a form of innuendo that I did not understand. I do not think that it was sexual.

Shortly after this coded message about the Street of the Weavers, Mr Barclay rose to take his leave of us. 'I will leave you girls to your revels,' was what he said, and that I do remember clearly, word for word, because not many people talk like that these days. Then he shook hands with us all round, with a compliment for each of us. 'Look after my Cynthia, dear teacher lady,' he charged Mrs Jerrold, 'because she means the world to me.' To Anaïs, he bowed low, and murmured that she would enliven the desert places. After saluting Julia, he held her hand up to the light, and warned her to watch out for her gems in Naples. Or, better still, to leave them at home in the bank. Naples may be restored by the brave Bassolino, he said, but it is not yet transformed, and its old traditions die hard.

These were wise words and I remember thinking that she would be wise to heed them. But I doubt that she will. She seems wedded to those jewels.

I forget what he said to me, although I suppose he must have said something. Did he mention something called Capital Gains Tax? I wonder what that is. Perhaps he thinks I ought to invest all my money instead of spending so much of it on what can only be described as a spree. But I think it is my turn to have a spree.

When he left the room, I knew that the time had come to unleash the subject of Sally Hepburn upon the scene. I had to brace myself, but I did it. I did not flatter her in my introduction of her, but I must have managed to make her sound acceptable, for they all agreed without a murmur that I should be allowed to invite her to join us. As Cynthia pointed out, she would make up the numbers and thus reduce the price per head. Cynthia, our organizer, had already found us a small air-conditioned minibus and a driver on the Internet. They belong to an Italian-based company called Parnassus that organizes trips to unlikely spots like Eritrea, Libya, Anatolia and French North Africa, as well as more obvious destinations like Greece and Italy. Tours with a Difference, they called themselves in their oddly translated brochure. The terms per person would be reduced, said Cynthia, if we were to make up a party of six plus driver, instead of five. So by all means invite your frightful friend Sally, they urged me merrily. We were all in reckless mood. In for a penny, in for a pound. I have offered to pay for the driver and the minibus. The others told me they were all happy to pay their share, but I was so pleased to be able to make this offer. It makes me feel better about Sally, too.

Sally, of course, leapt at the chance. Although she was the only one of us still in regular gainful employment, she anticipated no problem in getting time off. I uncharitably guessed that her employers would be glad to be rid of her for a bit. She sounded pleased to be asked, but not as surprised as in my view she ought to have been. She asked a lot of questions about her fellow travellers, questions which I parried with an expertise born of years of circumspection.

So it has all come together, and we shall go.

The girl without the lipoma is called Jenny, as I have now discovered. I also, on impulse, asked her to come with us, because seven is a lucky number, and Cynthia said there would have been room for seven. I didn't expect her to say yes, and she didn't. But I did ask her. Her face lit up. She said no, but her face lit up, and that was good to see. I see her at the Club now nearly every time I go. We always exchange a few civil words, and she bought me a retaliatory cup of coffee one evening. I think she looks a little better.

We'll be seven anyway, if you include the driver. The driver is a woman called Valeria. She is due to meet us at Tunis airport, to drive us around the ruins, and then to drive us on to the ferry, and off it again. We will retain the services of Valeria and the minibus to do the Bay of Naples and the Lake of Avernus. I am not sure what her qualifications as a guide are, but we know we need her as a driver, for there is nowhere to park in Italy. I hope that she and Mrs Jerrold get on well and do not contradict one another. I have no picture of this Valeria person in my mind, but I like her classical name.

It is a strange coincidence, perhaps, that four more of the seven of us have classical names. Julia, Cynthia, Ida, and myself. How long these names have endured.

It has been a busy time of preparation, although Cynthia has been doing most of the hard work. I have not bought cruise gear, despite the urgings of Anaïs, but I have treated myself to a few new clothes and they are not as drab as my usual wear. (I do like my new tie-dyed pink shirt with beige streaks, and I think it suits me quite well.) I have had to get myself a new passport, as mine had expired. A new passport, in my old name of Candida Wilton. I thought of reverting to my maiden name, but it was too complicated. (I was always teased about my maiden name, and Wilton is neutral and unexceptionable, after all.) I don't like the new maroon passports much. They are very unimposing.

The last time I went abroad was with Andrew, when we were still Mr and Mrs Andrew Wilton, seven years ago. We went to a conference in Chicago, on the subject of visual impairment and cognitive disorders. It was a vast affair, with several hundred delegates, occupying the whole of one of those functional modern hotels on what is known as the Magnificent Mile. Partners were given concessionary rates. It was rather a macabre gathering. The hotel seemed luxurious to me but others complained that it was sub-standard and poor value for money and not as good as the hotel the association had used the year before. (It is true that the elevators were unreliable and unpredictable, and sometimes led one many floors skywards into the wrong part of the building.) I avoided most of the functions and took myself for walks by the lake shore. The weather was atrocious. An icy wind howled round the sharp corners of steep buildings, and the lake was whipped into waves that crashed violently upon large geometric artificial rocks. Andrew was very charming to everybody, as usual, and people kept telling me how much they admired him. He gave a short paper on the history of the Hamilcar Henson Trust and attitudes to and treatment of the blind in the eighteenth century. He does speak well, I grant him that.

I think the weather will be quite different in the Mediterranean. I intend to sun myself. Anaïs warns us that when last she went to the Bay of Naples the whole place was shrouded in mist and remained foggy for the whole of her visit, but I'm sure that won't happen to us. We shall have fair weather and a calm crossing. It is set in our stars to be so.

We leave in two days' time. I have wondered whether or not to take this laptop with me and keep a record of our journey, but I don't think I will. It would be too much of a worry. I can write everything up when I get back.

Andrew rang me last night. He never rings. I have hardly spoken to him in three years, nor have I wished to do so. He rang, ostensibly, to ask if I had heard anything from Ellen, our middle daughter who lives in Finland. He claimed he was worried that she had not replied to his last phone message. He said it needed an early answer. He didn't tell me what the message was. I said I wasn't surprised Ellen hadn't rung back, as he must know how she hesitates to use the telephone.

I don't believe that his real purpose in ringing me was to talk about Ellen. He's never shown much interest in Ellen, because, unlike her sisters, she has refused to pay court to him. His real purpose was to pry. Suffolk Sally would, it at once occurred to me as soon as I heard his voice, have told him all about our excursion. I tried, as I spoke to him of little matters as calmly and coldly as I could, to remember what, if anything, I had told Sally about Northam Provident and my unexpected bonus. I wondered if he would dare broach the subject himself, and I gave him no opening, so he was obliged, after a little polite thrust and parry, to say openly, 'I hear you are off on a holiday?'

'Yes,' I said. 'I am going on an educational outing with my Virgil class to trace the latter part of the voyage of Aeneas.'

This sounded strange but was in a sense true. I enjoyed speaking those words. I think I have remembered them fairly accurately, also. (I admit to having fabricated some bits of conversation in this narrative.)

'Good heavens,' said Andrew. A tremor in his voice indicated that Sally had not told him much about the expedition. He sounded genuinely surprised. I was glad that I had it in me to cause surprise. Of course, even if Sally had told him or others on the Suffolk gossip network that she was going with me to North Africa and Italy, she would not have been able to give him much detail, for, despite her interest in the pornography of Pompeii, Sally is not a classical scholar.

Anaïs, Cynthia, Julia and I are not classic classical scholars either, but we are more scholarly than Sally Hepburn. Mrs Jerrold is a classical scholar, and also a published poet.

I relented a little, at the end of this conversation, and told Andrew that I was travelling with Parnassus Tours, and that if there was any real worry about Ellen he could contact me through their office in Milan. I gave him the phone number and our personalized tour reference number. I am not inhuman. I do not wish to cut myself off utterly from my family. It is simply that I feel a need to redefine what my relationship to my family should be, in these latter days, in these survival days, after biology has done its best and worst. I think that Andrew sounded relieved to have a contact number, but I may have been imagining that. He has done me such wrong that I don't know how to read him, how to speak of him, how to remember him, how to think of him any more. He is like a great blank in my memory. He is like a hole cut in my side.

We have arranged to meet at Stansted, Anaïs Al-Sayyab, Mrs Jerrold, Julia Jordan, Cynthia Barclay, Sally Hepburn and me. We all have our own tickets, in case we get lost or are late, but Cynthia has the Master Plan and all the booking details. She has organized us all brilliantly. The others still have not met Sally Hepburn. I know I ought to feel nervous about this, but I don't. I feel quite irresponsible about it. People of our age ought to be able to look after ourselves.

She makes her last entry before the voyage

Tomorrow we leave. I have done most of my packing, and I have played my last game of solitaire. I shall wrap up this laptop and hide it in the bottom of the wardrobe.

I have just reread the whole of this diary. I am not proud of it. What a mean, self-righteous, self-pitying voice is mine. Shall I learn to speak in other tones and other tongues when I leave these shores? Do I still have it in me to find some happiness? *Health, wealth, and the pursuit of happiness.* The new declaration of our human rights.

Let me write this down. *I am happy now.* I am full of happy anticipation.

Yesterday afternoon I went for my last walk along the canal bank. I passed the spot where my man in the Scrubs and his gang tormented and drowned that poor woman. He has explained to me that they were all out of their minds when they did it, and I daresay it was so. Drugs, he said. I notice that he doesn't, technically, express remorse. He expresses some emotion, but I wouldn't call it remorse. He speaks as though it was somebody else that did it.

There was a light breeze on the surface of the water, and floating plastic bottles were nudging one another and circling one another gently as in some mating ritual.

Darkness, dirt, despair.

The Lady Pond was a pretty place to die. Watercress, yellow irises, and water mint grew round its marges, and there was a rickety little wooden jetty you could walk out on over the water. You could gaze down into the shallows, and sometimes you could see fish below you. I liked it very much. The biology teacher, Miss Crawley, used to collect creatures from it and display them in the lab – caddis grubs, snails, daphnia. There were nesting moorhens at the far end of the pond, in the reeds. There are moorhens on the canal, too, but their nests are not so desirable. They have to build them from plastic garbage, poor things.

I have explained to my man in the Scrubs that I will be away for a while. I admitted I was going on holiday. He has been teasing me about my Lottery efforts and he says he guesses I have won a lot of money but that I won't tell him because it will make him jealous. I think I will tell him the truth when I get back. If I get back.

Last night I paid my last visit to the Health Club – well, not my last ever, I trust, but my last for a few weeks. I think it was significant that I was greeted by name as I went in. This rarely happens now. They are too busy now for personal names.

I dropped my engagement ring into the pool last night. I had thought of dropping it through the grid into the lapping sluice that surrounds the pool, but it occurred to me that it might cause an obstruction, and I do not want to be responsible for any damage. So I just pulled it off my finger and let it sink to the bottom of the pool. It drifted downwards rather than dropped, at a slight angle. It didn't spiral, as I had thought it might – perhaps a lighter ring might have spiralled? I couldn't resist seeing if I could have fished it up again with my toes. I could, easily. There isn't a deep end to the pool. It's all shallow water. Somebody will fish my ring out. It has probably been recovered already. I wonder what will happen to it? Will it be finders-keepers, or will there be an advertisement announcing its recovery? I've seen several notices for Lost Objects (usually said to be of Great Sentimental Value) in the Club, but I don't think I've seen any for Found Objects.

I don't care if I never see that ring again.

I have divorced myself from Andrew and married the blue water.

A strange memory came back to me, as I peered into the shallow depths to see if I could still see the ring. When we were girls, at St Anne's, we used to practise swimming underwater for bricks. The bricks were wrapped in cloth. They were drowned bricks, corpse bricks, bagged in wet canvas. Julia hated swimming, but I enjoyed it then, as I do now. I was quite good at brick retrieval and at life-saving exercises.

I wonder if we shall have a chance to swim in Tunisia and

Italy. Cynthia Barclay says she loves to swim. And I have packed my bathing suit. I meant to buy a new one, as the elastic of mine is perishing through overuse, but I have not yet done so. Maybe I will buy a new one on my travels.

So my ring lies drowned in the shallow deep.

PART TWO

Italian Journey

They assemble for their departure

You know that land. You have an image of that land. All the cold and bitter children of the cold north have an image of the warm welcome of that southern land. There the palm and the cypress cut themselves out in antique shapes for your delight against the blue sky and the noonday sun. Those are the very shapes and patterns that are carved upon the antique heart, and you know them as your birthright. From generation to generation, they imprint their shapes upon the human heart. It is the land where the pale jasmine blossoms in the sweet night air, and bright lemons hang like dim and secret lamps amidst the glittering and the gloss of the ever-green. It is the sunny clime where you breathe more freely both by day and by night, where your fearful lungs fill gently with the soft air, where you no longer huddle and shiver and wrap yourself into your own arms and clench yourself back into your own self. There you no longer need to dread the threshold between the body and the world, for all is mild, all flows easily, all is lightness. Your shoulders are without burden, your eyes are clear, your skin is soft, and your feet in their sandals are free. You stretch out your arms, you can see your toes. The sky is vast and blue, the sand is golden, and the horizon shimmers with pledge and with promise. You know that land.

That magical land awaits them now. Its dunes and its citrus and its oils and its jasmine await them. Their as yet unknown guide Valeria awaits them faithfully like a tall sentinel on the far shore. Queen Dido gazes from her battlements across the centuries for their approach, for she knows that they remember her. Remember me, she cried, and, against so many odds, through so much forgetfulness, through the death of so many empires, they do remember her. They keep their tryst.

The weather swirls and pulses in rapid coloured garish modern swathes around the turning globe, and around the globe we try to catch its passing, on screens, on charts, with laser lights. But it will not stay for us. It moves on.

A light northern English rain is now falling over the railtrack and the desolate brick arches of the Stansted Express, over the tender striped sowings of the spring green fields of Essex, over the busy bands of the carriageways of the M25 and the M11, and over Stansted airport, but nothing can dampen the spirits of our little band of travellers. They know that they are to fly southwards to that promised southern land, towards the sun. They do not know that the storm clouds are gathering over the Alps, and were they to know this, they would not care. The lightning may flash and the thunder may crash, but beyond those snowy peaks and that vicious howling in the heights, the sun's assurance awaits them.

So now they cluster, surrounded by their hand baggage, perched brightly, a little flock, about their cups of cappuccino and latte and espresso in the Costa Café. *Costa, Cuore D'Italia.* They are migratory birds, our friends, in their new spring plumage. They have travelled here separately, by car and by train, and they have checked in, and passed through security, and now they are waiting for the arrival of the last of their party. They are waiting for their wild card, Sally Hepburn. She has the shortest journey to make, and yet she is the last. Where is she? She is not yet late, exactly, for the Departures

Display Panel still instructs the Tunis Flight TP1082 passengers to wait for the gate number to be announced, but Sally has a reputation, even amongst those who have never met her, for being zealously overprompt. Is she waiting somewhere else, in the wrong place? The instructions to gather in this coffee corner have surely been unambiguous, and Stansted is not a large airport. Unlike Heathrow and Gatwick, Stansted is not a vast confusing maze of identical and identically repeating facilities. It ought to be easy enough to find one's way about at Stansted. It is, as they all agree, a well-organized architectural space, easy to negotiate, pleasing to the eye. Its light and airy cages remind Candida Wilton of the pale sky-green geometry of her Health Club.

So where is Sally Hepburn? Has she got cold feet? Has jealous Husband Andrew detained her? Has her train been derailed? Who will spot her first? Will her weight upset the apple cart? Will she prove an irritant?

This little group is already well bonded. The Virgil class has accepted Julia Jordan into its fold, and she sits amongst it, queenly, calm, a little detached, but apparently content. The Virgil class thinks it has understood why Julia had been invited. But it is still mystified by the inclusion of Sally Hepburn. Even Sally's friend Candida, the friend who asked her to join them, does not seem to know why she has done so. There is some strange unnatural compulsion binding the two women from Suffolk, connecting the spinster, Sally, and Candida, the abandoned wife.

Will the class be ready to take in Sally Hepburn? It is not sure. Will she be as tiresome and cantankerous as old Mr Wormald? Or will she play the game?

And here she comes, bustling, hot and bothered, lugging on squeaking wheels a suitcase which, although it has passed through check-in, looks far too big to be admitted as hand baggage. She is puffing and panting and talking, all at the same time, as she bears down upon her group. She is unseasonally and pessimistically clad in a stout tweed skirt and a short thick padded waterproof jacket. She is full of excuses. Her taxi did not arrive on time, the ticket machine at the station was not working, and her train was late. Her rail network is notoriously unreliable, so she had left herself plenty of time, but nevertheless it managed to delay her. She will write yet again to the manager.

Nobody listens to these tedious details, as they urge her to calm down, cool down, relax. She continues to breathe forth panic and heat and flurry as she is introduced, one by one, to her travelling companions. With her benefactor Candida, at whom she glowers rather accusingly, she is already long familiar, and Anaïs Al-Sayyab she has briefly encountered, in Candida's curiously anonymous London apartment off Ladbroke Grove. She grasps the hand of Anaïs, but is too flustered to register the effrontery of the long scarlet jacket of Anaïs, and the extremity of her grey peaked felt Mongolian cap. She is presented, a little calmer now, to the diminutive Mrs Jerrold, who is robed more discreetly in purple and black, although her bell-shaped silver earrings strike an eccentric and dissident note. (They tinkle and jangle faintly as Mrs Jerrold nods her head, and she nods her head frequently, possibly for the reaffirming pleasure of their music.) Cynthia Barclay, to Sally's eyes, seems at first glance to be a perfectly regular middle-class matron, dressed comfortably in a nice classic beige trouser suit, with a geometrically patterned silk scarf around her throat. (It is only on closer inspection that one notices the bold champagne-pink streak in her restored golden-grey locks, and the brazen interrogative tilt of her head.)

Julia Jordan is a writer, therefore one might expect her to

look odd, but Julia Jordan is as respectably dressed as Cynthia Barclay, in a checked yellow-and-brown cotton dress, largely covered by an unassuming lightweight Burberry raincoat. Sally cannot yet see the large amount of monogrammed luggage that accompanies Julia, for it is being loaded into the bowels of the aeroplane, along with the more modest bags of the other women. Sally had been nervous about meeting Julia Jordan, for she knows she is famous, and famous people make her talk too much. But Julia looks reassuringly ordinary. She looks less like a writer than Cynthia Barclay does, in Sally Hepburn's view.

Over the Alps, the electric lightning flashes. Deep below the airy pathways, squalls flurry the bruised purple waters of the Mediterranean. Far south, on the far African shore, the pale warm waves lap. Ruined temples, desert sands, dead languages, foreign tongues. These women keep faith with the past, they keep faith with myth and history.

All except Sally. Sally, unlike the rest of the party, has not been doing her homework. She is vague about their destination, vague about their route. She is here for the ride, wherever it may take her. She is a fellow traveller.

Her old friend and protégée Candida seems to have turned in the past few weeks into somebody else, somebody much less docile. Sally has, until this moment, been confident of her ability to 'get the better' of Candida Wilton, although she would not have described her confidence so brutally. She has long seen Candida as somebody whom she can manipulate, towards whom she can condescend, and whom she can embarrass or torment at will. And now here is Candida, sitting quite unruffled, and paying Sally Hepburn very little attention, despite the loud huffing and puffing of her advent. Candida seems to have disconnected herself. Moreover, her hair is a different shape, and much less wispy.

It is a more solid shape, and she seems to have got herself a new set of teeth. Sally, who wears partial dentures, has been watching the deterioration of Candida's teeth with interest and pleasure, but it seems that Candida has miraculously arrested their decay. How has she managed that? Can money work such wonders? How much money has Candida got? She had described her bonus to Sally as a 'small windfall', but that could mean anything, couldn't it? Had she come into a fortune or won the Lottery? The sight of her friend looking so undowntrodden is very irritating to Sally Hepburn. It goes against all the rules of age and entropy. It is not right.

Candida herself, freed from her own whining monologue, is also aware that she has turned into another person, a multiple, polyphonic person, who need not pretend to be stupid, who can use long words or make classical allusions if she wishes, without fear of being called a pedant or a swat or a semi-educated fool or somebody trying to be too-clever-by-half. Yet she is not so utterly transformed as to expect to evade the duty of sitting next to Sally Hepburn on the aeroplane. That she must do, although in other ways she has renounced her victim role. It may be, who knows, her last duty. It would not be fair to expect a stranger in this group to sit next to Sally. Sally is too large for an economy aeroplane seat. She will overflow, and therefore she must overflow on to Candida.

The group whiles away its waiting time at Stansted by looking at the brochure of the hotel where they are to stay in Tunis. It is called 'The Hotel Diana, the Hotel with a Difference'. The photographs display extensive beaches, colonnades and swimming pools, but all these travellers are cynical about brochures. It cannot be as nice as it looks, but never mind, they are determined to enjoy themselves, even if there are cockroaches and mosquitoes. Mrs Jerrold confesses that on her earlier trip to North Africa, with Eugene, in the 1950s, there had been many cockroaches and mosquitoes. But they had been younger then, and Morocco and Tunisia had had many other charms. Tangiers also they had visited. Eugene had known people in Tangiers – novelists, poets, dealers. Eugene had known such people even in the empty quarters of the world. It was said that if two literature-loving English-speaking people met in a bar in Eastern Europe or under a palm tree in Africa or at an oasis in the Near East, one of them would be Eugene Jerrold. He had been insatiably gregarious, greatly trusting, ever optimistic, and only rarely betrayed. I had to hide our money, nodded Mrs Jerrold, musically. I sewed it into my underwear and into the lining of my bags. He gave it away. He gave to beggars, and he always wanted to foot the bill. He liked the expansive gesture. He liked to play the host.

Cynthia Barclay has been appointed treasurer of the trip. She will settle the accounts and divide the expenses. She is good at that kind of thing. She has always been a spendthrift with her own money, but she is professional about organizing that of other people. She keeps Mr Barclay well in the black. And she assures them that her mathematics have been greatly improved by her new evening class. They can trust her to divide and subtract and keep a correct tally. They believe her. So far, her arrangements have been impeccable. Their allocation of pre-booked seats was waiting for them at check-in, just as she had said it would be. Sally Hepburn was in danger of losing her seat, but even she has found her correct place. They have great confidence in Mrs Barclay.

Mrs Jerrold recalls that on her earlier trip, she had been made very ill by a bottled mineral water called Ain Oktor, a chalky medicinal water of repulsive taste and a disastrous effect upon the bowels. She wonders if Ain Oktor is still to be purchased in Tunisia. If so, she warns them all to avoid it.

They fly onwards through the thunderbolts of Jove

Their disposition upon the aircraft is as follows:

Julia Jordan has a window seat. Next to her sits her admirer, Cynthia Barclay. Anaïs Al-Sayyab, on this row, takes the aisle.

In the row behind, Sally Hepburn takes the window seat. Next to her, in the middle, sits Candida Wilton. Next to Candida, Mrs Jerrold takes the aisle.

The aeroplane is named *Salammbô*, which Mrs Jerrold and Candida Wilton find disconcerting, though they do not say so. But despite the misgivings of some of her passengers, the *Salammbô* takes off smoothly, and gains height smoothly, as she should. As she soars through the calm skies above France, Cynthia and Julia converse with animation about television series they have seen or, in Julia's case, written, and actors they have liked or disliked. This conversation is mutually satisfactory. Their falsely golden heads bend together in the womanly gossiping intimacy of old friends. Occasionally Anaïs volunteers to add a remark, but most of her attention is given to embroidering a piece of fine canvas with a design consisting of a cross-section of a segment of a red cabbage. It is a convoluted design and requires a great deal of concentration. Occasionally she makes a mistake and has to unpick a thread. She deploys for this task a darling little pair of silver scissors with long golden crane-bird handles. They sparkle. The air hostess had looked at these scissors suspiciously, as though they might be construed as a dangerous weapon, but has decided to let them pass.

Behind Julia, Sally Hepburn is haranguing Candida, as is her wont, on various topics of the day. She begins with DVT (Candida eventually works out that this is an acronym for deep-vein thrombosis), which has been killing air passengers in the economy classes, and then moves on vigorously to her old favourite from Cromer days, nut allergy. She is sure there will be nuts in the vegetarian in-flight meal she has requested. Candida knows better than to say, 'Wait and see', because Sally is enjoying her apprehensions so much. Sally eyes with suspicious distaste the roasted peanuts which Candida is popping into her mouth, one by one, between sips from her glass of red wine. Sally sees them as a bad omen. Candida is not very fond of roasted peanuts, but, defiantly, independently, she is relishing these, even though they are a threat to her fine new bridgework.

Next to Candida, Mrs Jerrold seems to be reading a large paperback book called *The Death of Virgil*, which she has said she has been intending to read for years. It is a famous and famously unread novel by a German writer called Hermann Broch. Its moment, for Mrs Jerrold, has come. (Eugene claimed he had once had a drink with Hermann Broch just after the war in Princeton, and this may even be true, for Eugene was well known to have met some unlikely people in unlikely places.) But, although she appears to be reading, Mrs Jerrold's eyes are merely resting on the page. She is not listening to the nut rage of Sally Hepburn, for she has acquired over the years a finely tuned capacity for blotting out unnecessary noise. She is thinking about Goethe and Wordsworth. And why should she not?

She is thinking now of Goethe's love affair with antiquity and the classical south. *Kennst du das Land, wo die Zitronen blühn* . . . Yes, she knows that land. She is thinking of Goethe's southward Italian journey in 1786, and of his rapture as he encountered vineyards, maize, mulberry trees, apples, pears and quinces. How he loved the darting lizards and the noisy chirping of the cicadas. She is remembering that he wrote that he knew that these raptures would seem childish to the natives of the south, but that he, *who had suffered long beneath an evil sky*, was happy for a while to feel *a joy which should be ours as a perpetual natural necessity*. He was happy to bask in the perpetual natural necessity of the god-given and god-withheld sun. She is thinking also of young Wordsworth's crossing of the Alps, on foot, and of his mild astonishment when he reached the far side. She is thinking that she will never write another poem, for her muse had deserted her, as the muse in middle age deserted Wordsworth. She is thinking of her husband, Eugene, who had in their early days encouraged her to write, though his ebullience and energy had soon overwhelmed her and silenced her. She does not blame him for this, for he could not help his nature. She gazes out of the window at the bright clouds and thinks of sunsets, although it is midday. The light is strange up here in the empyrean.

And woven into these other thoughts, she is also thinking of her young friend Candida, who is sitting next to her and listening so patiently to her fat friend Sally's prodigal indignations. Candida has brought them all upon this pilgrimage. Mrs Jerrold is a seer, and she can see Candida walking forlornly by the dark canal with its scrubby weeds and its iridescent oils and its detergent odours. She sees her walk past the cemetery, with its broken wall and its cracked graves and its tilted funerary monuments. She sees her floating in the dank water, like Ophelia. *At evening by the sour canals/ We'll hope to hear some madrigals* . . . she often remembers these lines of Eugene's friend, Cecil Day Lewis. She wonders if Candida knows them. Does Candida read poetry? Did she ever listen to those tapes? She has never made reference to them. She is pleased that Candida is here with her, above the clouds. She is pleased that an accidental shower of gold has fallen upon the pale sad Candida.

The weather is beginning to deteriorate, and the stewards hasten with the meal, hoping to get it dispersed before the threatened turbulence. Sally's pre-ordered vegetarian lunch turns out to be some kind of lasagne, and when it arrives she discovers to her overt dissatisfaction and covert delight that there are what seem to be pine nuts in its portion of salad. She rings for the stewardess to complain. The stewardess offers to remove the offensive little boxlet of green leaves. Sally says she wants a replacement salad. The stewardess says that there isn't one. Candida offers to swap hers for Sally's, as hers seems to be nut-free, but this does not satisfy Sally, who wants attention more than she wants a nut-free salad. She embarks on a speech about how many vegetarians are also nut-allergic, and why the airline should know this. The stewardess, who is not English, does not follow this address very well, but as she leans over with her jug of orange juice, attempting, politely, to listen, the aeroplane lurches in the gathering storm, and she spills a few drops of juice on Candida's tray. Sally, officiously and clumsily mopping this up with her napkin, manages to knock over Candida's quarter-bottle of red wine. The wine colours Candida's chicken portion pink. It looks by now as though Candida Wilton has been very careless. Sally says the stewardess should fetch Candida a new meal and a new tray, but the stewardess says there isn't one. Sally is embarking on various offensively xenophobic remarks about the inefficiency of foreign airlines when the plane gives a great judder and the Fasten Seat Belts signs flash on and the cabin staff are told to return to their seats. Candida manages to make various placatory remarks in French to the stewardess, who gratefully grabs for her from her trolley a couple of little replacement wine bottles before disappearing to the safety of her own seat belt.

It is an electric storm of some violence. They can see the

forked lightning flash around them and above them. The snowy peaks and dark creased mineral clefts and ridges of the sharp Alps are ranged inhospitably below them. The plane shakes and shudders like a thin tin can, and other bottles of wine tip over on to other trays and on to other breasts of other chickens. Julia and Cynthia exchange worldly glances of comically exaggerated alarm, Anaïs shuts her eyes, and Mrs Jerrold placidly butters her bread roll. Sally Hepburn stares, transfixed, out of the window, at the galvanic display of heavenly fireworks, and at the white mountain summits, as though expecting to see the long-legged monster of Frankenstein loping over the crevasses beneath. Candida Wilton quietly resigns herself to death. If it be now, so be it, but she really would have liked to have seen Carthage and Cumae and Naples first. It seems a pity to get so far, and not to arrive.

Death does not yet choose to claim her or any of her fellow passengers. Death gives them a warning, but lets them pass through. The tumult abates, and the frail little metal craft sails on into calmer skies. The pilot broadcasts over the loudspeaker system a polite and perhaps faintly sardonic wish that they have not been too discomforted by the slight turbulence. The Seat Belt signs remain illumined, but the cabin staff begins to move around again, reassuringly, collecting trays, distributing coffee, offering Duty Free. The atmosphere still crackles with electricity. Candida can feel the crackling in her brain. Like some forms of electric shock therapy, it seems to have done her good. It has burnt up some dust. She feels dazzlingly, radiantly lucid, as *Salammbô* flies her south to Carthage. She ignores the unceasing conversation of Sally, which starts up again as soon as the thunderclaps fall silent. She feels that the rest of her life lies before her on a clear and shining track. Onwards and upwards, *nach*

Cuma, nach Cuma. She has left her earthly attachments far behind, and is sailing into the future. It lies before her like a cloth of dreams. All shall be made plain at last, in this bright new light.

The minibus driver and guide, Valeria, is due to meet them at Tunis-Carthage airport, to drive them to the Hotel Diana. They have speculated about what she will look like – will she be tall, small, dark, pale, old, young, foolish, sensible, silent, talkative, classical, romantic? Sally Hepburn has already professed her disappointment that she is not a man. Sally had, she said, been hoping for a gigolo, at last. But as she cannot even cope with a French-speaking Tunisian air hostess, Candida is thinking that she would not have coped too well with a gigolo either. A woman will be more congenial.

They arrive in Africa, and meet their stately guide

Valeria is very tall. Her flock spots her at once at the airport, for she stands head and shoulders above the rest of the mob greeting the passengers from the plane. She is even taller than Anaïs. She must be nearly six feet tall. This is unusual for an Italian woman, but, as she later reveals, she has Ethiopian blood in her ancestry. She is holding aloft a placard saying **WELCOME VIRGIL TOUR** in large bold black letters. The undiscussed but latent problem of whether she is guide or courier, and whether or not she will expect to be treated as a social equal, is solved at once, on first sight. For here is a lady if ever there was one. She is noble, and she inspires instant confidence.

Her appearance is in every way striking. Her skin is smooth and dark and unblemished. It is brown with mauve shadows. They all fall instantly in love with the beautiful Valeria. Her hair is twisted into little black ringlets in a halo around her face and tied into a thick braid at the back. She is dressed, at this their first meeting, in a long bright saffron-yellow tunic, with baggy trousers of a slightly darker orange. She looks a little like a priestess. And she drives, as they are soon to discover, like a charioteer.

Valeria extracts the Virgilian baggage with surprising speed, through some special channel, and leads her group to its waiting minibus. She organizes slaves to load the baggage into the back, and keeps a sharp eye on Julia's many monogrammed pieces. The late afternoon heat shimmers on the tarmac and the air smells hot. They clamber into the bus's air-conditioned interior and dispose themselves eagerly upon the banquettes. Candida does not sit next to Sally this time. She takes a seat of her own, with nobody next to her. She has deserved a little space. And the minibus hurtles off, with Valeria at the wheel, towards the Hotel Diana, the Hotel with a Difference.

By the time they reach their destination, the expert Valeria, without taking her eyes off the road, but with some cunning use of the mirror, has correctly identified Sally Hepburn as a troublemaker, Candida Wilton as a peacemaker, Mrs Jerrold as a tough old bird who will never tire and never complain, Cynthia Barclay as an organizing and sociable spirit who will thrive in a crisis, and Julia as a nervous prima donna. Anaïs Al-Sayyab she cannot classify so easily. She does not often have people who look like Anaïs on her desert tours. She likes the look of Anaïs.

And the Virgilians like the look of their hotel. It is neither as grand nor quite as close to the sea as the brochure had indicated, and its colonnades are by no means Roman in proportion, but it is bright and white and friendly. It is set on a hillside, and its sloping terraced garden is pleasantly planted with palms and cacti; great cascades of purple and pink bougainvillea fall lavishly from its parapets and balconies. It is luxury on a small, low-built and independent scale. It is not a Hilton or a Marriott or a Sheraton. It belongs to a second cousin of Valeria, a moustached gentleman about half her size, who is pleased to welcome in person his guests from England. It is just the place for them, he assures them, and happily they agree.

Their only problem seems to be how to spend the evening. There are too many delights on offer, and some of them sound rather exhausting. It has been a long day, and the aeroplane had been cramped as well as turbulent. Should they settle in quietly, and have a little supper, and so to bed, in order to wake refreshed for an arduous day of sightseeing on the morrow? Perhaps the more energetic could combine this modest plan with a little dip in the hotel pool, which winks at them seductively from its benevolent turquoise eye through a fringe of palm trees? On the other hand, would it not be fun to hit the town, and cruise along the Avenue Bourguiba, and take in a café, and see the night lights and the nightlife? Or Valeria could drive them up to the pines and eucalyptus and orange trees of the Belvedere Park, or around the lagoon or the bay? She is at their disposal, she assures them, and their wish is her command.

Cynthia longs to plunge at once into the sea. Julia and Anaïs want to hit the town – Julia likes the notion of a café, and Anaïs says she wants to go shopping. Sally wants her supper. Mrs Jerrold wants to retire to her room to read her book, although she is too polite to say so. Candida does not know what she wants. She wants everything. She wants it all.

It is Candida, however, who eventually suggests that they should celebrate their first evening together by holding a short seminar under the direction of Ida Jerrold. They will stay in the hotel, and take supper there, and then foregather with their Virgil texts for half an hour. This suggestion is accepted by all, for, though they do not like to admit it, even the more adventurous of them are tired, and not quite up to tackling a foreign city. None of them are quite as young as they were, though some of them do not like to admit that either. Valeria asks if she may attend the seminar, and is warmly invited to do so. Naturally, all the original Virgilians have brought their texts with them, and they offer to share them round with those who do not have them. Candida is highly satisfied with this eccentric arrangement. They will dine together at eight, and then do a little Latin.

None of the other guests in Valeria's second cousin's hotel with a difference seem to be Latin scholars. They are more outdoor sporting types, bronzed, lean-kneed, and muscular. They speak in French and Italian. Our group watches them, over dinner, and preens itself upon its refined classical credentials as it tucks into a copious meal of small pickled fishes, red-pepper salad, roasted chickens, oiled rice and fried flowers. Sally complains quite a lot about the piquancy of the peppers (and it is true that one or two of them are unforeseeably and randomly ferocious) but nobody listens to her. She calms down when a platter of pastries arrives. The pastries are excellent. Even those who never eat pastries are tempted by them. The wine is cheap and good. Mrs Jerrold is pleased to note that Ain Oktor is still on offer, all these decades later, so she can continue knowingly to avoid it. Her expertise has not been wasted.

The evening is so pleasant that they agree to meet outdoors, by the poolside, with their texts. An open fire with scented logs is flickering in a large brick oven, and insects gather around the living flames. The travellers make a little circle on white wooden chairs around Mrs Jerrold. To Candida's astonishment, she discovers that Julia has brought her old St Anne's school copy of Book Six. Julia clutches it, as a testimonial. Its stained blue and grey canvas cover is worn and marked, and its text is heavily annotated in several childish hands. Julia has remembered the innocence of her schooldays better than Candida would have expected. She has preserved its relics. Candida lost her school Virgil many moons ago.

Mrs Jerrold, however, does not wish to do Book Six and the Underworld yet. They should save that for its proper place in Naples. She thinks they should look at a few lines from Book Four – lines 259–78, to be precise – which describe Mercury's visit to Aeneas in the new city of Carthage. Aeneas, gloriously robed in a rich cloak of purple woven with thin threads of gold, a gift from Queen Dido, is busy laying the foundations of the citadel when Mercury descends upon him and tells him to remember his destiny as founder of Rome and Italy. Aeneas must not idle around here in the luxurious oriental land of Libya. He is chosen for a higher fate.

Earnestly they bend their heads over the Latin and attempt to disentangle the grammar. Their brains are rusty and dusty, despite the purging of the electric storm, and they find it is difficult to focus on the text. They can see the scene clearly enough – there is Aeneas, busily helping to construct (though not, presumably, with his own hands) the citadel stronghold of his mistress. He is suddenly recalled (as, in a later age, would be Mark Antony from the thrall of Cleopatra) to a recollection of his greater duties, and is struck, as by a thunderbolt, by the horror of the knowledge that it is his duty to betray and abandon Dido. Unlike Mark Antony, he will obey his destiny and sacrifice love for glory. He will become one of the great betrayers of history, and Dido one of the greatly betrayed. The group knows this story well, and has already spent much time considering the piety and propriety of the behaviour of Pius Aeneas. But the text itself is puzzling. They are glad they do not have an exam ahead of them in the morning.

They do not have too much difficulty with vocabulary. *Pulchram urbem* is 'beautiful city' in the accusative, and *magalia* (n., plural) they can well understand to mean 'humble Carthaginian huts', though this is not a very useful noun to learn by heart. *In tenuem auram* means, literally, 'into thin air', which is where Mercury vanishes when his mission is accomplished. Vocabulary is not difficult. Anyone can learn words. But as for the grammar – now that is another matter. Mrs Jerrold tells them that *oblite*, which means 'forgetful', is the vocative singular masculine of the perfect participle of the verb *obliviscor, –i, oblitus sum*, to forget, a verb which takes the genitive. This is double Dutch to them, at this time of night, after a three-hour flight through a thunderstorm, after a large meal and a few glasses of wine. They cannot get their old heads round it at all. Yes, they understand that Aeneas is being accused of being forgetful of his destiny and his kingdom, but they cannot understand how the words *fit together*. Patiently, Mrs Jerrold pursues the meaning, and teases out the golden thread, and suddenly, for a moment, they have it. *Heu, regni rerumque oblite tuarum!* 'Alas, you, of your kingdoms and fortunes forgetful!' Yes, the words fall into place, connect, and glow into transitory meaning. The students smile at one another, triumphant.

A light breeze rattles through the dry date palms, and a firefly dances in the shrubbery. Moths swoon into the flames. The air is scented with jasmine and aromatic wood. The lesson is over. They yawn and stretch. A thin moon rides high in the midnight blue above them, and vast Orion strides the calm sky with his shining belt. Cynthia is still eager for a swim, but acknowledges that it is now too late. Tomorrow they will do everything – the ruins, the city, the shopping for carpets and fabrics, the pilgrimage.

As they are about to depart to their separate rooms for the night, Mrs Jerrold, who has packed away her texts into her capacious bag, suddenly asks, 'Does anyone here play bridge?' Most shake their heads, but Cynthia Barclay and Valeria nod eagerly and hopefully. 'Would the rest of you like to learn?' asks Mrs Jerrold. High on their pride in having mastered the vocative singular masculine of the perfect participle of the verb *obliviscor, –i, oblitus sum*, they agree that it would be delightful to learn to play bridge. Even Candida Wilton, who was brought up to think card games wicked, says she would like to learn. They agree that it is too late now to take in anything new, but the next evening, after the Latin lesson, they will have a bridge lesson. Mrs Jerrold produces from her bag two packs of playing cards. 'You see,' she says, 'I came prepared. I can do card tricks, and I can tell fortunes, and I can play bridge.'

They congratulate her upon her foresight. Tired and happy, they take themselves to their rooms. None of them are sharing. All have paid for single-room supplements. Though they have not paid much extra, for Valeria's cousin has made them all a very good price.

Valeria, their custodian, is pleased with the way the day has gone. Her tour group has considerable potential. She lies flat upon her bed, doing her relaxation exercises, and remembers the tour on which she first learnt to play bridge. She had been in charge of a gaggle of lords and ladies from the House of Lords of Great Britain, gathered together to tour the ruins of Libya by day and to play bridge by night. Some of them were so much keener on bridge than on ruins that they played by day as well. They played in their bus as they rode through the desert, they played in cafés and hotel rooms and restaurants and at airports and railway stations, they played amidst the ruins of the amphitheatre of the emperor. And Valeria had been initiated into the mysteries of bridge. One weathered and pickled old peer, Lord Filey of Foley, had been gallantly eager to teach Valeria, and she had picked up the rules with what to him seemed surprising speed – he had never discovered that she had for a decade in an earlier manifestation been a postgraduate student attached to Cornell in the other Ithaca. She looks back, now, as she wiggles her toes in the air and flexes her ankles, upon the small sums of money she had wagered and won and lost in the Sahara, and she thinks of the endlessly fascinating cut of the cards, and she smiles to herself. Bridge is an amusing game, and these women would be right to add it to their repertoire. One can never have too many holds on happiness. Card games are the proper reward of the veterans of old campaigns. Lord Filey had played a tight hand.

Dutifully, her relaxation exercises completed, Valeria reads another chapter of her preceptor's revolutionary new work on the trade routes and silver coinage of the Etruscans. She likes to keep up with the past, and is sure Mrs Jerrold will be interested in the latest news of the Etruscans. Then she looks at her recently acquired photograph of the baroque monument to Doge Giovanni Pesaro in the Frari in Venice. It shows a massive sarcophagus, supported by four blackamoor caryatids burdened everlastingly by its overwhelming weight. She wonders whether they will so serve for ever, with their trousers so fashionably ragged at the knees, and their expressive and animated faces so hard to read. Ruskin hated this theatrical monument, with its 'grinning and horrible' figures, and milder critics still condemn it as bizarre. Valeria was entranced by these vigorous Titans supporting so much dead marble on their shoulders: does she have an Ethiopian chip on hers? She thinks she might never have noticed these black men, had it not been for her preceptor at Cornell, who is a white Englishman. What does that mean, she wonders? He taught her to use her eyes, and with them she has seen strange sights. Is the travel industry ready for a Black Athena Art Tour? Is there enough black money to support such a concept?

She is exhausted by her thoughts, and so she decides against trying to add another stanza to her epic poem on the theme of the Lioness of Judah, an elaborate and anachronistic work which she knows she will never complete. She shuts her eyes, and decides to drift into sleep. As she lies quietly, she hears a tapping at the door of the room next to hers. She guesses that it will be Sally Hepburn, popping in to borrow something from somebody. Sally, Valeria knows by instinct, is not good at demarcations. She is a born intruder.

Our heroine is threatened by an invasion

Candida has regained the peace and solitude of her room with an unprecedented sense of inner calm. Never in her life has she felt such delight. She is so happy with her room and with her journey. She has behaved so well throughout the day, she tells herself – she has humoured Sally, and calmed the flight attendant, and made a friendly contact with the handsome Valeria, and enthroned Mrs Jerrold in her rightful place as tutor. She has watched the flickering of the flames, and breathed in the sweetness of the night air. And now she stands at her open window, in her thin long white nightgown, gazing out across the sparkling waters of the Mediterranean, which spread below her and shimmer darkly northwards into the moonlit distance. The watery sheen delights and lightens her. She has always been drawn towards the water. She had had moments of peace even in Suffolk, walking the dog along the riverbank. She remembers them, and she remembers the urban gleam of the Grand Union Canal, and the place where the woman drowned, the woman whose rapist and murderer she has befriended. She has escaped both from that dullness, and from that dark destiny. She breathes deeply, and feels herself dying into life.

And then Sally Hepburn knocks upon the door.

Sally cannot resist it. Her pretext is aspirin. She will say she cannot find her packet of aspirins. She will say she has a headache from the thunderous Alps, and needs a tablet to settle her for sleep.

Candida hears the tapping, and turns away from the window and into the room, and crosses barefoot to the door across the wooden floor strewn with woven rugs, and cautiously opens the door a crack. A crack is enough for Sally, who heaves her way through, crying out, 'It's only me!' Candida backs away, towards her bed, and reaches for her black cotton kimono, and rapidly conceals her body from her friend's prying gaze.

Sally invades, examines, appropriates. She is not content with the proffered bottle of pills, which she snatches eagerly (but criticizes in passing for being insoluble) as she trips her way towards the window and the view. Candida is loath to let Sally see her view, although she cannot prevent her from gazing at it. Sally says that it is a better view than her own, and that Candida should draw the blinds to keep out the bugs, and that those loose rugs lying on the floor will surely be the death of somebody. The icy moon looks down disdainfully, the water blackens. Candida holds her wrap tightly round her small ageing drooping breasts. The whole bay changes colour under Sally's threatening eye. Then Sally bustles back into Candida's bathroom, and noisily pours herself a glass of water from the tap, and throatily swallows down her aspirins, and critically inspects Candida's modest array of cosmetics and toiletries. Candida thinks of pointing out that it would have been wiser to take the pills with bottled water, but refrains from this comment, because it is too like the kind of comment that Sally herself would have made.

Sally sits herself down, heavily, upon the end of Candida's bed, ready for a midnight gossip. As her eyes dart around the room, they alight, inevitably, upon the little basket of fruits that have been presented to Mrs Candida Wilton with the Best Wishes of the Manager and the hopes that she will Enjoy a Happy Visit. Sally is envious and indignant. She has not got fruits. Why has Candida got fruits? Eat my fruits, please take them, says Candida, wearily. But Sally does not want fruit, at this time of night. She wants to chat. She wants to discuss her fellow travellers. She wants to criticize Julia for her embarrassment of baggage, and Cynthia Barclay for the dyed pink streak in her hair. Sally, who had sat with such deceptive docility through the Latin lesson, has now summoned her resources, and is full of opinions about the pointlessness of teaching dead languages, and the parallel and distinct iniquity of the contemporary school curriculum, and the lack of grasp of successive Secretaries of State for Education. She wants to know more about Ida and Eugene Jerrold. Who *is* Mrs Jerrold? Why had she been teaching a class in W10? Where does she live? What does she live on?

Candida, out of weariness, finds herself describing Mrs Jerrold's little mews house. She wonders if this is treacherous, but despite her doubts she hears her voice speak on. Her voice tells of the potted shrubs and plants in the dead-end alley, and of the high-arched and smartly painted wooden doors where once the horses and carriages came and went, and of the cobblestones and ingenious stairways and balconies. It tells of

Mrs Jerrold's crowded walls with their many little paintings, and her sagging shelves of books, and her plump cats, and her wineglasses with their spiral stems. The voice does not speak of Mrs Jerrold's volumes of verse: Candida forbids it to do so, and it obeys her order.

Sally listens, greedily, and comments that Mrs Jerrold's little house must be worth a small fortune. A mews house, in Notting Hill. It's the kind of place where popstars live, says Sally.

I suppose it is, says Candida, who knows nothing of popstars and who had not thought of it in those terms. It's not really Notting Hill, says Candida. It's more Ladbroke Grove.

She almost says that Mr Barclay's house is really grand, but manages not to. What business would that be of Sally's?

Sally tries to move the conversation to Anaïs Al-Sayyab and her career in television, but this time Candida succeeds in giving nothing away at all. She remains silent, sitting defensively upright on the little stool by the dressing table. She wishes Sally would get up off her bed. She is making a great dent in it.

Candida yawns.

'It is time for bed,' says Candida, at last. She is beginning to fear that Sally will never budge. And indeed Sally seems remarkably reluctant to do so. But eventually she takes the hint, and takes herself off, although she produces many a threatening delay and manoeuvre as she goes. But go she does, at last, and the door shuts behind her, and Candida is again alone at last, in the blissful solitude of Africa.

Candida does not get straight into her bed. She pulls the covers straight, and smooths them down, so there is no longer any trace of Sally's bodily presence. Then she goes back to the window, and gazes out once more, for a while, at Orion and the night sea and the night sky.

In such a night
Stood Dido with a willow in her hand . . .

In her room, which is next to Candida's, Julia Jordan is not wasting time gazing at the view. She is still unpacking her suitcases. This activity reassures her. She has always enjoyed packing and unpacking. She is thinking about the plot of her Neapolitan novel, and wondering how on earth she has found herself here in Tunisia, when Naples is what she needs. Is there some twist to the plot that is waiting for her here? She has wandered here by mistake, but it doesn't seem to matter much. She shakes out her long silvery and gold evening skirt, and her black and gold silk shirt, and hangs them on a hanger from a hook on the back of the door. Then she adds her necklaces and a long printed silk scarf. Her shadow party-going self glimmers back at her, festively. She continues to arrange her underwear neatly in her drawers. She is a tidy person. She likes her things to be neatly arranged about her.

Anaïs Al-Sayyab is sitting up in bed, reading her Guide Book to Tunisia. She has a tumbler of duty-free whisky at her elbow, from which, from time to time, she takes a sip. This is a rum crew she has found herself with, she is thinking, but she is enjoying the spree. She is very taken with the look of Valeria. She has high hopes of the dusky Valeria, who will surely help her to find a more health-giving and mind-enhancing bedtime treat than duty-free whisky. The musky and dusky Valeria is a fine counterblast to the pallid English. Though, reflects Anaïs, as she pours in just a wee drop more into her tumbler, it is the pallor of her friend Candida that appeals to her. That washed-out, faded, luminous look of hers is in its own way so distinguished. Anaïs likes Candida. Anaïs feels Candida is on the verge of doing something really surprising – well, in a sense, she has already done it, by suddenly acquiring unexpected money, and inspiring this unexpected trip.

Ida Jerrold is also sitting up in bed, watching television with the sound off. She appears to be watching a religious ceremony of some unfamiliar denomination, presumably Islamic. On and on it goes. It is quite soothing. Robed men silently kneel and rise and chant and abase themselves before their Maker. It goes on and on.

Ida Jerrold is thinking about health and wealth and the pursuit of happiness. Her health is not bad, for her age, though during the thunderstorm she had experienced a strange wave of palpitations and had momentarily wondered if she were about to die, up there in the sky. She suffers from an irregular heartbeat, but she has suffered from this for so many years that she thinks little of it. Her heart is beating more calmly now, and so she stops thinking about it and moves on to the problem of money. Like Sally Hepburn, she is wondering how much her little mews house is really worth. She has been offered what seems to her to be a vast fortune for it. She has been offered, by a neighbour, more than £1 million for the little house that she and Eugene had bought just after the war for £3,500. Frankly, she could do with the money. She lives on a very small pension. Eugene had put nothing away. He had taken early retirement from his regular job at the BBC in order to do more freelance work, and then he had died, suddenly, in that stupid accident, before he had had time to take out any private pension. He and she had not thought much about pensions. People didn't, in those days. The BBC pension was pitiful. Candida Wilton had done much better from Northam Provident in one windfall than the widowed Mrs Jerrold would do in the whole of her lifetime from the BBC. So Ida Jerrold has to watch her pennies and shop carefully in Portobello market for cheap vegetables. And now she is too old to teach, and even if she were not too old, nobody wants to study the Classics any more, except for the odd bunch of eccentrics like her present companions.

So it would make sense for her to sell her little house to the photographer next door, whose wife has just had a second baby. They want to expand into her territory. She understands that. She has no idea of whether or not he has offered her a just price, but that is hardly the point. If he has offered, so would others. But then where would she actually *live*? She likes her house. If she had a million pounds, what would she spend it on? She does not starve, and she can afford to feed her cats, and she can drink gin when she wants to. She can still offer a glass of wine to a friend. She eats like a bird, and she feeds the birds. Her amusements are simple. She reads, and goes to lectures, most of which are free, and occasionally she goes to stay with a diminishing band of friends scattered around the country. She plays bridge, once a fortnight, with friends in South Kensington. She would in theory like to be able to afford to travel abroad more, but travel is exhausting, and at her age she is probably better off at home. She has had her travels. There is nothing that could give her as much pleasure as being in her little house, and drawing down the blinds in the evenings, and battening down the hatches, and stroking a cat upon her knee as she listens to the Third Programme. Her house is a jewel. It is beyond price. I will stay put, says Ida Jerrold to herself. I will ask Cynthia about house prices, for she is sure to know about such things, but whatever it is worth on the market I will not move. What is the market to me? My home is my treasure, and it is beyond price.

Ida Jerrold picks up *The Death of Virgil* in order to read

herself to sleep. It is heavy going, but she will finish it or die.

Quietly, secretly, Cynthia Barclay tiptoes barefoot along the corridor and out through the open side door near the restaurant and across the patio and through the shrubbery. She is wearing her bikini and she is wrapped in a large fluffy yellow towelling bathrobe. She discards the robe, revealing her hard, firm, London-sunbed-tanned body, and silently, making scarcely a ripple, she slips into the silky water, and breasts its smoothness. It is at once cool and warm, mild and refreshing, milky and soft. Weightless, she swims through its embrace. Godlike, it takes her.

The seven sisters see the sights

Sally Hepburn is not feeling too good the next day, and complains that the piquant peppers have poisoned her. (Is it, Candida wonders, the purloined tap water that has upset her stomach?) But Sally refuses to stay behind as the others determine to set off valiantly to see the sights.

Sally does not take calmly to the beggars of Tunis. They flummox her. Candida and Julia and Cynthia and Ida Jerrold do not like them either, but they do not respond to them with panic and hysterical distress. In vain do Valeria and Anaïs insist that, compared with many cities of the world, modern Tunis is relatively beggar-free. In vain does Candida remind her that London itself was well provided these days with its own complement of indigenous beggars. Sally continues to panic, even when surrounded by her Virgilian bodyguard. She begins to stumble, and twice she actually falls over, like a clumsy doll. When she falls, beggar children laugh and point. Candida continues to wonder whether it has been wise to bring Sally so far afield from Suffolk. But she helps her up, and dusts her down, and wanders eagerly onwards. She cannot afford to be dragged down or pulled over by Sally. She is too full of a naive and happy wonder.

Candida is enchanted by Tunis, and by its surroundings. Some of its streets smell divinely of the Goldborne Road. She sees now that this is how it should be. How can the denizens of the Goldborne Road bear to live in exile? How can anyone bear to live in the dark damp streets of London, beneath an evil sky?

For their allotted three days they gaze, wander, and pursue the new travelogue of their third age, of their free gift of after-time. The hours are crowded with glorious life. They chatter like parrots, they even sing in their minibus, as they had sung as children, on those rare school outings. They browse in museums, they are both charmed and alarmed by snake charmers, they wonder at scorpion swallowers, they decline to view the belly dancers. Mrs Barclay wonders whether or not to buy Mr Barclay a beautiful red fez.

Valeria watches her troop with an expert weather eye. She is accustomed to the little squalls that from time to time ruffle a group, and she is familiar also with the calms and the doldrums. So far, all are behaving well within the bounds of the reasonable. Even Sally Hepburn has confined her complaints to such matters as the noise of the air conditioning and the persistence of the mendicants and the uncertain prices in the souk. And Sally is much cheered when Valeria persuades her that in her purchase of an engraved agate ring set in silver she has acquired a veritable bargain. It had cost only the equivalent of a tenner, but Valeria assures her it is the real thing, and compliments Sally upon her sharp eye. Sally is flattered, placated, thinks better of the souk and the mendicants and the children who try to sell her scraps of embroidery. What does the Arabic inscription on her ring mean, she wants to know? Valeria inspects it, gravely, and says that she thinks it is probably something about the gardens of the just. Valeria, as she invents this rubric, glances anxiously after Julia, and wonders yet again whether or not she ought to warn her about wearing so many expensive rings so conspicuously. She does not want to spread alarm through her group, or to cast aspersions on the safety of the streets of North Africa, but, really, it is not wise. She assumes they are properly insured, but, even so, she would not risk it herself. It is an invitation to crime. She resolves that she will say something to Julia before they set off for Naples, if she can find the right moment.

They divide their time between the pleasures of the mind and of the body. Anaïs, who is at home in Africa, reveals herself to be curiously keen on shopping, and disappears on her own up side streets from time to time, returning occasionally seemingly empty-handed, occasionally with small packages. Valeria decides not to worry about her absences, for clearly Anaïs can look after herself, and knows her way back. Valeria thinks she can guess the contents of some of the packages, and suspects that Anaïs may be pursuing some private trade route of her own. Julia also enjoys shopping, but hers is of a more conventional variety: she acquires, under Valeria's supervision, a golden necklace and a silver brooch. Mrs Jerrold does not shop: she says she has too many objects in her life already. She takes herself off to sit in cafés, sipping mint tea from a tiny brown glass in a brass-filigree holder as she watches from afar the bargaining, and dips from time to time into the heavy works of Hermann Broch. She carries him everywhere with her in her bag. He is not going to escape her now.

Cynthia and Candida are the swimmers, seduced by the sea. Oh yes, they are interested in the ruins, and in the stories of Tanit and Salammbô and Hannibal and Dido, and they bend earnestly over their Virgil lessons and their bridge lessons of an evening, but they also wish to strike out from land. The pool cannot contain them, pleasant though it is. So Valeria is commissioned to find them beaches.

She is worth her weight in gold, they assure her, as they cast their eyes upon the little private cove she has selected for their delight. It is perfection. There is a small sandy stretch, where the non-swimming members of the party may sit and laze in the shade of Valeria's parasols, and there are rocks, over which Cynthia and Candida may clamber, and from which Cynthia may dive. Candida does not dive, she is too old and too timid and she is afraid of hitting her head on some hidden underwater danger, so she launches herself from the water's edge into the warm and waiting sea. And she stays near the shore, swimming, floating, thinking of her Health Club, and blessing it for keeping her in the habit of staying afloat. It is good that she has kept up the practice of swimming, and of revealing her ageing body to the gaze of others. She blesses Tamsin and Chelsea and Jenny and all her unknown and nameless friends at the Club.

Cynthia Barclay is not afraid of the sharp Alps of the underwater. She can see through the clear transparent brine that they are no threat. She climbs upwards, stands erect in the sun against the sky on a rock six feet above the Mediterranean, and gazes commandingly about her. Her figure is fine, and she flaunts it. The sun and sky acknowledge it, and the beach party acknowledges it. Then she plunges in, and strikes out to sea. She is a strong swimmer, and she ploughs her way forward freestyle and headdown through the water. No wonder the hotel pool could not hold her. She is like a dolphin in the wake of a fleeing sail. On and on she goes, northwards, in a straight line out from land, towards the far horizon and the invisibilities of Europe. Her dipping bronzed head grows smaller and smaller as she recedes from sight. Will she ever return? Valeria, hitherto confident, begins to wonder, for she is in theory in charge of this outing. She has never lost a client yet, unless you count old Mr Oliphant from Lincoln who died peacefully and gratefully in his sleep on the Nile. Candida, splashing in the shallows, has from her low water-level perspective lost all sight of Cynthia, and knows it would be vain for her to attempt to pursue her. Skilled though she may once have been in the long-unpractised arts of life-saving, now will not be her opportunity to display them. She would never be able to overtake the drowning Cynthia and to drag her back to shore. She knows she has not the strength.

It is late afternoon on their last day in North Africa, and the sun is sinking to the west. Candida swims her last ladylike breaststrokes, and turns to the shore. As she rises to her feet and emerges from the water in her perishing old black one-piece Speedo costume, she glances back out to sea, and there, far out, she spies Cynthia, who has turned, and is at last heading back to the beach. A murmur of relief rises from her companions, as Candida towels herself dry, and they all watch as the golden helmet heaves powerfully back towards their little assembly of parasols. How strongly Cynthia Barclay swims, and with what confidence! She had been so far out that she seems to arrive upon them from another continent. Larger and larger she grows upon their vision, until she is there before them in all her fleshliness, standing knee deep in the wavelets, shaking the glowing drops from her hair and from her body. 'More Juno than Venus, perhaps,' comments Mrs Jerrold, a little dryly, breaking the spell of their admiration.

Valeria emboldens herself to upbraid Cynthia with mock severity: what had she been thinking of, to frighten them all by swimming out so far from land? Sally Hepburn joins in the chorus of disapprobation, though without much conviction: she is somewhat overawed by such reckless boldness. Julia Jordan is silent, wondering if it is possible that those mighty brown breasts are reinforced with silicon, and, if so, whether Cynthia will divulge the name of her surgeon. Anaïs, who cannot swim, puffs enigmatically on her small brown cheroot, and keeps her own counsel. Mrs Jerrold, as Cynthia and Candida dress themselves, returns furtively to the pages of Hermann Broch. It is left to the two swimmers to praise the divine warmth and glorious clarity of the water. 'I thought that people said the Mediterranean was a dead sea,' says Candida, as they gather their bags for the short stroll back to the minibus. 'But it's as pure as the day of creation.'

Its purity is attested, it would seem, by a group of skinny barefoot boys who have spotted a sales opportunity and set up their stall by the waiting chariot. They have laid out upon a rock a display of riches of the deep which they claim to have caught for the beach party's delectation. Valeria is at first inclined to wave them away, but she sees that her charges are intrigued by the offerings before them, and allows the scene to develop. The boys have displayed live urchins, shellfish of various shapes and sizes, a dazzling scarlet starfish, and a small octopus. The octopus is a dead loss: nobody wants to gaze at its unattractive bluish suckers and its poor flabby grey corpse, so it is bundled unceremoniously out of sight. The starfish is wondered at, then replaced gently in a rock pool. The shellfish are named, in various languages, but the English ladies say they have no use for them: they are not here to indulge in home cooking, even of exotica such as these, and do not think the chef of the Hotel Diana will want an addition to his day's expert selections from the market.

The sea urchins present another proposition, and one with which Valeria has long been familiar. It will be a test of her Virgilians, and she does not know how they will respond to it. Some of the English are so squeamish, but some are so daring: one cannot always tell. The French on the whole are more adventurous than the English when it comes to eating strange meats and strange fishes, but sometimes the English surprise one by their enterprise. And this group, as she now begins to see, is ready for the challenge. One of the brown boy urchins has produced a pocket knife, with which he proceeds to attack one of the long-spiked bristling black sea urchins. He slices into it, and reveals its quivering soft bright persimmon-orange innards. He scoops them out, with his fingers, and devours them, to the accompaniment of much ostentatious smacking of the lips. Far from recoiling from this exhibition (which the boy is sometimes paid to repeat, sometimes to desist from repeating), the Virgilians surge forward curiously. Even Sally Hepburn, who faints in the presence of a peanut, does not avert her eyes. And Cynthia, fresh and still salty from the sea herself, is clearly keen to devour an urchin of her own.

Valeria assures them that it is quite safe to do so, and watches as, one after another, they sample this strange fruit. In the end, all but Anaïs partake. Anaïs excuses herself on the grounds that she thinks she has caught a touch of the sun, but in truth she is horrified and disgusted by the spiky little monsters. And it is Anaïs who is the first to notice the appalling behaviour of the sucked shells of the monsters. *They climb up on to their spikes, and they walk away from the scene of their own destruction.* Across the rock they stagger, although they are no longer alive, although their bodies and brains have been eaten up by the English ladies. Their skeletons walk. Anaïs catches Valeria's eye, and notes that she is already well versed in this striking natural phenomenon. The others do not yet notice, for they are too busy guzzling live flesh and wiping their dripping lips and necks with paper tissues and sandy towels, and laughing at their own temerity. Anaïs, austerely, believes that they should not be allowed to miss this astounding sight, and after restraining herself for a minute or two she cannot help but cry out, 'But look, darlings, do look, they're *still alive*!'

This produces consternation, but the consternation is mixed with mirth. The criminals are too deep in their crime to extricate themselves now. They watch in amazement as the empty shells of their impromptu feast stagger about in a vain and brave display of animation, before collapsing into perpetual inertia. Luckily, they do not last too long or walk too far. They will not follow them back to the Hotel with a Difference, in a little trail of prickly footsteps of damp reproach. They are dead and gone, really and truly dead and gone, and the boys demonstrate this by picking them up and pulling them about and turning them inside out and then hurling them back into their native element.

The boys laugh heartlessly, the English ladies laugh heartlessly, and there is great bonhomie amongst the group. Valeria settles the sea-urchin bill with a few small notes, and is ready to head back to the hotel for the last African supper, and the last African section of Virgil (the death of the pilot Palinurus, at the end of Book Five) and the last African game of bridge – Candida is hopeless but keen, Julia is keen and good and can't think why she's never played before, Sally is not very keen but better than Candida at remembering her cards, and Anaïs is keeping her cards close to her chest, as usual – but she is delayed by a sudden display of independent activity by one of the boy urchins. Activated by some kind query from Cynthia as to the dangers of his trade, he is displaying a scar on his knee. It is a wide, jagged, white-blue slash, frilled around the edges – an unstitched wound, sustained, as he now explains in many tongues, during a diving expedition for an octopus off the Rocks of Hercules. He is not complaining about it or begging for alms for it, he is proud of it, and Cynthia is in immediate sympathy: she rolls up her trouser leg in order to display to him a similar badge of honour on her shin, sustained, as she explains, during a rash attempt to climb over a broken-glass-bristled wall on her way out of some ladylike convent confinement of her youth. They compare wounds, with mutual satisfaction.

This moment of international communion is recalled with pleasure over supper, as they tuck into their sweet stewed lamb with apricots and couscous. They had been nice friendly boys, the urchin boys, and they had skipped away over the fierce sharp-edged foot-lacerating rocks like nimble goats. Valeria tells her flock about the Pillars of Hercules at Tangiers – had they been doing a tour of North Africa, instead of setting sail for Italy in the morning, they could have travelled westwards and visited the Pillars of Hercules. They could have seen the very point whence Ulysses set sail for eternity. And are the myths remembered, Mrs Jerrold wondered, by this generation reared on a mixed diet of Islam, Manchester United, and Madonna? (These last two alliterative items, they have discovered, are part of the *lingua franca* of initiatory small talk addressed to all tourists from the English-speaking world, though they achieve only a low recognition factor with this particular group.)

Valeria pauses, ponders her reply. Yes, she thinks some of the myths and stories are remembered, because they are preserved in place names, and, as they have seen, in the names of hotels and restaurants, of aeroplanes and ferries and trains and battleships – yes, memories of Diana and Dido,

Hannibal and Salammbô, Ishtar and Tanit live on. Even Marius and Regulus are not quite forgotten, though they are somewhat out of fashion. The British Victorians loved Hannibal and Marius, says Valeria, who knows a surprising amount about these things. They appropriated them and remade them in their own imperial image and painted historical paintings of them and wrote school-prize poems in Latin about them. And people trade still on these old names, and so they live on. We live in a palimpsest of memories, says Valeria. But if you were to ask the street boys who was Hercules, who was Hannibal – well, who knows what answer you might get? You should have asked them, says Valeria. There is no harm in asking.

Candida is remembering her many trips to the National Gallery, in the early months of her loneliness. She is thinking of Turner and wondering if he had ever been to Carthage. Just left of centre, in the foreground of Turner's painting of *Dido building Carthage*, a small toy boat floats on the wide shining path of water. A group of brown boys watch it, as they perch on the brink of the river. The classical columns and great façades soar above them and beyond them, and bare-shouldered, majestic Dido stands behind them, but they are intent upon their play. Candida tries to recall this image, but its details elude her. She thinks she sees boys dangling their legs in a river in a classical landscape, but she cannot see the little boat. But it is there, this image, in the palimpsest of her memory, and if she lives, she will revisit it.

She frequented galleries in her loneliness, but now she is no longer alone. She is one of a company. She is with her friends.

That evening, the seven sisters read, in Latin and in English, of the death of the pilot Palinurus, who fell asleep at the wheel. Candida Wilton and Ida Jerrold think of the death of

Eugene Jerrold, though they do not betray this consciousness to one another. They all discuss their forthcoming voyage – will it be a calm crossing? Or will a malicious god stir up trouble and seasickness for them? They will, on this occasion, be obliged to share cabins, as the ferry offers no single berths, but the prospect affords less alarm than it might have done three days earlier, for they know one another better now. Candida has thought it her duty to offer to share with Sally, but it has been decided to draw lots, in classical style. They agree that they will do this in the morning, at breakfast.

Julia and Candida do not take part in the last game of bridge: they watch for a while as Valeria-and-Cynthia battle it out with Ida-and-Sally, and then drift off to the bar, for a final *digestif*. (Anaïs has disappeared, as she does, to do whatever it is that she does when she disappears.) In the bar, they find themselves talking about their schooldays, and about Biology O level. It is the sea urchins that have stimulated these memories, for they vividly recall studying primitive life-forms with the aptly named Miss Moss – spirogyrae, amoebae, tadpoles, the difference between parasites and saprophytes, the structure and nature of the endoderm and the ectoderm. The sight of those walking husks haunts them. Life after death, the afterlife. They talk about chickens that walk after their heads have been chopped off, and remember tales of speaking heads that survive the guillotine and denounce the executioner. Miss Moss had been an animating teacher, in her way, and they have good memories of her tuition. She had managed to interest her girls in the mysteries of cellular life.

Candida finds that she is very much enjoying her conversation with Julia Jordan. She is enjoying it more than she would ever have expected she could. They are very old friends, and they have a long, shared past. Is it her imagination, or is Julia becoming more human, less odd, in her late middle age? Candida is reminded of the long, intense, after-lights conversations they had enjoyed, all those years ago, when they were young. Not all these interchanges had turned on Julia's sexual exploits, though those are the ones that Candida has, perhaps unfairly, tended to remember most vividly. No, they had talked of many other matters – of whether or not there was a God, of good and evil and right and wrong, of art and music and literature, of talent and privilege, and even, ignorantly, of politics. (Most, though by no means all, of the girls at St Anne's came from Tory-voting families, as did Julia herself: Candida's parents were distinguished by a religious objection to all political parties, a fact which had fascinated her schoolfellows, and a theme on which she was obliged, on many occasions, to expound and elaborate. Julia, in those days, had veered sharply to the left.)

It is good, surprisingly good, to be sitting here in a hotel bar in North Africa, peacefully, comfortably, with her old friend Julia Jordan. It is much better here than it had been sitting watching television alone of an evening in Holling House, while Andrew delivered a secular sermon about the visually impaired and disability allowances, or went through his papers in his study. Andrew's activities had always made her feel so unimportant, and here it does not matter if she is unimportant. And sitting here idly gossiping makes a pleasing change from watching the London skyline alone from her third-floor window through a flaw in the glass, though that had been satisfying, in its own strange dull aching way. This is what Candida is thinking to herself, so she is a little taken aback when her friend Julia suddenly remarks, into a companionable lull, 'Don't you think we're a bit like those poor creatures? Scuttling around after we're dead?' And Julia laughs her dry, bright, mirthless little laugh, and looks at Candida boldly and directly from her staring, protuberant grey eyes. Julia follows her intervention with a smiling, deprecating pout which says that she means exactly what she says, and realizes the implications of what she asks.

Candida does not answer at once: even in her head, she prevaricates. But she owes Julia an answer, for she, Candida Wilton, has instigated this journey, and it is on her account therefore that they scuttle and drift, if that is what they do. So, after a moment or two of reflection, and after glancing sideways at the card table where their compatriots are still intent upon their game, she says, 'No, I don't think it is like that. I don't feel that it is like that.'

'We can't pretend that we are young, any more,' pursues Julia. 'So what are we, after all?'

'Youth is not everything,' says Candida, sententiously.

'So what is the point of us?' insists Julia.

A long silence ensues, broken by a triumphant cry from Cynthia, and a 'Well done! That's the spirit!' from Mrs Jerrold.

Candida sips delicately from her tiny glass.

'The point is,' continues Julia 'that human beings weren't really meant to live so long. We weren't designed to age as we do. We ought to have been killed off long ago, by predators, or scarcities, or natural calamities. That's what happens to other species. Other animals don't age as we do.'

'Is that true?' inquires Candida, gently, playing for time. It is a new concept to her, and a shocking one.

'Yes, I'm sure it's true. I read an article about it in one of the weeklies. And there was that television series, about the ageing process. I didn't see it, but I read about it in the *Sunday Times*.'

'I didn't watch it,' says Candida, faintly.

'Nor did I, I can't get the BBC, but I got the hang of it without watching.'

'Miss Moss didn't teach us about the ageing process,' concedes Candida.

'They didn't know so much about it then. Life expectancy has seriously increased in the last forty years. People are living for longer and longer. They are testing the mechanism to its limits. And beyond its limits. It wasn't expected.'

'Cats age,' suggests Candida, in a propitiatory way. 'You meet quite a lot of old cats.' She is thinking of Ida Jerrold's cats, which are being cared for in her absence by the wife of the territorially ambitious photographer who lives next door.

'Cats age,' says Julia 'because human beings have domesticated them and artificially prolonged their lives with all sorts of unnatural creature comforts.'

'Like Smoked Salmon Sheba and Felix Crunchies,' says Candida.

'Exactly so. We keep them going to keep us company in the dark. Like grave goods in the ancient world. Like all those bronzes and tripods and fibulae and what not that we saw in that exhausting museum yesterday.'

This is such a satisfactory conceit that both women suddenly feel very much more cheerful, and Candida finds the strength to declare that she herself, speaking strictly for herself, does not feel at all like the discarded shell of a sea urchin. In fact, she says, she hasn't felt so cheerful for years. It may well be true that the human body wasn't designed to live as long as it now does, but the ingenuity of the human mind and spirit are the cause of this longevity, and they will find their own solution to its problems. As Hegel would have argued, says Candida.

'As *who* would have argued?' asks Julia, understandably.

'Oh, nothing,' says Candida, hurriedly. 'I don't know what I'm talking about. But I *do* know that I'm feeling just fine, and I'm very glad you agreed to come on this trip.'

'It's all a bit *spinsterly* and *grandmotherly* and *third ageist,*' says Julia, but her tone indicates that she is no longer in the dumps, and that she is glad that Candida is glad she is there. She proves this, a moment later, by reaching forward and impulsively squeezing Candida's hand. She squeezes it rather hard, and her splendid rings bite into her friend's flesh. 'Ow,' protests Candida, pleased by this gesture, yet affecting more pain than she has felt, and shaking her fingers vigorously when they are released.

'My hands', says Candida, insincerely woe-struck, 'are *terrible*. Look how wrinkled they are!'

And it is true that for some reason her hands have worn much less well than Julia's. They compare their knuckles and their fingers, spreading them out on the glass table before them. Is the deterioration of Candida's hands connected with childbirth or the washing of small garments? Surely not. Candida and Julia speak of gloves and hand creams (there was something called a Barrier Cream, in their mothers' day) and face creams and facelifts and arthritis. Julia demonstrates some anti-arthritis finger exercises which she occasionally practises in moments of boredom, and she claims that they work, though how would she know if they didn't? Candida, watching these exercises, which resemble the finger games about churches and steeples that one plays with small children, tells Julia that Valeria is worried that Julia will lose her rings in Naples, but is too polite to say so because she doesn't want to fuss. Julia says that Valeria is an admirably tactful person, and she promises not to blame her or anybody else if she loses her jewels – 'But I feel naked without them, quite naked,' she says, and Candida can see that this, though improbable, is true. Then Julia tells Candida about an elderly actress friend of hers who had delighted in dating her colleagues by the manner in which their hands appeared in press photographs – they touch up the face, but always forget the hands, or so this actress had always maintained. 'You can always tell by the hands!' had been her lugubrious, morbid, death-defying cry, as her own talons grew more and more claw-like, as the airbrush was obliged to work harder and harder on each wrinkled millimetre of her public image.

'Actually,' says Julia, at the end of this macabre evocation, 'I must say *you* look a damn sight better than you did when I saw you for that first time in London. You've lost years. It just shows what a bit of good luck can do. To be honest, I thought you were on the way out and closing down the hatches.'

Candida decides to take this as it is meant, as a compliment. And as they begin to stir themselves to go to their beds and their packing, Candida tells Julia about the drowning of her engagement ring in the ionized shallows of the Health Club pool. Julia is impressed and amused by this tale. 'Good for you, Candy!' she says. 'Good for you! I don't know why you married that self-satisfied wanker in the first place. You weren't pregnant, were you? No, I thought not. Not a virtuous couple like you two. Did he know how to do it, when you got into the marriage bed?'

'I'll tell you that story another day,' says Candida, yawning.

And they weave and wander their way, merrily, nostalgically, sentimentally, arm in arm, along the corridor to their rooms. At school, they hadn't been allowed to walk arm in arm. Any form of touching, apart from body blows on the battlefield of sport, had been against the rules. As they part, they kiss one another goodnight. They would never have done a thing like that, forty years ago. But the old school tie knots them still, and after all these years, they are pleased to feel its friendly bondage.

In bed, lying awake, Candida realizes that the solution to

the problem is death. It always has been, and it always will be. There is nothing to be done about this. Even Hegel must have known that. One can accept it, or fail to accept it. Acceptance is the better choice. The readiness is all. And she is certainly not ready to accept it yet.

The seven sisters exult in their first league out from land

The Transmed ferry is called *Arethusa*, after the nymph of the fountain of Syracuse: she is sister ship to the *Tritone*, named for the horn-blowing sea-god. But there is nothing of the antique or the classical in her line. She is a modern, handsome, heavy-duty, serious vessel, built to carry vehicles and cargoes and illegal immigrants, and she is painted a bright and functional green and white. Valeria drives her passengers into the gaping jaws of the *Arethusa*, and settles their ticketing, and leads them up from the clanking diesel-fumed car deck to their berths. The *Arethusa*, though cheerful in spirit, has little of the expensive brightly illuminated frivolity of the new ocean-going cruise liners of the Age of Idleness, of which they have glimpsed a fine example at anchor in the port of Tunis. They do not envy the holidaymakers their luxury. On the contrary, they are proud of the business-like simplicity of their craft, which bears witness to the superior gravity of their purpose. For they are pilgrims, not tourists.

Nevertheless, each pilgrim is privately relieved to find that the accommodations are not excessively Spartan. Valeria had assured them that they would not be uncomfortable, and they have come to trust Valeria's judgements, but one can never be quite sure of what others consider acceptable. There is nothing unacceptable about their two adjacent identical four-berthed cabins on B Deck. Each cabin is clean, and has a porthole looking out to sea, and numbered bunk beds, and a tiny triangular shower room with a lavatory, and a little desk with a little chair, and a supply of sea-sickness bags, and a closet not quite full of inflatable life-saving equipment. What more could reasonable people want? The only problem, both minor and soluble, is constituted by Julia's excess of baggage, for the storage space is severely limited, but Valeria manages to persuade her to leave most of it stowed in the minibus – Julia cannot want all of it on this short voyage, surely, she suggests, and Julia meekly agrees that this is probably true. Even Julia has succumbed to the benign authority of Valeria.

Once they have arranged themselves – Sally and Mrs Jerrold on the bottom bunks of Cabin 32, with Cynthia and Julia above them, and Anaïs, Candida, Valeria, and the possibility of an empty berth or an Unknown Traveller in Bunk 4 of Cabin 34 next door – they assemble on deck to watch the thrilling commotion of departure. Was it from this vantage point that heartless Aeneas cast his backward glance to gaze at the blazing funeral pyre of Dido, as he set out for Italy? Everlasting enmity she had invoked between the cities of Rome and Carthage, and she had refused to meet him for reconciliation in the Underworld. Aeneas had set forth from Carthage secretly at night, but it is the broad daylight of mid afternoon now, and the air is hot and still and quivering. There is no murmur here in the port from the western winds that blew Aeneas off course to his unintended sojourn in Sicily, though who knows what may greet them when they reach the open sea?

They ascend to the top deck and lean against the rails, gazing at the glittering oily surface of the water, at its mild sheen and its broken shallow sparkling, at the smaller craft of the harbour, at swirling gulls and marching cranes and vast containers swinging dangerously against the sky, like toys in the grip of giant pincers. All is action, movement, embarkation. Whose heart would not lift at such a scene? What painter has not wished to paint this shore? Surely we are bound for some glorious destiny, some sublime destination? Sicily, Naples, Cumae, what matter which?

They are all entertained by the important late arrival of a party of four foot-passengers, who stride along the elevated pedestrian walkway beneath them bearing bouquets, pausing, conversing with animation and much laughter with their farewell committee on the ramp. There are kisses, cries, embraces. This group too is in the highest of spirits. The four of them have the air of those who have just left a long, large, late lunch: they broadcast festivity and well-being. Two men, two women, all of the same middle height, all of the same late middle age, all of the same exuberance – the men could be brothers, though one of them, red-haired, smartly suited, and stout, is clearly the dominant male. His air of self satisfaction is delightful and his red face gleams with good will. His brother is darker, balder, more moustached; he is in shirt sleeves, he is the joker, he slaps backs and teases and is teased. The women, with their dyed well-groomed hair, their well-cut continental suits, their perilously high heels, their flamboyant and expensive silk scarves, are proud of their men. What are they doing, whither are they bound? They cannot be classical pilgrims, and they do not look like tourists. Perhaps they are on some kind of official trip? But if so, it is clear that for them business is pleasure. They are solid and happy in the fullness of their bodies. They are contented people. Happiness wafts around them, generously, in the hot afternoon air.

Mrs Jerrold watches them for a while, and exchanges appreciative comments on them with Cynthia. Then she moves away from the group, descends a deck, and finds herself a chair in the shade. Her mind returns to Virgil, and, again, to Goethe's love affairs with and within Italy. He had envied what he saw as the natural happiness of the southern nations. And she finds herself thinking about Goethe's death. It is in the nature of things that she, of this travelling group, will most probably prove the first to enter the Underworld, but she does not think she is very bothered about that. She hopes she will comport herself properly and not be a nuisance to others when the moment comes. Accounts differ as to the manner in which Goethe met his death. The legend that he cried out 'More light!' has been queried, and even those who accept that these were his last words have interpreted them in various ways. His doctor, Karl Vogel, claimed that he died in great pain, visible fear and mortal agitation. So what avails a lifetime of searching after wholeness and greatness and transcendence? Perhaps Eugene had had the better part, cut off suddenly in his prime.

Goethe had said, somewhere, that the only proper (or was it possible?) response to greater genius is love. Maybe he hadn't lived up to this precept, but he had been right to formulate it. Mrs Jerrold had never found the original location of this saying, but it had been often on Eugene's lips. And Eugene had, in life, lived up to it. How he had loved them, Wystan and Dylan and Louis and Stephen and Natasha and Peggy and Jill and all the great and famous ones. Suddenly, as she stands at the rail, she sees him so clearly – a big clumsy bear of a man, shambling, untidy, myopic, affable, with a large round red face, and grey wispy curls plastered over his shining broad-domed head. How the faces of these greater ones had lit up when Eugene entered a room! Eugene the comrade, ever welcome, ever accompanied by good humour, ever willing to stand his friends a pint. Eugene's friends were, for richer, for poorer, for better, for worse, his friends. He had been a loveable, exasperating man.

Mrs Jerrold closes her eyes in the shade.

Valeria trains her binoculars landwards towards the flat rooftops of the white city, and two storks flap clumsily across the field of her vision. Candida watches the officials below her on the quay, as they redirect traffic, and listens to the mounting thrum of the ship's engines. Their vessel is gathering its power. Julia has gone below to arrange her nightwear. Cynthia Barclay strikes a pose like a figurehead at the prow, and Anaïs is engaged one deck below in conversation with a handsome stranger who is leaning on the bar as though waiting for it to open. Sally is now nowhere to be seen, but we know she is on board. She has been feeling rather off-colour again. Maybe she will decide to be sick.

There is a hooting and a wailing and announcements are made in several languages. Visitors are requested to go ashore. A dashing little pilot ship called *Ascanius* comes alongside, like a sleek neat fish-dog, to shepherd them out to sea. Hawsers are uncoupled and coiled around capstans, and with a creaking and a groaning *Arethusa* frees her bulk and pulls away from the dock, and begins to inch slowly and heavily towards the open sea. Candida is transfixed by the metaphor of release, of departure. She watches the shifting line of the shore, the swelling of the horizon, and her heart is ready to break with joy. How blessed she has been in her life! As she stands there, what she at first perceives as great dark moths swirl and drift towards her and settle on her hair and her arms. They are not moths, they are large light black flakes of soot, the size of butterfly wings, issuing from the four stacked funnels of the *Arethusa*. They are pretty and endearing. She allows them to settle upon her as though they were living things. She does not think of the flakes from Dido's pyre, and the smell of Dido's burning flesh. Later, perhaps, she may, but now she does not. She is too happy now to think of death.

Once the link with land is broken, the watchers above descend to see what fun is to be had below. They discover Julia in the corridor of B Deck speaking with their steward, who is a grizzled and weather-beaten and elderly Neapolitan with a rich dark voice lower than the grumbling of gravel, a voice of bass majesty. Julia says she has negotiated extra hanging space in some mysterious private quarter to which he has allowed her special access: she pleads that she has done this only for the sake of her comrades. The steward admires Julia. Her old fires flare up brightly. They speak the same language, these two. Julia is happy. She has been saluted by a man who has himself seen some action. Her pride is satisfied, and so is his. It has been a satisfactory negotiation to both parties.

'Put out to sea, ignoble comrades. Our end is life. Put out to sea!'

It seems that a fourth voyager has joined Valeria, Candida and Anaïs in their cabin, for they discover there, modestly placed under the desk, a small, neat travel bag, which belongs to none of them. It has appeared as if from nowhere. It is made of a pale soft greenish leather, and it is neither old nor new. Its owner is not in evidence, but the bag promises well. It bears a label with an address in Sorrento, and the name of its owner, Anna Palumbo. It is, they think, a pretty name. What will she look like, their Anna? Will she become their friend? They have only one night at sea, so if they are to become friends, it must be done quickly.

Valeria has warned them that the food on the *Arethusa* is not up to the standard of the food at the Hotel Diana. It is canteen-style self-service, with prepaid coupons. There is a restaurant but she does not advise it. What she advises is a sundowner in the Caravaggio Lounge next to the DiscoBar on A Deck, where they will have a good view of the sunset. This will fortify them against the dull plateful of pasta and cutlet that will inevitably follow. There is no point in queuing early for this meal, as other passengers will, for the food gets neither better nor worse with waiting. It is always tepid, and there is always enough.

So there they assemble, as the sun lights a pink pathway towards them over the darkening sea. Yes, Valeria assures them, if they keep a lookout they may see dolphins. They are friendly to humans and they like to follow the boats through the water.

Which of the women on board is their cabin-fellow Anna? Can they guess? Is she looking out for them, as they for her?

Candida is happy to be in company, to be one of a group. She is glad she is not Anna Palumbo, travelling alone. She is glad she is not travelling with her one-time husband Andrew Wilton. She wonders if he has taken the trouble to find out her destination and her route. She wonders if there has been any news from Ellen. She does not think it likely that there can be anything much wrong with Ellen. It is much more probable that Andrew had been using her name as a pretext to satisfy his curiosity. But one cannot be sure. Candida is not given to worrying much about her daughters. They do not worry about her, and she will not worry about them.

But she cannot help but think of Ellen, for there, on the wall of the Caravaggio Lounge, is a series of framed photographs of the building of the *Arethusa* in a Finnish shipyard in 1995. The *Arethusa* had been assembled in the shipyard of Turku, on the southwest coast of Finland, and here are pictures to prove it, with shipbuilders building, and smiling officials in mayoral chains and fur hats, and champagne splashing. There is even an atmospheric picture of a Finnish forest in a bloody sunset in the snow. The *Arethusa* has sailed far from the land of winter to the sunny Mediterranean and the Tyrrhenian Sea.

The rest of the group thinks, if it thinks anything, that

Turku is in Turkey. Turku is nothing and nowhere to them. Only Candida knows that Turku is a serious Finnish port, on the Baltic, to the west of Helsinki. Only Candida can read and interpret these photographs correctly. But she has never been to see her daughter in Finland, because she has never been invited. A pang goes through her, as she sees the photographs of the snow and the pine trees. Her daughter does not live in Turku: she lives inland, in a village near the university town of Jyväskylä, in a region known as the Land of the Lakes. Candida knows this because she has wasted some time looking at the map of Finland. There is much water surrounding her daughter Ellen, but she does not live by the sea.

The meal is not good, as Valeria had warned them, but they are in too mild a mood to be cast down by lukewarm penne and dry escalopes. They are looking forward to their arrival in Italy, the land promised to the Trojans, and promised in turn, centuries later, to them. They sit up late, because the cabins, although agreed to be quite adequate, cannot be called commodious, and, anyway, it is fun watching their fellow passengers and plotting the sequence of their travels on shore. (Their first night will be spent at happy Arco Felice, to the west of Naples, and it is hoped that the next day will encompass Baia, Lake Avernus, and a visit to the Sibyl.) Their fellow passengers are amusing themselves in diverse ways. Many are chatting into their mobile phones, but some are actually reading books. Some are playing cards, and one young couple is playing dominoes, a game so old-fashioned that the seven sisters speculate that perhaps it is about to spring back into vogue. The group that they have labelled the Mayoral Quartet is enjoying itself immensely. It has dined à la carte in the restaurant, and now it orders round after round of drinks, and laughs, and talks with incessant animation, in a beautifully orchestrated manner – man to man and woman to woman, then brother-in-law to sister-in-law and sister-in-law to brother-in-law, then husband to wife and wife to husband, and then, beginning again at the beginning, man to man and woman to woman, and so on, throughout the long evening. Brandy follows wine and amaretto follows brandy. One of the women is now wearing her emerald-green silk scarf playfully in reverse, like a collar round her throat, its points flowing downwards over her back: she had placed it thus to avoid the spaghetti, and is clearly pleased with the effect. The seven sisters take note of this enterprising fashion tip. The darker brother has a silver hip flask, from which he occasionally offers a small additional infusion. The group is a pleasure to watch, and it is highly satisfied with its own satisfaction.

Anna Palumbo has not yet revealed herself. There are not many single women in evidence. Could she be that thin dark girl quietly reading a detective story? Or that stout older woman shouting angrily into her mobile? Or has she already shyly climbed up into her top bunk, to hide herself out of their way?

Yes, there she is, discovered, as they repair to bed. She has already tucked herself up in her thin pale blue nautical anchor-embroidered sheets, and is sitting up and reading a book. She is small and does not take up much space. Valeria, Anaïs and Candida enter, rather noisily, and fall into a respectful silence. Anna Palumbo, in possession of their bedchamber, smiles. She is small and white of skin, and her hair is very short and very dark. She is wearing a scarlet shirt with large pearl buttons. Is it a day shirt, or a night shirt? It is primly and discreetly buttoned up to her white neck and her pointed chin.

Shall they fall into conversation, or is it not necessary?

What is the bedtime cabin etiquette on board the *Arethusa*? Anna Palumbo takes the initiative. She addresses them first, tentatively, in Italian, then switches to English. She expresses the hope she will not be in their way. She has already made use of the shower room, she assures them. The space is restricted, but she will not disturb them, although she is a light sleeper.

Valeria, Anaïs and Candida mutter civilities. She makes them feel large and loud and gross. She is perched up there like a flat nun on a high ledge. Candida is to take the top bunk opposite, so she disappears into the triangular closet first, to wash her face and brush her teeth. (She does not need to use the lavatory: with forethought, she has visited the Ladies Room on A Deck, in order to avoid this intimate necessity.) Through the flimsy door, she can hear Anaïs pursuing a conversation with their guest, and when she emerges in her black cotton kimono a friendly rapport has already been established.

It is like a girls' dormitory in Cabin 34. They regress rapidly and effortlessly, and they talk for hours. Anna Palumbo is an art historian, and she is writing about Paul Klee's sojourn in Kairouan. She has been travelling in his footsteps. She is on this ferry because she is afraid of flying. She dislikes flying because her little brother and her grandmother were killed in an air crash when she was a child. She used to fly, but suddenly lost her nerve during an electric thunderstorm over the Atlantic when the plane's hydraulic system failed. She flies when she has to, but she prefers other forms of transport. She quite likes this ferry. She has been on it several times. It is beautiful, she says, to arrive in Naples from the sea, to depart from Naples on the sea. Paul Klee, she says, writes memorably of this experience. She lives in Rome but is going to stay with her sister in Sorrento for a few days on her way home. She had spotted their Virgil Tour luggage labels at once, and had seen their copies of Virgil on their beds. How unusual, she had thought, and how lucky to have such agreeable cabin-mates. Sometimes, says Anna, one can be very unlucky, with grumpy people who snore, or rude people who encroach, or small children who scream. Once, says Anna, she shared a cabin with a woman with a wooden leg. She had unstrapped it and hung it from the end of her bed where it had swayed around thumping and bumping all night long. This had been a little unnerving, although of course one feels sorry for a person with a missing leg.

Anna is very curious about their travels. She and Valeria exchange inside-information about ferries and hotels in Tunisia and Campania. Candida tells her about the Virgil class and Mrs Jerrold. Anna tells them a little about Paul Klee, who believed that the world was a large and fragile piece of clockwork, a giant and delicate toy. She says she wishes she could accompany them on their trip to see the Cumean Sibyl, for she has a big question to ask about her fiancé. Shall she marry him, or shall they remain unwed? They are happy apart, but maybe they are being cowardly. Maybe they should marry and have a baby? What do her new friends Valeria, Anaïs and Candida think? Anna Palumbo thinks her fiancé is not faithful to her, but this does not worry her if they are not married. It relieves her of the obligation to be faithful to him. She still has her freedom. Of mind, and of body. For married couples, fidelity becomes a more serious matter. What do they think about this? Do they have children? Are children a good idea?

Candida admits to her three daughters, but says that she is not the right person to ask about the virtues of maternity, as she is estranged from all of them. (She thinks of excepting Ellen here, but has not the courage to do so.) Anaïs says she is happily childless. She comes, she says, from a family of eight, and had spent much time avoiding efforts to make her look after her smaller siblings. That had been enough of that, for her. Valeria, also, denies progeny, but owns up to her years as a perpetual student at Cornell. It is the first that Anaïs and Candida have heard of this phase of their guide's life, and they cross-question her eagerly about the other Ithaca. She tries to explain to them about Mediterranean trade routes and revisionist thinking about geographical penetration of the hinterland, but it is getting late by now and they are too ignorant to follow her along these winding ancient ways.

Valeria and Anaïs are both too big for their beds. Their feet stick out. As Candida finally begins to doze, to the gentle rocking of the waves and the murmur of voices, she remembers Julia's contempt for those who make of marriage a Procrustean bed, and chop off their limbs to fit into it more neatly. They make marriage, said Julia, into a bed of blood. Instead, said Julia, of buying a new and bigger bed, or getting a different husband.

It had been easy enough to find a new husband, in those early days. And Anna Palumbo is young yet.

Infelix thalamus. Unhappy bed.

Candida and Anna fit neatly and trimly into their shipshape bunks, but those two big women below overflow and protrude. Nevertheless, they sleep soundly, as they make their slow way through the shoals and past the rocks and across the sea to Italy. They sleep as soundly as Palinurus, charmed by a vengeful god. Only Candida keeps the night watch, and even she dozes fitfully.

They reach Naples and the promised land of Italy

There is no other coastline like it upon earth. The golden islands and the volcanic mountains rise as though newborn from the turquoise waters. These mountains are young, and still in their springtime. The *Arethusa*, fashioned on the cold and distant Baltic, is now at home in these smiling southern seas, and she makes her way unerringly to shore across the friendly sparkling waves. Naples approaches, as Candida had dreamed she would. She sees her for the first time. She sees the citadel of the nymph Parthenope, and, rising above the city, the classic slopes of violent Vesuvius, her guardian and her betrayer. Candida leans upon the rail, sick with delight. If it were now to die, says Candida to herself, 'twere now to be most happy. Mrs Jerrold, who believes that she is seeing Naples for the last time, not the first, is in similarly lofty mood in the bright dawn. On the horizon, to the west, she sees a yacht in full sail, a sight to break the heart. She follows its course towards the horizon and out of sight. To see a beloved person sail away like that would surely make one die of longing. She thinks of Portunus, the god of harbours, the god of opportunities, who has given to herself and to Candida this unexpected voyage, and she considers herself to be blessed.

This elevation of mood cannot last. It is soon to be fractured by the confusion of disembarkation and landing cards. Julia is wondering how much to tip the steward, and Valeria is covertly studying an updated computer-generated map of Neapolitan one-way systems and roadworks. Anna Palumbo and Anaïs are exchanging addresses, and Sally thinks that she has lost her reading glasses. Cynthia is wrestling with the broken zip of her shoulder bag and the exchange rate of the lira. She is not happy with all those millions, and hopes Valeria has a better grasp of them than she has. Cynthia longs for the Euro.

It is easy enough to drive out of the exhaust-fumed gullet of the *Arethusa*, but it is not so easy to find one's way out of the docks. Valeria tells them all to look out for the motorway signposted westwards to Pozzuoli, as they weave round stretches of Ring Road and find themselves back almost where they started, on a parallel quay, by a basin full of the most rusted, unseaworthy, abandoned-looking ships that any of them have ever seen. They pause to admire their dereliction, and the indecipherable oriental hieroglyphs that adorn their rearing peeling metal flanks. Surely this ruined armada of junk will never sail again. The *Arethusa* has been a fine trim vessel, they tell themselves. They will remember her with pleasure.

Valeria consults her map once more, and sets off once more. She does not tell them that she herself has never been to Pozzuoli and Arco Felice and is very likely to get lost on the way there. She has done her homework and has good recommendations, but there are many things that could go wrong. Tunis and Carthage she knows well, and with Naples itself she is familiar, but the Phlegrean Fields, so particularly requested by her clients, are known to her, as to them, only through the literature. She does not betray her ignorance or uncertainty, because she knows that clients like to believe that their guides and drivers are infallible, but she will be happier when she knows she is on the right road.

She never finds the right road, the modern highway to the west, because none of them casts an eye high enough to find its super-signs. Instead, they find themselves following the signs of the old low road westwards through the shabby working-class suburbs of the burning fields. This road is clearly going in the right direction, so Valeria settles down at the wheel. It is an interesting though not a conventionally scenic route. It takes them past decaying high-rise apartment blocks, past gaping craters and building sites and gasometers and oil refineries and bus depots. Some of the rubbish reminds Candida of Ladbroke Grove. There is a pleasantly sulphurous stink, which reassures them that they are on their way. They seem to be travelling beneath the route of an abandoned attempt at a viaduct: they pause at red lights beneath a huge forgotten giant, hundreds of feet tall, reaching its pitiful empty arms up into the sky, its bald blind nub of a head staring sightlessly up at Vesuvius. Its arms are swathed in grey fabric that flaps in the morning light. It is a monster, but it is a tame monster. It lets them pass.

From time to time they stop at level crossings, to wait for the little local Solfatara train to pass. It is going to Pozzuoli too. They are getting near. Valeria cheers up. There is said to be a good lunch waiting on the birdless shores of Lake Avernus. And here at last is the sign to Arco Felice, and its welcoming hotels. They will soon be checking in.

The Hotel Santa Clara at Arco Felice proves to be a glorified motel, modern and of marble. What it lacks in character it makes up for in comfort and space. The Santa Clara is not quite the glamorous destination Julia Jordan had envisaged, but even she is pleased with it. The rooms are dark and large and cool and clean, the wardrobes are vast, and the bathrooms are fancy and full of pleasing gadgets and gold taps. Driving through those grim outskirts Julia had feared the worst. Julia is relieved. But Julia is not allowed to waste the morning hanging up her dresses. Already it is nearly noon, and the lake beckons them. She will have plenty of time to preen herself in the evening.

So now they head for Hades. Easy it is to enter her realms. *Facilis descensus Averno*, and easy indeed they find it, even though they are not armed with a golden bough. It is even nearer than Valeria had thought it would be. As she drives along a ravine of pink-barked umbrella conifers, she readjusts her sense of the scale of her map. There are ramshackle rabbit-hutch houses and barking dogs on one side of the steep ravine, and grander mansions on the other. She drives past a bespectacled red-haired Harry Potter-type boy punctiliously throwing plastic bags full of rubbish into a green-mantled ditch, and a man tinkering with a motorbike, and a large hand-written cardboard sign saying *Attenti al Cane*. There are no tourist coaches to be seen, but the signposts assure them that they are approaching the lake, and that must surely be Lake Avernus itself, lying before them and glinting blue and yellow in the sunlight at the end of the gauntlet. A crying of birds, a great flapping and mewing and screaming, announces their arrival.

This lake is by no means birdless. That is the first thing they notice. The accepted etymology of the word Avernus must be utterly false, or climactic conditions have changed beyond recognition since Virgil last came this way. They also notice, even before Valeria has parked their minibus on the shore, that it is very small. It is far smaller than any respectable English lake. It is more of a pond, really. And it is not dark, or gloomy, or in any other way sinister. It is a small and smiling lake, bright blue beneath a cloudless azure sky, and bordered by rich beds of tall tawny-gold and blanched feathery reeds. Green tree-fringed slopes protectively enclose it. A charming and modest *ristorante* juts out over the water: it is a little green wooden shed, of great simplicity. It calls itself *Calcetto del Lago*. It is a timeless little hostelry.

They are all hungry, but Mrs Jerrold insists that, before they embark on their lunch, they must seek the standing stone with the Virgilian inscription. This does not take very long, for it is conveniently placed on the lakeshore, less than two minutes' walk away from the restaurant. They stand there, solemnly, and read the message on the oblong plinth.

Spelunca alta fuit vastoque immanis hiatu,
Scrupea, tuta lacu nigro nemorumque tenebris . . .
Procul, o procul este, profani . . .

The message does not make any sense to them at all, on this late spring day at the beginning of the third millennium. Virgil's description no longer holds true. This is not a black lake surrounded by a gloomy forest, where the air breathes forth death, as he claimed. It is a blue lake, surrounded by green trees and yellow reeds, and birds are flocking everywhere about them. It breathes forth life, not death. They do not feel the need to stand aside. They feel at liberty to go in and order some lunch.

Their floral paper tablecloth wishes them a Good Appetite in many living languages, though not in Latin. They settle themselves in happy and hungry anticipation. The waters of the lake slop gently beneath their table. They can see it gleaming through the cracks between the rough wooden floorboards. Grey and white gulls swoop above them and little black coots and small pink-breasted ducks bob about below them. Sparrows perch and sway in the reed stalks, and cormorants on the distant stumps of drowned trees spread their wings to dry. It is an enchanted spot, but not in the ways they had expected. They order water, and red wine, which arrives in bottles of black glass, bearing the simple label *Vino Rosso*. They raise their glasses to one another, to Valeria, to the success of their expedition. This is a charmed and blessed place.

Most of them order the fish soup, for they have seen others at other tables enjoying the piled plates of mussels and tomatoes and parsley. Fat cloves of garlic lurk in the thick brew, and from the generous mounds of shellfish rear great pink mottled and suckered arms of octopus, as thick as the snakes that wrestled with Laocoon before the fall of Troy. Valeria reminds them of the urchin boys of Tunisia, and describes their octopus-catching technique, which is of a classical ferocity: they dive, spear, then plunge their teeth into the poor beast and bite out its brain. This is the best way to kill an octopus, the boys swear. In such a manner, centuries ago, died the squids and octopus grilled on the seashore and devoured by Aeneas and his wanderers. And so they die still upon the shores of the Mediterranean Sea.

Anaïs and Sally shudder delicately and avert their eyes from these creatures of the deep, and plunge their forks into their chaste mushroom risotto.

Valeria is relieved to have brought her flock to this safe landing stage, and is happy for them to linger over their luncheon. It is nearly closing time for the Sibyl's Cave, but they can go to see her in the morning. She has been there a long time, and she will wait.

The travellers are in expansive, storytelling mode. Ida Jerrold, who does not often speak of Eugene, is moved to describe the time he had his wallet stolen in Barcelona. He is present to her eyes as she speaks, and she makes her friends see him too – the affable, generous, friendly old buffer, wiping the pink ice cream from his jacket, telling the jostling pressing girls not to worry, it wasn't their fault, it didn't matter, it was only an old jacket, apologizing to them for their having spilled the ice cream on him, as though it had been his fault, not theirs – then discovering, twenty minutes later, that in their bumbling efforts to dab at him with paper tissues they had neatly extracted his wallet, his money, his passport, his driving licence . . . And he had continued to apologize for them, even after the event: they must have needed the money badly, he shouldn't have exposed them to temptation, he shouldn't have been such a fool as to encourage them to steal from him, there were too many tourists in Spain, it wasn't like that in the days of George Orwell, it was all the fault of General Franco . . . Oh innocent Eugene!

Nor should he have trusted that French philosopher at the wheel. French intellectuals have a bad driving record. They drive too fast, too showily, in powerful cars that they cannot control. Eugene should never have accepted that lift to Nîmes. He should have known better. They had careered into a poplar tree at ninety miles an hour and both had died instantly. Or so it was said in the police report.

Mrs Jerrold's eyes are sharp and bright but their lids are red and wrinkled. Sometimes she looks more like a tortoise than a bird.

Cynthia Barclay confesses that Mr Barclay has also on several occasions trusted those who were not trustworthy, but he tended to do this not because he was gullible, but because he liked the sense of danger. He had a penchant for bad boys and the thrills of the gutter. And so far, says Cynthia, nothing very terrible has happened to him. I think he doesn't take very *big* risks, says Cynthia, a little anxiously, and with her fingers crossed upon the tomato-spattered paper tablecloth.

Anaïs is moved to tell her own tale of trust and risk. She says she has not thought of this small incident for some years, but suddenly realizes, as she speaks, that it had done much to shape her life. For, says Anaïs, I have been a risk-taker. And this was one of the first risks of my life.

'I was on a train,' says Anaïs Al-Sayyab. 'A night train, between Paris and Milan. I was eighteen years old. Don't ask me how or why I got to be on this train. I can't remember. It must have been my first time in Europe. My Grand Tour. I was travelling alone. God knows how I got my parents to let me loose and finance this trip, but they did. They can't have known how risky it could be. Or could have been. I was in this first-class compartment – not a couchette or a wagon-lit, just an ordinary compartment, but I think it was first-class. I think it must have been first-class because I remember that the seats were quite large and plush. That was the cheaper option, in those days – you took a first-class seat for the night journey. It was cheaper than a couchette but not quite as squalid as third-class. It was romantic. And there was this young woman in my compartment. She was crying. She said her purse had been stolen and all her money was gone. She said she was an opera singer and that she was on her way to sing at La Scala. And how would she get from the station? What was she to do? So I said I would lend her some money. I think it was 10,000 francs I offered. I don't know why, but that's the sum that sticks in my mind. Of course francs were different then. Different size notes, different value, altogether different. Anyway, the point of this story, darlings, is that I didn't know this woman from Eve, and had no reason to believe her, and had hardly any money left myself. But I did believe her. I *chose* to believe her. And she brightened up no end, and took my money, and gave me her name and address, and I gave her the name of the cheap little hotel where I was to stay in Milan.

'I'd never been to Milan in my life. The hotel had been booked for me by a student friend in Paris who swore by it. I remember its name. It was called the *Hotel Commercio e Speranza*. The Hotel of Commerce and of Hope. And this woman said she would bring me back the 10,000 francs as soon as she could. I think she said she had a rehearsal that morning and would lose her job if she was late. The other people in the compartment were pretending this wasn't happening. They hated it. They disapproved of me even more than they disapproved of her. They muttered and frowned and were of little faith. And I remember thinking, I don't want to be like them, I want to be like me, even if I'm wrong and lose my last penny to a stranger.'

Anaïs pauses, for effect. Mrs Jerrold murmurs that Eugene would have backed her, had he been there.

'So what happened?' asks Julia, as the pause lengthens.

'We said goodbye to one another at dawn on Milan station, and she disappeared into the crowd. And I wondered if I would ever see her again. For two days, I heard nothing, and I began to realize how unlikely her whole story had been. I mean, the Scala, darlings? It was about the only building in Milan I'd ever heard of! An obvious lie! So I began to think I'd been a complete idiot, and to wonder if I'd ever believe anyone again. Oddly enough, I wasn't very worried, though I suppose I should have been. And then she turned up. With 10,000 francs in a brown envelope, and a ticket for *Tosca*. And do you know what, darlings? I never even bothered to go to *Tosca*. I didn't like opera, in those days. Well, I don't go for it much now, but I ought to have gone to see the show. I suppose she was in the chorus. If *Tosca* has a chorus. Does *Tosca* have a chorus? I've forgotten her name. I can remember the name of the hotel, but I can't remember hers. I don't suppose she became a great star, or her name would have come back to me, wouldn't it? Perhaps she was an understudy. She was wearing a dark green velvet coat and had a hat with a feather in it. Perhaps it was the feather that did it. I had faith in that feather.'

'You should have gone to *Tosca*,' says Mrs Jerrold. 'It would have been correct.'

'Yes, I know that now,' says Anaïs. 'I can't believe I didn't bother. But when you're young, you don't bother, do you? You don't do the obvious, do you? Or the correct? You think there's plenty of time for more adventures, and you don't bother.'

It is Julia's turn next. She tells of a man she met on a train on the East Coast line from London to Scotland, and the wild night she spent with him in strait-laced Pitlochry. He had been a manufacturer of egg boxes, and very sexy. Before going into action he had tied her up with hotel towels and read to her from an exciting naughty book he had bought in Paris about twin sisters in a convent and a visiting friar. Julia says she has been looking for this book for years, but has never found a copy. She thinks it was published by the Olympia Press. She should have made a note of the title, but she was too excited at the time. Do any of them recognize the story line? No? Well, she will just have to keep searching. She's forgotten the man's name too. She thinks he said he was called Arnold, but if he had any sense he was lying, so that's not much to go on.

Sally the Virgin, not to be outdone, introduces an anecdote about a meeting with a drunken BBC newscaster in a snowstorm in the station buffet at Manningtree. He had told her the secrets of the great. She has never told anybody this before, but according to this old roué the actress who plays Katie Kettlewell in *The Merry Widows* is the daughter of the Duke of Edinburgh – and when you think about it, when you look at them both, it might be true. What a resemblance!

Their stories intertwine and wreathe and weave themselves together.

Candida listens, and thinks she has not taken enough risks in her life. She has been too cautious, always. Even Sally has at times been braver than she. Is it too late, now? Yes, it is probably too late.

More coffee is ordered, and Candida boldly agrees to try

one of Anaïs's little cheroots. Only Valeria notices that a small cloud the size of a large umbrella is now floating on the horizon. She also spots a dead fish, lying belly-up in the lake beneath them. The wind is changing. Perhaps it is time to think of moving. She feels she could do with a siesta, and hopes they may all fancy one too. As she is summoning her forces to rouse them, her mobile phone bleeps and warns her that she has a message. She does not wish to disturb the gathering with it so she goes out to the little hut by the lake that serves as a lavatory, and discovers that the head office of Parnassus Tours in Milan is asking her to contact it. Valeria does not like this: such messages are usually bad news. But she obeys, and is even less happy to find that no less than three of her clients seem to have received messages from home. She is given numbers that they are requested to ring. Valeria is surprised: who can want to contact her charges? At their age, they are so thinly connected to life. That is why they are here, with her. Who can be recalling them, and to what? They are past the age for good news.

She combs her flourishing black curls in front of the tiny cracked silver sliver of mirror, and salves her dark lips, then steps out of the shack to take stock. She stands for a while by the lakeshore, irresolute, listening to the whispering of the reeds. The summonses are for Mrs Barclay, for Julia Jordan, and for Candida Wilton. Out there, somebody is asking for them. The harmony of the little group will be shattered. Shall she suppress the messages for a while? They have bonded so well. She does not want to disrupt them.

Of her group, only Julia Jordan has brought her own mobile, and clearly she has not had it switched on. Perhaps she has left it back at the hotel, in her voluminous baggage.

The sky is darkening, and the surface of Lake Avernus is

gently ruffled. The cry of the birds has changed its note. The great golden arches and stony ruins of the temple of Apollo on the eastern shore are dim amidst their scaffolding.

Valeria returns to the table, calls for the bill, rounds up her charges, and plants in their willing and receptive heads the attractive notion of a siesta in the hotel followed by an evening foray. Replete, they clamber drowsily back into their minibus, and do not notice that Valeria has trouble with the ignition. The battery seems a little flat, which it has no right to be. The van starts, but reluctantly. It needs attention. Some sort of trouble is brewing. A difficulty has entered their smooth and joyous journey.

During the short drive home, Valeria decides that she will not tell them that they are wanted until after their siesta. They will feel stronger after a little lie-down. If the news is bad, they will be better able to take it. She will contact each of the three, individually, discreetly. She will not make any public announcement.

Valeria is convinced the news must be bad. But she is not wholly right. Some of the news is good, some is enigmatic, some is bad.

She speaks to Julia first, rightly guessing that her news might be of a professional nature.

Julia Jordan's message is from her agent, and it is good. All of it is good news. An unexpected and surprisingly large repeat fee has been harvested from a public broadcasting company in the United States, a respectable deal is in the offing for her new Neapolitan drama, and the chief executive of Leone Films is in Naples and eager to meet her while she is in the neighbourhood. Julia's stock is rising. Julia stays glued for some time to her own mobile, in deep and highly animated discussion, so Valeria leaves her to it, and advances along the corridor to rouse Cynthia and Candida.

Candida's message is ambiguous. She does not know what to make of it. The contact at Parnassus Tours tells her that a person called Andrew Wilton has rung the office and asked her to ring him about their daughter Ellen who is in hospital, though Mr Wilton had wished to emphasize that the daughter is not seriously ill. He has left a hospital number, which Mrs Wilton may also like to ring, if she wishes to inquire about her daughter. The hospital number appears, from its dialling code, to be neither in Finland, nor in England. It is not a country code that Candida recognizes. Candida sits on her hotel bed, and motions to Valeria to sit down by her. Valeria, sympathetically, sits.

It is too complicated to begin to explain to this recent acquaintance the long story of her cool and distant family relationships and separations, but Valeria does not need an explanation. She guesses at once from Candida's response that this message is by way of a riddle. It is not a simple demand for action. It needs decoding.

Candida says she does not know what to do. She thinks it may even be a trick, or a hoax. It may be an attempt to ruin her holiday. She would not put that past Andrew. He would be capable of that. And, frankly, the thought of speaking to Andrew, the thought of ringing him and asking him for clarification, is in itself enough to destroy her valiant attempt at happiness. So what shall she do? Shall she ring the alleged hospital number?

Think about it, says Valeria. I'll go to speak to Mrs Barclay while you think about it. I'll ring the hospital for you if you like.

I haven't the courage, moans Candida faintly.

I'll be back in a minute, says Valeria, and strides on to Room 202 to deliver her third and last message.

This is the bad one. Cynthia Barclay rings Parnassus Tours,

and is at first struck dumb by what she hears. Then she lets out a cry. Valeria hovers, anxiously. 'Oh no,' says Cynthia, from time to time, then hands the receiver to Valeria as she sinks onto her bedside chair. Valeria instantly gets the gist of what has happened, despite her colleague Marco's confused, emotional and apologetic narration. Mrs Barclay's husband has been assaulted and is in hospital, dangerously ill. There is no doubt about this. He is in St Mary's, Paddington, and all the details are confirmed or confirmable. Here are the numbers, here is the police incident number, here is the name of the officer at Ladbroke Grove Police Station. Marco also has it all by fax and by email. In short, Mrs Barclay is urgently needed, and should take the next flight home.

'Oh God,' moans Cynthia Barclay, 'I should never have left him.'

She is in a state of shock. She has gone white under her tan and looks ten years older. Poor old boy, says Cynthia Barclay, poor, poor old boy. She clutches miserably at her frivolous hair.

Valeria is marvellous. Afterwards, they all agree that Valeria is marvellous. She is wonderful in a crisis. What would any of them have done, without Valeria? She informs the others of what has happened, she rings the airport, she soothes Cynthia. There is no direct flight from Naples available that night: there is an option via Milan, getting into Stansted in the early morning, but might it not be wiser to wait till the morning and fly direct? The morning flight is booked, indeed overbooked, but Valeria thinks she could wangle something. Valeria rings the British Consul in Naples. Cynthia rings St Mary's Hospital, where at first nobody will speak to her, and then she tries the police station. Then Candida rings St Mary's to check if Cynthia has understood what she was listening to. The hospital had not been wholly helpful, but in the end Candida manages to speak to somebody who seems to know what she is talking about. She is able to assure Cynthia that although Mr Barclay is in danger, it sounds as though he may well recover. He is not actually, to put it brutally, dying.

'Oh God,' moans Cynthia, 'he'll be so cross with me if I go rushing home. But I've got to go, I want to go. He won't want me to go, but I *want* to go.'

'You must do what you want,' says Candida, envying her this simplicity.

With a little string-pulling, Valeria finds Cynthia a seat on an Eagle flight at 8.50 the following morning. Cynthia concedes that this is the best thing to do, the most sensible thing to do. Valeria will drive her to the airport, leaving the others to fend for themselves for the morning.

The mood of the comrades is sombre as they meet for a drink in the bar. The bar is dominated by an enormous television set showing a football match between Napoli and Lazio. The vast square face of the set leans over them, aggressively, at a threatening angle. Although the hotel seems to have no other guests apart from three youths wearing jeans and guns, the management refuses to turn it off. Even the forceful and eloquent and finally abusive Valeria fails to quench it. It cannot be silenced. It yells on, high-pitched, like the unstoppable torment of a modern Hades. Eventually, it drives them out. They are not in a party mood, but they cannot sit in a room with that thing yelling at them. They will go down into town.

Valeria drives them down the hillside. The Bay of Naples glimmers in the distance, sweet in the night air. The old walls are blood red in the sunset. As the natural light fades, the floodlights pick up the arches and antiquities of Pozzuoli.

They pass the amphitheatre and the temple of Serapis and the temples of Augustus and Neptune. They drive beneath a huge triumphal arch, which a gang of youthful Pozzuoli artists is busy spraying with elaborate graffiti, while studiously and conscientiously consulting a large cardboard graffiti-design template. Valeria finds a parking place down by the harbour, and they smell the salt sea and see the coarse cobalt-blue fishing nets draped upon the shore. They sit on the harbour wall for a moment, and stare up at the sky. Where are the Pleaides, the Seven Sisters? Are they to be dispersed? Then they walk up the Corso to the Piazza della Repubblica, through the bustle of the evening *passegiata*, and find themselves a table on a sidewalk beneath an elaborate stained glass canopy.

The noise and bustle of humanity are soothing to them in their distress. Cynthia is calm now, resigned to her night of waiting, hopeful that Mr Barclay, who is a tough old boot, will fight back. 'After all,' says Cynthia, 'we didn't do too badly, Mr Barclay and me. I did my best for the old boy. He was well looked after. But I couldn't be there around the clock, could I? And I couldn't stop him going off on his wanderings, could I? He had the right. He needed a bit of excitement. I told him he was mad to go under the arches, but he wouldn't listen, would he? He couldn't help it.'

Cynthia Barclay nurses a beautiful misted goblet of cold blond beer. She raises a toast to Julia's success. Then she applies herself to the lesser problem of her friend Candida. She lays Candida's problem upon the table before them all. What is Candida to do? Should she ring the hospital? Should she ring her ex-husband Andrew Wilton in Suffolk? Should she ring Ellen's number in Finland to see if Ellen is there? Should one of the others ring Andrew for her? What does Candida think is really going on?

Candida finds that none of them thinks it odd that she had not immediately and spontaneously rung to inquire about Ellen. This is reassuring. They respect her hesitant diffidence. Candida says that she thinks Ellen would have contacted her directly had Ellen really wanted her mother to know where she was. Ellen would not have relied upon Andrew as a go-between, because she would have known how reluctant Candida would be to respond to any message from that quarter. So the likelihood is that Andrew is out to make trouble, is it not? Yes, the others nod in agreement. It seems that it might be so. But, even so, a phone call wouldn't hurt, would it?

Well, yes, it might, says Candida. It might ruin her mood for the next fortnight. Unnecessarily. On the other hand, the mood had been ruined already, by the news about Mr Barclay from Notting Hill. And it may not be unnecessary. For Ellen, it is possible, may really want to hear from her mother. It is not impossible that she might want to hear from her mother. *Unlikely*, thinks Candida, but not *impossible*.

Candida looks dim and miserable, the dimmest of the stars.

It is Mrs Jerrold who speaks out, and this time in no sibylline tone. Mrs Jerrold says that Candida ought to ring somebody, right now, and that if she won't, then she, Mrs Jerrold, will. I know what I'm talking about, says Mrs Jerrold. I lost touch with my only daughter for nearly twenty years. Through a stupid misunderstanding. It's just not worth it, says Mrs Jerrold. Life's too short.

So Candida is cajoled into trying the easiest option first. She rings her daughter's home in Finland from Valeria's mobile, from a sidewalk café in Pozzuoli, and receives a clear recorded message, in her daughter's somewhat clipped, dry and forbidding voice. 'Ellen Wilton is temporarily unable to take this call, please leave a message.' None the wiser, Candida leaves no message.

Does Ellen herself have a mobile, inquires Valeria? She understands that everybody in Finland has at least one mobile. Finland is the home of the mobile.

Ellen may have a mobile, but, if she has, Candida doesn't know its number. Mobiles are too modern for Candida.

The streets are full of strollers and idlers. Small children walk by, hand in hand with small grandparents. Motorbikes weave about on the Corso. Taxi drivers laugh and smoke in a cluster by their white cabs. The night air is benign. You would not think, sitting here, that this place was sinking slowly but inevitably and irreversibly under the water. But it is. It is not the new fashion of global warming that will sink Pozzuoli. It is an ancient natural phenomenon known as *bradisismo*, or, in English, 'bradyseism'. It is related to volcanic activity. Valeria has explained it to them, and they think they have understood it. They won't retain the explanation, but, for the moment, they have grasped it.

OK, says Candida, she will ring the hospital. Well, no, perhaps she won't, she'll ask Valeria to ring the hospital. Would Valeria mind?

The area code of the number given to Parnassus by Andrew is for Holland, Valeria says. For some reason, it seems that Ellen might be in Amsterdam. Valeria, fluent though she be in Italian, French, Spanish, English and Amharic, does not speak Dutch, but, as they all know, the Dutch speak English, so that won't matter. Candida, by this time, has acquired a little Dutch courage from a glass of grappa, and she is alert and attentive at the sober Valeria's elbow as the call goes through. It goes through instantly. It is amazing that one can phone a hospital in Amsterdam from a sidewalk café in Pozzuoli.

The phone rings, and the group listens, eagerly, holding its breath, as Valeria inquires if there is a Miss Ellen Wilton on any of their wards. There is a very short silence, and then Valeria's face lights up as a connection is made. 'Miss Wilton?' she says, in her delightful low guttural English. 'Miss Wilton? I am ringing for your mother, in Italy – yes, your mother – would you like to speak to your mother?'

This is a risky question, for what if she says no? But she doesn't say no, and Candida, taken by surprise, finds herself speaking directly across the whole of the continent to her own daughter. Her knees beneath the table have turned to water and her heart is pounding with fear.

But Ellen sounds quite calm. 'Mum?' she says. 'Is that really you, Mum? Where on earth are you?'

'In Pozzuoli.'

'Where on earth is that?'

'Near Naples.'

'What on earth are you doing there?'

'What on earth are you doing in Amsterdam?'

The group can hear Ellen laugh. It is a natural, responsive, normal laugh. They sigh with relief. It is all going to be OK, after all.

'I'm having an operation. Well, I've had the operation. It's over now. What for? Did you say what for? Do you remember that business with my cartilage? After that stupid ski disaster when I went into that tree stump? I've been having it fixed. What do you mean, why? Oh, you mean why Amsterdam? Because he's the right man for the job. He's the Achilles-tendon man. I've got a month off work. Yes, it's all going fine. And why are you ringing me out of the blue like this? Yes, of course I'm all right, what about you? You sound very odd. Are you all right? There's a lot of background noise. Can you hear me? I can't hear you any more. Look, ring me again tomorrow, yes, any time, they don't care what you do here, it's a wonderful hospital, it's liberty hall here – I said, it's a *wonderful hospital* – damn, I'm losing you. Mum? Hey, Mum? Damn it, she's gone.'

'She couldn't hear me,' says Candida, flushed and excited. 'How do I switch this thing off? She was only having her leg fixed. She sounded fine. Her Achilles tendon. In a Dutch hospital. She sounded just fine.'

'There, aren't you glad you rang?' says Mrs Jerrold.

'Yes,' says Candida.

They take this successful phone call to be a good omen for Mr Barclay's recovery. They decide to take their supper in the Restaurant of Serapis, which had attracted their attention on the drive into town. Cynthia and Valeria agree that although they will have to get up early, there is no point in going to bed early, as they will not sleep anyway. Over supper, they make more plans. Clearly, everything is different now. The Virgilians, like Aeneas before them, have been washed off course, and will have to plot another route. They are booked for one more night into the Santa Clara Motel at Arco Felice, and they will keep that booking, but they will have to think again about their onward journey. They had been intending to do Naples and Vesuvius and possibly the islands, while staying in a hotel in Naples that belongs to another of Valeria's second cousins. Then they had planned to recover quietly for a couple of days in Amalfi in a celebrated hotel, highly recommended and rather expensive, which had been patronized in earlier years by Goethe, Wagner, Ibsen and Mussolini. But, without Cynthia, do they still want to pursue this ambitious itinerary? And are they not also at risk of losing Julia to a movie mogul? They will be a diminished, possibly a dispirited band.

The meal is a last supper, but nobody has betrayed anybody. Everybody has behaved well. Even Sally Hepburn, so given to making a fuss about nothing, has proved remarkably adaptable and supportive now that there is something to make a fuss about. She has refrained from making any rude remarks about Andrew or Ellen, and has shown a shrewdly sympathetic insight into Mr Barclay's dangerous penchant for late-night roaming. Suffolk spinster though she be, she shows that she is neither ignorant nor judgemental about the ways of the world, and provides some interesting anecdotes about a couple of elderly and disreputable friends of the late Francis Bacon whom she knows in Suffolk. They are old now, and their wandering days are over, but they love to talk about them, and, in the absence of passing rough trade, they continue to persecute one another violently within their own small domain, regularly pushing one another downstairs, and locking one another out of the house in the snow. They hurl plates and carving knives at one another, and ring up the police and the social services to report one another's crimes. That was how Sally got to meet them in the first place, but now they have become friends, of a sort. They too are survivors. They like a drama. Sally serves from time to time as audience. They get bored when life is too calm.

Mr Barclay is not like that, says Cynthia. He is an angel to her, a domestic paragon of placid generosity. An angel in the house. But he goes out for the action. She had always thought that was fine, but look what's happened to him now, says Cynthia, with a darkening change of tone. Mugged, stabbed, robbed, and left bleeding under the motorway. The elegant Mr Barclay has been reduced to one of those yellow Police Serious Assault Witness Appeals that stand on every street corner in Candida's neighbourhood. It is too bad.

They encourage Cynthia not to be morbid. All may yet be

well. At least he hadn't been murdered in his own home, says Mrs Jerrold, like that poor Pope-Hennessy. 'Like who?' asks Julia, and Mrs Jerrold relates the cautionary tale of the death of the notorious risk-taker James Pope-Hennessy, who had been murdered at his maisonette at Number Nine Ladbroke Grove by the 'ruffianly associates of the unscrupulous youths with whom he chose to consort'. (This quaint old phrase, she says, comes from his entry in the *Dictionary of National Biography*, which she seems to know by heart: it had been written, she says, by an acquaintance of Eugene's.) James Pope-Hennessy was killed, according to Ida Jerrold, for boasting. He'd been telling the wrong kind of people that he'd been advanced a lot of money to write a biography of Noel Coward, and the stupid ruffians had wrongly thought he must have the cash stashed away under the cushions in Number Nine. They didn't know much about the ways of publishers, says Mrs Jerrold. This is a tale, says Mrs Jerrold, from the era before gay rights and AIDS – a tale of the bad old days, to which some of Mr Barclay's generation sometimes look back with foolish nostalgia. Eugene, she says, had known the pale, raven-haired and glamorous Pope-Hennessy quite well, and had adapted some of his travel writings for the BBC Third Programme. Pope-Hennessy, she says, was a very amusing man, and was much missed. He was, like Eugene, a great spendthrift.

Has Mr Barclay made a will, and if so, has he left anything or everything to Cynthia? They do not speak of this, for they are nice ladies. Some of them do not even think of it.

If Julia is full of selfish secret career happiness, she conceals it well.

If Candida is thinking angrily of her husband, or sadly of her daughter, she conceals it well.

If Valeria is worried about her minibus battery and about cancelling hotel bookings and claiming refunds, she conceals it well.

If Anaïs wishes she had never embarked with this ill-assorted crew, she conceals it well.

If Mrs Jerrold is longing to get to bed with Hermann Broch, she conceals it well.

As they call for their bill, Mrs Jerrold drains her glass of *acqua minerale*, and says, brightly, 'Did you know that Goethe believed that the Neapolitans invented lemonade?'

She seeks for the Sibyl and waits for her dismissal

Weeds grow tall in the quiet tracks of the Ferrovia Cumana at the bottom of the hill. Candida Wilton sits on a semi-derelict station on an old broken-down wooden bench in the sun and waits for a little train that does not come. She has bought a ticket, and punched it in the ticket machine, but the train does not come. She shuts her eyes and the sun beats down on her tired warm thin lids. It beats through them, from a clear blue morning sky, in a golden red wash. She can no longer fully shut her eyes against the sun. The brightness invades. A waft of warm breeze lifts her thin hair from her skull. The sun shines into the bone.

Valeria and Cynthia left long ago for the airport. Julia has stayed in the hotel, still busy wheeling and dealing on the telephone, in her prima donna mode. The others have gone down to Pozzuoli in a cab.

Candida is thinking about her daughter Ellen, and about the considerable difficulty she had found in forcing herself to make that simple telephone call. No, difficulty is too mild a word. It had been anguish. Without the support of her sisterhood, she would never have taken the risk. It had been far, far easier to ring and probe at St Mary's on Cynthia's behalf than to ring her own daughter. And yet, when she had got through to the hospital in Amsterdam, so unexpectedly easily, so quickly, Ellen had not sounded angry or estranged. Surprised, perhaps, but not angry. Why was Candida afraid of her own daughter? Was she afraid of rejection? Surely she had already been rejected, and therefore had nothing more to fear. What was this terror? What did it mean?

Candida has attempted to send flowers to her daughter in the hospital in Amsterdam, but has little confidence that her peace offering will arrive. She does not trust international credit-card transactions. Unless Ellen thanks her, she will never know if they reached her safely. And Ellen is not given to thanking people. Ellen is given to absenting herself.

Candida thinks she cannot take any more disappointment. She will humble herself, and ask the Sibyl what to do. If the little train ever comes. She almost hopes it will not come. She sits, and waits, and lets her mind drift, and thinks of Goethe and his natural pleasure in the natural world. *Starfishes, sea urchins, serpentine, jasper, obsidian, quartz, granites, porphyries, types of marble, glass of green or blue. Indian figs, narcissus, adonis, pomegranate, myrtle, olive.* He had been fond of lists and multiplicity.

But here, at last, is the little local train, bedaubed with richly massed graffiti. It stops for her on the poor hot neglected track. She is the only seeker to board it. She clutches her punched ticket.

Candida walks on sandalled feet up the Via Sacra towards the Sibyl's cave. Flowers grow by the wayside, the flowers that Virgil and Goethe and Chateaubriand saw and described. She is unworthy to follow in their august footsteps. Her guidebook tells her that the cave is not truly a cave, it is a galleried tomb, or possibly a defensive outpost. In the Middle Ages, it had become, says her guidebook, 'the fixed abode of robbers'. That is a pleasing phrase, and reminds her, momentarily, of the Ladbroke Grove 'ruffians' who set upon that poor old double-barrelled scribbler, may he rest in peace.

An antique headless statue and a fallen marble torso flank the path. Flakes of mica glitter like snow from the stone in the brightness, and red veins thread through the marble. At the top of the path, a great red earthenware pot is perched perilously upon a tripod. It leans towards the west.

Candida sits down upon a stone capital, and shuts her eyes once more. Chunks of fallen masonry lie about her, and tough-stemmed purple and yellow flowers clamber through them. She sits patiently, as if in prayer. There is a scent of thyme and lavender and juniper, and she hears the low sounds of bees and hover-flies moving monotonously, acquisitively, amidst the flowers and foliage. A lizard basks beside her upon a slab of limestone. She feels both the lightness and the weight of her own body in the sunshine. She is heavier than she was in her youth and in her young womanhood and in her middle age, and yet she is also lighter, for she feels herself to be nearer to the dryness of the sun and to the purifying of the fire. The fluids are drying out of her skin and her limbs and her entrails. She is turning into a dry husk, a weightless vessel. She feels with a new pleasure the ageing of her flesh.

She beseeches the Sibyl. She waits, patiently, for the message. The lizard rustles away into the pale dry grey-green sage bushes, over the yellow sulphur-loving lichen. She hears small twigs crackle and whisper, she hears the murmuring and the humming of the air, and she feels the turning of the earth. The sun is a blessing upon her tired eyelids.

Submit, whispers the wizened Sibyl, who lost her frenzy a thousand years ago. Be still, whispers the dry and witless

Sibyl from her wicker basket. Be still. Submit. You can climb no higher. This is the last height. Submit.

But it is not the last height. And she cannot submit.

Who is that waiting on the far shore? Is it her lover or her God?

PART THREE

Ellen's Version

What you and I have read so far is the story that I found on my mother's laptop, after her mysterious and unexpected death.

Her story was divided into two parts, as it is here – a first part called *Diary*, written in the first person, and a second part called *Italian Journey*, written in the third person. It was easy to find, because that's all there was in the machine, apart from a few miscellaneous jottings at the end of the *Diary* section, which I have not included in the text. There were no other documents. There were no other messages from the dead. My mother's laptop contents were very chaste. Like the contents of her refrigerator, which contained half a pint of sour low-fat milk, a carton of plain yoghurt three weeks past the sell-by date, some dried-up old pasta twirls, two canned plum tomatoes in a bowl, some olives and a few rashers of streaky bacon. The olives were those hard grey-green oval ones, a sort I particularly dislike, and they were covered with a thin white exuded crust of cold dried salt tears. Salt tears of bitter brine.

I am writing this on the same laptop machine. On my mother's machine.

She must have written the Italian section pretty damn quick, because I'd only just got my leg out of plaster when the news of her death came. She seems to have been meaning to continue the diary entries, and I suppose she may have deleted some material. But death intervened.

I still don't know whether or not it was suicide. I've been through what she wrote quite carefully, looking for clues, and I still can't decide. She was depressed, yes, from time to time, and with good reason, but she seems to have had a fair capacity for recovery. The coroner returned an open verdict, which was polite of him. He suggested that after the amount she'd drunk, she probably just fell in. I don't find that very convincing, though, do you? I think he was trying to be kind and to save us trouble. That's what coroners do.

The contents of her stomach had been less chaste than the contents of her laptop and her refrigerator. She'd drunk nearly half a bottle of gin, on top of several glasses of white wine, a couple of vegetable samosas, an onion bhaji, and a load of chips with curry sauce. I didn't know she went in for that sort of thing. Reading her diary, one wouldn't get that impression either. But maybe she lied in her diary. Maybe she edited out most of the samosas. Maybe she was ashamed of her weakness for samosas. It *is* rather shameful. The gin surprised me, too, as I know she didn't much care for gin. Mrs Jerrold thinks my mother may have bought this bottle of gin to entertain Mrs Jerrold. Mrs Jerrold says, if only she had been at home, on that last evening, when my mother rang, all this might never have happened. Mrs Jerrold reproaches herself, which is unnecessary of her.

Mrs Jerrold wasn't there to answer my mother's last phone call because she had gone to see her daughter, in Birmingham. She says she doesn't see much of her daughter. I think she was provoked into paying this rare visit to her daughter by the public exposure in Pozzuoli of the difficult relationship that my mother has with me and my sisters. She didn't exactly tell me this, but she hinted at it. So that's an irony.

It was a great shock to me, as you can well imagine. I wasn't expecting anything like this, though maybe I should have been. She'd sounded perfectly reasonable on the phone when she rang me in Amsterdam. She's never been exactly warm-hearted or cosy in her manner – I needn't bother to spell that out, need I – but she didn't sound any worse than usual, in fact if anything slightly better. I was surprised to hear from her at all, that's for sure, and I may have made that a bit too obvious to her, but I didn't give her the cold shoulder. I was pleased to hear from her. In my own fashion. Which is not unlike her fashion, when all is said. For, when all is said, I am, alas, her daughter.

I never got any flowers from her. She was right about fucking credit-card fucking international flora, they hadn't bloody delivered, had they. Actually that wasn't their name, they were called Blooms of the World, I found that out from her credit-card statement, and they'd charged her thirty-five pounds for their No Show. Maybe I'll prosecute them. And then again, maybe I won't bother. As the fabulous Mrs Jerrold said, life's too short.

Mum could have lived another thirty years. Grandma Pratt is still alive, though she hasn't got much to show for it. I don't think she knows Mum is dead. Somebody has probably told her, in that nice kind way that people have, but if so, it wasn't me. I think she's past taking things in. She sits there waiting for her God to call her home. I think her God never even noticed that she existed.

It was hell getting up all those stairs to my mother's apartment, for my last look around. Though she's right about the view when you do get up there. It's mesmerizing. Many-layered London town. It was just as she said, just as she wrote. I'd been there before, I went to see her just after she first moved in, but I'd been too distracted and too worried about her to look about me properly. This time I had all the time in the world and I took it all in. Eventually I even found the flaw in the glass through which she used to gaze, as she tried to change the shapes of her future. Poor Mother.

My leg isn't too brilliant, though Dr Cornelius swears it will be all right in the end. He says I'll be able to go cross-country skiing again.

She's right about the perils of the neighbourhood, too. She hadn't exaggerated them. Getting up her stairs wasn't easy, and getting into her street wasn't easy, either. The whole area was cordoned off. I'd just been to see Anaïs, to pick up the key and the laptop, and although she lives only a couple of streets away, I was cut off. There was a young man in scruffy plain clothes on the corner who said he was a policeman. He told me I couldn't come past the cordon. I said I had to get to my mother's flat, and he asked me to produce some ID. I hadn't got my passport on me – I'd locked it up, on purpose, in my suitcase, because I knew from my mother that the area was full of thieves and bag-snatchers. He didn't seem to like the look of my Finnish driving licence. I asked what had happened and demanded to know why I couldn't pass. He said there'd been a shooting. They'd found a gun but not a body. They were looking for the body. I'm not joking. I wish I were. I said I couldn't stand there all night, and eventually he offered to accompany me to the front door. At this point, I said, 'How do I know you're a policeman?' His opinion of me seemed to go up rather than down when I made this suspicious demand, and he became more friendly, and flashed his badge at me in a conspiratorial manner. He seemed to keep it stuffed away out of sight in his jeans pocket. For good reason, no doubt. There's probably a brisk trade in stolen police badges in those parts. Then he walked me to the door, and saw me in. The sirens wailed for hours, as I went through her refrigerator and her laptop. I wonder if they ever found the body.

Don't think I didn't feel intrusive, reading that diary. I did. But think of the anger that welled up in me while I was reading it. She may or may not have lied about how many samosas she was in the habit of devouring, but she sure as hell lied about a lot of other things. Lies of omission and of commission.

It was Anaïs Al-Sayyab who heard the bad news first. She rang me in Amsterdam, and introduced herself to me down the line, and told me what had happened. I said I'd come over, though I wasn't sure what use I was going to be to anyone. With my leg just out of plaster, and worried about missing yet more work. But I'm glad I went. I'd rather that it was me that got hold of the laptop than anyone else. I'd rather keep the bad news in the family. When Anaïs rang, I booked myself on the next cheap flight to Stansted. A funny thing happened on the way from Stansted to Liverpool Street Station. I didn't realize quite how odd it was at the time. The Stansted Express train stopped at Seven Sisters station, on the way into London. It's not scheduled to do that, but it did. There'd been a signal failure somewhere down the line. I'd been looking out of the window, in a desultory way, at Essex and the Hackney marshes, and at the encroaching desolation of London – that line has some weird high red-brick arches that would delight that brick connoisseur Cynthia Barclay – when we ground to a halt in this non-station. And I remember thinking, what a pretty name for such a dismal dump. An empty windswept platform, broken benches, tattered posters, boarded windows, brambles, buddleia. I wonder where the Seven Sisters Road got its name? I must look it up one day.

Anaïs had lifted the laptop from my mother's apartment. It seems she has a key to the apartment – she says Mum was always afraid of locking herself out. They'd registered the location of this spare key at the police station, so the police would know where to look in an emergency. It's a very high-risk crime area, as I think I've said already. Anaïs had gone round immediately, after the police called her, to remove anything of value. She doesn't seem to have a very high opinion of the morals or competence of the police. She'd taken the laptop, and a silver soup ladle, and a strange and rather sinister black metal crow that looked as though it might have been made in Mexico. She hadn't found anything else worth appropriating. I told her to keep the crow, as a memento. It looked at home with her.

Anaïs's flat, in contrast to my mother's, contains a lot of stuff that might well have attracted the attention of both police and burglars. She's got an impressive Danish music system, and a Beovision television set, and a vast library of CDs and videotapes, and a litter of expensive-looking bits of oriental carpet and tapestry and wall hangings. And hanging in there is the unmistakable perfume of high-quality North African hash, inadequately disguised by joss sticks and incense. The curtains are drenched with odour. It's a lovely smell. I wouldn't mind sharing a joint with Anaïs one day. I like Anaïs. When I met her, I found myself saying that I was sorry I looked such a mess – which I did; I'd rushed to the airport with whatever I could grab, and I seemed to be wearing an old, long, not very clean dark green cardigan that I'd been using as a bedjacket, and a pair of baggy trousers cut back to the knee. And she said, 'Well, darling, you do look a bit of a frump, but never mind, anyone looks a bit of a frump when they've had a leg in plaster for weeks, don't you think?'

The way she said that word 'frump' was very exhilarating. She managed to make it sound like a compliment. Yes. I think I could get on OK with Anaïs. Even though she was a friend of my mother's.

She pressed the laptop on me. I didn't need much pressing. I was quite curious to see what my mother had been up to, and to try to discover any clues to her untimely death.

I think I may have discovered them.

I suppose I could have deleted her documents, but I didn't. She'd put a lot of work into them. People don't write all that kind of stuff down without secretly wanting somebody else to read it, do they? I could have chucked her laptop after her into the canal, but I didn't.

I don't suppose she'd got it on disk anywhere. There's no evidence that she knew what a disk was. Poor Mum, she was sort of stranded between generations. She didn't belong to the old world, where nobody was computer literate, but she was too old to move into the new world.

I don't suppose this tragedy will have done my father's reputation much good. Two drownings in his near vicinity is two too many. He survived the affair with Anthea, but this might swing things posthumously in my mother's favour. Not that she's likely to be worrying about her reputation, wherever she is. She doesn't seem to have had much idea about what was really going on with my father and Jane and Anthea, does she? Or is she simply pretending not to know? She must have known about Jane and my father.

But maybe she didn't. Isobel and Martha know, but they pretend not to know. Maybe my mother really didn't know. I know I knew, but I didn't tell anybody, did I?

Of course, a great deal of what went wrong was my mother's fault. When I was younger I used to blame her for everything, but I got over that years ago. My father was also in part responsible, though there was a time when I suppose I wouldn't have admitted that. And I have to take on board the fact that I am now more critical of my father because of what happened with Jane and Anthea, and because Isobel and Martha have stuck by him in that sycophantic way that they have. But however you look at it, it's still true that it was my mother's frigidity that drove my father into the arms of other women. I don't suppose she ever slept with him, after Martha was conceived. Martha's conception was a bit miraculous. God knows how it happened. It must have given them both a shock. Unless, of course, they were trying for a boy. In the way that people are said to do.

Her frigid seepings have chilled me to the marrow. Walking under the motorway, where she so often walked on her daily route to the Health Club, I saw those 'crusted city tears of salt and nitrate and lime and droppings' that she described (described rather well, I have to say) and they seemed to me to be an emblem of the cold and cavernous home life of the Wiltons. She was drawn to them. Like to like.

You may wonder why, feeling this way, I took myself off to Finland, of all places. It is a good question. And there is a good answer, though you would get no inkling of it from my mother's account of me.

I cannot describe how annoyed I am by my mother's infrequent references to me. No, let me be honest, I don't mean just *annoyed*, I mean *wounded*. Hurt and wounded. Well, annoyed too. Hurt, wounded, annoyed, and *angry*. I took myself off to the permafrost in order to avoid this kind of pain but I don't seem to have managed it. She can still get through to me.

There is no reference, in my mother's entire narrative, to what I actually do. I can't tell you how offensive I find this. I have been through her text with a toothcomb, looking for any indications that she knew what I was doing in Jyväskylä, or why I was interested in going there and living there, but I have found nothing. All we get is a whimsical little fantasy about my playing the violin and living alone in a wooden house on the edge of a lake. Now, it's true that I used to play the violin when I was a child, though not very well, but I haven't touched an instrument in fifteen years. I sometimes strum to myself on the piano, but I don't play a violin. I repeat, *I do not play the violin*. And I don't live alone in a little wooden house by the edge of a lake. I live with my partner Clyde Hughes in an apartment in a large modern well-appointed house that belongs to the university. It is not far from a lake, but nowhere in that part of Finland is far from a lake. It is the Land of the Lakes. (She has got that bit of geographical terminology right, I concede. But the Land of the Lakes is not in the Arctic Circle, as she elsewhere, with what I suppose she thinks of as poetic exaggeration, suggests.) It is true that Clyde and I do dip into a lakeside sauna in the season, but I don't see anything wrong with that. Who doesn't? She seemed to have taken OK to her Health Club sauna, didn't she? There's nothing intrinsically comic or contemptible about a sauna, is there?

To be fair to her, she does at the very last, towards the end of the story, seem to have recognized that I have a proper job in Finland. When she refers to my having been given a month 'off work' for the operation. So she did know that I was working. But nothing, not a word, not a breath of interest in what I was working *at*. She knew about it. She can't not have known about it. It's interesting, my work, and I think it's important. To be honest, there was a time when I thought I'd been driven into it by a sense of over-compensation, or by an inability to get rid of that 'do-good' attitude that my father was always ostensibly so keen on. But I've come to think that whatever my motives, the work itself is important, in its own right. It's worth doing, whether or not I am worthy to do it, and whether or not I am successful at it.

I work as a speech therapist, in an international and multi-lingual research clinic attached to the university. Although my mother does not see fit to acknowledge its existence, it is a world-famous clinic. People come to us from all over the world. We do not promise sensational results, in terms of successful therapy, but people trust us, gain hope from us, and are anxious to volunteer themselves as part of our ongoing investigations. They know we have shown more dedication than any other institution in the world to the causes of some speech problems. We are investigating new theories of Mixed Cerebral Hemisphere Dominance (also known as MHD). These theories have been around in various forms for a long time, and in the past have resulted in some cruel and protracted experiments – there was at one time a fashion for attempting to force right-handed patients to revert to a hypothetical primal left-handedness by constraining them (and I mean physically) to use a variety of slings, braces, mittens and splints. This was better than the severing of the vocal cords and other experimental mutations that used to go on in earlier centuries, but it was never very helpful.

In the clinic, we don't go in for that kind of treatment, but we do observe closely what is happening in the areas responsible for speech production and comprehension. We have interesting new data on what happens in Broca's area and Wernicke's area while the actual process of stammering or stuttering or clustering takes place. We also work with stroke patients – we don't call them victims, and we aren't really supposed to call them patients, but personally I like the word 'patient'. And they have a great deal of patience, some of our clients. One of my colleagues, who has perfect pitch, thinks she has made a breakthrough discovery about the connections between pitch, tone, tune and speech. You can hear her chanting with her group. They enjoy their sessions. They learn new tunes, new tongues.

I wasn't very good at the violin because I haven't got a very good ear, I'm afraid.

It's not really wholly a coincidence, that we are based in Finland. Finnish is a very strange language. Strange historically, strange etymologically, strange on the page. It clusters, it hesitates, it rattles and spatters. I can speak only a few phrases. Clyde speaks it much better than I do, but that's because he's a native Welsh-speaker, and other languages come to him more easily.

Ours is a pioneering and yet a well-respected clinic. My mother may not have known much about us, but others do. If you look up any periodical connected with the field, you will find us quoted. I have even published a short paper myself, in association with Gunnar Tikkanen. It was called 'The Serpent of Zarathustra'. I sent a copy of it to my mother but she never even acknowledged receipt of it.

I admit that I am not very well paid. Speech therapists and research workers are not well paid. My partner and colleague Clyde Hughes and I are not rich. But we do well enough. The cost of living in Finland is extremely high, but benefits are good, and Clyde and I live comfortably, and are respected in our community. We like the landscape and the outdoor life. And, anyway, who is she to criticize? She never did a day's work in her life.

I don't have a mechanical speech problem myself, of the sort I work on, but I did find communication very difficult when I was little. I still do. And I was disturbed and haunted by the quota of blind and partially sighted children who were growing up around us. I suppose I have always been attracted by the deficient and the difficult. Maybe my mother was too. But, unlike my mother, I decided to try to do something about it.

Virgil was said to have a speech impediment. I wonder if the Virgilians knew that. And I wonder how it manifested itself. There is no detailed account of it in the record. So it can't have been very bad. The Romans used to cage speech defectives along the Appian Way, and torment them, for fun. There is also a story that the US Immigration and Naturalization Services used to classify people with speech problems as mental defectives, and ban them from entering the country, but I've never seen the evidence for that. It seems unlikely, to me.

It is quite untrue, incidentally, to say, as she does, that I was a fearful little snob. Isobel is a snob and a name-dropper, I grant her that, and she got sucked into county ways in a mysterious manner. Her ghastly husband is worse. He is always talking tediously about genealogy. He is very good on other people's great-grandfathers and second cousins. I blame England. It encourages that kind of rubbish, and once you've let it take hold, it grips you like bindweed. Isobel simply can't resist anyone with grand relations or a title. Martha is not a snob, though she is interested in all things smart and trendy. That's a bit different. Perhaps it's a more modern form of the same disease. But she's very young still. I don't blame her for that. She's still finding her way. I get on better with Martha than I do with Isobel. I wonder how she's reacting to this new drama. She does love a drama, but this one may be a bit too squalid for her. The Grand Union Canal isn't quite as nice or as select as the Lady Pond. On the other hand, it's topical. Notting Hill and Ladbroke Grove are fashionable places to live in, so they may also be fashionable places to die in, I suppose.

How can you not be a snob, when you're being brought up in an expensive boarding school with a father who spends half his time sucking up to the high and mighty?

I'll tell you another thing, there's plagiarism in that document. When she says her tears were 'as hot as tea', that's plagiarism. She lifted that phrase out of Robert Louis

Stevenson's *Treasure Island*. I happen to know that only because we did it as an example of a simile in an English lesson with Miss Gibson. Stevenson says something like 'the blood came over my hands as hot as tea', and we were all told to admire it as a vivid example of comparing the unusual with the commonplace, or something along those lines. I've remembered it all these years.

I suppose my mother needn't have known that, though. It's a pure fluke that I do. I'm not well up in similes and metaphors and metonyms. In fact I don't really know what a metonym is because we never got on to them with Miss Gibson. And although I agree that it is a striking simile, it's perfectly possible that she hit on it independently. That's not beyond the bounds of possibility, is it? Somehow, though, the coincidence, if it is a coincidence, makes me distrust everything she says. There are bits of Goethe and Virgil in there that I can check on, but there may well be other bits of Goethe and Virgil hidden away, unacknowledged. I suppose they are well out of copyright, so in theory she has a right to do what she likes with them. It makes me feel a bit uneasy, though.

That reference to Hegel threw me. I know for a fact that my mother has never read Hegel. Had never read Hegel, I mean. I've never read Hegel, and she never read Hegel. She wasn't clever enough to read Hegel. She wasn't well enough educated to read Hegel. Hegel is heavy going. So what was she doing, slipping him in there? Was she trying to impress herself? And if so, to what end?

Or was she hoping that someone – someone like me – would come along and get the impression that she had actually read Hegel? When she hadn't?

I can't imagine what she was up to.

But I think I've worked out what she was trying to do

with those first- and third-person voices. She kind of hints at it, though she doesn't spell it out. When she started trying to write the *Italian Journey*, she was trying to escape from the prison of her own voice. She didn't date the saving of her entries – she probably didn't know how to – so I've no way of knowing in what order or sequence she composed them, though logically I suppose she must have written the whole of the *Italian Journey* after her return. The two sections appear simply as two consecutive continuous texts. You can check on Windows Explorer that each was updated the day before her death, the day when she didn't manage to get in touch with Mrs Jerrold. (We know she tried to ring Mrs Jerrold because she left a short message on Mrs Jerrold's answerphone – her last spoken words, as far as we know.) I suppose there may be some clever way of working out the time scale of her composition in more detail, but if so, I don't know of it. It's no good my pretending I'm a genius with the word processor. I'm always getting into trouble, but when I do, I can run screaming to Zachary in the IT Department and he sorts me out. My mother didn't have anyone like Zachary. She wasn't part of an institution. She was all on her own. She didn't do too badly, for a loner.

She did learn to use colour, though. That last cryptic sentence in bold, the last of her bold sentences, she'd written it in bold red. Maybe it was the first line she ever wrote, not the last. How am I to know? And how am I to know if she ever saw him? Her lover, or her God.

She didn't seem to have a printer.

I don't think I ever forgot her birthday. I always sent her a card. Perhaps that year it got lost in the post.

I don't believe her story about the pet rat at Ladbroke Grove station, either. I don't think her account is very reliable. And that faux-naïf tone she adopts is very irritating.

She knows more than she lets on. Or does she pretend to know more than she really does know? Either way, something odd happens to her tone. That Hegel business is really puzzling. Why would one lie in one's diary?

I've met all her friends now, all except Valeria. They all came to the funeral. All except Valeria, who is somewhere in the wastes of Anatolia with a group of archaeologists from Poitiers. I did wonder for a moment whether Valeria was a real person, but the others confirm my mother's account. She's not six feet tall, but she is taller than any of the rest of them. Five foot ten, perhaps, says Cynthia, and statuesque. More Juno than Venus, says Cynthia. Juno, the guardian goddess of Carthage.

Of course, I remember Julia Jordan from my childhood. She was one of the few friends who visited my mother in her own right. She came to see us once or twice in Manchester, and she came once to Holling House. I didn't much like her. She wasn't good with children. She ignored us, and talked above our heads. She wasn't interested in us at all. No reason why she should be, I suppose. I enjoyed her books, when I was young. They were an easy read. At times I see moments where I think my mother is trying to copy her style. Julia was very pleasant to me, at the funeral. She spoke well of my mother. Things really are looking up for Julia. It seems it's never too late. Her film is really going to happen. And she seems to have struck up a friendship with a Neapolitan politician, Salvatore Masolino. Good for Julia.

Sally Hepburn I know quite well. I don't think Mum is at all fair to Sally Hepburn, though I agree that their mutual friend Henrietta Parks is a pain in the neck. Henrietta is the worst type of well-meaning amateur. I don't think she has any professional qualifications at all. Whereas Sally has a good track-record, and was very encouraging to me when I told her I wanted to train in London. From Mum's account, you'd think it was a crime to be fat. I think it's just self-loathing that makes her write like that about Sally. I mean, it all adds up, doesn't it? Low-fat milk and low-fat yoghurt and the Health Club, then a binge on chips and gin and curry sauce.

Sally's a good-humoured and broad-minded woman, interested in everybody and everything. She's fun. She told me some amazing stories about the goings-on of her clients in Ipswich. I suppose she shouldn't have done, but she did. She seemed to me to have a lot of common sense. I always thought it was very decent of her to be so nice to Mum. She had plenty of other friends. She didn't have to bother with Mum.

If anybody was kinky about sex, it wasn't Sally, it was my mother. At the very end of my mother's text, I found a couple of weird disconnected jottings. I think they may have been remarks she'd lifted out of the newspaper or heard on the news, and found offensive enough to record. One of them was, 'He's about as attractive as genital warts.' The second was, 'That, in a scrotum sac, is the message of Picasso.' Clearly the male sexual organ didn't appeal to my mother. She was an emasculating woman. It's not the fashion these days to call women emasculating. But I truly think that's what she was.

She has frozen up my sex life, that's for sure. I'm fond of Clyde, and I think he is fond of me, but nobody can pretend that what goes on between us is normal. It isn't abnormal, but it isn't normal. It's just, I suppose, inadequate. Perhaps I mean it's subnormal. Well, I suppose there are worse things than that. She neutered me. And I don't think Isobel has much fun in bed.

Anaïs and Mrs Barclay are ambiguous figures. Maybe

they are having an affair. Good luck to them, that's what I say.

Mr Barclay is recovering. I didn't meet him, because he was confined to his quarters. But Cynthia did mix me a drink. Candida Wilton, alias my mother, was right about the cocktails. Mrs Barclay is a dab hand at them. In Finland, in a stereotypical sort of way, we do tend to veer towards the beer or the vodka. Mrs B made me a White Lady. I've never had one before, though I've heard tell of them. She says I can have a Red Queen if ever I call again. It's a powerful invitation. I think Cynthia may even have liked me. I know my mother thinks I'm the least favoured of her daughters, and Anaïs called me a frump, but I'm not a complete disaster. I'm still functional.

My mother fell amongst friends. I can't work out whether this was luck or whether, sociologically, the odds were in her favour. There are a lot of nice middle-aged and elderly women about, at a loose end, and they are good at setting up little support groups for themselves. Not many of them end up in the canal.

Candida did try to be happy. She tried hard to describe happiness. I suppose I'm grateful for that. Perhaps she was happy, during that autumnal spring in Carthage and in Naples. It's just that she wasn't really up to writing about it. When she goes into the third person, it's uncomfortable. It's no good, trying to dress up your banal responses by classical allusions and references to Goethe, by using long words and broken-off bits of forgotten mythology. The Seven Sisters: Alcyone, Celaeno, Electra, Maia, Merope, Sterope, Taygete. The Seven Daughters of Atlas. A beneficent constellation, I gather. I looked them up in a Classical Dictionary. So what? Anyone could do that. What's that got to do with anything? I suppose I was most embarrassed by the bits when she tried to see herself as some kind of tragic heroine. But maybe, again, that's me being unfair. Most of the time she runs herself down, in a masochistic sort of way, and that's just as irritating. In fact, if one can be objective about her, she was really quite good-looking, for her age. Anyway, not bad-looking. She's right to say that she looked, at times, quite distinguished.

I keep on writing about her in the present tense. She seems still to be alive, in this machine. I wonder if it can tell the difference between us. Or does it think it's still her, tapping away here? Machines can be taught to remember frequently used words and phrases. Some machines can learn them spontaneously. This machine can spell the names of Valeria, Cynthia, Julia, Ida Jerrold, Sally Hepburn and Anaïs Al-Sayyab without any assistance from me. It even knows about the diaeresis on the name of Anaïs.

She retraces her mother's fatal footsteps

I went to see the place where she died. I thought I owed it to her.

I bought some flowers for her in Sainsbury's.

I think she spent quite a lot of time wandering pointlessly around the aisles of that Sainsbury's, so it seemed fitting. As I bought them, I thought, how naff. But I did it. I bought a blue bunch, mainly irises, nothing portentous or funereal. I felt a bit of a fool as I plodded along the towpath with this pre-packaged supermarket bouquet. It was quite a hot evening. The police had told me it happened just beyond the Canal Gasworks Conservation Area, and of course I'd heard all about it in the Coroner's Court. Unlike anyone else in the family, I sat through the whole grim show.

I'd forgotten that her Sainsbury's was also the scene of the Ladbroke Grove rail crash. There were some withered little tributes in cellophane with messages hanging on the wall, on the strands of barbed wire, over the railway tracks, on the left as you go in. I guess there are some there almost all the year round. It's always somebody's birthday or somebody's wedding anniversary. There was a cheap bunch of dead carnations, so dead you couldn't even tell what colour they had once been, and a fancier arrangement of ivy and ghostly faded large-petalled blue flowers of a more exclusive variety. I don't know what they can have been. I didn't recognize them. These dedicated bouquets were accompanied by many accidental tattered scraps and ribbons of plastic, also hanging from the wire, blown there by the wind – the relics of shredded plastic bags, I suppose. They looked from a distance like votive offerings, but really they were just scraps of airborne rubbish. We don't have so much rubbish in Finland. And there were two black and gold commemorative plaques on the wall, one from the staff of Sainsbury's, one with an inscribed prayer. If I remember rightly, the prayer said something about God holding the dead in the hollow of his hand. I don't know why such banal lies should bring tears to the eyes.

The tracks are wide and deep like a chasm. I remember seeing pictures of the crash on Finnish television and CNN. I rang my mother that week and we spoke about it. She said the whole area was at a standstill, with ambulances and police cars and television crews. She said she could smell burning.

It's quite untrue and unfair of her to say that I never rang her. I did, from time to time, but she never sounded very pleased to hear from me. And I'm sure I didn't forget her fiftieth birthday. I bet it was Isobel that forgot. I'm sure I sent a card and rang, and I think I also sent her some flowers. I suppose I could check my bank statements. But what would be the point in that, at this stage in the game?

I can see it must have been quite a pleasant walk, in its

way. There's a broad mown-grass verge, and some fancy brick and stone work, and there are quite a lot of brightly painted longboats moored along there, with geraniums and dogs and so on. They have names like Hero and Virgo and Andromeda. Mother was right, the classics are not quite dead. There are moorhens and herons, just as she said. People fishing, solitary, patient, hopeless. But it's also true that as soon as you leave the immediate vicinity of Sainsbury's, almost everybody, even the fishermen, looks mad or furtive. Nobody looks normal. I probably didn't look very normal myself. For one thing, I'm still limping. I'm a member of the walking-wounded brigade.

The watery field attracts despair.

You can hear the whine of the trains.

It was easy to identify the place where she fell in. It is marked – though not, of course, on her account – by a post, about three feet high. This post bears the label 'Canal Gasworks Conservation Area'. Near it there is a black metal bench, on which I sat for a few minutes, thinking of Anna Karenina. I think the whine of the trains had brought her to mind.

I laid my flowers at the foot of the municipal post. Maybe they will attract others, and the place will turn into a shrine. Stranger things have happened.

It's supposed to be a picnic area, I think. But you'd have to be brave to linger there. Some have. You can see their leavings. Cans, polystyrene boxes, cigarette ends, Kentucky Fried Chicken cartons. I sat there for a while, contemplating. It was neither pleasant nor unpleasant.

I don't understand why no witnesses have come forward. I don't understand how she managed to lie in the water for so long. It wasn't very long, but it was long enough for somebody to have seen her. Somebody must have seen her fall in. The towpath was full of people when I walked along it. Did they all pass by on the other side? I know people don't like reporting incidents these days, for fear of getting into trouble, or for fear of having to fill in endless forms at police stations, or of wasting time appearing at inquests, but this is ridiculous. A grown woman, floating in the water like Ophelia, by a public towpath, and nobody noticed? Is it likely?

Mrs Jerrold, Cynthia Barclay and Anaïs Al-Sayyab assured me that they thought my mother had been happy, in Africa, in Italy. She hadn't been making it up, to cheer herself up. I didn't tell them about her diaries, though I suppose I may, one day. Those three all come out very well from them, after all. It's Sally who gets the stick. And I'm not sure if Julia would like her appearance much, though she does end up better than she begins, and not many of us manage that.

Here's a bit of the story that I really don't understand. According to Mrs Jerrold, my mother never went to Cumae. She never walked alone up the Via Sacra and heard the immemorial bees. As Mrs Jerrold remembers it, Cynthia did indeed fly back on that Eagle flight at 8.50 a.m. or whenever, having been driven to Naples airport by Valeria. (Valeria's van broke down on the way back, but that's another story.) And my mother, according to Mrs Jerrold, sat around with the rest of them in downtown Pozzuoli, drinking coffee and killing time and gossiping about Mr and Mrs Barclay. None of them went to Cumae. None of them ever reached the Sibyl. Why should she invent a trip to Cumae?

PART FOUR

A Dying Fall

I don't think I've made a very good job of trying to impersonate my own daughter, or of trying to fake my own death. It's humiliating, but I'll have to admit that here I am, still alive. Here I still am, still sitting up here on the third floor back, locked in the same body, the same words, the same syntax, the same habits, the same mannerisms, the same old self. Looking through the same flaw in the same glass at the same constellations. I can't get out. I try, but I can't escape. There was no death, no inquest, no shrine. I'm back in the same old story. I had thought I could get out, but I don't think I can. I had thought £120,000 from Northam Provident could release me, but it can't. I had thought the soft sun of the south could melt the frozen patterning, but it couldn't.

Of course I won't end up in the canal. I won't even teeter on the brink. Did you believe, did I believe, even for a moment, that I might? I am condemned to life, to wearing out my life. All I can produce from my gaping mouth is a little tiny cry.

It's vanity, to think I could escape in that heroic manner. I haven't the courage. I cannot rise to the tragic mode. I must be humble and submit. I am just one of those small, insignificant, unfinished people. I respect those who can make an ending.

I suppose that we all have fantasies of our own death. Adolescents, even quite normal, happy adolescents, can spend a good deal of time dreaming of death as revenge. *'You'll be sorry when I'm gone.' 'You'll wish you never said that.'*

Parents weeping with remorse, teachers shocked, friends grief-stricken and sorrowing. That kind of scenario. The irony is that as we near death, there are fewer people left to be sorry, fewer left to miss us. Nobody would care, nobody would mind. So the self-pitying gesture goes unnoticed. And then we die, as quietly as we can, and people are merely relieved. So it will be when my mother dies, at last.

Our little, pitiful, feeble struggles. Sparrows and farthings, farthings and sparrows. Oh, we are the small change, and we know that.

But it was in its way a useful exercise, my effort to impersonate Ellen. It was only when I started to try to see things from Ellen's point of view that it struck me that Jane Richards probably did drown herself because of Andrew. I think the pseudo-Ellen is trying to hint that Andrew made a pass at Jane, maybe even that he seduced her, and I admit that that's a possibility, though I don't think it's very likely. I don't think that interpretation would have occurred to me on my own, without the help of an imagined Ellen. Andrew was quite scrupulous about not getting too involved with pupils. He liked them to admire him, but I'd be very surprised if he really overstepped the mark with anything other than a smile or a pat on the back or an innuendo. He'd have thought it too risky. No, I now think it's much more likely that Jane had *suspected* something was going on between Andrew and Anthea, and that she drowned herself because she couldn't bear to think about it, because she didn't know what to do about it. Maybe she saw something she shouldn't have seen, out of the corner of one of those ill-aligned eyes. Something nasty in the potting shed, as we used to say. But I'll never know the truth about that, will I? I'll never know what the poor girl was thinking about when she filled her pockets with stones. All I know is that she was braver than I am.

Her death was an act, not a gesture.

Maybe Andrew was carrying on with both mother and daughter. Such things have happened, I believe. That would explain a lot. I've only just thought of it, just now, at this instant, but now I've thought of it, the idea won't go away.

I wonder what the real Ellen really thinks. I wonder if I will dare to ask her, one day.

How impossible it is, to enter the consciousness of another person. How impossible, to escape from one's own.

Since I got back from my Italian Journey, I have been trying to mend the gap that had opened up between myself and Ellen. It is hard, so hard, and so humiliating. These have been painful months, more painful than I can say. I eat humble pie. I try to teach myself a new language, as she tries to teach language to those who cannot utter, but I am a late learner, and I cannot find the words. I make myself telephone her, and I hear myself mumbling banalities at her. 'How's your leg today?' 'I've been to the Club.' 'I've been to the library.' 'I'm having a cheese omelette for my supper.' Well, it's a start. It's an effort. She does answer the phone. She doesn't put the phone down on me, or pretend she isn't at home when she is.

Shall I dare to try to describe what happened on that evening by the Grand Union Canal? No, I do not think I have the courage. My tears were dried on my face and on my throat. Not hot, like tea or blood, but dried, like dried semen. Stiff, dried, papery. A thin encrustation of tears.

Ellen is right, I have always been afraid of the male organ. It has never seemed to me an attractive object, in any of its states, erect or dormant. Female genitalia do not attract me much either, although to me the female body is beautiful. My Health Club is full of beautiful naked women. But as I grow older, I find that some aspects of the womanly condition also disgust me. I used to be able to deal with my own bodily effusions: I do not think I was particularly squeamish, though I was always fastidious, and proud of being so. But now, the cloying dead smell of menstrual waste in the unemptied bins of a public lavatory repels me. The apparatus of menstruation fills me with a mild nausea. I am glad to have finished with the leaking and the blood. I now understand the nature of the taboo against menstruating women. The red stain in the pan or on the sheet is not pleasant.

Sexuality is omni-present, these days. One can't get away from it. It has leaked and spread into everything. People now use the word 'sexy' as a synonym for 'fashionable' or merely 'interesting'. It has lost its secrecy and its power. And women are supposed to go on looking sexy when they are into their sixties. That's all very well for people like Julia, who like that kind of thing, but it's not very good for the rest of us, is it? For some of us, it means nothing but a sense of unending failure and everlasting exclusion.

I have been forcing myself to think about the failure of my 'sex life' with Andrew. (I don't like that phrase, it's vulgar and it sounds as though it comes from the Personal Advice Column of a '50s women's magazine, but I can't think of any other way of putting it, and at least we all know what it means.) My sex life with Andrew was never satisfactory. When we were first married, we made love quite regularly, but I did not enjoy it much. I never had an orgasm. I began to expect and to fear failure and dissatisfaction. My body was lonely, and it never found company. At first, I hoped, but slowly hope faded, and then it seemed better not to begin to hope. It seemed better to lie quietly, and then to lie. I did not refuse, because I was a good wife, but I avoided. It did not cross my mind to blame Andrew for my dissatisfaction. I blamed myself. I was unhappy, and I felt guilty for being unhappy, because Andrew had given me no cause for complaint.

It did not cross my mind to think that I might be happier with another man. I was very backward in that respect. There I was, reading the racy novels of my friend Julia Jordan, and other sexually adventurous works of the '60s, but I did not think that anything in them could apply to me, because I was married to a good man. I had made my bed and I would lie in it. Infidelity would have been an impossibility to me. I wonder if there are any women in England left like that – younger women, I mean. I am sure there are a lot of women of my age who have lived monogamous lives, though I suppose we will die out eventually.

Andrew grew bored with me and his attentions became very infrequent. This, of course, was a relief to me. I now realize – and I mean *now*, as I write these words – that there must have been some extra-marital explanation of the temporary renewal of his sexual interest in me during that holiday in the Dordogne. This renewal of interest resulted in the birth of Martha, which neither of us had expected, and a certain rapprochement between us. For a while, he became kind and tender towards me. There was a truce. But I now think that he had begun to make love to me again because he had been making love to some other woman, and that he was kind to me for a while because of his guilt. I wonder who the other woman was? I don't suppose I shall ever know. What does it matter, anyway? It is all over, all in the past.

If this speculation is correct, and I feel it must be, then that would explain why I was less than responsive to his apparent interest. I must have smelt deceit without recognizing it. After Martha's birth, I became stubborn. At the time I blamed the shock of this fairly late pregnancy for my lasting revulsion from any sexual activity, but in truth it was his duplicity that finally alienated me. It took Andrew a long time to reveal himself for what he was and is. And I have been lying to myself, at quite a deep level, for most of my life.

It wasn't Martha's fault. She was an innocent victim. But I was a guilty party. I connived.

It is only in writing about these things that I discover what may have happened. That is odd.

She abandons reconstruction and returns to her narrative

Nothing much had changed, when I got back from Italy. Nobody at the Health Club noticed I had been away, but I suppose I wasn't away for very long, was I? I've been to see my man in the Scrubs. He's about to be moved to the Isle of Wight. He didn't seem to care about this one way or the other, though from what I hear and read in the press anywhere must be an improvement on the Scrubs. I think my going to visit him has been a complete and utter waste of time, from his point of view. It's given me a bit of exercise and introduced me to some new bits of rather disagreeable scenery. But getting myself a dog to walk would have done that for me just as well, if not better. I suppose talking to him merely added to my rather unhealthy obsession with the canal bank. He tells me I'm mad to walk there alone. There are people there looking for trouble, he says. He says I haven't got the sense I was born with. Miss, he says, you deserve what's coming your way. Don't say I didn't warn you, he says.

He has a strange, earnest, white-eyed look, and he likes to stare at me, eyeball to eyeball. I think he tries to make me look away, and often he succeeds. He is thirty-two years old. The whites of his eyes are larger than normal, and dazzlingly clear. His black hair is thick and glossy, and his eyebrows are proud and well defined. The whites of my eyes are bloodshot, and even my eyebrows now straggle strangely. I suppose I could pencil them in, but why bother? He has a life sentence but he will one day be released. He will have a chance to remake himself, one day. I wonder if I have had that chance, and wasted it.

Italy now seems like a dream. I think I was happy there, but the pseudo-Ellen is right, I can't describe happiness, either in the first person or in the third. I may have been happy there, but happiness is not for me. Happiness is for those who can live in a warm climate. And, anyway, it was a regressive happiness. It was a schoolgirl happiness, as dreams of drowning are schoolgirl fantasies. It is something different that draws me onwards. I must learn to grow old before I die. That, I think, is what the Sibyl tried to say, on her blank tapes and her withered leaves.

That dead Christmas tree is still lying under the motorway.

Ellen has pointed out that she has invited me several times to visit her in Finland, and that I have never taken her up on the suggestion. She doesn't acknowledge that I realize that she doesn't really want me to go. I can read the subtext. I'm not a fool. And I don't like her calling my style and attitudes 'faux-naïf'. I think that's offensive. Though she's right, of course, about the Ladbroke Grove rat. I only saw it twice. It's not really my friend. It probably wasn't even the same rat.

I've been looking for her paper on 'The Serpent and Zarathustra'. (I think I've reconstructed that title correctly.) I think I did receive it, but I am ashamed to say I never read it. I never even looked at it. I probably left it in Suffolk. I wonder how I could get hold of a copy? I can't ask her where it was published, because it seems so rude to have forgotten. I thought it might be too technical for me, but that's no excuse. I do know quite a lot about speech problems, actually, because I always read articles about them whenever I see them in the press – though that's not very often, because unlike autism or dyslexia or bulimia or other eating disorders they're not a fashionable subject. Not a 'sexy' subject, as one might say these days.

The pseudo-Ellen says she hasn't got a stammer. But she has. I don't know if the real Ellen would admit to it or not. We don't speak about it. My version of her version suggests that she's in denial. I think that may be unfair. I think it's me that's in denial. I was very upset by her speech problems when she was little and I probably did all the wrong things – interrupted her, listened to her too patiently, ignored it, looked anxious about it, sent her to the wrong kind of elocution classes. Let's face it, whatever I did was wrong. Who would have thought that at my age I could suffer such torments of remorse and of regret? I am in torment. I hope I make this clear.

I wonder if I do have an eating disorder, as Ellen suggests. Most women have one, so why not me?

Not all is bad. Julia, as Ellen correctly reports, is thriving. It was a happy trip for her, and I can take some credit, for without me she would never have gone to Naples and met her Masolino – well, she might have gone to Naples, but not at that precise moment, and timing is crucial in these matters. Julia has not much time to waste, and she did not waste it. She thrived rapidly in Naples. She met the mayor, and the dashingly bearded British Consul, and she went to Capri on a yacht and to Caserta in a Ferrari. She is back in luck, back in the money, and she says she is in love with the gallant Masolino, and he with her. I wish them well. It is a good story, and she deserves some luck. She is a brave woman.

Mr Barclay recovers, slowly. Nobody has been arrested

for the attack. Cynthia says he does not care about this. She says she thinks he is conscious of having been looking for trouble, and he promises to take more care in the future.

Anaïs and Cynthia see a good deal of each other these days. They go to the cinema together quite frequently. Sometimes I go with them, but when I am in low spirits, as I seem to be these days, I am conscious that I am not good company. I do not like to impose myself upon them.

I see Mrs Jerrold about once a week. She always seems pleased to see me. Since my prisoner said he was going to the Isle of Wight, I have not signed on for a new prisoner to visit. I think he's probably there by now. I don't think I was much use as a prison visitor.

I haven't heard a word from Sally since we got back. I'm a bit surprised. I don't much want to hear from her, but I'm surprised that I haven't. It will be a sad day, when even Sally Hepburn abandons me.

Valeria will have forgotten that we ever existed. She has so many groups.

The dreadlocked man has gone from under the bridge. He sleeps there no more. His bedroll, which he always folded and stowed with military precision, has vanished, so I think he will not return. The man with the crucifix still pursues his own path. I depend on him for continuity.

Last week a petrol bomb was thrown through the first-floor window of one of the flats just past the bridge. It is now sealed up with hardboard. And the plate-glass window of Mr Gordano Black's has been shattered in three places. Not broken, just shattered. It must be bullet proof. Well, around here, in a smart place like that, it would have to be. There are three little crazy splintered stars in the smooth surface of the streetwise window. Bricks, gun shots, who knows?

Yesterday I saw the handsome ruined Frenchman again,

walking along St Marks Road, by the hospital. Our eyes met. Our eyes meet always. I was surprised to see him, as I have not seen him for some time, and I was beginning to think he had been an hallucination. He might as well have been an hallucination. He is the glamour and the glitter of the dead city. He is the past that walks and stalks. He is the lure to the canal bank. He is not a real person. I know what he wants of me. He wants the coupling of the dead in the Underworld. We are both dead, and we walk through our afterlife.

I will go to my Health Club and swim my eight lengths and die a little in the sauna.

Perhaps I should speak to him, next time our paths cross.

She receives an unexpected summons

Several surprising things have happened. So it is not quite the end.

I had a postcard from Valeria. The seventh sister has not forgotten us yet. I was beginning to think I might have invented her. The card is very attractive. It came from Venice, and it pictures a geometric mosaic tile from the floor of Saint Mark's. So she may even have remembered how much I liked the Roman mosaics in the Musée du Bardo in Tunis. She asked me to give her love to all the group, and said how much she had enjoyed our company. Why don't we come with her to Venice next time, she said. I found this strangely touching. I don't suppose it means very much, but it is cheering.

Even more curiously, my engagement ring seems to have turned up at the Health Club. There is a Found Notice, describing what can only be my ring. I don't want to claim it, but I am astonished to discover that somebody actually handed it in instead of pocketing it. It's quite valuable.

And, strangest of all, I have had an invitation to visit Ellen in Finland. Not a mumbled, diffident, half-hearted suggestion, but a real invitation, in writing – well, in print, which in this case is more serious than writing. She and Clyde are to be married, and I am invited to the wedding party. It is a proper printed card – not expensively embossed or anything like that, but printed, nevertheless. On the back of it she has written

This is a very small private Finnish affair, but I do hope you will come. I haven't invited Andrew and Anthea, nor Isobel, so don't mention it to them (why would you?) but I've asked Martha. I don't know if she'll come or not. Come and stay a few days and we'll show you around.
Love,
Ellen.

I wonder why she is getting married. I wonder why she asked me to go to the party. I wonder if I shall go.

I've found her paper on 'The Serpent and Zarathustra'. I tracked it down in the Colindale newspaper library, and felt proud of myself for having done so, though I am still ashamed of myself for having ignored it in the first place. It is not easy to work the catalogue in Colindale, but I did it. The title is taken from an episode in Nietzsche's *Thus Spake Zarathustra*, which she uses as an epigraph. In this, the narrator has a hideous vision of a shepherd with 'a black and heavy' serpent dangling from his mouth. The shepherd is shaking and quivering as though in a trance of horror. The narrator tries in vain to tear away the serpent, and then, inspired, 'the voice of his horror' cries out 'Bite! Bite! Bite off its head! Bite!' And the shepherd bites off the head of the serpent, and as he does so he is transfigured, into 'one that was bright, and one that laughed'.

Ellen analyses this and other metaphors for dumbness and

speechlessness. She describes the phenomena of speaking in tongues, and considers epileptic fits and prophetic incomprehensibility – there is even a mention of my old friend the Cumean Sibyl. She explores violent solutions and pacific solutions to speech difficulties – solutions of the murderous will and solutions of surrender. Nietzsche in this episode went for the will and for the biting off of the head of the problem, but she says that others prefer to coax and tame the serpent. The pacific approach, the relaxation approach, is much more in favour now. But many still seem to respond to the command to 'Bite! Bite off its head!' Is it a question of individual psychology? This also she discusses.

Her paper is interesting. It is scholarly and I think it is original, though how would I know? I did not know she could write so well. I did not know that she could write at all.

I never liked Sports Day, at school. I always pitied the losers. I pitied them too much. All three of my daughters were good strong swimmers, but I did not like to go to the Swimming Gala, for fear my presence would make them sink like stones. I was not there to applaud them when they reached the finishing line.

She accepts the role of wedding guest

Candida Wilton decides that she will be brave. She will accept her daughter Ellen's invitation to go to Finland, even if that acceptance involves a meeting with her angry daughter Martha. She is learning, in her latter years, a bitter humility.

She sits on the aeroplane above the grey Baltic Sea, dumb with apprehension. There cannot be a happy ending. There is nothing but the next effort, and then, after that, the next. She cannot decide whether the effort is admirable or contemptible. It is the effort that is all, not the readiness.

Like a coward, she has allowed herself to become frightened of her own daughters. She attempts to confront the fear. She is not sure that she has the strength. She is too old for fighting and for confrontation, and yet what else shall she do? She is afraid to die, and she is afraid to live. She has lost her nerve.

Finland beneath her is bright in the sunshine with tawny autumn forests and pale green lakes.

She stays in a small hotel of Spartan simplicity. The slatted wood of her hard bed is a glossy varnished yellow, and the white linen blinds are decorated with bright and simple nursery flowers of red and yellow and blue. Poppies, cornflowers, sunflowers, marigolds. She lies in her stockinged feet on her hard bed, on top of the white duvet, and stares at the white ceiling. She lies very still, inert, like an effigy. She knows nothing about this northern country, where the *Arethusa* had been fashioned. The *Arethusa* gaily sails the southern seas with her cargo of cars and merrymakers, but Candida is out of time, out of place, alone. This hotel is like a sanatorium. She is a patient in a sanatorium.

With a great effort, she summons her strength. She arises from her bed and she dresses herself in her ladylike long dark blue wool skirt with its paler blue silk shirt. She pins a silver brooch to her bosom, and she attends the wedding party. Martha is there, her dark curls exuberant and her lips red, and she greets her mother with a false parade of affection. Judas-Martha kisses her mother's cheek with those red lips. Candida is white and drawn and dried with effort. Her mouth is dry. She can hardly speak. This occasion is very painful and distressing to her. She is not sure if she can rise to it. She feels near the point of death.

Ellen greets her mother with a more convincing gaucherie. Ellen has never been smooth of manner. Her limp is still quite noticeable at times. Nor is her new husband Clyde Hughes a man of much grace, though he manages to squeeze his new mother-in-law's hand quite warmly, and forces a smile at her, though she suspects he does not meet her eyes. (She cannot be sure that he does not meet her eyes, for she does not dare to meet his.) He is a tall, shy, ungainly, untidy, haggard-looking person, with a straggling beard. He is not wearing a tie. But he looks kind, and seems to mean well, which is a relief to Candida.

The whole occasion is lacking in grace and fluency. The wedding party takes place in an austere glass-walled function room in the clinic, with aluminium-grey venetian blinds. There is one cold crystal vase of tall blue flowers. Neither the hosts nor the guests are good at making introductions. Conversation is stilted, and punctuated by long silences. Some of those present, hazards Candida, are the serpent's victims and Ellen's patients, and cannot speak much anyway. Everything is blocked, everything is hesitant. Why has Ellen bothered with this ceremony? Is it important to her?

But despite the bleakness of the furnishings, there is a good supply of liquor, and the snacks are more than adequate. Candida takes refuge in an open salmon sandwich lavishly garnished with capers and some unknown dark red berries. She munches bravely on their resinous bitterness to allay her suffering. Eventually she finds herself talking about the berries and the mushrooms of the Land of the Lakes to a good-looking well-tanned expensively suited neurosurgeon whose manner is improving rapidly under the fiery influence of vodka. He is knocking back shot after shot of the cold clear liquor with ritual rigour. Candida allows him to refill her glass, and feels that the splinters of ice in her heart might perhaps one day begin to thaw. He tells her that the mushroom hunt is the sport of the season and of the region.

Will she be here long enough to embark on a mushroom expedition? There is nothing, he assures her, more exciting than tracking down the little creatures as they try to hide away in their lairs in the depths of the woodland.

He is, she discovers, a very entertaining man, this elderly middle-aged young neurosurgeon. He fantasizes bravely, he embarks on flights of invention, he pours her another glass and drinks her health, he invites her to a mushroom hunt if she is able to stay on to the next weekend. He is small and neat and puckish. She hears herself laughing at his jokes, to her own astonishment. He speaks warmly and with respect of Ellen and Clyde, and she finds herself filling with unexpected pride. Ellen and Clyde love the woodland, as she must know, says this winning man with his winning ways, as he bends the full power of his high-octane attention upon Candida Wilton. Every year, he says, they all join forces for outings, with one or two other keen fungus-hunters. My wife was a botanist, says the neurosurgeon, and she taught Clyde and Ellen the secret places. I have a summerhouse in the woods. You must come to see me there, he urges.

He is a widower. He lives alone.

The subdued, dull and decorous party grows noisier and more and more lively as the evening wears on. First there is laughter, then there is dancing. Candida and neurosurgeon Jan sit it out together, on an institutional plastic-backed settee, and watch the young people throw themselves about. Martha is dancing with a very tall Dutchman, and Ellen and Clyde are dancing together, surprisingly well. Ellen's limp seems to have been miraculously healed for the occasion. She has suddenly shed all her awkwardness. Candida has never seen either of her daughters on the dance floor before. Maybe they will find some happiness after all. Maybe they will be transfigured into those that are bright and those that laugh.

Jan Gunarsson continues to speak of the spell of the woodland and of the mystery of the long dark winters. Recklessly she tells him of the ghost orchid, and asks him if it is to be found in Finland. He gazes at her intently, eyeball to eyeball, and he tells her that he himself has seen it bloom, this very week, deep in the beech wood. With his own blue eyes he has seen this rare creature. Shall he take her to see it? Will she come with him? He stares into her timid soul.

He is a magician who needs someone to mesmerize. Tonight he has selected Candida as his subject. She submits. They make a pact to go together to visit the ghost orchid. She tells herself that he will have forgotten all about it by the morning. She is not nearly as drunk as this handsome wealthy healthy Finnish widower.

The wedding party lasts well into the early hours of the morning. It is years since Candida stayed up so late. Not even with her Virgilian friends has she seen so much of the night hours. She and Jan rise together to dance the last dance. It is years since Candida trod the dance floor. It is years since a man held her in his arms. They dance slowly, to the slow music of the last waltz. He holds her firmly and she does not stumble. She had been taught to dance the waltz correctly, all those years ago, at St Anne's, with Julia Jordan as her partner. (Julia had always taken the lead.) She had not thought to exercise this not very useful skill again, but it comes into its own at last. She finds that she has not forgotten the steps. It may be her imagination, but she thinks that Jan smells pleasantly of woodsmoke. He presses his smooth dry well-shaven cheek against hers. They are of the same height, and they fit together neatly. Nobody save the neon-lit dentist has touched the skin of her face for years.

It is long past midnight when she regains her narrow wooden bed. She is lonely in her body.

She meets the serpent's spoil

Jan didn't forget the woodland invitation, to my surprise. He'd left a message for me in the hotel before I even woke up. He must be an insomniac with a strong head and an iron constitution. But Ellen has more or less advised me not to accept it. He is, she says, a well-known philanderer. Well, I had guessed that. I wasn't born yesterday. Both Ellen and Clyde, however, like him very much, despite his philandering, and were much attached to his late wife. They were all good friends. But they say he is a wild card, and has been on the rampage since Valda's death.

'Of course, I know you can look after yourself, at your age, Mum,' said Ellen. 'I mean, he isn't a *rapist*. But he is notorious. For his woodland trips.'

At this, we both laughed.

Clyde has got a hangover.

'I just don't want you getting hurt, Mum, by his idle attentions,' said Ellen. 'I'd feel responsible.'

'I imagine he's been through all the local talent several times,' said Martha, who I think was rather jealous of the superficial and arbitrary interest I happened to have aroused.

'Of course,' said Ellen. 'He's run out of options here. This is a small community. But he also operates in Stockholm, Copenhagen, London and Paris. The world's his oyster on his neurosurgical tours. He's always been a bit of a rover. And since Valda died, he's been wicked. I think he's lonely, really, poor chap.'

We were having lunch, in Ellen's apartment. Scrambled eggs on toast, with, of course, wild mushrooms. They were strange and delicious, those little flutes and trumpets of orange and black. Martha and I savoured and admired. For a moment, it felt as though we were a family.

'Perhaps a notorious philanderer would be good for Mum,' said Martha. 'As a variation.'

At this, they both laughed. I think they were laughing, without malice, at their father, not at me.

'Jan's very rich,' said Ellen. 'Very, very rich.'

They began to tease me, and to tell me that perhaps after all I should go into the woods with Jan. I didn't mind their teasing me. I don't think there was any harm in it.

I didn't tell them about the ghost orchid.

I didn't go to the woods with Jan, but I did go to meet one or two of Clyde's clients at the speech clinic. He invited me. I didn't push my way in. He wanted me to see some of the kind of work they do there.

Clyde does not go in for the head-biting technique. He does not endorse the struggle. Nevertheless, there is struggle. However one approaches it, there is struggle. Clyde leads groups, and also has one-to-one sessions with individual clients. I sat in on one of the groups.

Afterwards, over strong coffee, in the clinical canteen, I talked to a man called Stuart Courage. He had been one of the group. He says it is his second visit to the clinic, and that he will be there for a fortnight. He describes himself as a successful entrepreneur, a product of the Thatcher revolution, who has made his money from fibre optics, copper wire, and the privatization of the telephone system. I couldn't follow the technicalities of all this and he didn't expect me to do so. He explained that he had suffered all his remembered life from a severe stammer (I did know, because of Ellen, because of my interest in the subject through Ellen, that boys tend to stammer much more than girls do) and as a consequence had always had a deep fear of the telephone, which he regarded as an instrument of torture. It was an irony, but not in his view a wholly accidental irony, that drew him to fibre optics, and, eventually, to the new world of emails and text-messaging, in which speech could be altogether avoided.

'It was then I realized,' he said, 'that although my name was courage, I was a coward. I realized that my real aim in life was to live a life without speech, but in such a manner that nobody would ever notice that I wasn't speaking. I was so deeply into avoidance and denial that I was about to disappear for ever into the shadows. And then I came to Finland – well, as you know, everyone in telecommunications has to pay homage to Finland – and it was while I was over here that I got to hear about the clinic. And I thought, it's now or never. And I made myself known to them. So that was last year. So here I am.'

Stuart Courage says that the admission of the severity of his problem was in itself part of the cure. 'I was like an alcoholic, at an AA meeting. The relief! The relief of confession, of not having to pretend any more! And now I've come back, as a volunteer guinea pig. I go to the meetings, and I confess my difficulties. And they wire me up with electrodes and give me passages to read aloud and they simulate social and professional speech situations, and then they record me to see what happens. In the brain. In my brain. They watch how my hemispheres confuse and double-cross themselves. I love it. This is my Health Club, my holiday resort, my working vacation, my dating agency. It's a wonderful place. They are wonderful people here. They are helping to change my life.'

Actually, that's not quite how he talks. Yet again I seem, relentlessly, inescapably, to have given the other person my own syntax and vocabulary. Though I don't talk quite like that, either, do I? But that's the gist of what he said. I think I've got most of the content right.

I probably shouldn't attempt dialogue. I can't mimic his style, and I wouldn't dream of trying to reproduce the struggles and hesitations of his speech upon the page. It would be rude to try. But they were there. He has a particular difficulty with the letters B, V and M. He told me this, but I had already observed it. (He made a joke about the Blessed Virgin Mary.) He struggles with the serpent. It is at times quite difficult to listen to him, but he assures me that it is less difficult when the problem is out in the open, and I am sure he is right about that. He says he is far more fluent in Finland than he is in England.

He is a very nice man. He is thin and wiry, and full of nervous energy. His eyes are grey, and so is his hair. His hair is crinkled and close-cropped, and it looks as though it is charged with electricity. I am full of admiration for his brave persistence. I don't suppose that we shall ever meet again, but I am glad to have had the chance to speak to him. I am glad that we have had the chance to speak together.

He did use the words 'dating agency'. I didn't make that up. I didn't put those words into his mouth.

He has never been married, he says. He lives in Southwark, in a modern development, overlooking the river. He says he likes to watch the life of the river. He asked me if I enjoyed the theatre. I said yes, though I don't, very much. I find the theatre rather boring. He said he would like to take me to the Globe. 'It's nice to have someone to go with,' he said.

Actually, I don't mind Shakespeare. He's less boring than most playwrights. But I don't suppose he will remember to ask me, though we did exchange addresses.

So I met two eligible and wealthy men during my Finnish visit, one a widower and one a bachelor, one drunk and one sober, one fluent and one tongue-tied. I accused Ellen of trying to be a matchmaker, and asked her when she was going to produce the Third Man, as things in my life tend to go in threesomes. I was only joking, of course, and she laughed, and said she'd run out of introductions.

Candida Wilton has finally taken up knitting. She bought the wool in Finland. There she sits, with her expensively, her sensuously handcrafted, her smooth ebony spears of needles, and her plain and her purl, and she listens to the radio as she knits. She has decided that she prefers knitting to playing solitaire, though she is not very good at knitting. The glowingly, boastfully natural colours and the extravagantly wild textures of the hanks of hand-dyed Finnish wools had seduced her as she wandered round the town on the last day of her visit. The wool shop had been filled with a cornucopia of colours, with lavish festoons of indigo, mauve, rust, grape, teal, rose madder, umber, amber and sap green yarn, in smooth and shaggy and rubbed and slubbed and silken strands. A lot of knitting still goes on in Finland. Candida had learnt to knit at school, and the knack returns to her, slowly. Like the steps of the waltz, the click of the needles returns. Knitting is better than sex, at her age. It wards off encroaching arthritis, and avoids social embarrassment. There is a lot to be said for knitting. Anaïs says it is a form of masturbation, but, says Candida to her friend Anaïs, so what? Anaïs is in no position to criticize. She embroiders cabbages. That's just as bad as knitting, surely. Anaïs claims that embroidery, unlike knitting, is art, but Candida does not accept this distinction.

She sits alone, high on a dark evening, in the fourth year of her sojourn

Candida does not think she is a prude, exactly, and words like masturbation do not rattle her. But, as she has repeatedly made plain, she is faintly and at times more than faintly disgusted by the way in which sex now permeates the culture in which she lives. Is this the sour grapes of an old maid? But she is not an old maid, she is the mother of three children. Is it the bitterness of an abandoned wife? No, she thinks not. She thinks it is a reaction against the triviality and the childishness of the world she lives in, which uses the word 'bonking' instead of the word 'fucking'. Really, says the reproving and censorious Candida to herself, each time she hears this silly word on the air waves. She sides with D. H. Lawrence on the use of the word 'fucking'.

Candida is listening to a radio programme where neither word is likely to appear. It is a gala performance of *The Trojans*, an opera, as she now knows, by Berlioz, broadcast live from the recently refurbished Royal Opera House. Some of the Virgilians had thought of trying to get together to go to see this opera, for old time's sake, but they hadn't managed to book tickets: the seats had been spectacularly expensive, the performances few. So, instead of taking part in a group outing, she is listening to it by herself, for free.

Candida is glad to have an evening to herself. She has been far too busy of late. Her social calendar is full. There is bridge in South Kensington with Mrs Jerrold, on alternate Tuesday evenings: Candida is even worse at bridge than she is at knitting, but she is learning, slowly, and her presence on the sidelines is tolerated, because she is young, and brings new blood and new gossip to the ageing gathering. Then there are the weekly cinema outings with Cynthia and Anaïs. Mr Barclay sometimes joins them these days, for he has wisely given up his solitary forays into the night, or so he says: they politely tease him when he makes deliberately ignorant remarks about Film, or drops bits of what he insists on calling Feng Shui from his chopsticks. Mr Barclay has decided to dress for these occasions as an honorary lady: he has acquired a priest's cassock, in which he thinks he looks very fetching. He has always wanted to wear skirts. After all, why not? is his line. If not now, when? The skirt suits him. His ankles are bony.

Mr Barclay's first name is John. Candida had hoped he

would prove to be called something more exotic. She will never be able to bring herself to address him as John.

Last night Candida went to the National Theatre with Stuart Courage, and sat silently and patiently through an interminable production of *Peer Gynt*. They had dinner afterwards in the theatre restaurant and tried to make sense of Ibsen as they ate their smooth little ramekins of spinach soufflé and their dog-bowls of fisherman's pie. Stuart Courage has been very pressing with his invitations, and says he is looking forward to taking her to the Globe when it opens again for its next season. One day soon she will have to ask him back to her side of town, for a pot of rillettes and a quail from the smart Holland Park butcher, but not, she thinks, just yet. If he wants to spend his money on her, why not? They had both been baffled by *Peer Gynt*: was this great classic really as rambling and ill-constructed as it seemed to them to be? What was it all *about*? Stuart is quite interesting on the subject, and his speech, with her, is almost normal. He is not exactly transfigured by light in her presence, but he does laugh, and he can make her laugh. A witty man has been living inside him for years, trying to get out.

Candida suspects that Stuart Courage is more keen on her, or her company, than he is able or at this point willing to show. She does not know what she thinks about this. She has a hunch that he will pluck up the courage to propose marriage to her before the following year is out. She likes him, and she likes his fine view of the Thames, but the idea of marriage is unappealing. There would have to be strict ground rules and bed rules before she committed herself to any association of that sort. But if Cynthia and Mr Barclay can rub along together, why not she and Stuart Courage?

Occasionally she feels a wish to pass her hands over the

magnetic field of Stuart Courage's hair. She has not yet indulged it. She wonders if this is a sign of incipient sexual attraction. Stuart Courage, so far, has not made any physical overtures towards her. He has not even pecked at her cheek in greeting. But she senses that he has an interest in her.

So last evening had been more than fully occupied by Stuart Courage and the National Theatre, and today Candida has had a healthy lunch in the AIDS restaurant at the London Lighthouse with Martha and Martha's new boyfriend from the LSE: baked potato with tuna for Candida, green spaghetti for Martha, and curried parsnip soup for the boyfriend. It had been a bright, crisp, sunny day, warm enough to sit and rock backwards and forwards for a few minutes in the swing-seat in the scented garden by the fountain. Martha and Timothy had liked that, they said. And tomorrow morning she has to see an accountant about her Capital Gains Tax, a subject that fills her with disbelieving but detached hysteria.

On top of all of this, she is trying to plan a trip next spring to Petra with some of the old crowd, under the shining aegis of the shining and faithfully eager Valeria. *Rose-red Petra, half as old as time.* Candida had always thought Petra was in Syria, but according to Valeria it is in Jordan, and Valeria must know. Valeria is urging the rival claims of Leptis Magna in Libya, but Candida has still to be persuaded. She is enjoying the luxury of indecision. She doesn't care what the taxman says. There's sure to be enough money left over for at least one more trip, and she'd like to fit it in, before old age or world terror overtake her. Anaïs and Cynthia and Mrs Jerrold are all keen on the plan, on any plan, but Sally seems to want to opt out, and Julia seems to be far too busy to plan ahead. Shall they recruit, and if so, whom? Anaïs thinks Anna Palumbo might like to join them. It seems that

Anaïs and Anna Palumbo email one another constantly. Candida still hasn't got to grips with email, but she's thinking about it.

Candida tries not to be jealous of Anaïs's friendship with Anna Palumbo. Jealousy is childish. She is not at school now, playing the game of 'best friends'. She is slightly ashamed of the fact that she has secretly looked into Anna's field of study, Paul Klee, and discovered to her astonishment that he had spent only fourteen days in Tunisia. He had been there in April 1914, with fellow artists Louis Moilliet and August Macke. She had imagined, from the way Anna had been speaking of its effect on him, that he had been there for years. But no, he had rattled through Tunis, Sidi-Bou-Said, Hammamet and Kairouan, as rapidly as any package tourist. How can Anna justify spending so much time and money on this brief incident, even if it was very formative? Candida is not sure if she likes Paul Klee very much, as a person, although she likes his paintings, and can see that North African cities are, as he suggested, built on cubist principles. Better not to read too much biography, better not to read other people's diaries, thinks Candida. Though Anna was right: his description of arriving in Naples from Africa was as good as Goethe's. And she likes it when he says that the African moon will rise within him for ever, and that each pale and muted Northern moonrise will recall it to him. 'I am myself the moonrise of the South,' he wrote. In Swiss-German, presumably. She can't be bothered to check the original. She knows a little French, yes, but she does not pretend to know German. Or to read Hegel, come to that. Ellen is right. She has not read Hegel, and would not understand him if she tried.

Candida does not know why she feels ashamed of her curiosity about Anna. Is it because she fears she is becoming a second-hand person, like Sally Hepburn, with an obsessive displaced interest in the private lives of strangers?

Sally Hepburn has remained very quiet of late. It almost seems as though she has dropped Candida. Candida wonders what she has done right, or wrong, to receive the brush-off. She is slightly disconcerted by Sally's neglect, though she does not like to admit it to herself. The admission would be too problematic.

Then there is the Health Club, and the Yoga class at the Health Club. Candida seems to have joined a Yoga class, though she is not sure how this happened: she has temporarily suspended her attendance, because of her leg, but she thinks that it remains a commitment. And she has, despite her own misgivings, taken on a new prisoner, at a different and less convenient prison. He is a sanctimonious and religious old ruffian who tries to convert her to his own brand of Born Again Christianity. She suspects he is a double-dyed hypocrite, but is not yet quite sure. She quite enjoys seeing him, and speculating about his motivation.

She has had a postcard from her man on the Isle of Wight.

Ellen is expecting a baby. Whether this is the cause or the result of her marriage to Clyde Hughes is not clear. Even Martha does not know. So Candida will become a grandmother, at last. She thinks she is very pleased about this, and she is relieved by this evidence that her fears about Ellen and Clyde's relationship have been unfounded. She does not intend to be an intrusive grandmother, but she does intend to try to be attentive. She will not lose touch again. She looks forward to her visits to Finland, where she will be able to replenish her stocks of wool.

How nice Candida Wilton looks, as she sits there, quietly, calmly, complacently, knitting away and thinking in a humble and attentive spirit about her plans for the future. The music swells triumphantly around her, and her spirit expands in its vastness. She is slightly surprised by its note of overpowering joy, for surely this act is intended to represent the fall of Troy? Or has she somehow been transported to join unknowing Dido, as yet resplendent in Carthage? Can the chorus be singing so gloriously about impending death?

Candida's face is serene in the dim evening light.

You can't see, from here, can you, that she has a vicious and newly stitched gash along her right leg? It is nicely covered by her nice wool skirt. But if she were to lift that skirt, you would see that she has acquired a three-inch scar on her right thigh, a scar almost deep enough to rival the scars of Cynthia Barclay and the Tunisian urchin, and a great deal fresher. Where did she get this wound? Has somebody attacked her with a knife? She has always said that the neighbourhood was colourful: has she, like Mr Barclay, been courting danger? Has she too met her destiny? Who would want to carve up the aged right thigh of a nice lady like Candida Wilton?

She climbs over the fence in search of salvation

It was all my own fault. I think it was connected with Jenny's disappearance. You remember Jenny, the girl who had that lump in her lower back? I'd noticed when I got back from Italy and the Parnassus tour that she wasn't around, and I'd sort of mildly missed her. I wouldn't say I'd *positively* missed her, because I was always worried about her, and she wasn't all that much fun to be with, but I had missed her. I'd missed her presence. But then I'd got depressed myself, and went through that bad period when I felt like throwing myself into the canal, and had all those really bad dreams about lying in the gutter on Ladbroke Grove with the pigeons and the sparrows, and I sort of forgot about her. (In the dream, I lie there, on the pavement, and I cannot move, but I can watch the birds pecking in the gutter, and I tell myself, in the dream, that this at least is a small mercy. It is a very low and lowering dream. Maybe it is about my mother.) Then I went to Finland, and slowly stuck myself together, and when I got back I began to think about Jenny again, and to register that she wasn't around. I'd got used to seeing her at the Health Club – we always used to have a pleasant and pointless little chat. And I found that I couldn't remember when I'd last seen her.

I was nervous about asking after her. I didn't want to seem to be prying. After all, we weren't close friends. And I couldn't remember her last name. I knew she was called Jenny, and I was almost sure that her second name began with an A. Agutter, Asher, Arditti? Various famous names beginning with a J and an A kept getting in the way. It was stupid of me, but I was afraid to ask. So I did a typically surreptitious and cowardly and devious thing. I started to look discreetly through the Workout Sheets, those stiff green record sheets that they keep in a sort of filing system next to the gym. I found mine – it was too tragic. *Wilton, C.*, attended twice for instruction two years ago. After that, nothing. No record of any further activity at all. It was clear that Wilton, C., had abdicated, gone off, done her own thing. Who cared? Nobody. I paid my annual sub. That was OK by them, and that was OK by me. It wasn't like school, where they chased you and bullied you and made you play netball in the rain. I love my Health Club. Though I have to say that my Health Club, like me, is showing signs of wear and tear, although it's so much younger than I am. It is no longer pristine. The swimwear spinner keeps going wrong, and the other evening one of the large oval mirrors fell off the wall and crashed to the floor. It splintered into many small shining silver shards. It seemed a bad omen.

I couldn't find a *Jenny A.* in the Workout file that might have been my friend. I decided that her card had been removed.

After three searches, I decided to ask. I asked so politely, so tentatively, that the good nature of Chelsea and Tamsin overcame their respect for the Data Protection Act, and I learnt that Jenny Argent was no longer a member.

Jenny Argent. Of course that was her name. As soon as I heard it, it came back to me.

Jenny Argent, I discovered, was no longer a member because she was dead. This took a little longer to ascertain. It was kind-hearted Tamsin who told me. Jenny's subscription had lapsed, and they'd sent her a reminder, and the envelope had come back with one large red hand-written word on it. DECEASED, it had said. They'd checked with her Notting Hill Barclay's bank account, and found that it was true. In principle, she might have been due for a two-month refund of unused membership, but she wouldn't want it, would she, being dead? So young, said Tamsin, looking at me from her great startled brown healthy eyes. She was so young, wanner she? Tamsin was shocked.

I said yes, she was young.

As I walked home, I wondered how many Health Club members die *per annum*, on average, and whether the Health Club, if alerted in time, sends wreaths to their funerals. They send you a card and a free gift on your birthday, so why not a wreath? The free gifts, when you look at the small print on the accompanying birthday card, are rather disappointing – all you get is a free guest visit, or a free roast on the sunbed. I can't think of any of my friends who would like a free visit, except Anaïs, and she's a member already. And I don't fancy the sunbed. I think sunbeds can give you cancer, even though Cynthia swears by them and says they are completely harmless.

I suppose that's what Jenny Argent had. She had some kind of malignant tumour. I knew it from the very first. I knew it wasn't a lipoma.

It was while I was walking home, taking in this revelation about my sad, dead and lonely comrade, that my eye fell on that small brown Christmas tree. Three whole years that dead tree had been lying there under the motorway bridge. I don't know why, but suddenly, as I walked past, this really really pissed me off. I went home, and I poured myself a glass of wine, and I switched on the telly, but I couldn't get that stupid tree out of my mind. I made myself some supper, and I had another glass of wine, but I still felt angry about that tree. You can't just let things lie.

It was about eleven when I went out to rescue it. That's late for me. I'm usually in bed by then. It was dark, of course, and damp, though it wasn't actually raining. There was a light veneer of slippery dampness on the surface of the street. A dark sweat of city water.

The solid spiked metal railing that runs along the side of the pavement under the high arch of the motorway is about four feet high. But that wasn't the only hazard. Behind the railing is a barrier of broad-gauged wire mesh, festooned by various random coils of barbed wire. These nasty bits of dangerous hardware aren't doing anything in particular. They don't connect with or protect anything. They're just there. Somebody just dumped them there, long ago. All they are defending is this two-foot-high dead tree in a cheap broken terracotta-coloured plastic pot, and some beer cans and plastic bags and sweet wrappings. These are the priceless treasures of my celestial city. The tree was lying beyond one layer of wire mesh. But I thought that if I could just get over the spikes, I could get at it.

It's a long time since I tried to climb over a railing. Not since I climbed in to St Anne's after an evening escapade with Julia Jordan. But I did it.

You might think I might feel foolish, standing on the wrong side of a railing, holding a small dead tree. But I didn't feel foolish, I felt triumphant. I think it would all have been all right if people hadn't tried to be helpful.

Of course I'd hoped that nobody would see me, and I'd waited for the road to look empty in all directions before I'd made my attempt. But, somehow, getting back on to the pavement seemed more difficult and perilous than climbing over in the first place. I chucked the dwarf tree over, on to the pavement, and considered my position. There I was, stuck, like an animal in a zoo, and when I stepped back to take stock I backed straight into the barbed wire. From this side, there wasn't enough room to manoeuvre. I kept getting tangled up on the wires behind me, as I tried to get my knees up on to the top of the spikes. I still think I'd have been able to manage it fine by myself, but just as I was bracing myself for another assault these two chaps appeared. I suppose they thought I was mad, but in fact they were quite polite, and asked me if I wanted a hand. I had to say yes, didn't I? One of them gave me a leg up, from his side, through the railings, and I managed to get astride on top of the railings. It would all have been OK, but then the other one began to pull me over the top and down, and I lost my balance. I told him to stop pulling, but he wouldn't. That's when I scraped my leg so badly, on the way back down. And I gave one of my ankles a nasty jolt, when I landed, though I didn't pay that much attention to it at the time.

And that's when the police arrived. The police car pulled

up just as I was inspecting the damage to my leg. Blood was slow to ooze, but it was beading up to the surface. The police must have seen some of the incident. I suppose we did look rather a suspicious little gathering. Drunk and disorderly, at best. Well, I suppose I was a little drunk, or I wouldn't have been clambering around like that at midnight, would I?

I ended up in the Accident and Emergency Department of the hospital down the road. That was quite an instructive experience. There was a lot of blood there. My wound was very insignificant, compared with some of the injuries I saw. I've had to go back to the hospital several times, to have the stitches out, and for ankle inspections. I've done something to my Achilles tendon, but it isn't as bad as Ellen's. They say it isn't going to need surgery. I'm not booked in for Amsterdam. I haven't dared to tell Ellen.

They do quite a good lunch in the Friends of the Hospital Canteen. I've made friends with the volunteer lady with the library trolley. It seems she once knew Eugene Jerrold.

Nobody got charged with anything. I suppose I could have been charged with trespass. And those two chaps could have been charged with aiding and abetting me. It looked bad, for all of us. But it ended up with a caution. I don't think a caution counts as a criminal record, does it?

That tree is back there, back where it was, under the motorway bridge. It's a few feet from the very place where it was when I rescued it. Somebody must have chucked it straight back over the railings, into the terrible hinterland. It will probably lie there for another three years. I don't suppose anyone else will try to rescue it. I don't think I'll bother. I don't want to be condemned to climbing over railings to rescue trees, in endless repetition, like a latter-day Sisyphus. I'm getting too old for that kind of thing. I should have taken the tree to the hospital with me, but I wasn't thinking straight, was I? Maybe it wants to be there. Maybe that is its home.

As for me, I have no home. This is not my home. This is simply the place where I wait.

The sky, tonight, is streaked with blood above the dying city. It bleeds for me now that I bleed no more. I am filled with expectation. What is it that is calling me?

Stretch forth your hand, I say, stretch forth your hand

Leabharlanna Atha Cliath